P9-CAE-940

THE SUDOKU MURDER

THE SUDOKU MURDER

A Katie McDonald Mystery

SHELLEY FREYDONT

RUNNING PRESS
PHILADELPHIA • LONDON

© 2008 by Shelley Freydont
All rights reserved under the Pan-American
and International Copyright Conventions
Printed in the United States

This book may not be reproduced in whole or in part, in any form or by any means, electronic or mechanical, including photocopying, recording, or by any information storage and retrieval system now known or hereafter invented, without written permission from the publisher.

9   8   7   6   5   4   3   2   1
Digit on the right indicates the number of this printing
ISBN 978-0-7624-3492-3

Previously published as a hardcover from Carroll & Graf, an imprint of
Avalon Publishing Group, Inc.

Sudoku puzzle image on page 167 is from *The Mammoth Book of Sudoku* (c)
2005, Constable & Robinson, Ltd.

Puzzles throughout from *The Mammoth Book of Kakuro, Wordoku and
Sudoku, ed.* Nathan Haselbauer, reprinted by kind permission of Constable
& Robinson Ltd., London.

Cover design by Whitney Cookman
Interior design by Maria E. Torres
Typography: Berkeley, and Interstate

Running Press Book Publishers
2300 Chestnut Street
Philadelphia, PA 19103-4371

Visit us on the web!
www.runningpress.com

To my mentors,
Julia Cauthorn and Maggie Cousins
Gone now but not forgotten

CHAPTER

ONE

TWELVE HOURS AGO, this had seemed like a good idea. A no-brainer, which in itself was almost unheard of, for Kate McDonald, BS, MS, PhD and member of a highly classified government think tank, The Institute for Theoretical Mathematics.

She'd left Virginia without a backward glance, passed the WEL-COME TO NEW HAMPSHIRE sign without a qualm. Felt only marginally nervous when she entered the Granville town limits. But now, sitting in the driveway of her childhood home, even with the tinted glass of her Toyota Matrix hiding her from curious eyes, her heart was pounding in her throat and she wondered why on earth she'd been so rash.

Just go inside, she told herself. It would only take a minute to change from her frayed jeans and oversized "Geeks Do It by Numbers" sweatshirt into something that looked more professional, more confident . . . less geeky.

The professor needed her. His letter had said it was urgent. And she was sitting here, wasting time.

She slipped on her sunglasses, opened the car door, and slid her feet onto the pavement. She glanced around; no one in sight. She threw her purse over her shoulder, bumped her suitcase over the seat back, draped her navy suit over her arm, and scooped up the stack of Sudoku puzzle books off the passenger seat. Balancing this unwieldy bundle, she made a mad dash across the lawn to the white clapboard bungalow where she'd grown up.

She ran up the front steps and across the porch, the bag banging against her thigh, the books sliding precariously from side to side. She shouldered open the screen door and had just fitted the key to the lock when a loud shriek pierced the quiet neighborhood.

Kate jumped. The suit jacket slipped off the hanger, and the puzzle books clattered to the porch floor.

A very tall, very thin woman with blue sausage curls piled high on the top of her head was barreling down the sidewalk, one arm raised in the air. "Excuse me, Miss. Young lady. What are you doing?"

Kate stared. It couldn't be her Aunt Prudence. Not the Aunt Prudence who'd lived three houses away for as long as Kate could remember. That Aunt Pru wore sensible shirtwaist dresses and L.L. Bean walking shoes. This woman was wearing a red and white jogging suit and pristine white sneakers. But she was definitely her aunt.

Kate waved. "Aunt Pru. It's me."

Pru skidded to a halt, then screeched, "Katie? Katie!" She started up again, the running suit flapping like semaphores on a skinny mast. She made it across the lawn and up the steps before Kate realized what she had in mind. Too late, Kate braced herself for impact just as her aunt launched herself toward her.

"Oof," said Kate, staggering back and falling into the open screen door. "How did you know I was coming? Did Dad call you?"

Pru released her and stepped back. "James knew you were coming? Why that scoundrel. I talked to him last week and he never said a word. I think that Florida sun has baked what little brains he was born with." She cocked her head and smiled. "I saw you from my window." She stopped to peruse Kate from head to toe. Kate had to repress the urge to squirm under her aunt's scrutiny.

"You look different," said Pru.

"So do you." Kate hadn't seen her aunt in nine years, but her father had warned her. His incorrigibly straight-laced sister had gone through a "life change" a year ago. "Off her damn rocker," her father had pronounced, and promptly fled to the golf courses of Florida. But Kate hadn't expected this.

"Have to keep up with the times."

Kate nodded. She wanted to ask why Aunt Pru's hair was blue. Nine years ago, she'd been a redhead like Kate and her father and all the McDonalds. But that would have to wait; Kate had things to do. She leaned down to pick up her suit jacket and books. Pru took the jacket from her and smoothed it out.

"How long are you staying? Are you on vacation? I wondered if that Washington think place would ever give you time off."

So had Kate. The "tank" had begrudgingly given her three weeks' emergency leave. Mathematicians weren't supposed to have emergencies.

"And how about your young man? I hope you brought him with you."

Kate shook her head.

Pru lifted an eyebrow at Kate. "James *said* you were seeing a nice young man. Is he joining you later?"

This time Kate did squirm. "Uh, no." Walt, her CPA ex-boyfriend, had dropped her for a blonde of indeterminate IQ. Kate had discovered them one night in the backseat of Walt's BMW in the Alexandria

Food Town parking lot. "Actually I came to see Professor Avondale—and you, of course."

Pru tsked. "Did you scare him away?"

"The professor?"

"Don't be smart. Your young man."

Don't be smart. She'd heard that enough times growing up. From her father on the few occasions when she was "giving him sass." But from Aunt Pru, the admonition was literal. Don't act too smart or the boys won't like you.

Kate probably had scared Walt away. Once a geek, always a geek, even to a CPA. She was beginning to fear that geekdom might be a terminal condition.

"Well, not to worry. There are plenty of eligible men in town. Good catches, too. Real gentlemen with job security."

Kate shuddered and opened the front door.

Aunt Pru followed her in. "You're not planning to stay here?"

"It's my home." And always would be. Her father would never sell, not as long as there was a chance Kate might come back for good.

"But honey, you can't stay here all by yourself." Pru sniffed the air and wrinkled her powdered nose. "You'll be much more comfortable in my guest room."

Kate remembered Pru's guest room, an unbelievable mix of New England *Field and Stream* and American Gothic. Had it also gone through a life change? Kate imagined beaded curtains and lava lamps. Not a pretty image.

"Thanks, but I really mean to stay at home."

Aunt Pru pursed her lips and raised her eyebrows, and Kate began her mental recitation. *Katherine Margaret McDonald.*

"Katherine Mar—"

"Really, Aunt Pru. I'll be fine. Now I have to get going or I'll be too late to see the professor."

"Ah. Poor soul. Penniless, I hear. That old mansion is falling down around his ears. I don't know why somebody doesn't do something. Maybe he *should* sell."

"Sell? He would never sell."

"Just about everybody else has. Whole town's gone nutty over this mall rumor." Pru snorted. "Like we need an outlet mall. What do we have Maine for?"

"An outlet mall?" The professor hadn't said why he needed her. But an outlet mall? "They're going to build a mall in the historic district?"

"Not in but *on* the historic district. At least that's the scuttlebutt. The more fools they." Pru frowned, walked past Kate, and ran her hand over the hallway credenza. She held up a finger. "See?"

"A little dust," said Kate. "But—"

"And to think Jimmy pays Merry Maids to come in once a month." Pru wagged her dusty fingertip at Kate. "Does this look like dusting to you?"

Since Kate never dusted but hired the Alexandria Cleaning Service to do it for her, she just shrugged.

"Well, it doesn't to me, and if you're planning to stay—"

"Aunt Pru. I really have to get dressed and get over to the professor's."

"You run along," said Pru, and she started down the hall. Kate grabbed her suitcase and puzzle books and followed her into the kitchen.

"Go on. I'll just do a little touch-up." Pru took the Sudoku books from Kate and looked them over. "Don't see how you can figure these things out. Though I suppose you're a whiz at them."

Kate winced. Actually she held several East Coast titles for speed and accuracy, but she didn't tell Pru that. And she wasn't going to tell her that she spent most of her nights at home alone with a glass of wine and a puzzle book.

"You won't have time for puzzles while you're here," Pru said, and stuffed the books into the utility drawer. "And I hope you're not planning to wear blue jeans every day. We'll have to do something about your wardrobe. Men like to see a little leg."

Well, some things hadn't changed. Being unlucky in love, Pru had always been determined to find Kate a good husband. Her good intentions had been one of the reasons Kate had left town in the first place. But she knew the futility of arguing with her aunt once she got something in her head. Or as her father described it, "a bee in her backside." Kate took her suitcase and suit and hurried to her room.

When she came out a few minutes later, dressed in her suit and high heels, her short hair pulled fiercely back from her face with two ivory combs, Aunt Pru was standing at the counter with a dish towel in her hand.

"You look very nice."

"Thanks." Kate kissed her aunt on her cheek and got a nose full of overpowering cologne. "I have to run. I'll call you when I get back."

"Take your time," said Pru, and she began to scrub the sink.

Kate let herself out the front door, and with a sense of growing unease she drove across town to Granville's first and only claim to fame: The Avondale Puzzle Museum.

The old section of town was two blocks from the downtown center and ten blocks from the "new" section of 1830s bungalows where the McDonalds lived. The houses were all huge and exuded longevity and old money. Extensive gardens backed onto the river on one side of the neighborhood and the valley on the other.

The museum was on Hopper Street, the main drag of the historic district. It was a three-story home built in the Colonial style and separated from its neighbors by high privet hedges. The museum took up the first two floors, and the professor lived on the third.

For fifty years, Professor P. T. Avondale, the town's reclusive genius, had unwittingly kept tourism alive with his obsession with puzzles from around the world. And just as unwittingly, he'd created a refuge for a ten-year-old girl who had more brains than were good for her and who'd just lost her mother in a freak auto accident.

He'd discovered Kate one day, sitting among the Japanese puzzle boxes, furiously working a Rubik's Cube while tears spilled over the brightly colored toy and splashed onto her overalls.

He'd sat down beside her, tall and lanky and slightly bent at the shoulders, and pulled his own cube from one of the capacious pockets of his old tweed jacket. They worked their puzzles side by side without speaking. And finished at the same time.

Kate looked up at him and he smiled, hazel eyes twinkling beneath bushy iron gray eyebrows, and Kate threw herself into his arms.

Almost twenty years later, Kate's throat tightened just thinking about that day. He certainly hadn't expected her reaction, and he sat awkwardly patting the top of her head until the last sob died away. Then he stiffly got to his feet, pulling her up with him, and took her into his second-floor office where he made hot chocolate and they sat in two big wing chairs by the fire, sipping and staring into the flames.

She hadn't known then how out of character his gesture had been.

After that, she came to the museum every day after school, first thing on Saturday mornings, and would have skipped church on Sunday except the museum was closed for the Sabbath. If her father thought it odd that his daughter was spending all her time with a sixty-year-old semirecluse, he didn't say. Though Kate suspected he hadn't noticed. He was too tied up in his own grief to have any comfort to offer her.

So while other girls her age giggled, learned to polish their nails, and spent hours down at the drugstore sipping cream sodas, Kate was taking up tickets, dusting showcases, working Rubik's Cubes with the professor, and learning everything in the world about puzzles.

The receptionist and majordomo of the museum, Janice Krupps, merely tolerated her. She looked askance at Kate's uneven pigtails and wrinkled T-shirts and overalls, and she did her best to make Kate feel like an interloper. Kate hoped she'd retired by now.

Kate parked on the street in front of the museum and got out of the car. She didn't go in immediately, but stood looking at the house where she'd spent so many happy years.

It was surrounded by a porch-rail fence nearly hidden beneath a sprawling rosebush. Beyond two giant elm trees, she could see gables, windows, and cornices peeking through the branches.

She could also see that the paint was peeling.

She opened the gate and walked up the mossy flagstones, past the sign with fading letters that spelled out AVONDALE PUZZLE MUSEUM. As she stepped onto the circular porch, a thrill passed over her. She used to feel like Cinderella every time she stood in front of the paneled front door with its regal crown molding and recessed columns. She felt a little like that now.

She took a deep breath. She had the professor's letter in her purse. It was short, a mere page. And it begged her to come home. And now she knew the reason. A mall—as if the world needed another one. What the world needed was a puzzle museum, a place where children and adults could come and learn, be amazed and delighted. Where they could lose their worries and stretch their imaginations and find solace for their deepest sadness.

And here, she realized, was her chance to extricate herself from the world of numbers, numbers, and nothing but numbers. Living with equations, fractals, and chaos was exhilarating, but lonely. Her fellow think-tank members lived numbers, breathed numbers, dreamed numbers. Even when they went bowling, they calculated strike and spare percentages, predicted the mean scores, estimated the time it would take to finish a game. And when they went for a beer afterward, they talked about numbers. Argued about numbers. No wonder Walt had traded her in for someone who could barely balance her checkbook.

She was boring and out of touch. Well, that was about to change. The professor needed her—the children of Granville needed her. The town needed her. This might be her chance to become a people person at last.

She pushed open the door. A bell jangled overhead as she stepped inside. The foyer was spacious and empty. And, thank goodness, there was no Miss Krupps at the reception desk.

Beyond the ornamental archway, a wide staircase rose to the second floor. Alongside it, a hallway led to the first-floor exhibition rooms, but she could only see a few dim shapes of furniture before it faded into darkness.

A sole light shone from the pedestal candelabrum, casting the entrance into twilight. The atmosphere felt rarefied, empty, as if the museum were already gone. Well, that wasn't going to happen, not if she had anything to say about it.

She tiptoed past the empty desk and hurried toward the stairs.

A figure stepped out of the shadows. "Young woman, the museum is closing. You'll have to return another day."

Kate stopped with her foot on the first tread. She'd never forget that brittle voice. She turned to face it. "Hello, Miss—Hello, Janice."

Janice Krupps stood with her feet spread, looking ominous from the rounded toes of her sensible black shoes to the tips of her black-rimmed eyeglasses. She was wearing a raspberry-colored skirt and cardigan set. The skirt had lost its shape and the sweater was tighter, but Kate recognized it.

Janice pursed her lips. The gesture accentuated the spider lines of lipstick that had collected in the wrinkles around her mouth. Then her eyes rounded beneath the thick lenses of her glasses. "Katie McDonald."

Kate could feel the chill across the room, but she was grown now, could pay her way if she had to, and she had no intention of letting this sour old lady intimidate her.

She'd never figured out why Janice disliked her so much. She had since the first day Kate visited the museum. She'd been a lonely little girl who missed her mother. She wasn't loud, didn't touch things, just came to see the puzzles. Any other woman would have taken pity on her. But Janice had taken an immediate dislike, and she'd never softened.

Kate summoned up a smile. "You can go ahead and close up. I've just come to see the professor. Is he in his office?"

Janice took a challenging step toward her. "Yes. But you can't go up there. You don't have an appointment."

An appointment? The woman not only had gotten meaner, she had turned loopy. "He's expecting me," said Kate, and started up the stairs.

Janice hurried after her. "You'll just have to make an appointment and come back tomorrow or next week."

Kate kept climbing. She could hear Janice huffing up the stairs behind her, mumbling under her breath. "Rude . . . upstart . . . never had any manners." Kate got the point. She and Janice would never be friends. No surprises there. No loss.

When she reached the top of the stairs, she crossed the hall to the professor's office and knocked on the door. Janice jumped in front of her and plastered herself against the door. "I said—"

Kate reached past her and grasped the doorknob. She hoped that Janice couldn't see how her hand was shaking. She hated confrontations, but she wouldn't be stopped now. Not after she'd come this far.

"I'm going to see the professor." She turned the knob and pushed the door open.

Janice stood her ground. "You can't."

Kate slipped under her arm, shut the door, and locked it.

The knob rattled a few times, then stopped. Kate waited until she heard Janice walking slowly away, then she released her pent-up breath and turned to the room.

The professor was sitting at his desk, his head bent, his shoulders slumped. He still had a full head of hair, only it was snow white instead of the salt and pepper gray she remembered.

His shoulders rose and fell in rhythm to his deep, steady breathing. He was asleep. Kate tiptoed closer. There was an open book on the desk, a pencil nestled in the fold of the binding. And Kate recognized one of the popular series of Sudoku puzzles.

She bit back a gasp of pleasure mingled with a deeper emotion. He'd moved on from Rubik's to Sudoku, as she had. If Kate had been a superstitious person, she would have believed this was a sign that she had done the right thing in coming back. She wasn't superstitious, but suddenly she was so certain that this was where she belonged that she would have shouted it out the window if there had been anyone to listen.

She touched his shoulder. "Professor Avondale?" she said quietly, not wanting to startle him.

The professor twitched. His head came up. "Harry? Are you back?" He turned and saw Kate. His eyebrows quirked. "You're not Harry."

"No, sir. I'm Kate, Katie . . . McDonald." She waited for a sign of recognition. She'd changed but not that much. "Remember? You wrote to me."

Slowly the professor's eyes lost their vacant look, and the lines of confusion left his face. His eyes sparked to life, and Kate felt a rush of immense relief.

"Katie. My dear." He struggled to his feet, took both her hands in his, and shook them. "Thank you. Thank you for coming."

While the professor made tea on the office hot plate, Kate wandered around the room looking at the familiar objects on the tables and letting her eyes roam lovingly over the books on the built-in shelves. It had always been a cozy room, with dark wainscoting and intricately patterned carpets. The heavy walnut desk was still piled with books and papers in apparent disorder, but she wasn't fooled. The professor knew where everything was. He had a photographic memory.

She stopped by the pedestal that held the crystal ball, a present from a Roumanian gypsy, or so the professor had told her. She'd never been allowed to touch it. She didn't touch it now.

When the tea was brewed, they took their places before the unlit fireplace as they had hundreds of time in the past. The wing chairs seemed smaller than before, a little faded, rubbed threadbare at the armrests.

Slowly the professor began to tell her about the harassments, the petty acts of vandalism, the anonymous threatening letters. With each incident, Kate grew more outraged. They were obviously intimidation tactics to force the professor and the other owners to sell.

"Have you notified the police?"

The professor snorted. "The police. Three deputies, barely old enough to shave. Old Benjamin Meany who empties the parking meters when his rheumatism lets him get out of bed. Not that they haven't tried. But we have a new police chief."

"He won't help?"

"Comes from Boston," he said as if that explained everything.

It did. The new chief was an outsider.

"This house has been in the Avondale family for generations." The professor shook his head, looked into the empty grate. "What's going to happen to the puzzles?"

"But if you refuse to sell—"

"I can't," he said, desperation tingeing his voice.

"But why?"

"The bank is going to foreclose. I thought you might be able to help." The professor hung his head, already defeated. And Kate swore to herself that she would not let anyone take the thing he loved most in the world. But she also knew better than to offer false hope. First she needed to understand exactly what was going on.

"Do you mind if I ask? I thought you owned the house."

The professor continued to gaze into the empty grate and nodded his head. "I do. But the museum board wanted to make improvements. I had to cosign the loan."

What improvements? Kate wondered. They hadn't painted. As far as she could tell, nothing had been improved.

"They haven't spent all the money?"

"Tied it up. I've been making the monthly payments, but the bank says I haven't." The professor pushed his teacup aside and reached for the Sudoku book lying on the table next to his chair. He pulled a pen from the pencil caddy and turned a few pages before rolling them back against the back cover. He clicked the pen and frowned at the book page.

"Professor?"

He didn't answer. He was already engrossed in solving his puzzle. She knew what he was doing. Puzzle solving was an escape as well as a tool for focusing your thought process. She used puzzles in much the same way, and she understood the professor's need. But she also needed his full attention, and without wrenching the book from his hands, she didn't know how to get it.

"Have you been to the bank?" Then she remembered who the bank president was. Jacob Donnelly. She got a terrible sinking feeling.

"I tried to tell Jacob, but his mind is . . . " He filled in a box of the puzzle grid.

"Jacob Donnelly? What did he say? Did he approve the loan?"

"It was his idea." He filled in two more blanks.

"I don't understand."

Finally the professor looked at her. "He's president of the museum board."

Kate stopped the teacup halfway to her mouth. "But I thought . . . " She foundered. "But why?"

The professor didn't answer, just continued to fill in the blanks. Kate could only watch while her mind tried to assimilate the absurdity of the situation, and the professor retreated further into his realm of safety. If the professor had tried to sabotage himself, he couldn't have found a more effective method. His beloved museum was now controlled by his most bitter enemy.

None of it made sense, but Kate knew she'd learn no more from him now. When he turned the page and began a new grid, she stood up. "You're tired. I'll come back in the morning, and we can decide what's best to be done."

Slowly, the professor looked up. His eyes had that blank look she'd seen when she'd first entered the office. She forced a smile to her lips, while inside she was crying for her dearest friend.

He didn't return her smile, just looked at her like he was surprised to find her there. His face cleared for a moment. "I knew you'd come, but where's Harry?"

CHAPTER

TWO

SO WHERE WAS Harry? *And who was Harry?* wondered Kate as she drove back across town. At first she'd thought the professor was talking about a new game, like Where's Waldo? But it quickly became clear that Harry was a person.

Unfortunately the professor had volunteered no more information. And she wasn't sure that Harry was in any way involved in the professor's dilemma. And even if he were, there wasn't much she could do about it until he showed up again.

It was nearly ten o'clock when she turned onto Porter Street. Most of its inhabitants were in bed, and all the houses were dark, except for one white-framed bungalow in the middle of the block. Lights blazed from every window. The porch light broadcast into the front yard.

Aunt Pru had made sure she wouldn't come home to a dark house. Kate could almost hear her saying, "It's a dangerous world out there. No young woman is safe on her own." Not that there had been a violent crime in Granville in the last decade. But

Kate appreciated her aunt's concern, even though it would soon become annoying. She'd have to find a way to gently but firmly convince Pru that she was capable of taking care of herself.

She pulled into the driveway and, out of habit, locked the car doors. The first thing she noticed when she stepped inside was the pervasive smell of lemon Pledge. Every surface shone with polish. The carpet showed the tracks left by recent vacuuming. There was a vase of late-blooming asters on the hall credenza, and the smell of cooking wafted down the hall.

The rattle of pans sounded from the kitchen, then water rushing into the sink. The combined smells and sounds made Kate a little dizzy, and she realized that she hadn't eaten since morning.

Aunt Pru stepped through the kitchen door, wiping her hands on a faded apron that Kate recognized from her childhood. Memories swept over her. Her mother, fine boned and petite, coming out to meet her, ready with a warm snack for Kate when she returned from school. Then the image faded, and Aunt Pru's red running suit came back into focus.

"Dinner's on the table. Wash your hands and come into the kitchen before it gets cold."

Kate did as she was told. She suddenly felt dead tired and not up to the task that lay ahead. Afraid that she had jeopardized her job at the tank without taking necessary precautions for her future. What were the odds of saving the museum?

She scrubbed her hands, even ran water over her face, and went to the kitchen. Her place was set, the place where she always sat as a kid. She slumped into the chair, then quickly straightened up. *Coming home is a bitch,* she thought as she watched Pru pour a glass of milk and set it beside her plate. She made a mental note to check the cellar for her dad's stash of French wines.

Pru sat down opposite her and watched her eat. "You'll never guess who I ran into at the Market Basket."

Kate's mouth was full so she made mmming sounds and moved her head around to show interest.

"Lou Albioni."

Kate drew a blank.

"You remember him. Antonio's middle son."

Kate still drew a blank, but she was beginning to get a frightening suspicion about where this was going.

"He was just made manager. Such a lovely young man. Always so polite." She got up to serve Kate more stew.

"Aunt Pru—"

"He's going to call you."

"Aunt Pru—"

"Great future. Job security." Pru wagged her finger at Kate. "Everybody's got to eat."

By the time the food was put away and the dishes washed, it was after eleven. Kate stood on the porch, watching until her aunt was safely inside her own house. Then she hit the cellar and found a Pinot Noir 1998. She uncorked the bottle, rummaged in the top cabinet for a wineglass, and found one right where she expected it—behind the cookie jar. She poured herself a glass of wine, selected one of the puzzle books from the utility drawer, and carried both into the living room.

Minutes later, she was engrossed in numbers. The tension that had been building all day melted away as one number followed another and rows and columns took shape across the grid. Her mind retreated into a comfortable, familiar world where stability and the laws of probability reigned. Where she could free associate, regroup, and theorize. By the time she had successfully entered the last digit into the puzzle grid, she had a plan of action.

* * *

Kate spent the next morning at the professor's desk, poring over everything that related to the bank loan. Unfortunately, she didn't find one endorsed check that would prove that the payments had been made. The professor was no help. He thought that Janice had filed the endorsed checks. Janice said she had returned them to the professor.

When Kate asked about computer statements, they both looked blankly at her. They didn't use computer banking. *Or anything else,* thought Kate. She hadn't seen a computer anywhere in the museum. She was forced to depend on the hard copies of what she had.

It was early afternoon when, armed with copies of the loan, the letter of payment due, and other miscellaneous papers, Kate walked the three blocks to the Farm and Mercantile Bank.

Granville was a typical New England town. A jumble of ill-assorted clapboard buildings, looking as much like houses as businesses. Most had steep roofs to accommodate the snow and covered entrances to keep the elements out. Many dated from the early 1900s or earlier.

The bank was situated in the center of downtown. It was a brick building constructed around 1900. Across the street, a triangle of grass, commonly called Granville Green, grew up around the statue of Abelard Granville, the founder of the once-prospering town. Behind it, the old town hall had a fresh coat of paint.

Cars were parked at an angle along the curbs; shoppers walked along the sidewalk, entering and leaving the various stores. Some, like the General Merchandise and Timothy's Hardware, Kate recognized. Others were new. But she recognized none of the people she passed, and they seemed oblivious to her.

She had to admit, Granville was a pretty town. The air was crisp and invigorating, free of car exhaust and garbage smells. A hint of fall wafted in on an occasional breeze. Soon the leaves would turn to red and gold. The sun shone steadily, casting short shadows as the morning passed into afternoon. And now that she was here, she couldn't remember why she'd been so afraid to return.

Her life here hadn't been so bad. Except for her mother dying and the kids making fun of her. But other than that . . . *Katie is a ge-ek.*

She pushed the thought away and stopped for a moment to compose herself before she entered the bank. She hadn't called in advance. She'd decided surprise was her best tactic. She readjusted her sheaf of folders and stepped inside.

It was darker inside the bank, and it took a moment for the shadows to take form. A row of teller stations ran across the back. Several desks were set apart in new glass cubicles. There was a receptionist's desk near the door. She walked over to it.

A middle-aged woman looked up and smiled. "May I help you?"

"I'd like to see the loan manager," said Kate. She knew her nerves made her voice sound brusque. She tried a smile on the woman and was immediately rewarded.

"Certainly." She picked up the phone and pressed a button.

"Carol, there's someone to see Mr. Donnelly."

Kate's smile fractured. Surely she had said loan manager and not bank president. Well, she'd correct her mistake before she had to confront Jacob Donnelly. She turned to the receptionist, but before she could say a word, a door that led to the back of the bank opened and a man stepped out, smiling in her direction. Not Jacob Donnelly. She felt almost giddy with relief.

He was about her height, dressed in a conservative gray suit that pulled slightly at his stomach. His hair was receding, leaving a thinning peninsula at the top of his forehead.

She straightened the hem of her jacket and walked toward him, assuming her mathematician-in-command posture and stretching out her hand. "Good morning, I'm Katherine McDonald and I—"

"Good God." The loan manager's smile faded, then ratcheted back up. "Katie McDonald. What on earth brings you back to Granville?"

Confused, Kate stared at the man. Did she know him? One of her schoolmates? He looked older than that.

The smile broadened into a grin. A not-very-nice grin. "Don't you recognize me?"

"I . . ." And suddenly she did. Not Jacob Donnelly. Not even his son, Jacob Jr. But his grandson Darrell, the bully of Granville Valley High School. And Kate's nemesis.

Her stomach flip-flopped and tried to tie itself in knots. "I'm sorry?" The words came out okay. Let him think she didn't remember him. It would give her time to pull herself together. He couldn't taunt her. He couldn't hurt her. Not anymore. But he could hurt the professor, so she'd have to be on her guard and not let him get to her—if he attempted to. Surely they had grown past that.

"Oh come on now, Katie. You haven't forgotten your old friend Darrell." He smiled.

She smiled back as *Katie is a ge-ek, Katie is a ge-ek* looped through her head. And it was Darrell Donnelly's voice she heard. Darrell's names for her had grown much worse during high school, but they never hurt as much as that first childish taunt.

"Darrell," she managed. "What a surprise." She had to fight to keep her tone light. *Remember the professor,* she counseled herself. *Just state your business, don't let him push you into losing your temper. And don't let him intimidate you.*

"Come back to my office and tell me how I can help you." He led her across the room and down a hallway lined by doors with brass name plaques. They stopped at a door at the end of the hall. Kate just had time to read *Darrell Donnelly, Loan Manager,* before he ushered her inside.

He motioned her to a seat in front of a wide cherrywood desk, where a computer screen sat off to one side and a pristine green blotter was centered in front of a high-back leather chair.

As soon as she was seated, Darrell sat down behind the desk.

Kate placed her folders carefully on the desk, lining them perfectly one on top of the other and placing the bottom edge parallel to the edge of the desk. When she looked up, Darrell was watching her, a quizzical expression on his face.

"Actually, Darrell, I'm glad to see you." *Liar, liar, pants on fire.* She swallowed. *Get a grip.* She was reverting to childhood. Not good. She picked a place on Darrell's forehead and focused on it. A trick she'd learned from the speech consultant she'd once hired to help her with her delivery when she had to present a paper in front of an audience. She was counting on the technique to see her through her talk with Darrell. "I'm here to clear up some confusion about the Avondale Museum's bank loan."

Darrell leaned back in his chair, rested his elbows on the chair arms, and templed his fingers. Attentive, sympathetic. Kate kept her benign expression carefully in place. She knew better than to relax.

"What seems to be the problem?"

"Well," said Kate, opening the top folder. "It's my understanding the museum took out an improvement loan eighteen months ago. It says here"—she turned the loan paper toward him and pointed to a place on the page—"that it was for a thirty-six-month period. And yet, the professor received"—she flipped through the next folder, extracted the collection notice, and handed it to Darrell—"this notice that the loan is being called in. Why is that?"

Darrell took the letter and looked at it. Then he dropped it to the desk, rolled his chair back, pulled out a keyboard drawer, and began typing. He stared at the computer screen, waiting for the account to appear. At least that's what Kate supposed he was doing since she couldn't see the screen from where she was seated.

He clicked the mouse several times while Kate sat, straight-backed, her hands folded in her lap. She could feel her palms growing damp, and she surreptitiously wiped them on her skirt.

"Ah, here's the problem."

Kate felt a flood of relief. Maybe there was a simple explanation. Darrell swung the computer screen around so she could see. Financing wasn't her field, but it only took a quick glance to see that withdrawals had considerably diminished the line of credit and that the interest and finance charges had increased instead of the loan being paid off.

Darrell was watching her complacently. He knew she understood what she was seeing. Even in high school, she could figure out problems like this before most of the kids had finished reading the question.

"I don't understand," she said, stalling for time.

"Of course, you do." Darrell flashed his teeth at her. It was feral, not friendly. "Old P. T. is three months behind in his payments. You gotta pay to play."

Kate clenched her fists, refusing to be baited, holding on to her temper with every ounce of willpower she possessed. His smarmy attitude had turned blatantly disrespectful. *Don't do it. Don't let him do it to you,* she warned herself, as countless trips to the principal's office rose to her mind. And the cause was sitting in front of her. She turned to the screen, just to break eye contact. She studied the account figures while she counted to ten. It did little to assuage her anger or fix what was staring back at her.

There was no mistake. The balance left in the account was negligible. No payments had been listed since June. They were up the creek.

"I see," she said slowly.

"Of course you do."

Darrell was barely concealing his contempt behind his veneer of civility. This was about more than a child bully and his prey. What was going on? Had the feud between his grandfather and the professor filtered down through two generations? It didn't make sense. But then she didn't know what had caused the fight in the first place. As far as she knew, no one did.

She made another stab. "It was my understanding that the museum board took out the loan and is responsible for the payments."

Darrell didn't answer but took the copy of the loan she'd handed him and flipped through the pages. He turned it around and shoved it across the desk at her. "Section VI, paragraph three."

In the event of forfeiture, Peter Thomas Avondale assumes all responsibility, etc. etc. It took Kate longer to grasp than usual, since she had stuck on the most interesting fact of the paragraph. P. T.'s name was Peter Thomas.

Kate had always called him Professor. She didn't know why learning his given name had moved her the way it did. The brilliant, reclusive P. T. Avondale had once been a boy named Peter Thomas. Had his friends made fun of him, too?

Slowly, she returned the pages to the desk. "There must be a bookkeeping error. It is my understanding that the loan payments have been remitted in a timely fashion." She now felt sweat rolling down her armpits. Even mathematicians didn't talk like this. She hadn't learned it from her speech coach. She must have picked it up from television.

"Well," said Darrell, "as you can see, the last payment was made in June. The balance remaining in the account is not sufficient to offset dereliction. If the payment schedule isn't brought up to date by the end of the month and the remaining principal paid off, the bank will have no option but to foreclose on the house and auction it off in order to recoup the losses."

You can't, she thought, but she bit back the words before she blurted them out loud. She took a steadying breath and looked him in the forehead. "I'll need an extension to give me time to analyze the museum's books and correct the error."

Darrell leaned back in his chair again, templed his fingers. It seemed to be a favorite position of his. "I thought you worked for one of those . . . " He paused, and Kate mentally inserted the unstated "geeky." "Hush-hush government think tanks. Is accounting one of your hobbies?"

His smile was in place, but Kate didn't miss the sarcasm beneath his words. What had she ever done to him that he should carry a grudge all these years? Like grandfather, like grandson?

"I'm merely trying to help out an old friend."

Donnelly shrugged, assuming the expression of one whose hands were tied. "Sorry. There's nothing I can do to help you. I suggest you have the old man find the money to pay."

For a crazed moment she considered demanding to see the bank president but managed just in time to remember that the president was Jacob Donnelly. There wouldn't be any help coming from the bank. She'd have to come up with some other way to stall the fore-closure.

Kate gathered her papers and stood up. "Thanks for the clarifi-cation," she said through clenched teeth.

"Sorry I couldn't help. But business is business." Darrell swung his chair around and went to open the door.

When he started to follow her down the hall, Kate stopped him. "Don't bother to see me out. I've taken too much of your time already."

There was a minute slip of his obvious satisfaction. And during that split second, Kate declared war. She was no longer a motherless, gawky child-genius. She was one of the most respected mathemati-cians in her field. She was a member of a classified think tank. She lec-tured all over the country. She had top-priority government clearance.

And she was pissed.

"Good day, Darrell." She didn't look back as she made her way down the plushly carpeted hall, but she could feel him standing in his doorway, watching. And she could imagine the satisfied smirk on his face. She'd seen it often enough as a kid.

She nodded to the receptionist as she passed. The woman smiled back and returned to her work. Kate stepped onto the street.

She paused outside to calm her jangled nerves and put a lid on her anger. She glanced back inside the bank and saw that Darrell had followed her out and was watching her from the receptionist's desk. She smiled at him. Waved. Then walked off down the street.

She was glad he was losing his hair, the little toad.

When Kate returned to the museum, Janice was not at her desk. Like the day before, the front door had been left open with no one to guard the exhibits. They should really hire a security guard. Some of their puzzles were very rare and worth a lot of money.

There was a Ming Dynasty puzzle box; a hand-cut cast of "The Smashed Up Locomotive," the first jigsaw puzzle Milton Bradley had ever produced; several original crosswords and conundrums dating from the seventeenth and eighteenth centuries; and a World War II puzzle that was part of a series sent to German prisoner of war camps, which contained a hidden hacksaw and compass.

And there was a display of Dell Magazines where the first Sudoku puzzles appeared in 1979. They were called Number Place puzzles then. The professor had acquired the issues before the Japanese renamed the puzzles Sudoku. The collection must be valuable now that Sudoku had become a worldwide obsession.

At least, she assumed everything was still on display. She hadn't had time to take a good look at the exhibit rooms. She'd been too busy trying to figure out how to save them.

She went upstairs to the office. The professor was sitting in his chair by the fireplace working a Sudoku puzzle. He looked up expectantly. His interest dimmed only slightly when he saw that it was Kate. And she felt a little hurt because she knew he was hoping that it was Harry, whoever he was.

It was ridiculous to feel that little stab of hurt. No. Call it what it was. She was jealous of someone she didn't even know. She was being unfair. She'd moved away. Gone on with her life. She was glad that the professor had someone new to care about.

Someone had placed the small writing table in the center of the room. It was set for two with china, crystal wineglasses, and cloth napkins. It must have been the professor's work. Janice would never condescend to doing something nice for her.

Unless he was expecting someone else. Once again that unfamiliar little prick of jealousy hit her. She ruthlessly pushed it away.

The professor got stiffly to his feet and gestured toward the table. "Rayette over at the bakery heard you were in town. She sent lunch."

"Rayette? The sticky bun lady?" Rayette owned the local bakery and was famous for miles around because of her sticky buns, apple fritters, and other sweets.

He led her to the table. He hadn't even asked how the bank visit had gone. Perhaps he was just too old to care.

"Aren't we missing something?" he asked.

She looked at him and saw the old twinkle in his eye. Not so old. But what? And then she saw. "There's no silverware."

She laughed, and the professor went to the cabinet and opened the door. He lifted out a shiny silver-plated casque. The Cofanetto by Berrocal. Actually it was a copy based on the original chest puzzle, the individual pieces of which made up a place setting for two.

He placed it in the center of the little table.

It had always been her job to set the silverware, ever since the first day he showed her the key to releasing the parts and opening the "Coffin" to reveal knives, forks, goblets, and candlesticks.

"Let's see." She rubbed the tips of her fingers together. She could hear the professor chuckling, and she felt a surge of optimism.

She disassembled the outside of the box and reassembled the pieces into knives and forks. But when she would have continued, the professor laughed and said, "Our luncheon will get cold before you remember the rest." He removed the partially opened casque and returned to pull out Kate's chair.

She sat down, and he began taking out covered foil containers from a shopping bag that was placed on the floor nearby.

Salad, pasta, and a chicken dish covered in a sauce of capers and mushrooms. And a bottle of sparkling water that the professor poured with the aplomb of a sommelier. They could have been sitting on the Rue de Pais in Paris or the Piazza Navona in Rome instead of Hopper Street in Granville, New Hampshire.

"It smells wonderful," said Kate as the professor sat down opposite her. She knew they should be discussing what to do about the loan, but it was such an enchanting moment that she let herself float along on the illusion. She knew it would end soon enough.

1		6		7			4	9
			3	4	2			
2						7	8	
		1			7	9	3	8
	2		9		4		7	
7	9	5	1			6		
	7	8						1
			4	5	9			
6	4			1		3		2

*PUZZLE SOLUTIONS BEGIN ON PAGE 344.

"THE BANK TURNED down my request for an extension," Kate said from her chair by the fireplace.

The professor handed her a cup of tea and placed his cup on the side table next to his Sudoku book. He lowered himself into the chair. "Hmm." He glanced at the puzzle book.

Oh no you don't, thought Kate. *I need some answers if I'm going to be able to help.*

"What about the board? Can't they do something? How is the money tied up? How were they intending to pay back the balance?"

The professor reached for his puzzle book.

Too many questions at once, she thought. Her frustration was driving him away. Her hand closed over his, preventing him from picking up the book.

"Who's Harry?"

The professor's fingers relaxed beneath hers.

"He . . . helps at the museum."

"Like I did?"

"Yes. He's not as smart as you were, but almost." His face softened, and a smile hovered on his lips. "The kid's brilliant at ciphers and codes and cryptograms. Never could interest him in Sudoku, though." Then the smile disappeared and his fingers grew restless.

Kate increased the pressure of her hand on his. "And he's disappeared?"

The professor nodded slowly.

"Or has he just not been in lately?"

"He always comes. Right after school and stays until closing. Sometimes he stays here overnight. Whenever—" He shook his head as if to clear it. "He's done something to him."

"Who, Professor? Who has done something to him?" Was he becoming paranoid? Or just getting old and forgetful. "Maybe he's sick or on vacation."

The professor laughed, a bitter sound that sent a chill down her spine.

"If he were sick, he'd come here. He's never had a vacation."

"Have you called his parents?"

"There are no parents. He lives with his uncle. He's a mean bas— man. But Harry wouldn't let him stop him from coming here."

"Did you call the uncle?"

"He doesn't have a phone. I asked the chief of police to go out and see about him."

"And?"

"He went. So he says. But Perkins said he didn't know where Harry was."

"Well, if he's been missing for over forty-eight hours . . . "

"Almost a week, but Chief Mitchell says he can't do anything until the uncle files a missing person report. He thinks Harry ran away. He wouldn't run away. He would run here." He slipped the puzzle book out from under her hand.

"Do you think someone might have scared him away?" *Or hurt him*, thought Kate, her imagination racing faster than the incoming data. The professor had mentioned anonymous threatening letters. He'd thrown them away before she arrived, but she had no reason to believe he was making them up.

"Never."

"Did any of the anonymous letters mention Harry?"

The professor's hand paused over the pencil caddy. He shook his head, then he snatched a pen from the caddy. "No." His voice was barely a whisper. He opened the book, filled in a number.

She was losing him, and she knew she needed to find Harry if she was ever going to get the professor to concentrate on saving the museum.

"Why don't we drive over to his uncle's house and see for ourselves."

The pen hovered over the page. Kate held her breath.

He clicked the pen shut and stood up. The Sudoku book slid off his lap. "All right."

It was a long drive. "Buck" Perkins lived several miles out of town. The stately old homes of downtown Granville gave way to a two-lane macadam road that cut through the surrounding fields, and Kate tried not to imagine the golden grasses being replaced by acres of mall parking lot. They passed an occasional farmhouse, a fish and tackle store, and an old boarded-up roadhouse.

"Turn right up there," said the professor, pointing past an abandoned one-pump gas station where weeds grew high around the pump and sprouted from the cracks in the concrete.

Kate turned onto an even narrower road and came face to face with a tractor coming toward them down the middle of the road. She swung the Toyota to the shoulder, and the tractor driver raised his hand to her as he bounced past.

She pulled back onto the pavement. They drove another few minutes between fields of freshly mowed hay. Ahead of them, she saw a line of rural mailboxes and slowed down to read the names. No Perkins. She sped up again. The fields gave way to copses of trees, and the road began to meander uphill until the pavement stopped and the road turned into a rutted track of hard-packed dirt.

Kate was beginning to think they'd missed the Perkins house, when they came to a dilapidated wooden shed set back a few feet from the track and two long rows of chicken coops. She saw a clearing ahead and slowed down.

A dented mailbox leaned at an acute angle from the ground. It had once been white, but now blotches of the original aluminum were bared by peeling paint. She stopped in front of it and leaned over the professor to read the broken letters. She made out a P and a stroke that could be part of an L or a K.

"I think we're here," she said, feeling sick.

Behind the mailbox, a patch of dusty ground was littered with abandoned cars, stripped of most of their usable parts and left to slowly corrode. Twisted bicycles lay in a jumble in the dirt. There was an old, tubular washing machine, several mesh crates, and a bin of misshapen hubcaps.

A sagging, wooden garage sat at the edge of the yard. A muddy truck with monster tires was parked in front of it. On the far side, a square outbuilding was in even worse condition except for the shiny new padlock on the weathered door. And behind it all was the worst-looking, most disgusting, god-awful excuse for a trailer Kate had ever seen. It was something you might see in a movie, but nobody should really live this way. Especially not a child.

She turned into the yard and cut the engine. The professor stared straight ahead, as horrified as she. "Harry," he murmured, and fumbled with the door handle.

Kate released her seatbelt and was about to get out when the trailer door opened and a man stepped out. Two mongrel dogs leaped past him and raced for the car, bearing their teeth and growling.

Kate grabbed the professor's arm. "Wait."

The man didn't call off the dogs, but walked toward the car. His hair was dark and shaggy. A beard hid most of his face; his eyes were deep set under thick brows.

Kate shivered. He was wearing an army jacket and holding a shotgun at the ready.

She could feel the professor vibrating beneath her hand. Not fear, but anger. "Do not antagonize him," she whispered.

"I'd like to kill him," said the professor, and shook off her hold.

His vehemence stunned Kate. She'd never heard him utter a violent word in his life.

She hurt for him. She'd been longing for him to take an interest, show some initiative. But this was not the time or the place.

The man swung toward the passenger side. Kate opened the professor's window but leaned across him to talk to the man herself.

"Hi," she said, trying to look friendly.

"You're trespassing."

"Are you Mr. Perkins?"

"Who wants to know?"

The professor stirred. "What have you—"

Kate pushed him back and leaned farther over him, willing him to be quiet. She should have researched the situation better. They could be killed and their bodies dumped, and no one would find them for . . . forever, maybe.

"We're concerned about Harry."

"Harry's gone. And you better get going, too."

"Gone?" she persisted, weighing the odds of getting shot before she asked another question.

"Ayuh. He run off. Ain't the first time, but I'll tell ya, lady, if you're from the truant office, you can forget about coming out here again. 'Cause I won't have that ungrateful little bastard back. He's run away his last time. So you can just scratch him off your list." He backed away from the Toyota and raised the shotgun.

He didn't exactly aim it at them, but Kate got the point. She moved back to the driver's side, started the engine, raised the window, and hit the automatic lock button practically in the same motion.

She backed out of the yard and threw the car into drive. She pushed her foot down on the gas pedal, and the car lurched forward. The professor looked back over his shoulder, but Kate didn't even bother to check the rearview mirror. She was getting them out of there. Fast.

As soon as they were out of sight of the shack, she slowed down and concentrated on missing the worst of the ruts in the road. They didn't speak until she turned onto the county road and they were headed back to town.

Then the professor said, "We should have looked for Harry."

"He had a shotgun, Professor. And I doubt he would have any qualms about using it."

"If he's hurt the boy—" The professor didn't continue. He didn't have to. She felt the same way. Because she was pretty certain that Buck Perkins was capable of violence. But why harm— she couldn't bring herself to say kill—his nephew?

"I didn't know people really acted that way," said the professor, staring at the road ahead.

"I know," Kate agreed. She gave a nervous laugh. "I kept expecting to hear dueling banjos any minute." She glanced at her mentor, but he had dropped back into brooding. "We'll find him," she said, "if I have to talk to the police chief myself."

* * *

Janice was waiting for them when they returned to the museum. "Where have you been?" she asked, jumping to her feet as they entered the front door. She ignored Kate but ran to the professor and took his arm. "When I got back from lunch and saw the dishes just left on the table, I thought something awful had happened. Are you okay?"

She turned to Kate. "You shouldn't have coerced him into leaving the museum. He doesn't go out. No telling what kind of trouble you've caused."

The professor extricated his elbow from her grip. "I'm going for my nap." He headed across the foyer but stopped at the foot of the stairs. "Thank you, Katie." He smiled at her, a tired smile, then turned and slowly climbed the stairs.

"If anything happens to him, it will be your fault." Janice spit the words at her, then turned on her heel and marched up the stairs after the professor.

Kate watched them go. She was worried about the professor, too, but not in the same way as Janice. She hoped Harry had indeed run away. She was afraid that if he was found injured—or worse—the professor might not survive the shock.

She kept forgetting that he must be close to eighty. His intellect was still remarkably quick. Puzzle solving had kept his mind active. And even if he did have moments of confusion, so did she and everyone else she knew.

Puzzles and the professor had seen her through difficult times. He'd always been there for her. Never once became irritated with her constant presence. Never acted bored. He was the only adult who let her talk about her mother and who offered her a safe place to grieve. There had been days when his tutelage and their shared joy in puzzles was the only thing that kept her from crawling back under the covers and pulling them over her head.

Now she was the one to be there for him, and it felt like time was running out.

When she was sure Janice was a safe distance away, Kate climbed the stairs and went into the office. Their dirty luncheon dishes were still on the table, but the bag of leftovers was gone.

Kate gathered up plates, silverware, and glasses and carried them down to the kitchen. She found the bag of leftovers in the fridge. Janice must have put them there.

She filled the sink with sudsy water, dismantled the silverware, and carefully washed and dried each section. She was drying the last piece when she heard the front bell jangle. She hadn't seen one visitor in the two days she'd been back. She hurried down the hall to see who it was.

She checked when she saw that Janice had returned to her desk. But when she saw the mailbag hanging from the man's shoulder and recognized him as Izzy Culpepper, she rushed toward him. There might be another anonymous letter in today's mail.

Izzy dropped the stack of mail on Janice's desk just as Kate reached the foyer.

"Well, Katie McDonald. Heard you were back in town. Gonna stay awhile?"

"Hi, Mr. Culpepper. It's good to see you."

"Same here. You stick around for a while. Give everybody a chance to say hello." He tipped his cap to the two women and left.

Kate reached for the stack of mail at the same time Janice reached for it.

"Thanks, Janice, but I'll see to these."

"I always—"

Kate scooped up the pile of mail. She didn't want to inflame their already adversarial relationship, but with the anonymous letters and missed bank payments, someone needed to take charge. She tried for a smile; it didn't come close to being friendly, but it was the best she could do. She really needed to work on her people skills.

She retreated upstairs, sat down at the professor's desk, and turned on the lamp. It cast a pool of yellow light over the green blotter. She reached into the desk drawer for a letter opener.

And found it just where she knew it would be. The professor had received it as a gift years before from an expert on Thai pattern puzzles. It was inlaid with nacre and jade and opened by a secret catch in the seam of the ornamentation. Kate had to search for a second before she found the catch. Then the sharp double-edged blade sprang out of the handle and glinted in the lamplight.

She quickly sorted the stack of mail into bills, junk, and personal, until she came to an envelope addressed to her. A frison of anxiety passed over her. She hadn't told any of her friends or coworkers where she was going. There hadn't been time.

Cautiously, she eased the blade under the tab and slit open the envelope. Using her fingernails, she pulled out the paper. Not that she expected there would be fingerprints. Anybody who watched television knew to wear gloves.

She knew even before it was fully opened that it was one of the anonymous letters. The message was constructed with letters cut from magazines and newspapers. Kate could tell that from the different texture of the paper and the variety of type. It was a quaint method, more provocative than a computer-generated threat. She shivered as she read the words. *Leave town now. You're not wanted here. You will only harm those near to you.*

Someone in Granville knew she was here and why.

Well, of course they did. Besides the professor and Aunt Pru, there was Janice, the people at the bank, Rayette, Lou Albioni . . . and the number of people they told probably grew exponentially. Hell, everybody in town might know she was here and why.

All the letter writer had to do was put the letter into the postbox by last night and it would be delivered today. But who would want to frighten her away?

The room suddenly felt dark and eerily still. She pushed the letter away. She needed more light. But before she could get up to turn on the lamps, she heard a thud.

She glanced toward the door, hoping it was the professor, but the door stayed shut. She listened but heard nothing more. *Because there's nothing to hear,* she told herself. That nasty letter had spooked her.

Still, she looked around the room. The books were lined up evenly in the bookcases. Sudoku books were stacked perfectly on the tea table. The fortune-teller's globe gleamed from its mahogany pedestal. Everything was in order.

Something brushed against her leg. Something furry. Kate squeaked and pushed the desk chair away from the desk—and caught a glimpse of gray fur slinking past her feet.

"Ugh. Go away," she cried, pulling up her knees, her heart pounding.

And then it jumped and landed in her lap. Kate's heart stopped as claws grappled at her skirt. Then it leaped onto the desktop, turned, and stared at her with glassy, beady eyes.

She froze, too paralyzed to run or scream—or even stand on her chair. Slowly her brain kicked in. Not a rat. Not a rat. A cat.

Her breath whooshed out.

The cat sat back on its haunches and fixed her with a curious look.

She laughed nervously. "You scared me to death. You're huge. You *are* a cat, aren't you?"

The cat made no response. Not a meow or a flick of the tail. Just sat there watching her. He was covered with long, silky gray and brown fur. It fell smoothly across his rump and spread onto the blotter, turning his tail into a feather duster. Tufts grew out of his ears; more fur created a ruff around his neck. Long white whiskers arced from his face, which gave him the appearance of a Chinese guardian figure.

She leaned forward, peered at him. Surely it couldn't be . . . "Al? Is that you?"

The cat trilled, a sound much too small for a cat of his size. He must have weighed close to thirty pounds.

Kate made a quick calculation back to the day she and the professor had found a tiny powder puff of a kitten caught in the newly pruned bushes of the backyard maze. Fourteen, fifteen years ago? They'd carefully extricated his long fur from the privet branches and taken him inside for a saucer of milk. He'd fit into the professor's palm.

Kate named him Aloysius after the wooly mammoth on Sesame Street, Aloysius Snuffleupagus.

He hadn't stayed small for long. Within weeks, he tripled in size and continued to grow. He came and went as he pleased, but he was loving and curious. He was forever jumping onto the checkerboard, or knocking the professor's Rubik's Cube off the table, or sitting on the jigsaw they were working.

"It *is* you. Where did you come from? Where have you been?" As she watched, Aloysius grew limp and melted onto the ink blotter, spreading himself across the threatening letter.

He looked back at her with a "what next?" expression on his face that she knew well and rolled bonelessly to his back.

She stroked his stomach and scratched behind his ears until his fur coat vibrated with his satisfied rumbling.

"Okay. I'm sorry, but that's enough. You're destroying evidence." She pushed him off the letter, and he let out a disgruntled "yeow" before rearranging himself on the ink blotter.

The two of them studied the letter. Al soon lost interest. He jumped down from the desk and sauntered across the carpet to sit on the windowsill.

The professor came in a few minutes later, looking refreshed from his nap.

Kate slipped the letter beneath the ink blotter. She didn't want to upset him further.

He crossed the room and turned on the hot plate for tea. When it was brewed, Kate joined him in front of the fireplace for their afternoon puzzle time just as they had each afternoon when she'd been a young girl. Al left the windowsill and sprang to the arm of the professor's chair, where he settled down to kibbutz.

The room took on an aura of stillness as they worked their puzzles separately, and yet together, like so many times before. The night drew on as Kate and the professor slipped into their old ways. And for a while, Kate forgot the troubles they faced and drifted back to a time when she was the one who took his strength and he was the one who gave.

It was late when she finally left the museum. And it wasn't until she was halfway home that she remembered the anonymous letter under the blotter. She'd have to retrieve it first thing in the morning. She turned the corner and once again saw lights shining from her house.

She slowed to make the turn into the driveway and saw Pru standing in the doorway.

Watching for me, she thought with a feeling of inevitability. But when she got out of the car, Pru ran to the edge of the porch and frantically waved both arms.

For a moment Kate couldn't move, her mind conjuring fires and heart attacks. The professor? Her father?

"No," she cried, and raced toward the house.

THE FIRST THING Kate remembered once she had slapped the alarm clock silent the next morning was that she had accepted a date with Louis Albioni—for tonight. Aunt Pru's hysterical waving was not because the house was on fire, her dad hadn't suffered a heart attack, and no one had died . . . Louis Albioni was on the phone.

And with Aunt Pru standing over her while she took the call, she couldn't do anything but graciously accept his invitation to dinner.

Well, wasn't that what she wanted? A chance to be a normal person. And what was more normal than a date on Friday night? It would be a harmless diversion from the problems at the museum. It might even be fun.

She dressed quickly and stopped in the kitchen long enough to make a cup of instant coffee and grab an apple from a bowl of fruit on the counter.

Aunt Pru had stocked the fridge and cabinets with food. Kate made a mental note to repay her. She knew that Pru lived on a limited budget, from her stocks, her social security, and the money Kate's father sent her every month.

Kate felt a little stab of guilt—a really little one. She hadn't asked her aunt to buy all this stuff. But she appreciated it. As overbearing and meddlesome as Aunt Pru could be, she had a good and generous spirit. She was just lonely. She should be the one going out on dates.

Kate grabbed her bag, laptop, and purse and, balancing apple and coffee cup, walked out to her car.

The door to the museum was unlocked when she arrived, and Janice wasn't at the reception desk. Kate locked the entrance door behind her and went upstairs.

Janice was standing just outside the office, her ear pressed to the closed door. She must have heard Kate, for she jumped back and turned around. The two women stared at each other for a split second, then Janice gave her a spiteful look and slinked away.

Kate started to knock, but stopped when she heard voices coming from inside. Janice had been eavesdropping. Had Harry returned? The professor would be so relieved. And Kate had to admit she was curious to see the boy who had taken her place in the professor's life. She wondered if Janice was mean to him, too.

One of the voices raised to a shrill pitch. Not a boy's, but a woman's. "It's either a nice condo in a retirement village or I'll have you committed. I swear I will."

Kate pulled back from the door. The woman was threatening the professor. But who would have the power to have him committed? And why?

Over my dead body, thought Kate, and she turned the knob. She pushed the door open and walked inside.

The professor sat at his desk, slowly shaking his head as if he couldn't believe what he'd just heard.

A woman was leaning over him. She was in her mid-fifties, Kate guessed, dressed in an expensive black-and-white checked suit cinched by a blood red belt that accentuated her carefully maintained figure. Crimson spike heels made her seem taller than she was, which Kate estimated to be around five foot six. A matching crimson purse sat upright on the professor's desk.

The professor was staring at the purse like it was a malevolent animal, and Kate realized that it was sitting on top of his puzzle book.

The woman stepped forward. "This is a private conversation."

Kate swallowed. "It was too loud to be private."

"Just who do you think you are?"

"A friend of Professor Avondale's." Kate waited for a reaction. Getting none, she added, "Who won't let him be threatened or bullied."

"Well, you little—"

"I'll have to ask you to leave now. The professor and I have work to do." Was it her imagination, or was the woman smirking at her? Granted, Kate didn't have great people skills, but she thought she'd sounded pretty forceful.

Support came from an unsuspected source. The professor's quiet voice broke in. "Yes, Abigail. You've made your point. Now please leave. Katie and I have work to do."

The woman turned on him. "Katie. Don't think she'll be able to help you. You can make this easy or hard. But the outcome will be the same."

She snatched her purse from the desk, and the professor reached for his Sudoku book.

She stopped at the door and turned back to Kate. Kate lifted her chin, though her knees were quaking.

"Either he agrees to the retirement home or I'll have him declared incompetent." She whisked through the door and left.

Kate listened to her heels clicking on the hardwood floor, then she turned to the professor. Her heart was pounding, her mouth dry. And for a second she longed for the quiet, rarefied atmosphere of the think tank where their arguments were philosophical, theoretical, or about whose turn it was to make the coffee.

Kate quietly closed the door, then turned to the professor. He was engrossed in his puzzle. She sympathized with his need to withdraw into a world where logic prevailed and the outcome was known, but she needed answers.

"Professor, who was that woman?"

At first he didn't answer. He filled in another blank. "My daughter."

Kate literally stumbled backward. Daughter? She didn't know the professor had ever been married. He'd never spoken of a wife or a daughter. And no one else had ever mentioned them. She certainly didn't live in Granville. So why was she here now? And why was she threatening to commit him? Coincidence?

Not likely. Events in nature might be random, but intent rarely was. Someone must have warned her that Kate had come to look after his interests.

The professor's head was bent over his puzzle book. He'd tuned the world out, including Kate. She tiptoed out of the office.

She spent the morning looking through the museum and was appalled at what she saw. She began with the first-floor exhibit rooms that housed the jigsaws and the mechanical puzzle collection. Most of the display lights were burned out. There was a layer of dust over everything.

The only room on the first floor that was clean and obviously used was the Paper Puzzle room. The lights were brighter, and the framed displays of crosswords, acrostics, griddles, and Tangrams displayed on the wall were all clean. There was a new wall display dedicated to Sudoku.

A long table ran down the center of the room, and its hard surface shone with polish. But the hoppers that usually held copies of puzzles for visitors to work were empty. She guessed that Janice or somebody kept this room clean for the various clubs that still met at the museum. If they still met. Once there had been a Jigsaw Club, a Crossword Club, and a Rubik's Club. Did any of them still exist?

Kate went down the hall to the kitchen. The counters were clean but scratched by long years of use. The linoleum floor was worn down to the floorboards in some places.

Through the window, she caught a glimpse of the maze where they'd discovered Al. It was completely overgrown. She turned away. Everywhere screamed neglect, and Kate knew it would take months, not days or weeks, to set the place to rights again.

She went upstairs, past the office and bathrooms. The larger display room had been turned into storage. It was filled with cast-off furniture and an assortment of cardboard boxes that Kate hoped didn't hold priceless puzzles. The other room was empty of anything but rolls of discarded carpet. She pulled a corner back, unleashing a cloud of dust into the air. The pattern was barely discernible, but she recognized it as the stair runner.

So that's why the stairs were bare. They'd have to replace it. Hardwood stairs would be slippery in wet weather and loud and distracting at all times. So why hadn't they thrown the old carpet out? And why stop when they'd just gotten started?

Only one more question to add to the many questions she needed to ask. She'd have to call the board. And soon. She dreaded it. The idea of speaking to Jacob Donnelly made her knees quake.

It was obvious the professor expected her to deal with things. She'd watched as he increasingly submerged himself into his private world of Sudoku. She could sympathize, but she was afraid that one day he wouldn't come back.

Was that why his daughter threatened to have him committed? Did she think he was getting too absentminded to take care of himself? But he could. He'd served Kate lunch. Was ready to take on Buck Perkins. But he'd lost interest in the museum. As far as she knew, he hadn't visited the rooms once since her return.

Was he aware of the state to which they'd fallen?

Kate stopped at the base of the stairs that led to the third floor. The professor lived there. She'd never been allowed to visit him there, and it was still sacrosanct.

She turned off the lights as she passed back down the hall. No need to pay for electricity when there was nothing to see. She stopped at the ladies room, a large Victorian-era washroom that overlooked the hedge between the houses. She washed her hands. The cabbage rose wallpaper was peeling above the sink. She turned off the water with more force than necessary.

How could the board have let things fall into such a state? Why didn't Janice pay more attention to the daily operations? Why had the professor let them do this to him?

By the time she walked into the office, her stomach was roiling with anger. The professor had moved to the window and was looking out at the street.

"Professor?"

"Yes, my dear?" He turned to her, his eyes mild and trusting. Her words of indignation died on her lips.

She bit her lip struggling with the anger and the love and frustration that warred inside her. "Have you been into the exhibition rooms lately?"

His expression changed, and he looked away. Finally, he shook his head. And Kate understood with a blinding clarity that he had already said good-bye to the objects of his life's work and love.

She stood helpless. It would take a quantum leap to make the museum viable again, and all she had was mundane Euclidean geometry. "To get from point A to point C, you must go through point B."

Of course. What had she been thinking? Quantum leaps were out of the question. Step-by-step process was the only thing that would see them clear of this dilemma.

She'd gotten waylaid from what she knew best. Logic, process, the scientific method. She was reacting, not acting. Aunt Pru's matchmaking, Janice's dislike, the missing Harry, his detestable uncle, the professor and his threatening daughter. All people problems—she didn't have a clue about how to fix those things.

Maybe normal life wasn't such a great thing after all.

At noon, Janice announced that she was going to lunch. "We always close an hour for lunch." She took her purse out of the bottom drawer of her desk and locked it. Without another word, she left the museum. Kate heard the rattle of her keys.

Locked out, locked in. It all amounted to the same thing. Kate was floundering. She hadn't come up with any facts, much less a solution. She had no access to the bank accounts. No way to make the loan payments except out of her own savings. And she didn't think she had enough to make up the difference.

Besides, she would need the money to live on, because saving the museum was going to take more than a few weeks. She'd be forced to take an extended leave from the institute, if they would allow it. And if not, well, she'd deal with that, too.

While Janice was at lunch, Kate and the professor enjoyed a peaceful hour eating leftovers from Rayette's and reminiscing. It was the most lively and comfortable he'd been since she'd returned, but it came to an abrupt end when Janice walked into the office carrying a paper bag.

Kate could feel the professor stiffen.

Janice stopped and eyed the trays of food. "Leftovers. About what I'd expect."

"They were quite sufficient," said the professor, catching Kate's eye.

"You can't live on leftovers. I brought you a real lunch."

"That's very thoughtful of you, Janice. Perhaps you could put it in the kitchen, and I can have it for dinner."

Janice shot Kate a seething look, then walked across the room and out the door without another word.

"She means well."

"I'm sure she does. But I could never be as patient as you are."

The professor smiled. "No, dear. You were never one for patience, except when it came to numbers and puzzles. Janice can be overbearing, but I've learned control over the years. And besides, it's very convenient to be served lunch instead of climbing the stairs to make it for myself." His eyes twinkled, making him look years younger. "Don't let her upset you."

Kate shook her head.

"Katie." He coaxed out her name like he'd done when she was a girl. "Promise?"

"Promise." That was easy enough to do. But she wanted to promise him more, promise him anything and everything. If only she could.

Kate carried the dishes down to the kitchen, taking the narrow back staircase in order to avoid passing through the foyer and risking another confrontation with Janice. When she came out, she saw the professor was standing in the doorway of the Jigsaw room. He was clutching something in his hand, and Kate realized that he was holding the letter that she'd hidden under the desk blotter. Without speaking, she came to stand beside him.

The late afternoon sun slanted through the windows above the wooden shutters, catching dust motes as they sat in the air.

He didn't look at her, just stared into the exhibit room. "I sent Janice to the post office. You should have told me that another letter had come."

"I was going to, but we were having such a nice time yesterday. . . . "

"Yes, we were."

He crumpled the letter in his hand. "This one was aimed at you. I shouldn't have asked you to come."

"Yes, you should. I'm glad you did. I wanted to come. And the letter is just some nasty prank."

He shook his head. "I was wrong. I want you to leave. Go back to Alexandria where you have a real life."

"No," said Kate, stunned. "I won't leave. I care about the museum." She hesitated. There was more she wanted to say, but she didn't know quite how to do it. So she just blurted it out. "I care about you."

Finally, the professor turned to look down at her. "And I care about you."

"Then don't ask me to leave."

He sighed and walked into the room; Kate followed him. He stopped by the display case and wiped a smudge from the glass with the elbow of his tweed jacket.

"You'll take care of the puzzles."

"Of course," she said, confused. "We'll both take care of them. We'll get this sorted out. I'm staying until the museum is back on its feet."

The professor shook his head. "You have your own work."

He was right, of course. She couldn't really walk away from the institute. She did important work, sort of, and they depended on her.

So does the professor, said an inner voice, not the one in her head that she usually listened to. "It can wait."

He shook his head. "I've let this go on for much too long. It has to stop now."

"Professor? Do you know who wrote these letters? Or what happened to the loan money?" What had he been keeping from her?

"Not a clue." He smiled at his puzzle humor. "Now then. It's Friday night, and surely there's some young man who wants the pleasure of your company tonight."

Kate groaned inwardly. She'd forgotten all about Louis Albioni. "Well, actually, Aunt Pru . . ."

The professor chuckled. "Up to her old tricks, is she? Well, run along. We wouldn't want to keep him waiting. And Katie." He reached into his pocket and took a key off his key ring. "You should have this." He held out the key to the front door.

Slowly, she took it from him.

They stood in the semidarkness, the room weaving a magical spell over them. "I'm glad you came. I've missed you." He lifted her hand and pressed it to his lips, then he turned and strode out of the room.

When Kate left a few minutes later, he was at his desk, working a puzzle.

The first thing Kate noticed when she opened the door to her bungalow was the large vase of flowers on the hall table. The second thing she noticed was that there was no Aunt Pru. She'd been worried that her aunt was planning to play chaperone, and she breathed a sigh of relief.

Of course it was only six-thirty. There was still time for Pru to make an appearance. With that motivation, Kate hurried down the hall to her bedroom. There were clothes laid out on the bed—a khaki skirt that Kate had bought last season and never worn and a new white blouse with a large, soft bow that looped down the front. The price tag was still pinned to the cuff.

"Oh, Aunt Pru," said Kate, exasperated and yet touched by her aunt's concern.

She wouldn't wear it. She'd look like a librarian from the fifties. She went to the closet and picked out a black knit sheath with three-quarter sleeves and a hemline that stopped mid-thigh.

It could be dressed up or down.

Forty minutes later she was showered, dressed, and sitting in the living room waiting for her date. She'd decided on low-heeled shoes, just in case he was short. She added a heavy gold-link belt and matching hoop earrings for a bit of flash. She exchanged her shoulder bag for a small clutch. Her Blackberry wouldn't fit inside, just her driver's license, some spare change, and a small pad and pen in case she was hit with any brilliant hypotheses during dinner.

She looked good. She'd copied the ensemble from a spring fashion magazine. Always trust the experts. But as she sat on the couch, waiting for the doorbell to ring, she began to have doubts. If he showed up in a suit, she would be all right, but what if he showed up in jeans and a flannel shirt and took her to the Granville Bar and Grill.

She'd have to lose the belt on the way out the door.

The doorbell rang, and she catapulted off the couch. Her shoe went flying, and she hopped across the room while trying to put it back on her foot. By the time she reached the door, she was flustered and out of breath.

Smoothing her hair back, forcing a smile to dry lips, she opened the door.

"Hi. I'm Louis." He was tall with dark hair that gleamed back from his forehead. He was wearing brown slacks and a plaid sports shirt with a brown knitted tie.

He was holding the duplicate of the bouquet that was sitting on the credenza.

She stepped in front of it.

"Hi. I'm Kate. Please, come on in." She took the flowers. "They're beautiful."

Louis stepped past her, and Kate got a whiff of serious aftershave.

"Sit down. I'll just put these in a vase." She gestured to the living room. When he was out of view, she scuttled the bouquet and the table arrangement into the kitchen. She stuck the arrangement in a water pitcher, replaced it with the bouquet, and took it back out into the hallway.

"Well," she said. "Shall we go?"

Louis drove them to the outskirts of town, past the Bar and Grill to a new strip mall. All the stores were closed except for a single restaurant. The green neon sign in the window spelled out ALBIONI'S ITALIANO.

Louis smiled sheepishly. "I couldn't decide where to take you for dinner, then I thought, what the heck, I know the food's good here."

Thank God I didn't wear that white blouse, thought Kate, imagining marinara disasters as she waited for Louis to come around the car and open her door.

They were shown to a window table with a view of the parking lot, and Kate just caught the wink that the maitre d' gave Louis before walking away.

She suddenly felt nervous. She was on display like a fish in a bowl, like a teenager meeting the boy's parents. A waiter brought bread and filled their water glasses.

Louis ordered for the both of them. "I'm kind of an expert," he said.

"Yeah," said the waiter, a husky young man who couldn't be older than twenty. He looked at Kate. "He's got great taste."

Kate smiled uncomfortably. She didn't think he was talking about Louis's taste in linguine.

The dinner was pretty good. The conversation wouldn't merit one star. Once Louis had finished an explanation of achieving the perfect al dente pasta and she'd tried to explain about the vertices and graph probabilities of Sudoku, the conversation sputtered out, and they spent most of the meal looking at their own plates or out the window.

Breathe, Kate told herself. *This is pleasant. Just think of something to say.* She asked him about produce, and the evening picked up. They bonded over the ratio of cost versus overhead expenses versus shelf life. But by coffee, they'd exhausted the subject of lettuce and had moved back into silence.

Kate began to worry about how to end the evening. She was tired from all the emotional stress of the last two days, and she longed for a Sudoku and bed.

The silence grew more uncomfortable as they drove back to town. Kate began to formulate excuses for not asking him in.

They were standing on the porch fumbling for a way to end the evening, when the hall telephone rang. Aunt Pru hadn't wasted a second, though it did make the goodnight easier.

"You'd better get that," said Louis at the same time Kate said, "I'd better get that."

"Thanks for the lovely evening. I had a wonderful time."

"Me, too," said Louis. He stalled after that.

"Well, thanks again." Kate grabbed his hand, shook it, and hurried inside. She heard his car drive away as she picked up the phone. He'd been as anxious to end the evening as she had been.

"Hello?"

"Katie . . ."

"Professor, what is it?"

"There's something I need to tell you. Tonight."

2		5		4			3	
		7	6	1		2		8
					5	4	9	1
	6			7	8			
8	5						7	9
			3	9			6	
1	4	6	2					
9		3		8	1	5		
	8			3		7		4

THE OFFICE LIGHT was on. The rest of the museum was dark. Kate parked at the curb and ran up the sidewalk. She was worried. What could be so important that the professor couldn't wait for the morning.

She hurried up the front steps, fumbling for the key she'd added to her key ring. But as she reached the door, it opened. For a second, a dark figure loomed before her. Then it brushed past her, knocking her off balance, and ran down the steps to the street.

Kate watched, open mouthed, then reality hit. Something was terribly wrong. Had she surprised a burglar? Had the professor? She rushed inside. The foyer was pitch black, but she didn't waste time fumbling for the switch. She took the stairs two at a time.

The office door was open. The professor was sitting at his desk, shoulders sagging.

"Professor?"

He didn't answer. She looked for the rise and fall of his shoulders, hoping he was asleep. But she didn't see any movement at all. "Professor?" she said more loudly.

There was something wrong with his neck. An optical illusion. A trick of the light.

"Professor?" This time the word was barely a whisper, because suddenly she knew for certain what she was looking at. The letter opener, the nacre catching the light, stuck out at a right angle from the professor's neck.

Her breath caught, refused to come in or out. Then logic kicked in, overriding her horror. She felt his face, warm but a ghastly yellow in the light of the desk lamp.

With stiff fingers, she lifted his wrist; his arm was heavy. She couldn't find a pulse.

She shook her head, refusing to believe what she already knew. Mechanically, her hand reached for the phone. Punched in 911. She gave the address. Told them there was an accident. Begged them to hurry, then hung up before they could tell her to stay on the line. She needed to act.

She pushed the chair away from the desk; the professor's body flopped forward. She grabbed him under the arms and lowered him to the floor. The weight of his body dragged her down with him, trapping her arms. She pulled them out from under him.

She stumbled blindly across the room, grabbed the dish towels from the drawer beneath the hot plate, and rushed back to the body.

Not the body. The professor. Her friend and mentor. She folded the towel, and with the bile rising in her throat, she slid the opener from his neck. She pressed the folded towels to the wound, but she had already seen that the blood was not flowing.

She dropped the towels, stacked her hands, and pushed on his chest. Hard. Five times in succession. Put her ear to his nose, felt nothing. Lifted his chin, blew into his mouth, then returned to his chest.

Five more thrusts to his chest, three breaths into his mouth, again and again, until someone dragged her to her feet and thrust her toward another person who moved her off to the side.

The EMTs had arrived. She hadn't even heard the sirens.

"Save him, please save him," she murmured.

No one answered her. She didn't expect them to. They were busy over the professor's body. She watched as if from down a long hallway. Willing him to breathe again.

She felt a tear slide down her cheek. Brushed it away and then stared at her hand. It was covered with blood. Both hands were sticky with it. Her dress was wet with it. Her nose was suddenly filled with the smell of it.

She swayed as her dinner rose to her throat. She forced it back down. She couldn't be sick now. The professor might need her.

The professor does need you, a colder, more clinical voice told her. The professor was dead. He would need her to find out who had murdered him. And suddenly without conscious intent, she began to look around the room.

The actions of the EMTs, the thunk of the defibrillator, the voices all faded into the background. Other details appeared in total clarity. The desk, the chair, the rug beneath. There was a book opened on the desk. One of those larger spiral puzzle books. She stepped toward it. Recoiled when she saw the splatters of blood across the page. And her mind began to add up facts. If the book was covered with blood, the attacker would be, too.

The person who'd pushed her aside as she'd opened the front door. Had she smelled blood, felt wetness, when he passed? She couldn't remember. She hadn't expected it.

She forced herself to look more closely at the puzzle. She didn't know why. The professor hadn't scrawled the name of his killer across the page. She doubted if he'd even survived the attack. Because she knew in her head that he was dead.

She peered at the page, but it was hard to make out the numbers through the spatters. She stepped closer. Her foot came in contact with something on the floor. The professor's pen? She stooped to pick it up, but it was the letter opener. Covered with blood.

She reached out for it, wanting to hide the obscenity of it all. But a large hand clamped down on her wrist. She cried out as much in surprise as in pain. She tried to wrench it away.

"Stop struggling." The voice was low, threatening.

Then she was yanked to her feet. For a moment panic overrode intelligence as the image of the figure on the porch rose in her mind. She raised her free hand to protect herself and came face to face with a dark blue uniform that seemed to stretch across her entire field of vision.

A policeman. She sagged with relief. He started to catch her, then thought better of it.

"Come on. There's nothing you can do." His voice was more gentle than his hold on her wrist or the look of anger on his face. He nudged her toward the door.

"No. I can't leave."

The EMTs were packing up. She heard the metallic scratch of a zipper. Her knees buckled, and this time he held her on her feet while he barked orders to the EMTs.

"Leave the bod—the professor," he said. "And don't touch anything else. The county crime scene van is on its way."

He guided Kate out the door.

He's irritated, she thought. *The professor is dead and he's irritated.*

They stopped in the hallway long enough for him to say something to a man with camera equipment hanging from his shoulder. A photographer who stopped and stared at Kate, openmouthed, until the policeman yelled at him. Then he backed up and hurried into the office.

More men came up the stairs, and she found herself counting them. Strange details popped into her vision, then receded. One of the patrolmen was carrying a metal case. It was aluminum. One had freckles across his nose. Someone had turned on the lights, because she could see.

They stopped and stared. The policeman motioned one of them over and barked orders at the rest.

He seemed to be in charge. Was he the new chief of police?

"Are you—" Kate started to ask, but he thrust her toward the young patrolman with the freckles.

"Take her downstairs so she can sit down. Don't let her get away." He went into the office.

"Ma'am?" said the new policeman, glancing at the office door.

Kate nodded and went down the stairs. He walked beside her but kept his distance. She didn't blame him; the professor's blood was caking on her skin. She stumbled.

He reached to help her.

She shook her head. "I'm okay."

She heard his sigh of relief.

She made it to the foyer, then couldn't go any farther. She sat down in Janice's chair, and fog seemed to descend over her. Her mind drifted out of her control. She didn't know how long she sat there.

There were more sirens. More men. More equipment.

Then the policeman was back. He reached into his pocket and pulled out a notepad and a pen. Kate bit back a sob as an image of the professor reaching for his Sudoku book and pen overlaid the officer's actions.

He narrowed his eyes at her. He had a scar on his lower lip.

"Your name?"

"Kate—Katherine McDonald."

"You found the, uh, deceased?"

Kate shook her head, her last ditch effort at denial. Her lip quivered. The policeman looked away. "I know this is difficult, but could you please just answer the question?"

"Yes."

"You placed the call to 911?"

"Who are you?"

His jaw tightened. "Chief of Police Brandon Mitchell. Did you place the call?"

A commotion above them made Kate look up. The EMTs were carrying a stretcher down the stairs.

"Jesus Christ."

The EMTs stopped. "Crime Scene said we could take the body."

Chief Mitchell pushed his fingers through his hair, a brown almost as dark as his eyes. "Fine. Do it quickly, please." He stepped in front of Kate, blocking her view.

"Yes," she said.

"What?"

"Yes, I called the EMTs. Where are they taking him?"

He scowled down at her. "I think we'd better continue this conversation downtown."

What an odd thing to say, thought Kate. They were already downtown. And it wasn't a conversation, more like an interrogation. He couldn't think that she—

She clapped her hand over her mouth, remembering too late that it was still covered with the professor's blood. "Could I wash my hands first?"

"No," he said. "Curtis," he bellowed. Kate had to fight the urge to cover her ears.

A head appeared over the banister above them. "Yes sir?"

It was the boy with the freckles.

"Secure the scene."

"Yes sir."

"Seal the door and have someone stand guard outside." He turned to Kate. "If you please." He gestured toward the front door just as the EMTs rolled the body bag out the front door.

"Oh God. I have his blood on my hands."

He leaned down, bracing his hands on the arms of the chair, and peered down at her.

She blinked up at him.

There was a moment of silence, then, "You have the right to remain silent . . ."

She didn't hear the rest. The chief droned on, then he led her outside and put her into the back of a squad car. It wasn't until the siren churned up and they were speeding away that she realized. They weren't going downtown. They were going to the police station. She'd just been arrested.

9	6					8		
	1	7		8		4		5
			1	3	2			
8					6	9	5	2
	4		2		1		6	
3	2	6	8					7
			5	1	4			
7		8		6		2	1	
		4					9	6

"GOOD HEAVENS, KATIE McDonald, what happened to you? Are you all right?"

The dispatcher at the Granville police station jumped up from her chair and hurried toward Kate. Kate didn't recognize her at first. Then remembered. Aunt Pru's bridge partner, Elmira Swyndon. And suddenly Kate couldn't control her emotions any longer. She shook her head, spraying big tears out in front of her.

"Chief Mitchell, can't you see the girl is about to faint? Get her some water. Now, Katie, you just come over here and sit down." She put her arm around Kate's shoulders, led her over to the waiting area, and sat her down on the bench.

"Don't—" said the chief. Then with a huge sigh he crossed over to the water cooler. He came back with two cups filled with water. He handed one to Kate.

She took it with shaking hands. Water sloshed over the rim.

"Here, let me help you." Elmira reached for the cup, but the chief snatched it away. The rest of the water splashed onto Kate's dress.

"Give her this one." He handed the full cup to Elmira and carried the other one away, holding it by the tips of his fingers.

He just took my fingerprints, thought Kate, as Elmira held the cup to her lips and helped her drink. *Stupid man. He should have just asked; they're on file with the government. I have a classified job.*

"That's right, honey. You just drink up. Then we'll get you cleaned up and call Pru."

"Ms. Swyndon," said a harsh voice from the doorway. "Please bring Miss, uh, McDonald back to the inter—back to room C."

"I will not. You can ask your questions tomorrow. When she's feeling more the thing."

"Elmira!"

Elmira looked reprovingly at him and patted Kate's hand. "He's new. Just can't seem to get the hang of things. Don't let him bully you. We don't." And with another pat, she helped Kate down the hall to room C.

It was a small room, with plaster walls painted metallic gray. A small, rectangular table was placed in the center with two straight-back metal chairs facing each other. The light was harsh. The tape recorder ancient.

And all Kate could think was that she had the professor's blood on her hands—and on her arms and dress and probably her face.

Elmira stood next to Kate until the chief of police crossed his arms and glared at her. Giving him a look that she'd take no sass from him, she said, "I'll go call your aunt."

When they were alone, the chief sat down across from her. He looked at her without flinching as if seeing a blood-covered woman in a knit dress were an everyday occurrence for him. He *was* the police chief, but Granville didn't have any serious crime. Until now.

He clicked on the tape recorder. It whined for several seconds before gears finally caught and the steady click of the tape threading over the heads took over. He gave the time and date and case number. "Witness has waived the right to attorney."

Had she done that? It didn't matter. She didn't need an attorney.

"Please tell me exactly who you are and what you were doing at the museum after hours."

"My name is Katherine McDonald. I'm a friend of the professor's."

"That would be Professor Peter Thomas Avondale."

She nodded.

"Please answer verbally for the recording."

"Yes."

He nodded for her to go on.

Kate took a shaky breath, not wanting to revisit the scene of the professor's death.

"Oh God," she murmured, then bit her lip until she felt able to continue. "He, the professor, called me and asked me to come to the museum."

"And what time was this?"

She shrugged. Caught herself. "Around eleven, I think. I had been on—been out to dinner."

"And you were dining with . . . ?"

Now she was going to get poor Louis Albioni in trouble. "A friend."

She could tell the chief was losing his patience. His face remained impassive, but his energy arced across the table at her like particles in a cyclotron.

"If you must know, it was Louis Albioni."

"The guy from the groc—" He stopped the tape. Rewound it to her last statement. They waited for the recorder to whine up again.

"No fair," she said.

He raised one eyebrow, and Kate thought of Aunt Pru. She'd be so upset. But she wished she'd get here.

"So Professor Avondale called and you left your date and immediately went to the museum. The house is located at Sixty-three Hopper Street."

Kate frowned at him. Realized he was talking for the benefit of the report.

"Yes."

That skeptical look again.

"Well, it wasn't that interesting. I mean, we didn't have a lot to talk about." What was she saying? She didn't have to explain her social life to this man.

His scarred lip twitched. Annoyance or laughter?

Katie is a ge-ek.

She lowered her eyes. "So I went, and when I got there—" She jumped up. The chief reached for his holster.

"Don't shoot," she cried. "It's just that I remembered something. There was a man."

A commotion outside the door interrupted her. The door burst open, and Aunt Pru, dressed in a hot pink sweat outfit, descended on the room, followed by Elmira and a thin man, who was nearly bald except for a tonsure of gray hair. Even though it was past midnight, he was dressed in an old-fashioned three-piece suit. He and Pru looked ridiculous together. Kate felt the onset of hysterical giggling. She had to pull herself together.

"Chief Mitchell," he said in a gravelly tenor voice. "I don't know how they do things in Boston, but around here a man—or woman—has right to counsel."

The chief turned off the tape recorder and sighed. "She's been read her rights. Go ahead and counsel."

"Rights! Rights?" shrieked Aunt Pru, bearing down on the chief, who'd stood up when they'd entered the room. "How dare

you arrest my niece? On what charges? Forgetting to use her
napkin? Turning on her car before she buckled her seat belt?
Squeezing the tomatoes at the Market Basket?"

She turned to Kate, and her expression went blank. Her face
turned pale. "Oh my Lord. She's hurt. Why haven't you called a
doctor? Katie, honey. Are you hurt? Get up. We're going to the
emergency room."

She glared at the chief, defying him to stop her.

"Aunt Pru. I'm okay, but the professor is dead." Kate's mouth
twisted. A sob shook her. Pru was beside her in an instant and
enclosed Kate in protective arms.

"Jesus Christ," muttered the chief.

Pru turned on him. "Don't you use the Lord's name in vain,
young man. Simon, we're leaving."

A muscle in the chief's jaw jumped. "She was found at the crime
scene standing over the body. She was covered in blood. She was
trying to dispose of the murder weapon when I stopped her."

Kate jumped up. "What?" she exclaimed at the same time Aunt
Pru said, "Murder?"

"I was not trying to dispose of the murder weapon. I called the
EMTs. I tried to save him. And you're wasting time. There was a
man who came out just as I went in. He'll be covered in blood, and
you should be looking for him."

"Murder?" said Aunt Pru, and sank into the chair Kate had
vacated.

"Katie. Don't say another word," said the lawyer.

"But—"

"My client is obviously distraught. I'm taking her home. If you
want to question her after she's rested, you may call me tomorrow
and I'll arrange it for you."

"Now just a damn minute."

The lawyer held up his hand. "Come along, Katie."

Kate scuttled over to him, leaving a wide swath around the chief, who looked like he was considering the odds of taking them all on at once. Which was ridiculous, two sexagenarian ladies, one old lawyer, and a geek covered in blood. She almost felt sorry for him.

Kate stayed in the shower until the water ran tepid. Then she dressed in a long flannel nightgown, a terry cloth robe, and a pair of heavy wool socks and padded down the hall to the living room.

Pru and the lawyer, whom Pru had introduced as Simon Mack, were drinking tea. A plate of sandwiches sat on the coffee table between them.

Pru patted a place on the couch next to her. "Come sit over here. I'll get you some tea. Or would you rather have some warm milk?"

"Tea's fine." Kate sat down and pulled her knees up. Pru didn't even give her a disapproving look, just poured out tea and filled the cup with sugar.

"Do you think you could tell us what happened tonight, Katie?" asked Simon in a gentle voice. "We can wait until tomorrow, but details get lost as time passes. And I think I should be aware of the facts before the chief of police questions you again."

"That big—"

"Now, Prudence. He's just doing his job. Can't blame the boy for lacking finesse. Murder's an everyday thing where he comes from."

"Then he should go back there," said Pru.

Simon reached for a sandwich. "Perhaps he should. But since he shows no signs of doing that, we'd best learn how to deal with him."

"But I don't have anything to hide," said Kate, feeling the tears well up again. "And I want to talk to him. If I could just make him listen."

"Well, you can't," said Pru. "The man's about as approachable as a wounded bear."

"Pru, that kind of attitude is not going to help Katie."

"Well, he makes me so mad, I could spit. Giving decent folks traffic tickets and practicllly accusing their niece of murder."

"Pru, you ran the stop sign."

"Just a little bit. Everybody does. And if he thinks Katie—"

"Pru," Simon coaxed.

Pru huffed out a sigh. "I'll stifle myself . . . somehow."

Simon nodded. "Good. I know you will." .

Kate told him about going to the museum, the intruder, the letter opener. "And if he'd only listened to me, he might have found the murderer by now. He's out there somewhere." Kate collapsed against the couch cushion. "How could anyone murder such a wonderful man? Who would do such a thing?"

Simon and Pru exchanged glances.

"Who?" Kate repeated.

"There's no telling," said Simon. "A lot of tempers are flaring over this mall thing. Maybe someone just boiled over. The professor is one of the last holdouts."

"But not the last," said Kate. "There are others. He said so."

"About three."

"Is this person going to murder them all? For a shopping mall, for Christ's sake."

"Katherine Mar—"

"Sorry, Aunt Pru." Kate put down her cup. Aunt Pru refilled it, adding even more sugar than the last time.

"So you moved P. T. to the floor."

"I was trying to start his heart."

"That was a very brave thing to do," said Pru, and pursed her lips at Simon.

"Prudence. Just let me do my job. We don't want any surprises at the police station tomorrow."

Pru's eyes widened. "She's not going down there. She's a heroine, not a common criminal. She tried to save P. T.'s life, and I'm going to make sure everyone, including that know-it-all Brandon Mitchell, knows it."

"Excellent," Simon said, "but be sure not to divulge any of the details you've heard tonight."

"My lips are sealed," said Pru, and she pressed them together to prove it.

Simon smiled, stifling a yawn. He stood up. "I imagine the chief will want to see you first thing tomorrow morning. I'll pick you up about nine."

Kate nodded.

"Goodnight, Prudence. No need to see me to the door. Goodnight, Katie."

"Mr. Mack."

"Simon, please."

"Simon. Where did they take the professor? What are they going to do to him? Who's going to arrange the funeral?"

"Well, they've most likely taken him to County General, possibly to perform an autopsy. Standard procedure, though from what you told us, it's clear how he died. I'm not sure who will handle the arrangements." He looked at Pru. She shook her head.

"I think I should."

Aunt Pru protested. Then Kate suddenly remembered Abigail Avondale. "He has a daughter."

They both looked at her.

"How do you know that?" asked Pru.

"She came to the museum, yesterday. She threatened to have the professor put away."

"Well, there's your murderer," said Pru with a snap of her head. "Never laid eyes on a harder, more bitter woman, except her mother. Two of a kind and double the nasty. But we don't talk about her," she added as an afterthought.

"Why?"

"You get some rest," said Simon. "Morning will be here before you know it, and we want you thinking clearly."

Kate nodded. She always thought clearly. Even in her sleep. Except for a few minutes tonight when it counted most.

She heard the soft *snick* of the front door as Simon left.

Aunt Pru returned the cups to the tea tray and stood up. "Simon's right. Let's get you to bed."

For once, Kate didn't mind her aunt's fussing. She let her pull back the covers and tuck her in. "Thanks for rescuing me."

"As if I wouldn't take care of mine," said Pru, and flicked off the light. "Now, go to sleep. Things will look better in the morning."

No they won't, thought Kate, and she closed her eyes.

She didn't drift into sleep. She didn't toss or turn. She wasn't visited by images of her murdered friend. One minute she was awake, the next, the door shut on the world and she was plunged into darkness—unthinking, unforgiving darkness.

When she began to emerge from this abyss of sleep, she was dreaming about coffee.

Her eyes were heavy-lidded, and she had to force them open. She smelled coffee.

It was light outside. She looked at the bedside clock. Eight o'clock. Morning. The day was . . . Saturday. She was in bed in her own room in Granville. The professor was dead. All the horror of the night before flooded over her.

And Janice didn't know. She would arrive at the museum to crime scene tape and policemen. Someone had to stop her.

Kate pushed the covers away. She pulled on jeans and a sweater and was halfway down the hall when Aunt Pru stuck her head out of the kitchen doorway. She was wearing the same pink sweatsuit she'd worn the night before.

"I thought I heard you."

"Have you been here all night?"

"Well, I couldn't very well leave you alone. Do you feel better? I made coffee. Sit down and I'll make some toast. Do you think you could eat an egg?"

Kate's eyes clouded with tears. With grief and for her aunt's generosity. "I'll take some coffee with me."

"You have plenty of time. Simon isn't picking you up until nine."

"I have to go to the museum."

Pru's face slackened. "Katie, hon, don't you remember?"

"Yes," said Kate, forcing herself to make the word audible. "And I'm so grateful to you and to Simon. But could you please ask him to meet me at the museum? Janice will come to work. She doesn't know—She'll—she doesn't know. I should be there."

She shouldn't care. But she did. No one, not even Janice, should have to face that alone.

Janice was already at the museum when Kate pulled up to the curb. She was standing on the sidewalk staring up at the house. The gate was padlocked, and there was yellow tape pulled across the entrance way. Two police cars were parked on the street, and one of the officers was standing next to her.

Kate got out of the car and hurried over to them. "I'm sorry I wasn't here. Someone should have told you."

Janice didn't look at her. Didn't even seem to notice her. Just stared at the closed door of the museum.

The young officer must have been up all night. His eyes were mere slits. A stubble of blond beard sprinkled his chin. He looked young and innocent and awkward. He saw Kate and visibly slumped with relief.

"I've tried to explain," he began.

"They won't let me in," said Janice. "Me. I've opened the museum every day for twenty-two years. And they won't let me in."

She was wearing the raspberry skirt and twinset, and the morning sun accentuated the snags and stains from years of wear.

What would she do now that she no longer had the museum? Would she be able to find another job at her age?

Kate didn't want to feel sympathy, but suddenly their past differences no longer mattered. They both loved the professor in their own way. She touched Janice's shoulder.

Janice jerked away and turned on her. "This is your doing. You killed him. Bitch! Bitch!" She lunged at Kate.

The officer, his reflexes slowed by fatigue, made a belated attempt to stop her.

But it was another pair of hands that grabbed her and handed her off to the helpless young policeman.

Kate turned stricken eyes up to the chief of police. She shook her head, trying to dislodge Janice's accusations. Wanting to tell him that Janice hadn't really meant what she said. But she couldn't speak. Just stood looking at the chief while Janice's sobs filled the air.

"I didn't," she finally managed in a voice that didn't sound like hers. "I didn't." She needed him to believe her. She needed someone to tell her that her return, her good intentions, hadn't set this awful thing in motion.

But the chief's hard, dark eyes merely looked back at her, his number one suspect.

"Drive Ms. Krupps home, Owens," he said, his eyes never leaving Kate's face.

"Yes sir." The officer led Janice toward one of the police cars.

"You killed him" was the last thing they heard before the car door slammed shut.

"I thought Simon Mack was bringing you to the station."

Kate nodded. "He was—but I remembered—" She gestured toward the empty parking space where the patrol car had been. "Janice. I didn't want her to—Oh, I don't know what I thought. He's meeting me here."

"Then we'll wait for him." He gestured toward his own car.

CHIEF OF POLICE GRANVILLE POLICE DEPARTMENT was painted across the door.

Kate shrunk back.

His eyes flicked again. "You can sit up front." And he opened the door.

Simon arrived a few minutes later. He swerved in front of the chief's car and parked at an angle to the curb. He jumped out and strode toward the police car.

The chief opened the door and got out to meet him. "I didn't ask her one damn question, so crawl off, Mack."

Kate was shocked. Not at the damn but at the *Mack,* then remembered it was Simon's name. What was wrong with her? She had to pull herself together, get her mind working or she was going to find herself in jail while the professor's murderer went free.

She closed her eyes. Thought of the puzzle book in her purse. If she could just work one. Seeing numbers fall into logical order would set her mind back on track. But she knew it would appear callous and unfeeling. So she visualized a blank grid, entered digits arbitrarily throughout the cells, and keeping the process of elimination in her head, she began to fill in the boxes.

"What have you done to her?"

"Nothing. She's fallen asleep."

Kate's concentration broke. The numbers changed, and the page began to fill with blood. Her eyes flew open, realized someone had opened her door. The last image of the bloody puzzle faded away. She swallowed, said, "I was just resting my eyes." *And I need you to leave me alone. Because there was something about that puzzle . . .*

"She can drive with you. I'll meet you there in half an hour. I have to check in here first. Come on." The chief took her by the elbow and hauled her out of the car. He passed her off to Simon and walked toward the gate, which he vaulted over without hesitation and continued on toward the house.

"You should have waited for me," said Simon. "I don't trust that man. He's not one of us, and he may try to entrap you."

"But I didn't—"

"We know that, but he doesn't, and he needs to find a suspect or this town will ride him out on a rail." Simon nodded, a quick little action that punctuated his statement. "And darn it, I'll be the second one in line."

Distracted, Kate asked, "The second?"

"Right behind your Aunt Pru." He nodded again.

And Kate found herself actually smiling.

		7	9	6	1	3		
	9				8			1
	4	3			5	9	8	
6			8				9	
	5	2				6	7	
	1				7			4
	3	1	4			5	2	
7			5				6	
		5	7	2	9	8		

9		1
	CHAPTER **S E V E N**	
2		

KATE WAS ONCE again sitting in Interview Room C, only this time Simon Mack was sitting beside her, and there were three mugs of steaming coffee on the metal table. Elmira had tried to put a plate of donuts down, but the chief stopped her, much to her disgust and to Simon's amusement.

"They'll be outside, getting stale. For when you're finished." Elmira huffed out the door. The chief closed it behind her and sat down. He clicked on the whining tape recorder and looked down at his notes.

Kate repeated the events of the night before with the chief occasionally stopping her to ask for clarification. All the time, Simon sat poised to spring. He made Kate more nervous than the police chief did.

"The man you say ran out of the house—"

"I suppose it could have been a woman, but he ... or she ... was wearing some kind of overcoat, like a dress coat, or a raincoat."

"Which? Dress coat or raincoat?"

"I don't know. It was dark. I didn't expect someone to open the door and knock me over. And by the time I did look, he was running down the street."

"Which way did he run?"

"To the left . . ."

And so it went for an hour. At which time Elmira knocked on the door and said she was sure Kate needed to powder her nose.

Kate could see the chief's jaw clench. But he allowed her a quick bathroom break. Kate caught the look of triumph on Elmira's face. She was pretty sure the chief had seen it, too.

He really needed to take charge or he'd be looking for a new job before he knew it. And what did she care? She used the facilities and went back to the interview room.

Only Simon was sitting at the table.

"Is it over?" Kate asked hopefully.

"Not quite, dear. The chief had to take a phone call. Evidently there's some problem over at the professor's house."

"What kind of a problem? Have they arrested someone?"

"Not yet, but don't you worry. They will."

Not at the rate they're going, thought Kate.

The chief came back into the room.

Slow seethe, thought Kate. One of the guys at the institute was so well known for it, they called him SS Grigoriev. He thought they were referring to his fear of flying.

What had happened to piss off the chief?

He clicked on the tape recorder. It whined to life.

She wasn't going to find out.

"Interview with Katherine McDonald, nine forty-seven, September—"

There was a knock at the door. The chief punched off the tape recorder. "Come."

Elmira opened the door. "They called again, chief. No one can get the cat down."

"Then tell them to call animal control."

"No," said Kate. "It's Al."

"Who?"

"Aloysius, the professor's cat."

"Not your concern." He turned on the tape recorder. "This person you allegedly saw—"

"I did see him. And Al is my concern. And you can't let animal control take him away."

The chief ran his fingers through his hair. Turned off the tape recorder. "Ms. McDonald . . . "

Elmira knocked on the door. Simon dropped his chin to hide a smile.

"Yes, Elmira."

"Animal control says it's a pet and they won't remove him without the owner's signature."

"The owner is—" The chief cut a look toward Kate. "Get them on the phone and explain the situation, will you, please, Elmira."

"I can get him down," said Kate. "He's on the top bookshelf, isn't he. He's just trying to protect the professor's space. Maine Coons are very loyal."

"She's right," said Elmira from the doorway.

"Ayuh." Simon nodded in agreement.

A vein began to throb in the chief's neck.

"Tell animal control to take a hike. Tell everyone else to stay put. I'll deal with the cat myself as soon as I finish this interview."

If ever, Kate finished for him. Not even an outsider deserved this kind of treatment. Why didn't he take control? *Because if he did,* warned her internal voice, *you'd be charged with murder.*

The chief turned on the recorder again.

Kate told him about the letter opener.

"And only you and the professor knew how it opens."

"I didn't say that. I don't know who else knew. I've been gone for nearly ten years."

"Why did you return now?"

"I told you. The professor wrote and asked me to come."

"Why?"

She was tempted to say, none of your business. "He didn't say in the letter. But I think because he needed help with some financial matters concerning the museum."

"You're a CPA?"

"A math—mathematician."

"You teach?"

"No. I . . . just do math."

Both his eyebrows rose.

She was used to the reaction, and they were getting off track. "It doesn't matter. We need to find that man—or woman."

"*We* don't have to do anything. *I'll* find him—or her."

"Chief Mitchell," warned Simon.

The chief glanced at him. "Just being politically correct." He refocused on Kate.

"It was someone he knew."

"Speculation, Ms. McDonald."

"Speculation often precedes theorem," she snapped. Then cringed when she saw his expression. "What I mean is, the professor was stabbed with his letter opener. It can only be opened by a hidden catch. The killer had to know how to open it."

"You, for instance?"

"No!"

"Chief Mitchell. If you continue to badger my client—"

The chief waved him off. Calmed his voice. "Continue, please."

"That's all." Should she mention the puzzle? He would think

she was crazy. "And there was no sign of a struggle. The professor was still sitting in his chair."

"Until you moved the body."

"I was trying to save him. He was working a Sudoku."

The chief stopped her. "The interviewee is referring to the paper of gridded numbers found on the desk blotter." He moved his hand for her to continue.

"He must have been working it while the murderer was there."

"Or was interrupted by the killer."

"Possibly. But he often worked them to focus his mind or when he was upset."

"Denial mechanism."

She looked at him, startled.

He gave her an ironic look.

"Well, yes." Her mind flashed on the puzzle. Could almost see the numbers through the splatters of blood. Something wasn't right. She was seeing the wrong numbers.

"What? Have you thought of something?"

The image fled. "No."

They finished the interview. The chief released her with the instruction to stay in town.

"I'll come back to the museum to help with Aloysius."

"Not necessary."

She made Simon take her anyway.

The chief was already inside when they arrived at the museum. *He* didn't need to obey the speed limit.

Patrolman Curtis was coming out the front door when they got out of the SUV. He met them at the gate and shook his head.

"Lord, what an uproar. The darndest thing I ever saw. Two immovable forces. Cat and chief."

"He isn't hurting him, is he?"

"The cat or the chief?" he asked, not quite hiding his amusement. Then he seemed to remember the seriousness of the situation. "No. When I left, the chief was standing on a chair trying to get him down from the bookcase. He may have been a hot-shot big-city detective, but he's a little out of his league up here."

Kate stifled the urge to stick up for the chief. Aloysius was no ordinary cat. "Let me inside. I can get him down."

"The chief will skin me alive if I do."

Simon grinned. "The chief will be skinned alive if you don't."

The patrolman unlocked the gate. "Step this way."

The scene was so ridiculous that Kate hesitated a moment before stepping into the office. The chief was standing on a straight-backed chair, his arms stretched toward the top shelf, where Al was arched like a Halloween cat.

The chief's left cheek was marked by two long scratches that were dripping blood down his jawline. Papers and magazines littered the floor around the chair. Two police officers were watching from a safe distance and doing nothing to help.

"Al," Kate said softly.

Al's ears twitched. His head swiveled toward her voice. He launched himself from the bookcase, flew past the chief's head, and landed with a thud on the carpet. He padded leisurely over to Kate and butted his head against her ankle.

She picked him up, staggering a little under his weight. "That's a good boy." She scratched him behind the ears and was rewarded by a low, rumbling purr.

"Who let her in here?"

Al's head jerked around. He zeroed in on the chief, who was climbing down from the chair. The purr turned to a growl.

"Shush," said Kate, as much to the chief as to Aloysius. "We're going to the kitchen now. You can follow us, chief, if you feel the need. But keep your distance." She turned on the last word and carried Al out of the room.

She heard the sounds of suppressed laughter behind her. She'd made the chief appear ridiculous in front of his men. When, oh when would she ever learn to deal with people? Especially ones that mattered so much to her continued way of life.

"At least *you* like me," she told Al, and buried her face in his fur.

"You should have listened to me," Kate said as the chief crossed to the sink and splashed water on his face. She handed him a paper towel, and he gingerly patted it across his cheek.

"That's all I do. Listen to you people. I should never have come to this godforsaken town."

"Then why did you?" Kate snapped. It was one thing for her not to like Granville; it hadn't always been kind to her. But for an outsider to attack it—What was she saying? She'd been an outsider all her life.

"Because I was sick of homicide. I thought I would get in a little fishing and hunting on my days off, except that I haven't had any days off." He stopped abruptly, realizing too late what he was saying and who he was saying it to.

"Sorry. Don't know why I said that. Lack of sleep. No excuse."

"I do," said Kate.

He looked confused.

"Know why you said that."

His look of confusion turned to a frown.

"It's okay. I know what it feels like not to fit in."

The chief snorted. "You? The whole town is up my—on my case because I asked you a few questions."

"Really?"

"Yes, really. Can we get on with this? I'm trying to conduct a murder investigation. Where is that cat?"

Kate looked around. Aloysius was gone.

"Hiding, most likely. He'll come out when I've put his food down. But your men should hurry with whatever they're doing. They won't be able to keep Al out of the office. He has his ways. And we've never been able to find them all." Memories rushed in. Al tangled in the maze. Lost in a storage area under the eaves. Al trapped in the laundry chute until he'd trained them to keep the doors unlocked.

She bit her lip and put the food bowl on the floor. Al nosed open the dumbwaiter door and headed for his breakfast.

"He'll have to stay here. He belongs here. And someone will have to feed him and make sure he has fresh water."

"He'll be taken care of."

She turned on him. "You wouldn't."

"I just mean I'll make sure he gets fed. So put *your* claws away. I've had enough for one day."

Had that been a joke? Or just exasperation?

"I'd like you to do one more thing before you leave."

"Certainly."

He took her downstairs to walk through her actions of "the night in question." The chief stood in as the killer, and Simon and Aloysius followed her every move. She went through it unemotionally, counting off each step on the way.

She only faltered once, when she reached the office and found one of policemen slumped over the desk. He lowered himself to the ground.

"I started CPR," said Kate. "And then the EMTs came and moved me away." She stepped back. Stood there unmoving.

But when she stepped toward the desk, Chief Mitchell stopped her. "Why did you go back to the desk?"

"Because . . ." Kate knew she should tell him about the puzzle. He'd probably think she was nuts. "It's just that something seemed off about the puzzle."

"How so?"

She tried to see it, but it kept eluding her. "I'm not sure. Maybe if I could look at it again."

"Thank you, Ms. McDonald. You've been a big help. Take her home, Simon."

1		9		2	3		4	
					5		7	8
	4	5			1	9		
		8			7		5	9
3			6		4			7
9	6		5			2		
		1	4			3	6	
6	2		3					
	7		1	8		4		2

THE FUNERAL WAS held on Wednesday at the Presbyterian Memorial Cemetery a block from the church. Kate hadn't been allowed to return to the museum. Officer Owens was put in charge of feeding Al. She'd only left home once, when Pru insisted they go to Lily Love's dress shop to buy something for the funeral. Kate had no idea how the investigation was progressing. The chief hadn't contacted her again.

The day was cold and overcast, though it was early October. Kate couldn't help but think that even the heavens were angry at the professor's passing. She shivered inside her coat.

"Cold?" asked Pru.

Kate shook her head. *From the inside out,* she thought.

"A real nice crowd," Aunt Pru murmured in her ear. "Half the town is here. I'm glad to see it."

"Me, too." Kate looked over the crowd. Found Louis Albioni, who nodded back at her. Found a few other familiar faces. Some more that she probably knew but who'd changed since she'd last seen them. Several people nodded her way, or smiled sympathetically.

It seemed as though everyone was looking around them. Wondering which one of their neighbors had killed the professor? Wondering if she had?

Abigail Avondale sat in the first row of folding chairs beneath the tent that was set up over the open grave. She'd brought no one with her. But Darrell Donnelly had joined her soon after she arrived, and he was sitting next to her as they waited for the service to begin.

"Why is Darrell sitting next to Abigail?" asked Kate in a whisper. "Does he know her?"

Aunt Pru leaned closer and said in her ear, "Don't know, but I suspect it's because of his grandfather. On his right."

Kate looked at the man next to Darrell. She remembered Jacob Donnelly. He'd presented her with a scholarship when she was in the eighth grade. But mostly she remembered him as the professor's enemy.

He seemed older now. Of course he would be. He was fleshier than she remembered, with puffy cheeks, a sagging jawline, and heavy bags beneath his eyes. "Is he sick?"

"His wife, Willetta. Degenerative disease. Taking its toll on Jacob." Aunt Pru lifted her chin. "There's Reverend Norwith." She straightened up, clasped her gloved hands, and looked solemn. For a moment Kate saw the old Aunt Pru. She had to admit that she liked the new one better.

"Dust to dust," began the pastor. Kate blinked back tears and looked across the rows and rows of markers that lined the hill. She saw Chief Mitchell standing off to the side. He was wearing a charcoal dress coat. A scarf was tucked inside the lapels. He looked very distinguished and very out of place.

He scanned the mourners as they listened to Pastor Norwith's eulogy. *He's looking for the murderer,* Kate thought, and felt better.

The service ended. The coffin was lowered into the grave. Abigail stood and picked up a handful of earth from the pile that would soon cover the professor. She tossed the grains into the open grave, then brushed her hand off on the handkerchief she'd been holding but had not needed.

Did you kill you own father? wondered Kate. She must have shuddered, because Aunt Pru linked her arm in hers. "Do you want to leave?"

"No. I'm fine."

They joined the line waiting to add their bit of earth to Abigail's.

When it was her turn, Kate knelt by the grave. "I'll find who did this," she whispered, before tears made it impossible to speak. She opened her fingers and let the dirt fall onto the casket.

She felt a hand on her shoulder and looked up to see an elderly woman smiling sadly down at her. She was wearing a slim-fitting black suit and a black, wide-brimmed hat that hid her eyes.

"Come, Kate. There's no more you, or I, can do here."

The voice was so sympathetic, so understanding, that it was all Kate could do not to burst into tears.

She turned from the grave, almost stumbled in the spongy grass. Pru took her arm. "Simon's waiting for us in the parking lot."

"Who was that woman, behind me? At the grave."

"Marian Teasdale. Incredible fortitude. Very sad." And with those enigmatic words, she led Kate to Simon's SUV.

They drove the two blocks to the Bowsman Inn for the after-funeral reception. The inn dated from the Revolutionary period but had been added to over the years and was now a bed and breakfast situated coincidentally, but conveniently, near the Presbyterian church and the cemetery. "Got 'em coming and going," her father would say and then chuckle to himself.

The current owners, Nancy and John Vance, were doing extremely well. They'd added a huge banquet room across the back with panoramic windows that overlooked the river.

Simon related bits of history about the inn on the ride over, in an effort, Kate suspected, to take her mind off the proceedings now taking place at the cemetery.

She was touched, but it made no difference. She'd turned off her emotions with her handful of earth. She was going to catch a murderer.

The banquet room was beautifully decorated, and food and drink were plentiful. Kate begrudgingly had to adjust her feelings about Abigail Avondale. She'd come through in spades.

For once, she hoped that there really was a heaven and that the professor could see the love and thought his daughter had put into his funeral. She even smiled at the thought of the professor in wings and his old tweed jacket looking down at them.

Simon and Pru returned from the buffet table laden with plates and cups of punch.

Simon handed her a cup. "A penny for your thoughts."

"I was just thinking that the professor would be so gratified to see what a lovely funeral and reception Abigail made for him. Especially after their horrible last scene."

"Pooh," said Pru. "This was all Marian's doing. She won't take the credit for it, of course. But everybody knows."

"Marian Teasdale arranged this?" asked Kate.

"Orchestrated the whole darn thing," said Pru. "I heard it from Agnes Mortimer over at the funeral home. There was a huge row, she said. With Marian telling Abigail that if she didn't pay for an elegant send-off, she'd let everyone know. And she'd never get so much as a toehold in this town."

"What do you mean, toehold?"

"I don't know. Agnes didn't know either. That's just what she heard Marian say." Pru nodded her head once, sharply putting paid to the subject.

A toehold, thought Kate. That was why she threatened to have the professor committed? She wanted his house. His property. She was going to sell it to the mall consortium.

And what would happen to the puzzles? Kate was sure Abigail wouldn't want them. She might sell them—or she might be bitter enough to have them carted away.

Kate experienced a moment of sheer panic. Then good sense prevailed. First she'd ask the board if provisions were made to keep the exhibit intact. If not, Kate would offer to buy them herself. At least as many as she could afford.

And then what? She couldn't stay here indefinitely. She'd have to donate them to another museum.

"Katie, how are you holding up?"

"What?" Kate realized that Elmira Swyndon had joined them. She was smiling sympathetically.

"Fine. Thank you, Mrs. Swyndon."

"Honey, you're a grown-up now. You just call me Elmira. And don't you worry. We'll get that so-and-so and hang him up by his thumbs. Right on Granville Green." She frowned, pursed her lips. "As soon as Chief Mitchell catches him."

"Pooh," said Pru disdainfully. "If you ask me, that man couldn't find his own behind in the mirror. Just gives tickets to decent citizens who don't deserve them."

"Oh, he's not dumb. Except when it comes to making himself likable. I bet he'll get his man—or woman."

"No," exclaimed Pru. "You don't think a woman would do such a thing."

"Ladies," Simon interrupted. "Such speculation should be saved for a more private venue."

"You're right," said Elmira. She gave him a contrite look and went straight back to her narrative. "I hear things around the station, mind you. And I know that the chief hasn't ruled out any possibilities. And my nephew Sam says he requested copies of all the photos Sam took. I bet he's been studying them with a magnifying glass."

"Photos?" asked Kate, suddenly interested.

"That's right," said Elmira. "Sam's the police photographer."

"As well as owning his own photography shop in town," added Pru. "Is he at the reception?" She leaned closer to Kate and whispered, "Great catch."

"No, he had to get back to the shop," said Elmira.

"Do you think he could get me a copy of the picture he took of the puzzle the professor was working?" asked Kate.

"Why?" asked Pru.

"Kate." Simon's voice held a warning note.

"Just for sentimental reasons," she said.

"I don't see why not. I'll ask him." Elmira looked around and lowered her voice. "Don't think we should tell the chief, though." She pulled a long face and shook her head. "He's just gotta learn to lighten up." She looked past Kate. "Oh, there's Rayette over there. I have to beg her to make one of those big cannoli things for Elise's christening." She hurried away.

Guests were beginning to leave. Kate wanted to go, too. She wanted to get out of her shoes, she wanted to be alone, she wanted to think. But she knew that they would be among the last to leave. Too much opportunity for gossip. She sighed and resigned herself to the wait.

Time dragged on. Abigail stood at the side of the room with Darrell and Jacob Donnelly in attendance. People stopped to offer condolences, but they didn't linger. They seemed to be drawn to Marian Teasdale, and she always had a small group around her. It seemed to Kate that Marian was the real bereaved at this funeral.

Kate saw Chief Mitchell on the far side of the room. He was standing alone, watching. She'd seen him before, but not once did he have a plate in his hand, not even a cup of punch. No one spoke to him.

So maybe he was there officially, but still. It must be awful not to be accepted, not even liked, when the success of his job depended on it.

It wasn't fair. Kate had been gone for years, and the minute she returned it was like she'd never left. Because she was a local. A local who had been treated pretty cruelly as a kid, she reminded herself. But Darrell Donnelly was the only ex-schoolmate she'd seen so far. Maybe they'd all moved away.

And for a spiteful moment, Kate hoped they were unable to fit in wherever they were.

Let it go. It's over. And besides, now that she could look back on it with some distance, Darrell had usually been the ringleader.

"We should get going," said Simon. "Kate is exhausted."

Aunt Pru whirled around. "Why didn't you say so? I'm ready to leave. Let's just pay our condolences on our way out."

Again? thought Kate wearily. Then she saw that Marian Teasdale had joined Abigail and the two Donnellys in what looked like a serious conversation.

Pru marched right into it, and for once Kate was thankful. What could those four have to say to each other?

"So sorry for your loss," said Pru.

"Thank you." Abigail barely looked at Pru. She'd zeroed in on Simon. "I've been meaning to talk to you. You're my father's attorney."

"Ayuh," said Simon, his accent thicker than usual.

"When have you scheduled the reading of the will?"

"Haven't."

Abigail's eyes flashed. "And why is that?"

"Don't have his will."

There was a moment of shocked silence, then Jacob Donnelly said, "You mean there is no will?"

"Oh, there could be," said Simon, dropping back into his normal voice. "P. T. had his own way of doing things. Unfortunately, it often made things more complicated than not. He may have made one. It might be in the house somewhere."

"It hardly matters," said Abigail. "I'm his only heir." She snapped her head toward Marian. "Which means I have the right to close the museum until I decide what to do with house."

"As if she doesn't know already," said Pru in an undertone. "She'll sell it and take the money and run. Just like her mother."

"Shh, Aunt Pru. She'll hear you."

"I don't care if she does. It's the honest to God truth. He had to pay her mother a small fortune just to get rid of the two of them. Don't think he ever recouped *that* loss. If you know what I mean." Aunt Pru's eyebrow arched.

Kate looked at her aunt in surprise. She had no idea what she meant. This news didn't compute at all with the professor she knew.

Kate turned her attention back to Simon.

"Ultimately that may be true," said Simon. "When and if a will is found, it must be proven to be valid, then there's the public notification, and the legal waiting period for other possible heirs to come forward." He opened his hands. "These things take time."

"There are no other heirs," said Abigail. "My mother is dead."

Beside Kate, Aunt Pru snorted.

"Well, the board does have a legal document," said Marian. "You'll have it on file, Simon."

Simon nodded.

"And it is valid."

"Yes, it is."

"And," said Marian, turning to Abigail, "it states that in the event of P. T. being unable to fulfill his duties for any reason as curator, the board will be responsible for maintaining the operations of the museum."

Kate felt movement behind her. The police chief was standing in the arched doorway, barely noticeable. It was a good trick for so large a man. Their eyes met for a split second; he stepped back into the shadows cast by the archway.

"Where is Chief Mitchell?" asked Darrell. "I saw him not long ago."

On cue, the chief stepped into view.

Jacob Donnelly motioned to him. "Chief Mitchell, a word please."

The chief looked surprise. *As if he hadn't just heard every word of the conversation,* thought Kate. He sauntered over, his face expressionless.

"When will your men be finished with the museum?"

"In the next day or two."

"Then you might let Simon look through P. T.'s papers for a will."

"Certainly."

"Thank you." Jacob turned his back on the chief, dismissing him. Nothing registered on the chief's face as he turned away. He didn't seem to care how everyone treated him or do anything about making himself more amenable. But Kate's cheeks burned with indignation all the same.

"At that time," Simon continued, "I will set the process in motion. Until the will is found or the appropriate waiting period has terminated, it's business as usual."

A quick look passed between Abigail and Darrell.

Simon smiled at Abigail, and behind that smile Kate saw the same attitude they all showed toward the chief. *Not one of us.*

How far would a town go to protect one of their own?

Abigail hesitated, then with a terse "I'll expect to hear from you," she swept out of the room.

"Find that will," said Darrell. He and his grandfather hurried after her, passing Nancy Vance, the inn's proprietor, without a glance.

Nancy was holding the leather visitors book in her hand. "Oh dear, I'd hoped to catch Ms. Avondale before she left. She forgot to take this. I think it must contain the names of half the inhabitants of Granville." She held out the book.

"I'll take it," said Marian. "I doubt if Ms. Avondale will mind."

Aunt Pru nudged Kate in the ribs. Kate understood and had to agree. Marian had arranged for the funeral. She deserved the book more than the professor's ungrateful daughter.

Marian's hands closed gently over the volume. "Well, shall we go?"

They thanked Nancy and started together toward the parking lot. When they reached the bottom of the steps, the chief of police appeared.

"May I see you to your car?" he asked Marian.

She looked surprised, but delighted. "Thank you, Chief Mitchell. That's very kind."

Kate watched them walk off together. They made a handsome couple, even if a good forty years separated them. *Now what was he up to?* she wondered.

Simon drove them home. The leaves were beginning to turn, the tips tinged with a splash of color. In a few weeks, the town and the surrounding countryside would be blanketed in fiery oranges and reds.

Sightseers would flock from all over the country to witness fall in New Hampshire. Kate wondered if she would be here to see them. There was no longer a reason to stay. She wouldn't even have access to the museum anymore.

She'd return to Alexandria and her numbers. The old house and museum would go under the backhoe to make way for progress.

And when, if, she came again, there would be a mall where her dreams had once been.

"Simon."

"Yes, dear?" he said, glancing at her through the rearview mirror.

"Can the bank foreclose on the loan with the estate tied up like this?"

"They'll have to submit a legal writ and go through the estate executor."

"Who is the executor?"

"The court will appoint one. Probably me, if no one has any objections. Why?"

"Just curious." A spark of hope flickered inside her. It wasn't a large one. But maybe the museum could still be saved.

Pru chuckled. "Simon, you may be Granville's oldest living lawyer. But you're also the smartest."

"I'll take that as a compliment."

"As well you should. I thought I'd bust when you pulled that tight-lipped New Englander routine with Abigail."

"You were outrageous," agreed Kate.

"Thank you."

He was also crafty. A good man to have on your side.

Simon dropped her off at her door and waited in the car until she was inside. Then he drove Pru three doors down to her own house. Kate let herself inside, silently thanking Simon for insisting Pru go home and rest. Kate needed time alone.

She kicked off her shoes as soon as she was inside, then changed out of her black dress and put on jeans and her "Geeks" T-shirt. She opened a bottle of wine, took out her notebook, and settled down on the couch to make a list of people who'd been at the funeral and reception.

Didn't they say that killers often came to their victim's funeral? Had the murderer been there today?

There had been more than two hundred people at the funeral, nearly a hundred at the reception—not half the town, but certainly a good percentage of it. The professor may have been reclusive, but he'd touched the lives of many, many people.

She frowned at the blank page of her notebook. Pictured the banquet room that afternoon. Methodically began to list the attendees. The professor wasn't the only one with a photographic memory.

She started with the ones whom she knew had a connection to the professor.

Abigail Avondale, who had climbed back to the top of Kate's mental list of possible suspects.

Jacob and Darrell Donnelly, who'd stuck by Abigail's side throughout. What could be brewing there? And how could she find out?

Marian Teasdale. She'd certainly been the focus of condolences at the reception. She and the professor were longtime friends, that much was obvious.

Janice had attended the service but had been noticeably absent from the reception afterward. Someone said she was too distraught to stay.

And Chief Mitchell. He could hardly have a motive, but Kate knew the importance of objective research. She wrote in his name. It looked good on the page.

There was a blip in her concentration. She quickly filled in Pru, Simon, and herself. Added Elmira.

There were the Franklins who owned and operated the *Granville Free Press* and put out the *Nickelsaver*, possible sources for the letters used in the anonymous letters. Not that it mattered now. As far as she knew, the professor had destroyed the one sent to her as he had the others.

Alice Hinckley. She'd been the town's source of homemade jam for as long as Kate could remember. She also lived in the historic district. Had she sold her house, or was she one of the holdouts? Kate needed to find out. She placed a question mark by her name.

The Saxons, the Phillipses, the Renquists. The Houlihans.

The list grew longer until she no longer had names for faces. They didn't really interest her. And wouldn't until something pointed to one of them as the murderer.

Fatigue seemed to seep into her bones. And she knew it was ineffective to work with a less-than-acute mind. She tossed the notebook aside, took a sip of wine, and reached for her Sudoku book. She worked one puzzle after another until the light grew dim and she had to turn on the table lamps.

She found herself keeping one ear out for Pru. She didn't want company exactly. But here she was working puzzles by herself in an empty house. She picked up the notebook again. Looked over the list. Just a list of names. She needed to know more about their relationships.

And she knew just who to call to find out.

Pru answered on the first ring. "Of course, honey, I'll come right over."

	4	8		5		7	2	
	6						1	
		2	1		6	3		
			3		4			
	1						4	
			7		5			
		5	4		9	2		
	7						9	
	9	4		3		6	5	

PRU ARRIVED FIVE minutes later, carrying a bulging bag of groceries. She handed Kate the bag and shrugged out of her car coat. Underneath she was wearing turtle fur sweatpants, an L.L. Bean turtleneck, and bunny fur bedroom slippers.

"Excuse my shoes," she said, taking the bag back from Kate. "All that standing around today just set my bunions off."

"You look fine." Kate closed the door and followed her to the kitchen.

"I didn't know if you'd eaten," said Pru, lifting a pie tin out of the bag, "so I just brought over a little corned beef hash."

Kate took it from her. "Thanks. Maybe later. I'll just put it in the fridge for now."

When she closed the fridge door, Pru was holding up a brown bag that looked suspiciously like the ones used by liquor stores.

The old Aunt Pru had strong ideas about "spirits," an unending source of humor and exasperation for Kate's dad. "She once was sweet on a drinker. Told her no good would come of it. Didn't listen. Never did. Took her awhile to figure it out on her own."

Kate had corked her bottle from earlier in the evening and put it in the cupboard, then washed and dried her glass and put it away before Pru arrived.

Pru pulled out a pinot noir and held it toward Kate. "Didn't know if you'd discovered Jimmy's cellah. Larry down at Bottle Depot said you'd like this. It's French, and it has a cork."

Kate didn't really want another glass, but she was so touched by her aunt's gift that she meekly took the bottle. "This is a good wine," she said, looking at the label. She set it down on the counter and rummaged in the utensil drawer for the corkscrew, which was sitting right on top where she'd tossed it a few minutes ago.

Kate uncorked the wine and reached for the kettle. "I'll put on water for tea. Or would you prefer coffee."

"I think I'll join you for a little sip. Just a little one, mind you. Don't want you drinking alone. That's how it starts."

Kate hesitated, wondering if fatigue was blurring her senses. Had her teetotaling aunt said she wanted a glass of wine? What other surprises were ahead from this new Aunt Pru?

"You just get down the glasses. Jimmy keeps them on the top shelf above the canned goods, behind the cookie jar."

"But you don't drink wine. We could both drink tea."

Pru ruffled the air with her fingers. "A little glass won't hurt me."

Kate got the glasses down and handed them to Pru. Then she picked up the bottle of wine and followed her aunt into the living room.

Pru sat down on the couch and picked up Kate's notebook. "What's this?"

"Just a list of people at the funeral today."

"You should have asked Marian to borrow the guest list. Course, you could always remember everything you ever saw."

Kate poured out two half glasses of wine. She handed Pru a glass, which she held up in front of her, frowning at the deep burgundy color. Then she lifted her glass in a toast. "Here's to P. T. May he rest in peace." She took a sip. Her mouth puckered up and her face twisted.

"It's an acquired taste," said Kate. "I'll put on water for tea."

"No. My mind's made up." She took another sip. This time her reaction was less violent.

Kate was still deciding how to ask questions without making her aunt suspicious when Pru decided for her.

"Imagine Jacob Donnelly sitting in the front row like he was family. And Marian standing off to the side. That no-good daughter never even offered her a seat. Not that you'd expect her to."

"Why?"

"Long story."

"Who was Abigail's mother? I never knew the professor was married."

"Well, he was. For a heartbeat. And that was too long. Everyone thought he and Marian would make a match of it. Two fine old families, but . . . " Pru shrugged, took a sip of wine, and fell into contemplative silence.

"Why didn't they?"

"Dunno. The four of them, Jacob, Willetta, Marian, and P. T., were like this in high school." Pru squeezed four fingers together. "Jacob and P. T. both went down to Harvard. Marian went to Smith, but it was close enough for them to get together weekends. Willetta stayed home like a lot of girls did in those days. She had an invalid mother to care for." Pru sipped more wine.

"But she married Jacob Donnelly."

"Right after he graduated. She'd always been sweet on Jacob. No accounting for taste." Pru emptied her glass and stuck it out for Kate to refill. Kate poured an inch, then put the bottle down. She didn't want Pru to get tipsy and not be able to tell her everything she wanted to know.

"Then P. T. comes home from college, already married. Met her in Boston. A little thing with a wasp waist and high notions. We called her the gadabout. Loved to party. P. T. didn't.

"Nobody took to her." Pru lowered her voice and leaned so far over the coffee table that Kate was afraid she might fall. "She started showing almost immediately after they moved into the family house. Ayuh. People got the drift of things pretty quick. Abigail was born two months early, only she was as healthy and big as any full-term baby you ever saw."

Pru nodded, held out her glass again. Kate filled it without thinking. Filled her own.

"She should have been thankful to P. T. for doing right by her, but she treated him like he'd made that baby all by himself. She made his life hell. Flirted with anything that wore pants. And her a young mother. That's when P. T. started collecting puzzles. Finally he paid her to leave town and take the child with her."

"Are you sure?" asked Kate. "He really paid her to leave?"

"Ayuh."

"His wife and his daughter." It didn't sound like the professor she knew. But a man could change in forty some-odd years. Maybe he thought of Kate as the daughter he'd given up so many years before. Had he been kind to Kate to make up for the way he'd treated Abigail?

"And Marian Teasdale?"

"She acted like nothing happened. You can't buy breeding like that. She married Arnold Compton the following spring.

"He died of a heart attack back in Seventy-seven. Or maybe it was Seventy-eight. They never had children. She took back the family name. There's always been a Teasdale in Granville, and she's the last." Pru yawned.

"Why didn't she and the professor get married after her husband died?"

"Not the Teasdale way. Doesn't mean they didn't . . . " Pru lifted her eyebrow, only this time the other one came up with it.

More information than I needed, thought Kate. But Marian Teasdale and the professor. She could see them together. She hoped they'd been happy.

"And how does Janice fit into all of this?"

Pru snorted. "Janice Krupps. That sour old— She's originally from up near Berlin. Came to town one day looking for work; took the job at the museum and has been there ever since. And just like you'd expect, she fell in love with P. T. Not that I think he ever noticed. He could always ignore what he didn't want to see.

"She never had a chance. Not with Marian around. Don't know why she stayed on. Turned her mean." Pru pressed her fingers to her lips. "I shouldn't have said that. Not my business."

As if you don't know everybody's business, thought Kate.

"What happened between the professor and Jacob Donnelly?"

"Why all these questions?"

Kate willed herself not to fidget. It always gave her away. "No reason. It's just that with the professor gone, I want to learn everything I can about him. To remember him better."

Pru nodded sympathetically. "They fell out years ago. Nobody remembers when or why. They've hardly spoken since. These men. Nothing but playground nonsense."

"But Mr. Donnelly is chairman of the museum board. It doesn't make sense. Why would he support the project of a man he hates? Unless he was trying to sabotage him."

"Don't be silly. He and the professor were puzzle nuts since grammar school. So they say. But that was before my time," she added quickly.

"Oh."

"It's not Jacob's fault that the museum is in such a state. He's the one that convinced P. T. to renovate. Unfortunately Willetta took a turn for the worse right around the same time, and he had to leave things in P. T.'s hands. Too bad. Jacob always had a head for business. But P. T." Pru shook her head, but it was more of a wobble. "Never could cope with the real world. Too many brains, you know. Oh." Pru clapped her hand over her mouth.

"It's okay, Aunt Pru. I know what you mean."

Pru took another sip of wine; her glass was empty again.

By Kate's count—and she knew how to count—that made two and a third glasses. They were small glasses, but she was sure Pru had just reached her limit.

"What's wrong with his wife?"

Pru slowly shook her head. "Has one of those deteriorating diseases. Her mother had it, too. Forget the name. Something nobody can pronounce. Jacob takes her down to Boston twice a month for some kind of treatments. Gotta cost him an arm and leg."

A vague picture of the professor's past was beginning to emerge. But Kate was still no closer to finding out who had a motive for murdering him. And she was afraid that she was getting her aunt drunk. Pru's eyes weren't very focused. Kate would feel awful if she were responsible for her aunt's first hangover.

The telephone rang. Kate and Pru both jumped. Kate narrowed her eyes at her aunt. Who had she seen at the funeral? When did she have time to set Kate up with another date? She doubted if Louis Albioni would be calling this late. She doubted if he'd ever be calling again.

The phone rang again.

"Well, hurry up and answer it," said Pru. Her eyes were gleaming, but Kate wasn't sure if it was with anticipation or from inebriation.

Reluctantly, Kate stood up. If she walked really slowly, maybe they would hang up before she got there.

But the phone kept ringing, and at last she was forced to pick it up. When she hung up a few minutes later, she stood looking at the old black receiver, wondering if she were losing her mind. Still in a state of bewilderment, she went back into the living room.

Aunt Pru was sitting on the edge of the couch, knees together and back erect. "That was a long conversation," she said, pretending not to be curious and not succeeding in the least.

"Yes," said Kate, still not believing what had just happened.

"Anyone I know?" Pru prodded.

"Yes, actually it was."

"Oh?"

"It was Jacob Donnelly. The board has asked me to be acting curator of the museum until the will is probated."

The two women looked at each other, speechless, then Pru said, "That's wonderful. You can stay home now."

Home, thought Kate. This wasn't her home anymore. She had a co-op and a job in Alexandria. She'd have to be back there in a few weeks. And yet . . .

"They're holding a special board meeting tomorrow night to make it official. It's only until the will is found and probated. Then I guess we'll know what the fate of the museum will be." She dropped into her chair. "I can't believe they asked me to take over. It seems crazy."

"No it doesn't," said Pru. "You're the best qualified. You know that museum inside and out. And you love it, which is more than I can say for any of the others, except maybe Marian." She chuckled. "I'd love to see Abigail Avondale's face when she hears about this."

"I wouldn't."

"Well, pooh on her." Pru frowned. "But you can't work in the museum alone. What if the murderer comes back?"

Kate swallowed. "I won't be alone. Janice will be there. I guess. Besides, the museum will be full of people."

Pru pursed her lips. "That museum hasn't been full of people in years. Janice wouldn't be any help in an emergency if she even bothers to come back. Don't think people didn't notice that she wasn't at the reception.

"You need an armed guard. That snotpotty chief of police can provide you with one. I'll call him first thing in the morning." Pru snapped her head down in a final nod. Then raised a hand to her forehead. "I'm not sure I'm really made for strong spirits."

"Not for you," Kate agreed.

Pru hoisted herself off the couch and swayed on her feet. "You're looking tired. You'd better get to bed." She began gathering up the glasses.

"I'll take care of those," said Kate. "I'll watch you home."

But Pru wasn't going to let her off so easily. "Promise you won't set foot in that museum until I talk to that new chief." She wagged a finger close to Kate's nose. Kate stepped back, imagining that finger being wagged at the chief.

"I'm sure the board will take precautions. And there's no reason to bother the chief. He'll be busy finding the murderer."

"Well, I suppose we should let him *try* to do his job. But I don't want you in that museum alone."

Kate stood on the front steps and watched Pru tilt her way down the street and up the steps to her house. A minute later the porch lights went out, and Kate went back inside.

She was going to be curator. Even if it was only for a few weeks, it was an honor. One that she didn't deserve. She'd let the professor down. And now he was gone. She gathered up the glasses and wine bottle and carried them into the kitchen. She rinsed out the glasses, wondering at the turn her life had taken and sad that she wouldn't have the professor to share it with.

And that's when it hit her. She'd come back out of the blue. The professor was murdered, and she was made curator. Chief Mitchell would have a field day with that. She'd be lucky if she didn't end up in jail instead of the museum.

CHAPTER

TEN

IT WASN'T UNTIL the next morning, when Kate was standing outside the museum, that Jacob Donnelly's phone call really sank in.

She was curator of the museum. A shiver of pride and pleasure skittered over her, mixed with a subduing sense of loss.

But this was not the time for sadness or insecurity. She had work to do. She was dressed in a navy blue pantsuit and pin-striped, tailored blouse. She knew it made her look older and more formidable than she really was. She often wore it to conferences. It should work on the board of directors. It might even give her an edge with the police chief, though she doubted it. He probably ate women in business suits for breakfast.

She was relieved to see that the crime tape had been removed from the door. The house looked perfectly normal, not like a place where murder had been committed.

She let herself in and flipped on each light switch she passed. A few more dollars on electricity was not going to make or break them, but presenting a lively bright atmosphere might.

She went upstairs but paused outside the office door, her knees suddenly feeling weak.

"Coward," she murmured, and opened the door.

Inside, the office looked perfectly normal. She half expected to see the professor sitting at the desk, his head bent over one of his puzzles. But the chair was empty—and new. The desk blotter had been removed along with the puzzle.

Someone had cleaned the room. She dropped her purse and briefcase by the desk chair and stared at the desktop. The books had been arranged carefully around the edges. It left a gaping emptiness where the blotter had been. She stared at the space until the puzzle appeared in her head. She tried to picture the numbers that had been there. Saw several sevens and a circle. It must have been the beginning of an eight, a nine, a six? Zeros weren't used in Sudoku.

She needed a copy of that puzzle. But she didn't believe that Elmira's nephew would really agree to something that couldn't be legal.

It wouldn't bring the professor back. But for her own peace of mind, she had to know what was on that puzzle. It was an intuitive, irrational desire, but something had struck her subconscious. Something she couldn't dredge up by herself.

She sighed and walked to the center of the room, then just stood there watching the sun cast dappled light on the carpet. The professor's Sudoku books were stacked neatly by his chair as if waiting for him. The Cofanetto still sat on the cabinet top. No one had thought to put it away, and the sight of it made her breath catch.

She swallowed, steeled herself. Tears wouldn't catch a murderer or save a museum.

She walked toward the bookcase, looking for a sleeping Al. But he wasn't in his usual place. She listened for a thump that would tell her he was nearby. But all was silent.

She was standing close to the pedestal that held the gypsy's crystal ball. She didn't touch it. Maybe she never would. She looked deep into its milky glass. *Tell me the future,* she whispered. *Tell me who murdered the professor. Tell me . . . anything.* But no message disturbed the opaque whiteness of the ball.

She forced herself to sit down at the desk. Her initial pleasure at being named curator, even as interim, had come and gone. Her decision to make things right seemed silly. Silly and stupid. She fisted her hands, brought them down on the desktop.

Enough of this. There was work to be done.

She pulled her laptop from her briefcase and booted it up. The power bars lit to full range. One of her neighbors had a wireless system. That would come in handy, since the museum wasn't connected. She opened a new document and typed in *Buy a new desk blotter. Buy a printer and a copier. Fax machine.*

She saved it and opened a new document. Started a new list. *Find missing checks, pay utility bills.*

Fire Janice. She deleted that, but it had felt good just to put it down.

Ask board about an inventory list. She hadn't seen one among the papers in the file cabinet. *Ask about insurance. Deal with loan default.*

Change lightbulbs to brighter wattage. Catalog repairs that can't wait for the renovation. Ask board for money to hire a handyman.

She deleted the handyman. God only knew how many single handymen Aunt Pru was acquainted with. She could change the lightbulbs herself. There was a ladder in the cellar, though she didn't relish going down there. It wasn't like her bungalow cellar that had been partially finished to accommodate her father's wines. This one was dank and creepy. Maybe she'd make Janice get the ladder.

And where was Janice? It was almost nine-thirty. With any luck, she wouldn't show up.

Kate opened Excel. Set up a spreadsheet with four columns. Across the top she filled in People, Motives, Opportunities, and Additional Data.

She should have thought of doing this while she was wallowing in grief for the last week. She'd wasted valuable time.

In the first column, she listed the names she'd written down the night before. Then she typed what she knew about them, thanks to Aunt Pru. The spreadsheet began to take shape.

She was in familiar territory now. All she had to do was put down the known information, consider the possibilities, and arrange them in a logical pattern. Use deductive logic. Just like in Sudoku. Just like in math. When the grid was filled in, she'd know who the killer was.

Abigail Avondale. Motive: *Hated father/for the past? Property/Mall consortium?* But when Kate came to Opportunities, she stalled. She had no idea how and when Abigail had been with the professor. The professor had been alive when she left the museum.

She moved to the Additional Data column. *Threatened him with commitment/Power of attorney? Ask Simon.*

Jacob Donnelly. Motives: *Longstanding animosity/unknown reason.* That had an ominous ring to it. Revenge for something that happened fifty years ago?

Janice Krupps. Kate got a certain satisfaction from adding her to the list, though she couldn't see any reason for Janice to murder the professor. She doted on him. Had his inattention finally pushed her over the brink? Would she rather see him dead than have to admit the hopelessness of her situation. But once again, why now?

She stalled after the first three names. Then reluctantly considered Marian Teasdale. Came up with no motive at all.

On a whim—she couldn't call it more than that—she added Darrell's name to the list. He seemed to know Abigail, he refused to help with the loan situation, and she didn't like him. Not exactly proper method.

She looked at the spreadsheet and realized that, except for her impromptu addition of Darrell, she'd listed her suspects in alphabetical order. She added a cell between Avondale and Jacob Donnelly and moved Darrell to it. The list should really be in order of probability. But she'd have to wait for more data.

She had stooped to guessing. And how could you guess what someone would do if pushed to their limit? You couldn't build a theory on guesswork. But how else could you understand what would make a person act irrationally? She was out of her area of expertise. People didn't always react the way they should.

She wondered if Chief Mitchell used the same method to narrow down his suspects. Of course, he had access to more information than she did. But he'd never share that information with her.

"Which is fine, if you'd just catch the killer."

Belatedly she thought of another name. She was loathe to type it in. But she had to be objective, and for once, she hated having to be that way. Because the professor had cared about him. She created a new cell for Harry Perkins. She knew nothing about him except that he spent time at the museum and lived in squalor with a hateful uncle.

And he was missing. That was the most damning thing that she knew about him. Chief Mitchell might already be looking for him—not as a missing person but as a murder suspect.

The downstairs bell jangled. Janice must have come to work after all. It was nearly ten o'clock. Did she know that Kate had been appointed interim curator? Was this her first test on the job?

"Okay, Professor, give me patience." Kate dreaded the confrontation, but she knew it had to be done, and the sooner the better.

She'd be considerate but firm. She wouldn't let Janice continue to bully her. She was the boss now.

She locked her laptop in her briefcase and ran her fingers through her hair, dislodging one of the combs that held her curls back. She readjusted it with nervous fingers. Ran her tongue over suddenly dry lips and went downstairs.

Janice fixed her with a sullen look before she'd even reached the bottom of the stairs.

Kate fought the urge to turn and run. "Good morning," she said in what she hoped was a curator's voice. Just a hint of authority that she didn't have before. At the same time she smiled, cuing Janice that she was willing to be, if not friends, at least civil. But Janice was having no part of it.

As Kate reached her desk, Janice pulled the newspaper out of her tote bag and opened it.

Kate took a deep breath. "I suppose the board called you to let you know that I will be acting as curator until the museum's future is finalized."

Janice continued to ignore her. Kate had to force herself not to retreat. There was nothing Janice could do to her. In fact, Janice was at her mercy.

Janice glanced over the top of her newspaper. "You may have gotten what you want, but it won't last."

The words stung. "Janice, I don't know what—" She stopped herself. It didn't matter that Janice hated her, or why. Her patience snapped. "I'll expect you to continue at your position until further notice. Please be on time from now on. Without the newspaper."

And to Kate's utter surprise, she snatched the paper from Janice's grasp. Somehow she managed to fold it and shove it under her arm. "And please try to make visiting the museum an enjoyable experience."

She turned on her heel, and knowing she'd never make it up the stairs without betraying her nerves, she strode down the hall to the kitchen.

She dropped the newspaper on the table and stood at the sink, drinking tap water, trying to relieve her parched mouth and throat. What had possessed her? Certainly not the professor's patience.

Outside the window, the maze rose like a stockade, a snarl of unkempt boxwoods that blocked out the sun. And although boxwoods were evergreen, yellow leaves appeared among the green.

Kate put down her glass and went out the back door. The grass had been cut near the back stoop. Someone had even attempted to cut back the boxwoods. A ragged patch of pruning marked the entrance to the maze.

Without thinking, Kate walked over to it, ducked her head, and slipped through the overgrown opening. She was immediately engulfed by green. As a child, she used to walk with her head flung back, following the blue maze of sky above her instead of the graveled path. Now, the branches were nearly thatched over above her head, and the gravel was packed into the dirt.

She twisted to the side and eased farther inside. She'd gone only a few feet when she realized that she'd never be able to find her way out again. The paths and turns she'd known like her own backyard were unrecognizable now.

She backed out until she was once again standing on the outside, looking in. She mentally added *landscaper* to her list.

She used the back stairs to get to the second floor. She had no desire to face Janice again so soon.

She stayed in the office for the rest of the morning, the door open to hear if anyone visited the museum. No one did. When Janice went to lunch, she ventured downstairs.

She wandered from room to room. The museum felt empty and

lonely, and she wasn't accomplishing a single thing. She found a granola bar in her bag and ate it. She couldn't bring herself to leave the museum even for lunch.

During the afternoon, she began to worry about how to approach the museum board that night. She couldn't exactly say, "What did you people do with the professor's money?" or "Where were you on the night in question?"

So what *was* she going to say to them? *Thank you for making me curator, even for a little while.* She didn't want to be curator. She wanted the professor back. She stood up and looked out the window. *Good evening, I'm glad you could come.* No. They had invited her.

It didn't matter. She'd just go in and meet the other members. They would apprise her of her new duties. She would ask her questions about the budget, the inventory. She might even find out the reason for the loan default. It would be fine.

CHAPTER

ELEVEN

AT SIX O'CLOCK, Kate went downstairs to unlock the door for the meeting. She was surprised to see Janice still at her desk.

"I always stay late for board meetings," Janice said. "I take the minutes."

"Oh," said Kate. "Are you the board's secretary?"

"Willetta is the secretary/treasurer, but she's become too ill to fulfill her duties. And with Jacob absent so many times, I felt I had to help out."

I bet you did, thought Kate ungraciously. The professor's voice echoed in her mind. *Patience*. She bit her lip. She was letting Janice bring out her two worst qualities—impatience and a hot temper. She had to do better.

The doorbell jangled.

Kate felt that familiar frisson of panic begin. *Not now*, she demanded. *Just think of them as mathematicians*. Janice jumped up, but Kate beat her to the door.

Jacob Donnelly stood at the door, looking even more haggard than he had at the funeral.

"Good evening, Mr. Donnelly. Please come in."

"Katie," he said. "Bad about P. T. Lucky you were here to take over for him." He began unbuttoning his coat—a beige, all-weather coat.

Don't be stupid, thought Kate. *It's fall. They'll all be wearing coats.*

He nodded to Janice. "Please send the others back as soon as they get here." He continued down the hall to the boardroom.

The next to arrive was Marian Teasdale. Her coat was camel colored. She was hatless, and soft gray curls framed her head. She had the bluest eyes that Kate had ever seen. They seemed to light up the room. And Kate understood how the professor could love her. And why Janice never had a chance against her.

She held out both hands to Kate. "I'm so glad you accepted our offer. P. T. would be so pleased."

"Thank you," said Kate. "I'm glad I could be of service." She sounded like an ass. Why couldn't she be natural like this woman?

"So am I." Marian squeezed Kate's hands and stepped into the foyer. "Good evening, Janice."

Janice's nod was arctic. Kate blushed for her. Marian was in her late seventies; Janice couldn't be much past sixty. The man they both evidently loved was dead.

The others arrived soon after that. A round man entered, puffing from his climb up the five steps. He was in his sixties, Kate guessed, and brusquely introduced himself as Erik Ingersoll. He handed her his raincoat and hat and proceeded to the back room.

Another coat, thought Kate. But in his physical condition, he couldn't have run off down the sidewalk the way the killer had. She carried it to the coat closet where Marian was hanging up her own coat.

She glanced at the raincoat and gave Kate a wry smile.

The next two men arrived together. One she recognized as Jason Elks, the fifteen-year newcomer to Granville.

"Katie McDonald," he said, and shook her hand. "Prudence, I'm sure, is delighted to have you home for a visit, even under such terrible circumstances. I've known P. T. since we were at college together. I'd never expect something like this to happen to him." He introduced her to his companion, Daniel Crowder, another older gentleman who hadn't bothered with a suit and tie but wore khaki pants, a checked shirt, and a quilted hunting jacket.

The whole board is bordering on ancient, thought Kate. None of them could be younger than their late sixties. The museum could use some young, energetic blood.

The last member arrived, and Kate was glad to see a woman about her own age. She looked familiar. Reddish brown hair wisped about her face, then fell straight to her shoulders. She had hazel eyes and full lips.

"Katie, you don't remember me, do you? I saw you at the reception, but I didn't want to intrude. Ginny Sue Bright."

"Ginny Sue?" Kate's mouth opened. Ginny had been a plain girl, but her friendly personality had made her lots of friends. *Unlike me*, thought Kate. "You look so different."

Ginny grinned. "I hope that was a compliment."

Kate's cheeks flared. "Yes, I mean, you look great."

Ginny shook her head. "You look exactly the same. Only you're taller."

Kate blushed hotter.

"I love the short hair. Is it true you work in one of those hush-hush Washington think tanks?" She started walking inside, carrying Kate along with her.

"I . . . work with a team of mathematicians."

"That must be exciting."

Kate looked at her incredulously.

"I mean to be with people you can relate to."

Kate nodded. A geek among geeks.

Ginny stood smiling at her.

Belatedly, Kate blurted, "What do you do?"

Ginny laughed. "I teach fourth grade at Valley View Elementary. I only got as far as teacher's college, then came back again." She shrugged. "But I like it. The kids are great, most of the time. And it's got good benefits."

Kate nodded, trying to think of something to say. The thought of teaching fourth graders made her queasy.

"So are you back for long?"

"I'm not sure. The professor . . . I'm just not sure."

"A terrible loss, for the community as well as for his friends. I hope you'll stay." She lowered her voice. "The board is ancient and the last bastion of Granville's old-boys club. It takes forever to get anything done. The renovations are months behind. And with that damn mall hanging over our heads, and P. T.'s murder—"

"Ginny Sue. The meeting is about to begin." Jacob Donnelly stood in the doorway of the meeting room, motioning to them. "Katie, if you please."

Kate grabbed the stack of folders she'd left on Janice's desk, and the two of them hurried down the hall.

As they entered the room, Kate heard Marian Teasdale say, "I'm so sorry Willetta isn't feeling up to the meeting tonight." Then all conversation ceased, and five board members turned to look at Kate and Ginny Sue.

"Sit here, Katie." Marian gestured to the seat next to her and to the left of Jacob Donnelly, who sat at the head of the table. Kate wondered if this was where the professor had sat. Would she be able to fill his shoes, even temporarily?

She sat down. Erik Ingersoll sat directly across from her. Ginny Sue was next to him. Jason Elks and Daniel Crowder sat across from each other at the foot of table.

Janice was sitting in a folding chair several feet from the table, her steno book opened on her lap and her pen poised above the paper.

"The meeting will come to order." Jacob Donnelly glanced down at the sheet of paper on the table before him. "Janice, will you read the minutes from the last meeting?"

Janice straightened up. "The meeting of the . . . "

Kate listened to every word but found nothing out of the ordinary. It seemed to her the meeting had accomplished nothing.

"Move to approve the minutes."

The minutes were approved. Donnelly, Sr. cleared his throat. "First, I'd like to thank Katie McDonald for agreeing to serve as pro tem curator. P. T. and I didn't always see eye to eye on things, but his passing will be a loss to the community."

Was that all it was, wondered Kate, *not seeing eye to eye?* Had the Granville gossip mill blown their disagreement out of proportion?

"And since this is an emergency meeting, I suggest we dispense with the usual agenda and get straight to the point. We're in a pickle."

Kate bit her lip to keep from laughing. It was a ludicrous phrase from such a distinguished man.

"First and foremost, there is the issue of the unpaid bank loan. I've had Darrell scrutinize the account. There have been no loan payments for three months. But there have been considerable withdrawals."

"There's the retaining fee we paid to Balboa and Sons," said Ginny Sue.

"Peanuts compared to what's missing." He reached into his jacket and pulled out a folded computer readout. He opened it and passed it around the table.

"Great God in heaven. There's close to two hundred thousand missing," said Jason Elks. "What the hell is going on? You can't tell me P. T. was skimming. Hell, his house and the museum are at stake."

Ginny looked at the paper and turned pale. By the time it had made its way around the table, everyone was talking at once.

"You're out of order." Janice's voice was shrill. No one paid any attention.

Jacob raised his hand. Everyone fell silent.

"I know Katie consulted Darrell about the situation. Have you been able to discover where that money is?"

"No," Kate said, taken by surprise. "There seems to be some confusion about who—where the endorsed checks were filed. And I haven't found them." She glanced quickly at Janice. She was bent over her steno pad, and Kate couldn't see her expression.

Everyone in the room looked at Janice.

"Janice, did the professor make the payments?"

Janice didn't look up. "As far as I know. I was not privy to the professor's financial affairs."

The hell, you weren't, thought Kate. She was in charge of the mail before Kate had taken over. Responsible for sending it out as well as opening it. But she didn't think this was the time or place to accuse Janice of carelessness or, worse, subverting the payments to the bank.

"Katie, we need to find that money."

Kate nodded. She'd do anything she had to do to keep the museum.

"I know you're what they call a theoretical mathematician, but can you handle basic bookkeeping?"

Kate felt the heat rise to her face. *Katie is a ge-ek.* "Well, I can add and subtract and balance income and expenditures. But who oversees the expenditures?"

"P. T." He paused to look around the table. "The board thought that since he was the cosigner and since Willetta was . . . was unable to continue her duties as treasurer, he should be responsible for the loan."

"That's what comes of trusting your finances to someone with his head in the clouds." Erik Ingersoll laced his fingers and rested them on his belly.

"Out of order."

"Thank you, Janice." Jacob's tone was dismissive. "That money has to be somewhere. Even P. T. couldn't lose track of that much money."

There was a hint of bitterness in Jacob's voice. Had their original fight been over money? Did Jacob still hold a grudge even though the professor was dead?

Marian raised her hand. "Jacob, I offered to make up the back payments. P. T. refused to let me. But I'm offering the board the same."

Kate stared at her. Marian's eyes were sparkling but this time with unshed tears. Kate looked away.

"That's very generous of you, Marian. But it won't solve the problem of the missing funds. Fortunately, the bank will not be able to foreclose as long as the estate is tied up."

"Have they found a will?" asked Jason Elks.

"Not to my knowledge. Finding it will expedite matters considerably, but it will also put the museum in jeopardy."

"I don't believe there's any question about what Abigail will do with the house," said Ginny. "Sell it to the mall people."

"But not the puzzle museum. We're incorporated," Marian said. "And unless something else is specifically stipulated in the will, the puzzles will continue to belong to the corporation."

"Which means we'll have to find a new location," said Ingersoll, "if we plan to continue with the museum."

Kate looked at Marian. The puzzles belonged here just like Aloysius belonged here.

"Possibly," said Jacob. "But since Balboa and Sons have postponed the start date on the museum renovation again, and until we hear the outcome of the will—if there is a will—the subject is moot. In fact all subjects pertaining to the museum are moot. This meeting is adjourned." He got up and left the room.

Everyone sat for a minute. They seemed as surprise as Kate to be so summarily dismissed.

"I drove thirty miles for that?" said Daniel Crowder.

Jason Elks slapped him on the back. "Come over to my house for some chess. I'm right around the corner."

Kate took her unneeded folders and followed the others out of the room. She hadn't had the opportunity to ask her questions or find out about her duties.

Ginny Sue was waiting for her in the hall. "Are you free for lunch tomorrow?"

"Me?" said Kate.

"Yeah, you." Ginny Sue gave her a broadcast smile. "I bet you haven't had a moment to relax since you arrived."

"Not really," said Kate.

"So what do you say? There's no school tomorrow—a religious holiday—and we can catch up."

"Okay," said Kate. "I'd love to."

"Great," said Ginny Sue, buttoning up her cabled sweater. "One o'clock? Rayette's? The early lunchers will all be finished and we'll have the place pretty much to ourselves." She finished buttoning her sweater and shifted her purse to her shoulder.

Kate walked her to the door.

"Gee, it's turned cold. See you tomorrow." Ginny Sue pulled up her collar and hurried down the steps.

Shivering, Kate closed the door. They'd have to turn on the heat before long. The boiler would probably need servicing. And she hadn't had a chance to ask what kind of operating expenses she had to work with. Or for how long.

Janice was sitting at her desk with her coat on.

"Are you going to be long? I have to lock up."

"That's okay, Janice. You go ahead. I'll lock up."

"But you—"

"Have my own keys, and I know what to do. See you tomorrow."

Janice hesitated, and Kate hoped she wouldn't continue to argue. She suddenly felt bone tired. The obstacles set before her seemed insurmountable. But she had to establish her authority.

"Goodnight."

Reluctantly, Janice selected a key off a large ring and unlocked the bottom drawer of her desk. She lifted out her purse and locked the drawer. She stood up and, without another word, walked out the door.

For the first time in her life, Janice's rudeness hadn't bothered Kate. She'd been more interested in what was in the drawer. Why would she need to lock it while the museum was closed and she was the one to open the museum in the morning?

Kate suddenly had an overwhelming desire to see what was inside.

She hurried to the front window and drew the edge of the drapes aside. She was just in time to see Janice open the gate and step through. She closed it tightly behind her, checked the latch, then took off down the sidewalk.

Kate stood there until she was sure Janice had really gone. Then she let the curtains drop and went upstairs to get the professor's keys. She'd seen them in his desk that morning. Now if one of them would just fit that drawer.

She took the ring downstairs and, checking once more to make sure no one was returning to the museum, she sat down at Janice's chair.

Even in burglary, she proceeded systematically. She started with the wide center drawer. It wasn't locked, and she found only the usual office supplies: pencils, paper clips, stamps, a roll of Tums, and several bills marked paid. One of them was the utility bill. At least they would have lights and heat for another month.

The top right drawer held a stack of typing paper. The second, manila envelopes, an appointment calendar opened to August, a roll of faded red tickets, and a hole punch.

She hesitated when she came to the bottom drawer. She'd never broken into anything before. Had never rifled through another person's possessions. But whatever was in that drawer most likely belonged to the museum, and if Janice wasn't going to volunteer what she knew about the missing checks, Kate had no choice but to look for them herself.

A nifty rationalization for rifling through another person's belongings.

Nerves made her clumsy, and her fingers shook as she tried each key. It was the last one, of course. It slipped smoothly into the lock and turned with a click. Kate pulled the drawer open and almost laughed when she saw the curved glass bottle of cologne next to a paperback titled *Love's Slave*. She moved the cologne aside and lifted out the paperback. What she was interested in lay underneath.

A blue canvas ledger. She listened again, certain that Janice would barge through the door and catch her. So what if she did? Kate had every right to look at the museum's books.

So why are you sneaking around like this?

Because she was a coward. This way she could look for discrepancies without having to accuse Janice to her face. If she found nothing, no one would ever have to know.

She picked up the book and opened it. *Petty Cash* was written across the page in a fine pointed script. Kate quelled the disappointment. There might be something useful in it. She turned the page: Typing paper, $100. Ink cartridge, $250. *But no computer and no printer,* thought Kate. Unless the professor had one in his apartment.

Kate didn't even consider using her keys to find out. That was a violation she wouldn't commit. She'd have to ask Simon if he would look when he was given permission to search for the will.

Stationery, $400. That couldn't be. She hadn't seen any stationery, and surely that would be downstairs. She looked again. The decimal point was definitely in the hundreds place. She scrolled down the page. More items, whose prices seemed in a normal range. Then Bulletin Board. Also nonexistent and costing nine hundred dollars.

It was becoming clear why Janice kept the desk locked. What was not clear was why anyone helping themselves to huge amounts of money would leave a paper trail.

Kate turned the page. More running expenditures sprinkled by obviously padded amounts. Janice was systematically helping herself to the petty cash. Was she doing the same with the loan funds?

If only Kate could find those endorsed checks. Anyone who had cashed them would be smart to destroy them. Then again, Janice kept a running account of her thefts.

Stupid or arrogant, it amounted to the same thing. Janice was stealing from the museum. And it had to stop.

The only other things in the drawer were two magazines. *Country Homes* and *Glamour. The sum of a lonely life,* thought Kate, looking at the items before her.

And suddenly Kate understood why Aunt Pru was so eager to get her married. Was Aunt Pru lonely? Was she afraid Kate would be? Maybe. But at least neither of them would grow bitter, the way Janice had.

Kate began to return things to the desk, replacing them exactly as she had found them.

Something thumped against the front door. Her heart caught in her throat. Her hand knocked against the bottle of cologne, and she fumbled to upright it. When she drew her hand away, her fingers were wet. She looked in horror at the bottle. Nothing appeared to have spilled, but the fragrance permeated the air.

Kate quickly shut the desk, listening for the rattle of keys in the outside lock as she fumbled to fit the desk key into the tiny keyhole. It slipped into place and clicked. She yanked the key out and shoved the ring into her jacket pocket as she hurried to the door.

There she waited, holding her breath, trying desperately to think of an excuse if Janice opened the door. There was no way she could deny having been in the desk; the room still smelled of Janice's cologne. And so did her fingers.

Then she heard the muffled complaint from the other side of the door. And she nearly sank to the floor with relief. She unlocked the door and looked down. Aloysius was sitting on his haunches, looking impatient.

She laughed unsteadily. One of the board members must have let him out when they left. But now that she thought about it, she hadn't seen him since the afternoon. He would have been first to the door when they arrived. Mr. Curiosity. But he hadn't been there.

"How did you get out, you rascal?" She opened the door, and Al pranced past her.

Something moved in the shadows. Janice stepped into the light and followed him inside.

9   1

CHAPTER

TWELVE

2

"I FORGOT MY book."

Kate opened the door wider, hoping that the night air might dispel the smell of cologne.

Janice brushed past her, paused, sniffed, gave Kate a dark look, and rushed to her desk.

Kate took a surreptitious inhale. The smell had lessened—at least by the door. She considered just standing there until Janice got her book and left again. But curiosity got the best of her. She walked closer to the desk and caught a faint, but condemning, smell of cheap cologne.

"You've been in my desk," said Janice.

"Don't be ridiculous." Kate's response was pure prevarication, and she didn't think it fooled Janice for an instant. Good. Let her sweat.

Janice scowled at her and pulled at the bottom drawer. It didn't open, and Kate had to force herself not to sigh with relief.

Janice fumbled in her purse, pulled out her key ring, and opened the drawer. She stared into it for a long time, and Kate thanked the fates for giving her a photographic memory. But the drawer reeked of perfume.

"What's that smell?" she asked innocently.

"Nothing," snapped Janice. She took her book and slid it into her purse. She locked the drawer and stood up. "I'll be going now."

"Goodnight . . . again."

The door slammed behind Janice, and Kate heard the jangle of keys as she locked the door.

Kate sank against the desk.

"Yeow," said Al, waiting at the hall entrance.

"No kidding."

"Yeow."

"All right, I'm coming. But if you ask me, I don't know if this people-person business is all it's cracked up to be." She'd been nasty to an employee, broken into a desk, and practically lied.

When was she going to get to the good people-person stuff?

By the time she fed Al, turned off all the lights, and locked up the museum for the night, she was beginning to feel easier. She'd acted out of necessity. She had wrongs to right, and she couldn't be squeamish about how she accomplished it.

She locked the front door and looked around. It was only eight-thirty, but there was no moon, and she began to feel a little spooked.

She hurried to her car, jumped inside, and locked the doors.

On the ride home, she tried to piece together what she'd learned that night besides the fact that Janice read romances, used cheap perfume, and was definitely helping herself to some major petty cash.

Could she really be the perpetrator of the loan theft? You'd have to be pretty clever to pull that off. Janice didn't strike Kate as particularly clever. Stupid maybe, arrogant, but not smart enough to hide over two hundred thousand dollars.

But Darrell Donnelly was smart enough, and he had access to the accounts. He could get to the checks before they were actually posted to the loan account . . . and take the money for himself?

The idea was so disturbing that she nearly missed the stop sign at the corner of Main Street. She slammed on the brakes. All she needed was to get ticketed for rolling through the stop sign. The chief of police might think it was a family trait.

Did Chief Mitchell know about the loan default? That could be a motive for murder. If only she knew what he knew about the case. He would never tell her. She knew the rules of classified information.

She looked both ways on the empty street and pulled out into the intersection.

She had absolutely no proof of anything, not even the petty cash theft. There might really be a printer, mountains of stationery, and an expensive bulletin board on the third floor.

When Kate arrived at the museum the next day, she was astonished to find two surveyors set up along the sidewalk. At first she thought they were measuring the property lines of the house next door, until she saw a third man appear out of the bushes alongside the museum.

Kate hurried forward.

"Excuse me." She stepped in front of the man, preventing him from rolling up his tape measure. "You're on private property."

"I know. This is the Avondale house. We're supposed to confirm the property lines."

"Who told you to do that?"

"My boss did. Lady that owns the place hired us. Ms. Avondale. Who are you?"

"This is a museum. I'm the curator. And Abigail Avondale doesn't own this house." At least not yet. Then a terrible thought struck her. Had Simon found a will?

"Well, she gave us the go-ahead. Told us she owned it and paid us to fix the property lines." The surveyor walked over to a truck where a spec sheet was spread across the hood.

Kate flipped open her cell phone and realized she hadn't programmed Simon's number in. She hurried to the porch, reaching into her bag for the keys as she went.

"Damn females. Bring that tripod over here, and we'll do the south boundary."

Kate closed the door on the surveyor's complaint and went immediately to Janice's desk to phone Simon.

"I'll be right over." He hung up, and Kate went back outside where she watched helplessly as the men continued measuring.

A few minutes later, Kate saw Simon's SUV coming up the street. He double-parked his SUV beside the truck. He jumped out and strode over to them. "You're a bit premature, fellahs," he said, shaking his head. "The town send you over?"

The man Kate had talked to shook his head.

"Well, I'm afraid you'll have to wait until the town does its own surveying, when and if the property is up for sale."

"But we have a work order for this. Our boss'll spit nails."

"Who's your boss?" asked Simon, looking at the unmarked truck. "Nobody local I bet. I know 'em all."

"Nah. Come over from up Berlin way. And just who are you?" The man jutted his chin at Simon. He was taller, brawnier, and younger than Simon, but Simon didn't seem intimidated at all.

"I'm the lawyer for this museum, and if you know what's good for you, you'll be going on about your business. I'd hate to have to call the new chief of police. He's from down south, ayuh."

Simon smiled, and suddenly Kate knew why he was considered the best lawyer in the county. It was the kind of smile that said I know something you don't and you'll be sorry if you have to find out.

The man scratched his head and looked at his two coworkers who'd stopped what they were doing to listen to the conversation.

"Down south, huh?"

Simon nodded. "Boston."

The man expelled a breath. "Okay, but if we get docked for not finishing this job, I'm having the boss call you."

"Ayuh." Simon reached into his vest pocket and pulled out a business card.

The man took it, stuffed it into his shirt pocket, and nodded at the other two. Simon moved his car, and within minutes they had loaded the truck and were driving down the street.

"Sorry I had to call you," said Kate, "but I wasn't sure I had the right to kick them off the property."

"You're my client. You're supposed to call me. But you could make me a cup of coffee. I had to leave the house without mine." He took her elbow and was escorting her up the steps when Janice arrived. She nodded to Simon and rushed past them, fumbling with her keys.

"It's unlocked," Kate called after her. Janice hesitated, then opened the door and stepped inside.

"Katie, dear, she just gave you a look that could fry hash."

"I know," said Kate, heat flaring in her cheeks.

"You two on the outs?"

She shrugged. She didn't think she should tell her lawyer that she'd broken into Janice's desk and found evidence of theft. "Ever since she's known me. Come on, I'll get you that coffee."

While Kate made the coffee, Simon called the police station and asked for an officer to accompany him while he searched for the will. "I'm here. Might as well get it done if the chief can spare a man to oversee the process."

Twenty minutes later, they heard the echo of the doorbell and went to meet the policeman.

Janice was staring at him as if he'd just stepped off a spaceship.

She thinks he's come to arrest her. And Kate was happy to let her sweat a bit. She hurried to meet the officer and gestured him toward the hall.

Simon shot her a perceptive look and followed them to the back stairway.

Kate handed him her key ring. "The office is open, but one of those must fit the professor's apartment. And Simon, let me know."

The two men took the back stairs. Kate wandered through the exhibition rooms, feeling at loose ends, not wanting to make an inventory or even clean the counters if they were about to discover that Abigail did indeed inherit.

But she couldn't stay idle for long. She gathered up Windex and paper towels from the kitchen and began to ruthlessly clean the glass display cases. That's when the first visitors arrived.

Gratified and excited, Kate hurried out to meet them. They didn't stop at any of the rooms, but climbed the stairs.

Kate had left the office unlocked as usual. She sprinted up the stairs after them.

They had stopped outside the office and were peering inside, talking in low whispers. They hadn't come to view the puzzles but to see the crime scene.

Kate felt a wave of revulsion. "Excuse me," she said, stepping up to them. They stared back at her as if she were a murderer. Maybe that was what the Granville grapevine was saying about her.

"I'm sorry, but this floor is closed for inventory. The first-floor rooms are open, and these should be open again soon." *I'm becoming pretty good at lying,* she thought. "This way, please."

They grumbled but obeyed. She locked the office door, put the key in her pocket, and followed them downstairs.

They were already leaving.

"Janice, please tell all visitors that the upstairs is closed until further notice." Without waiting for an answer, she went back into the exhibition room to her Windex.

The police needed to solve this soon if she were ever to turn the museum back to the magic place it once had been. She couldn't do it with murder hanging over their heads—over her head.

An hour later, Simon poked his head in the Jigsaw room. "Looks great in here."

"Thanks." She looked up expectantly.

Simon shook his head. They hadn't found a will. There was still time to save the museum.

Twice more Kate was interrupted by patrons who stood in the hall talking in low whispers. So when she heard the bell jangle for the third time, she immediately expected the worst.

What she found was a Girl Scout troop—twelve girls and two leaders solemnly listening to Janice's recitation of the museum rules: "No talking, no eating or drinking, no touching."

Jeez, though Kate. *You forgot to mention no fun.* She put on a smile. "Hi, everybody. You're going to love the museum. If you have any questions, just ask."

Janice gave her a sour look. The Girl Scouts looked dubious, and the leaders looked like they wished they'd gone to the bottling plant instead.

Janice ushered them into the ground-floor exhibition room. Kate watched from the doorway as they glanced quickly through the room with their troop leader pointing and whispering softly, while Janice stood back with an eagle eye ready to point out any infractions. No wonder the museum got few visitors.

They didn't stay long; the room wasn't conducive to lingering and neither was Janice's forbidding presence. They were already looking bored.

Kate knew that if she interfered, Janice would only make things worse, but she couldn't let what should be a wonderful experience turn into tedium.

She met them as they came out the door. "Thank you, Janice. That will be all."

At first she thought that Janice would defy her, but she just shrugged and went back to her desk.

"You're going to love the next room," said Kate. "It's called the Hidden Picture room." She got several flicks of interest. She herded them into the center of the next exhibition room.

"Tell me what you see," said Kate, wishing she'd changed the light-bulbs instead of polishing the display cases. The girls stood where they were and looked around at the walls. No one said a word.

"Come closer to the picture."

They moved en masse. She pointed to a landscape painting hanging on the wall. The Scouts craned their necks to look at it, and Kate made a mental note to hang a few pictures lower for smaller people.

"Look straight at the picture and tell me what you see."

"A tree," said one of the girls.

"Shh," said the girl next to her. "We're not supposed to talk out loud."

"It's all right," said Kate. "You can talk in here. What else can you see?"

"A cliff."

"Some cows."

"A meadow."

"That's right. But this is a puzzle picture."

"What kind of puzzle?"

"There's another picture hidden in this one."

The girls stared hard. Even the leaders appeared interested.

"I can't see anything."

"That's because you have to look in a special way." Kate's voice caught as she remembered the professor teaching her to shift her eyes until the landscape blurred and another picture emerged. She shifted her eyes and the landscape disappeared. The face that appeared leered out at her, accusing, before it became a landscape again.

"I see a face," exclaimed one of the girls.

"Me, too."

"Me, too. Me, too. Me, too."

One of the leaders smiled. The other one looked relieved.

"How do they do that?"

"Well," said Kate, moving them to the next picture. "First you draw a dim outline of your hidden picture. When you have that, you turn it into something else, like a forest or pieces of fruit."

"Can we do that?" asked one girl. Then they were all asking. "Can we do that?"

Oops. She'd wanted to instill some enthusiasm, but she hadn't counted on this much.

"Unfortunately, the museum used up all its crayons, but Saturday . . . um, after next . . . or the next . . . is a special puzzle day. You can come back then and do all sorts of things." What was she saying? They might not even be in business by then. "You'll see the posters for it around town. And you don't have to pay a thing, so bring all your friends."

She'd have to call Ginny and ask her to help. "But the Japanese puzzle boxes are in the next room, and you can try some of them now."

The group converged on the door, chattering and skipping with excitement. And Kate thought, *This is what it should be like.*

She sat them on the floor, just where the brightest lightbulb would shine down on them. She took out one of the least fragile boxes and held it up. "The Japanese were the masters of the puzzle box. It can only be opened in one way." She tried to lift the lid but it wouldn't open. "But not the normal way."

"Can I try?"

She handed the box to a girl in pigtails, who tried in vain to open it.

"Let me try." The next girl took the box, turned it upside down, and frowned at the bottom. It went around the group until it came back to Kate.

"Told you it was a puzzle. Now watch." Deftly she slid back one section after another until the sides fell away and they were looking at a jade bird's egg, centered on a square of red velvet.

This discovery was met by oohs and ahs and several wows. Kate let them come up one by one to gently run a finger over the smooth, hard stone.

She demonstrated on a few more boxes, then pointed out the largest box. It was decorated in black lacquer and gold gilt. It sat in a glass case by itself.

The girls crowded around it.

"We can't touch this one. It's very old and very fragile. And . . . no one has ever been able to open it. The secret was lost hundreds of years ago."

The girls stole up to the table and gazed at the box in awe.

"What do you think is in there?" asked a girl with braces.

"Something wonderful," said Kate, and was shocked at the mystery in her voice. And the past flooded in, and she was as young as these Scouts and alone until the professor had rescued her.

She shook herself and the spell broke. "We have lots more exhibits, but they're in storage because we're renovating the rooms. But when everything is ready there will be a big grand opening, and everything will be on display, and there will be a room for you to work puzzles and even make your own."

"My dad says they're going to tear down the museum. That's why we came to see it, before they put up the mall."

"A museum doesn't have to be a place. It's the things in the museum and the people who come to see them. So if that does happen, and I hope it doesn't, we'll move the puzzles to another place, and that will become the museum."

"I like this place."

"So do I," said Kate. "So do I."

	6			4				
2		3	5		1			
9		4	2		8			
3		1	7		9	6		
	9						1	
		6	4		5	7		3
			3		4	2		1
			1		6	8		7
				2			4	

IT WAS ALMOST one when the troop left, full of smiles and thank-yous and promises to come to Puzzle Saturday.

Kate nearly called Rayette's to cancel her lunch date. She'd had a great time with the Scouts. They'd almost made her forget the first three groups of people who'd come to see the murder scene. And she knew that at Rayette's, everybody she met would be wondering, talking, speculating. She'd had enough of the Granville curious for one day. But she would have to face the town soon enough, and Rayette's seemed like the friendliest place in which to do it.

She washed her hands and face, ran a brush through tangled hair, and set off toward downtown.

Kate walked past the bank, drug store, the fabric store, and the Village Shoe Store where there was a big postboard sign in the window: FOR LEASE. Next to it, an antique store advertised UNDER NEW MANAGEMENT.

A computer store had opened up across the street. She went in, bought a fax, scanner/copier/printer combination, and asked them to deliver it to the museum that afternoon.

She almost walked right past Rayette's, which, to give Rayette her due, was almost as famous as the Avondale Puzzle Museum. But she hardly recognized the old bakery. The plain plate glass windows had been embellished by swags of lace curtains. The window case that Kate had lingered over as a child was gone, and two tiny, round, iron tables with filigree chairs had replaced them. New gilt lettering arched across the glass: RAYETTE'S BAKERY AND CAFÉ.

Kate opened the door and stepped into the comforting aroma of baking and brewing coffee.

The stainless steel shelves of the old bakery case that had once held pans of molasses cookies, lemon squares, and Rayette's sticky buns were now filled with cut glass platters of French pastries and nouveau desserts resting on white paper doilies.

Kate was glad to see one section was reserved for Rayette's Unforgettables and still held all the old favorites. In the center was a pyramid of Rayette's famous sticky buns.

The bakery had expanded into the building next to it, and an archway led into a chic little bistro. A maplewood counter held menus and a shining antique cash register. Behind it, a giant copper cappuccino maker belched out steam. A chalkboard propped on an easel listed the lunch specials. Round tables were covered with white lace tablecloths, and each had a centerpiece of silk flowers.

Kate was looking over the heads of the diners to find Ginny Sue when she saw Rayette moving toward her through the tables. Her platinum hair was swept back from her round face in two wings indicative of the local beauty parlor. She was wearing a white princess blouse and a navy blue skirt that had probably fit better several sticky buns ago.

"Katie." Rayette wiped her hands on the linen towel that hung from her belt. It must have been a fairly new replacement for the oversized aprons she used to wear, because there were culinary fingerprints all over her navy blue skirt. "It's about time. Ginny Sue's got a corner table. This crowd should be clearing out in a few minutes, and you can have some peace and quiet."

Quiet? The buzz of conversation had stopped the minute she'd entered the room. She could feel everyone looking at her. Well, maybe not looking but wanting to look. She felt the sudden urge to cut and run.

Rayette placed her hand in the small of Kate's back and gently propelled her through the room. "They're just curious. You just smile and nod, and things will get back to normal."

Kate nodded and smiled and finally sank gratefully into the chair across from Ginny Sue.

"You're a celebrity," she whispered.

Kate made a face. "They probably heard I was the police chief's number one suspect."

"No. Are you?"

Kate shrugged.

"Well, I wouldn't let it bother you. Nobody would believe you'd do something like that. And nobody listens to what he says anyway."

"I've noticed that," said Kate. "Why doesn't anyone like the chief?"

"Need you ask? He's an outsider," Rayette said. "Specials are on the chalkboard. I'll send Holly over in a minute to take your order. And as soon as the rest of these folks clear out, I'll join you for a cup of coffee."

Kate looked around the room. It didn't seem like anyone was thinking about leaving anytime soon.

"Don't worry. There's no such thing as a leisurely lunch around here. I'm lucky to have trained most of them to take off at all.

Heaven save me from the brown bag lunch." Rayette shook her head, sending off a spray of confectioner's sugar. "See?"

Two men in sports coats were standing up at a table nearby. Across the room, four women were gathering up shopping bags. There was already a small line at the cash register.

"Back in a flash," said Rayette, and bustled off toward the register.

"Amazing," said Kate.

"Like clockwork." Ginny Sue opened her menu.

A petite girl with a blonde ponytail, dressed identically to Rayette, set a basket of muffins on the table.

"Hi, I'm Holly and I'll be your server. Our muffin of the day is lemon poppy seed."

"I'll have the prosciutto and avocado salad," said Ginny Sue.

"Sounds good to me," Kate said.

Holly left with their orders. Rayette bustled over. "Told ya."

She'd been right. There were only a couple of tables still occupied, and those patrons were nearing the end of their meals. Kate glanced at her watch. One-thirty.

"Pull up a chair and join us," said Ginny Sue. "We can fill Katie in on all the local dirt."

"Thought you'd never ask." Rayette dragged a chair over from the next table and sat down. "Now where are we?"

"Katie was just asking why nobody liked the new police chief."

Rayette snorted. "Outsider. And if that weren't bad enough, he enforces laws that we've been ignoring for years."

Ginny Sue took a muffin and handed the basket to Kate. "Lord, you've never seen such a ruckus as when he confiscated Roy Larkin's truck for not having an inspection sticker. I thought Roy was going to have a stroke."

"He confiscated Roy's truck?"

"Sure did," said Rayette. "Hell, he hadn't gotten it inspected in ten years. Nobody ever stopped him for it before."

Kate shook her head. "Not very safe. And Aunt Pru got a ticket for rolling through the stop sign. She's pretty bent about it."

"Well, what do you expect. People've been rolling through that stop sign for as long as I can remember. Don't know why they bothered to put it up. Between the elm tree and the climbing roses, you can't see a dang thing until you're halfway out in the intersection."

"So if everyone intends to ignore the laws, why did you hire an outsider? Why not just get someone who knows the lay of the land?"

Holly returned with their food. Rayette picked up the thread of the conversation as the other two dug into their salads.

"Some jackass on the town council decided if we were going to become a big, tourist town, we'd need some tough law enforcement. Never occurred to them that it would also apply to us. Sent out an Internet search. Brandon Mitchell applied, poor unsuspecting soul. And he got the job."

"I don't think they had that many applicants," said Ginny Sue, spearing a slice of avocado. "Granville's reputation precedes it."

"Ayuh," said Rayette in an exaggerated New England accent. "We've been doing things the Granville way since the thirteen colonies."

"Plus," added Ginny Sue, "he doesn't play well with others."

"I noticed," said Kate. "I don't envy him."

"Well, if he can solve the professor's murder, people might change their feelings toward him."

"As long as the murderer isn't one of us," said Rayette.

"But who else could it be?" said Kate.

The two women shrugged.

Conversation stalled while Ginny Sue and Kate concentrated on their salads. Then Kate asked, "Will he be able to find the murderer? If it is . . . " She hesitated. "One of us?"

"I don't know. Everybody's curious, but nobody's saying nothing."

"Even about me? I caught several people this morning in places they had no right to be."

"Well, don't take it personally. This is the most exciting thing to happen in Granville in years. Though it's a crying shame it had to be the professor. He was a good man."

"Yes, he was," said Kate. She put down her fork. Her appetite was gone.

"You should make them sign up to be patrons before they leave," said Ginny Sue. "That way at least the museum would get something out of their bad manners."

"Good idea," said Kate. "I was too floored at first to even think, but I'll take your suggestion to heart." She'd turn the job over to Janice. Let her start earning her paycheck.

"I've got lots of good ideas," said Ginny Sue. She took a bite of salad. "Not that anyone but Marian pays me the least attention. The board is a bunch of old farts. Couldn't look to the future if you gave them a telescope."

"But the renovations . . . "

"Do you see any?"

"No."

"And it doesn't make sense," added Ginny Sue. "They didn't even take out the loan until the rumors about the outlet mall started."

"That's crazy. Maybe they thought the museum could benefit from the proposed mall?"

Rayette groaned. "Except the mall will be where the museum was. And all those beautiful old homes."

Ginny Sue nodded. "It didn't make sense to me, either. But I figured maybe they knew something, I didn't. Jacob was adamant about improving the museum. Then Willetta took a turn for the worse, and he's had to pretty much drop out of the board meetings. We're a ship without a captain."

"You or Marian should take over."

"That'll be the day," said Rayette. Her head swiveled to the side. "And here's another Granville resident who doesn't like our chief of police."

A huddled figure in a trench coat, head scarf, and dark glasses scuttled into the bakery, carrying a heavy, ancient, beige suitcase.

"Who is it?"

"Alice Hinckley," said Rayette, getting up.

"Alice Hinckley? Why is she dressed like that?"

"Ginny Sue will fill you in. I'll be right back." Rayette took off across the now-empty dining room.

Kate turned to Ginny Sue.

"The new chief fined her for selling her jams without a food handler's license."

"You're kidding." Kate watched Rayette take the heavy suitcase and carry it into the kitchen. Alice followed behind her, looking furtively in all directions.

"She's been selling those jams for years. Why would he do such a thing?"

"Hell, I don't know." Ginny Sue shook her head. "Just trying to do his job, I guess. But he sure isn't making any friends."

"How much does a license cost?"

"About fifteen dollars."

"So why doesn't she just pay for one?"

Ginny Sue barked out a laugh. "You *have* been gone a long time."

When Alice came out of the kitchen, the suitcase was considerably lighter. She went directly to the door, opened it a crack, looked up and down the sidewalk, then slipped outside.

Rayette came back to the table. "Mission accomplished." She sat down. "So are you planning to stay long?"

"I don't know. I'm supposed to be back at work in a few weeks. There's a new project starting then, and if I'm not there at the beginning, they'll find someone else. Jobs for theoretical mathematicians are few and far between. But I'm staying here until the murderer is caught." She grimaced. "Plus I've been told not to leave town."

"Well, you should stick around. We could use some brains in this town. People are losing their minds. Greed'll do that to you." Rayette shook her head; more confectioner's sugar lifted into the air. "An outlet mall. Hell, we're just down the road from Maine. What do we need one for? I don't want to have to compete with a food court. I just got this place fixed up how I like it."

"We don't need one," said Ginny Sue. "But we're going to have one if the last holdouts give in. With P. T. dead, that only leaves the Phillipses, the Motts, Roy Elkins, and Alice Hinckley."

"That's right," said Kate. "I'd forgotten she lived on the east side."

"Right next door to the museum," said Ginny Sue.

"And she's holding out, too?"

"You bet, and she has the GABs to back her up."

Kate glanced at her watch. It was after two. She should get back to the museum and make sure Janice had opened for the afternoon. "Who are the gabs?"

"The Granny Activist Brigade," said Rayette. "A force to be reckoned with."

"You're kidding, right?"

"Nope. You should talk to Alice. She's the one that organized the brigade. She might be able to help you with the museum."

She might indeed, thought Kate. Had Alice received threatening letters? Been harassed? Had she seen anything the night of the murder? The houses were separated by high hedges, but if she were anything like Pru, she might have been looking out the front window. Had the chief questioned her? And if he had, had she been willing to talk to him?

"I'll go talk to her this afternoon."

"Does that mean you're going to stay? The museum needs you," said Ginny Sue. "If you need to pick up some extra cash while you're here, we always need math tutors and substitute teachers."

"I'm okay for now, and there's something else I want to do."

"What's that?"

"Set up an interactive room in the museum. Using puzzles not only for fun but for developing logical thinking. Sudoku for remedial math students, crosswords for vocabulary building, Rubik's Cubes and other mechanical puzzles for small motor skills. But mainly for fun. A real hands-on experience."

"That's a fabulous idea. We could put together an afternoon program. We could run it in conjunction with the school system." Ginny Sue's hand went to her mouth. "Sorry. I tend to get carried away."

"Not at all. I could use some good ideas—and some help. Actually, I know I should have waited until they find the will and we know the fate of the museum, but I sort of promised some Girl Scouts that we'd have a free puzzle Saturday."

"That's a fantastic idea. It'll get people interested again. Maybe make them realize what they'd be missing if they let the museum be torn down." Ginny Sue stopped, frowned. "But how soon could you do it?"

Kate played with her napkin. "Two weeks?"

"Okay," said Ginny Sue, a little subdued. "We could do that. Yeah. Sure we can do that."

"Only if you're interested and have the time. I know I shouldn't have made a promise I couldn't keep. But the girls were so enthusiastic that I spoke before I thought."

Ginny Sue grinned. "I believe you always had that problem."

She looked at her watch. "I've got to run. I promised my mom that I'd drive her over to Ossipee to visit her sister, but I'll come by the museum on Monday or Tuesday, and we'll get cracking."

"Thanks. I really appreciate it." Kate reached for her purse. "I'd better be going, too."

"Lunch is on me," said Rayette. "Get the GABs to make you some posters. I'll put one in the window."

ALICE HINCKLEY'S HOUSE was no more than a hundred feet from the museum, but the two houses were separated by a tall privet hedge, an overgrown garden, and an ancient oak tree with low branches that created a latticework between the houses. It was white clapboard and stone, and like the museum, it showed signs of wear.

Kate rang the bell and listened as the peals echoed through the house. At last the door opened a crack, and an eye peered past the brass security chain.

"Mrs. Hinckley? I'm Kate McDonald. Could I come in and talk to you for a minute?"

The eye blinked. The door didn't move.

"You Jimmy McDonald's girl?" The voice was light and wobbled slightly; the tone was suspicious.

"Yes. Remember me?"

"I remember you. Didn't kill P. T., did you?"

Kate stood nonplused for a second. "Of course not. How could you think—"

"Just asking. So don't get all pissy. Can't be too careful these days."

"Well, I didn't kill him. But I do want to find out who did."

The door closed.

Damn. She'd probably scared the poor lady. She heard the chain rattle, and the door opened again. Alice Hinckley squinted out at her. Her face was pink and crinkled and framed by wisps of white hair.

"Come in then." She opened the door wider, and Kate stepped inside. She led Kate through the entrance hall and into the parlor. It was filled with Queen Anne furniture and the requisite cross-stitched pillows and doilies. But what got Kate's attention were the stacks of paper lined up on the étagère, the fliers that covered every available surface. A row of hand-lettered posters were propped against the wall. PROTECT OUR QUALITY OF LIFE. DOWN WITH MALLS.

Alice motioned for Kate to sit down. Then she pushed away a stack of fliers and sat down on the edge of the couch, primly crossing her ankles above black orthopedic shoes. She smoothed her skirt over her knees and looked up with perceptive blue eyes.

"So you came back, did you? P. T. said he was going to write you. Shouldn't have waited so long. Those people will stop at nothing to get what they want."

"That's why I came to see you. Rayette said you're one of the owners who refuses to sell."

Alice cocked her head. It reminded Kate of a robin. "Ayuh, I am, and I'm going to fight this thing to the finish. They'll have to carry me out feet first before I let them tear down my house. So if you've come to try to persuade me to sell—"

"No," said Kate, "just the opposite. I want to save the museum—and all the houses."

"Good for you. And you can count on the GABs to help."

Kate smiled. She didn't think a bunch of grannies and a few signs could do anything to save the museum. But their hearts were in the right place.

"And I'd like to ask you some questions."

"Ask away." Alice clasped her hands in her lap and leaned forward.

"Has anyone been harassing you to sell?"

"Harassing me? I'll show you *harassed*. Come with me." She popped off the couch and waved at Kate to follow. Then she took off down the hall. Kate had to hurry to catch up.

They went into the kitchen and out the back door. Alice stopped on the porch and pointed into the yard. "That used to be my shed. Someone set fire to it, and by the time the fire department got here it was nothing but ashes. Wasn't any vandals like that patoot of a police chief said. It was those no-good mall people. But if they think that a little smoke will change my mind, they can think again."

She turned abruptly and went back inside.

They returned to the parlor, and Alice crossed to a mahogany writing table. She picked up several envelopes and waved them at Kate. "And what about these?" she asked, sounding triumphant. "Saved every last one of them." She shoved them at Kate.

Kate knew immediately what they were, but she slid the top one out of the envelope and shuddered. The same cutout letters. How could someone write those things to a harmless old woman? She returned it to the envelope and opened the next.

"Nasty, aren't they?"

Kate nodded. Nasty, malicious, threatening. "Did you show these to Chief Mitchell?"

"No. I. Did. Not. Wouldn't give him the time of day. He'd just figure out a way to fine me for possession of filthy literature."

The chief had certainly won no friends in Granville. How would he ever solve this case?

"There's one other thing I wanted to ask."

"Don't be shy. Ask away."

"Well . . . did you see anything the night of the—the murder?"

Alice pursed her lips, shook her head. "Not a darn thing. The garden is too overgrown. Just can't do what I used to do. Because of my work for the GABs taking up so much of my time," she added in case Kate mistook her inattention for the rigors of old age.

"I can see the lights through the trees, and I know that the only light on that night was in P. T.'s office. Can't see the front because of that old oak tree being in the way. But I'll be more vigilant from now on. If they come back for me, they'll get a surprise they won't forget."

Kate just hoped Alice wasn't packing a loaded shotgun somewhere nearby. "If anyone threatens you, you'll have to call the police. And you should really show those letters to the chief. He might be able to trace the source."

Alice hmmphed. "Don't watch much television, do you? They wear those latex gloves. And you can buy those gloves anywhere. The grocery store even. I learned that on *CSI*."

"Thank you," said Kate. "I really appreciate your talking to me." She started for the front door.

"Glad to help. And you can count on the GABs to help, too. You just be at the town meeting on Monday. You'll see some real action."

Kate nodded, though the thought of a bunch of old ladies sitting in the back row, their signs bobbling back and forth as they dozed off during the speeches, didn't give her much hope.

"I'll be there."

"Good. And you tell that aunt of yours she'd just better get over it and join us."

That stopped Kate. "Aunt Pru refused to join the GABs?" Surely her aunt wasn't pro-mall.

"Said she wasn't a granny. I told her she would be if she'd ever bothered to get married. But that's Prudence McDonald for you. More stubborn than God, she is."

"I'll tell her," said Kate. "And thanks again."

She walked out to the sidewalk and turned back. Alice Hinckley was still standing on the porch. "Mrs. Hinckley, if you ever need any help, please call the police, even if you don't like the chief." She waved good-bye and stepped past the overgrown rose bushes to the sidewalk.

The chief's police car was parked at the curb.

With a sense of impending doom, Kate walked up the steps to the museum. She passed Izzy Culpepper coming out.

He tipped his hat to her. "That new chief of police is waiting for you. Want me to wait around and make sure he minds his manners?"

Et tu, Izzy, thought Kate. Though she didn't know what the five foot three Izzy could do against the six-plus feet of muscle of the new chief. "Thanks, Izzy. But I think I can handle him."

"Well, I'll just be down the street if you need me." He hoisted his mailbag over his bony shoulder and trudged toward the gate. Kate went inside to see what the chief wanted.

He and Janice were faced off across the reception desk. The stack of mail lay between them. Kate hurried over. "Can I help you, Chief Mitchell?"

He turned his scowl on her. He considered her for a moment, then said, "Could I see you . . . privately?"

Kate's stomach dropped. Had he found out she'd asked Elmira for a copy of the puzzle? "Certainly. Come upstairs to my office." She reached for the mail.

He beat her to it. "I'll carry it for you."

She gave him a tight smile. "Thanks." She walked past him, defying herself to turn back and see if he was following. She didn't need to look to know he was right behind her. She could feel him, strong, determined, with not one friendly bone in his body.

She shivered involuntarily as she opened the office door and gestured him in.

"Please sit down."

"I'd rather watch you open your mail."

She stared at him, then took the envelopes from him. She went through them one by one, discarding some and dropping the others to the desktop to be dealt with later—in private—after the chief had gone. But she'd only made it halfway through the brochures and junk flyers when she saw a letter addressed to her. And she knew that it was another anonymous letter.

She let the rest of the mail drop to the desk, opened the drawer, and absently reached for the letter opener. Froze with her hand hovering over the empty tray. The letter opener wasn't there. It was tagged evidence somewhere in the police station. She glanced quickly at the chief to see if he'd noticed.

He had. There was a curious expression on his face. Not exactly accusatory, maybe a little compassionate? Probably a trick of the light.

"For you?" he asked, his eyes shifting to the envelope and back to her.

"Yes. It's addressed to me."

"May I?" He took the letter from her hand before she could protest. "If it's personal, I won't read it."

She nodded. She was glad to relinquish it. She didn't want to know what was inside.

He reached into his pants pocket and brought out a pocket knife. He slid the tip beneath the flap.

"Shouldn't you wear gloves or something?"

He tilted his head, his eyes narrowed at her as if he were discovering a new species. Then his eyebrows lifted. "It's been through the mail, been touched by god knows how many mail handlers. Izzy was carrying it; Janice already looked through the stack."

"And me now."

"Yeah, but if I thought you were dumb enough to leave prints in the first place, I wouldn't have let you touch it."

"You—You think I sent that to myself? That's outrageous. What does it say?"

He carefully unfolded the letter. Kate noticed that even though he'd dismissed the possibility of prints, he held it by the corners. He read the letter, then silently turned it toward Kate. *See what happens when you meddle?*

Kate's breath caught. The letter writer was accusing her of causing the professor's death. Rationally, she knew it wasn't true, but she'd been fighting the same feelings since the night of the professor's death. She'd tried hard not to listen to the tiny suspicion that her return was the catalyst that had caused someone to go amok and turn into a murderer.

"I'll catch him—or her."

Kate looked up. "Then you don't think I . . ." She couldn't even finish the sentence.

"That you sent the letters? No."

At any other time Kate might have been gratified, but now she just wanted the nightmare to end.

"And the—" She couldn't say it.

"Murder? That remains to be seen."

Blood rushed to Kate's cheeks. "You know, Alice Hinckley was right. You just use the evidence to turn it on the recipient. Even if she's innocent."

"So that's where you were." He pinned her with accusatory eyes—rich chocolate, accusatory eyes.

Kate broke eye contact.

"What were you doing there?"

"Being neighborly."

"I just bet. Has she received these letters, too?"

"If she has, she probably won't tell you. You have no sense of graciousness whatsoever."

He leaned over and braced one hand on the desktop. "Grace is the last thing you need in a homicide investigation. Trust me. You people might not like me, but I sure as hell will try to protect you."

"Until you cart me off to jail. Thanks a lot." She was going to cry. And she was appalled that he would see her do it. So far, she'd nearly fainted, practically collapsed, and made herself his main suspect. She had to get a grip. "Would you like to state your business?"

He straightened away from the desk. "Actually, I came to see Janice Krupps."

"Janice? Why?"

"Standard procedure."

Kate flopped back in her chair and braced her forehead on her hand. "Can't you tell me anything? It's horrible not knowing what's happening. And what about poor Harry Perkins? He doesn't even know the professor's dead. What if he reads about it in a newspaper or hears it on the news? He'll be devastated."

The chief didn't answer, but his look spoke loud and clear, and it said, *If Harry didn't kill him.*

"Oh, just go away."

"What else did Alice Hinckley say?"

"Ask her yourself, Mr. Go-it-alone."

He spun her chair around so fast that she nearly fell out of it. He grabbed both chair arms, trapping her. "I know you people don't like outsiders. And you'd like nothing better than for me to admit defeat and leave town. But I'll be damned if your prejudices are going to prevent me from solving this case."

"I'm not prejudiced."

"The hell you aren't. So you can tell your friends that I'll solve this case, no matter how uncooperative they are. I'll find the killer. No matter who it is."

He pushed away from the chair. It rolled back and hit the desk. The chief was already at the door.

"Alice got letters, too," said Kate. "She kept them all."

The chief slammed the door behind him. No *thank you*. No nothing. The chief was one angry man, but he might just be the man to find the professor's killer.

She reached for the anonymous letter. It was gone.

				4			6	8
		7	9		6			
					7			5
3		1			2			
8				6				4
			7			3		6
6			5					
			6		1	2		
5	9			8				

KATE SPENT SATURDAY trying to concentrate on her work at the museum and trying not to worry about the future. But the professor's death hovered over everything she did.

When she went to bed that night, she dreamed of anonymous letters and Sudoku puzzles. Sometimes they were clear enough for her to actually see the words and numbers. Sometimes they morphed, and the words aligned themselves into grids and the numbers became strings of cryptic symbols.

She awoke to sunshine and a headache. It didn't get better when the phone rang and Pru announced that she'd pick her up for church within the hour.

They were one of the first to arrive for the service. They took their seats in the third-row pew, where the McDonalds had sat for three generations. The Donnelly family pew was right across from them, and Kate saw Jacob and Darrell sitting together. There were familiar faces wherever she turned.

There were only three churches in Granville—Christ Presbyterian where they were members, the Methodist church a block away, and an Episcopal church on the other side of town. It seemed like the whole town was attending the Presbyterian church today.

The professor was a Presbyterian, too, though Kate had never known it until she saw Reverend Norwith at the funeral. She'd never seen the professor in church.

But the real reason that the church was full was because the professor was dead and she was here. She had no doubt about that. The Granville grapevine had been busy. Surely they didn't really suspect her of killing her mentor.

"There's Louis over there, third pew back," said Pru, and waved at him.

Louis waved and smiled.

Kate flushed. Waved and smiled.

"Now I want you to be sure and say hello to him after the service," said Pru, looking straight ahead with a pious expression on her face. "This murder thing is a tragedy, but that's no reason to let it mess up your social life."

"Aunt Pru."

"I know P. T. and you were close, but life goes on, and thirty will be here before you know it."

"Thirty? Oh." Her birthday. Not until March, at which time, according to Aunt Pru, she would become an old maid. She didn't want to grow old alone, but this seemed liked an inappropriate time to be worrying about it.

"Now don't turn around, but Ellis Grumwalt is sitting directly behind us two rows back. You remember him."

Kate fought the urge to turn around. "I don't think so."

"Crew cut, sandy hair."

Kate couldn't help herself. Slowly reaching for a hymnal, she turned her head so she could glance at Ellis Grumwalt, then settled back on the pew.

"What do you think?" asked Pru.

"I think the service is starting."

"Roto-Rooter. Job security." Pru opened her hymnal.

The choir filed into the choir loft. Elmira caught Kate's eye from where she stood in the soprano section. She nodded her head and winked.

Elmira had gotten the photos. Of course, now most of the congregation would know that something was up. Kate just hoped the chief of police wasn't a Presbyterian.

Reverend Norwith took his place at the lectern. Organ music filled the sanctuary, and the congregation stood to sing.

When the final chords died away and they had returned to their seats, Reverend Norwith opened his hands. "Welcome. And may you find solace in the house of the Lord." He looked down at his notes and up again. "This has been a sad week for the good people of Granville. We have lost a dear member of the community. Peter Thomas Avondale, fondly known as P. T. to his friends, was killed by an evil intruder."

Kate clutched the hymnal. She hoped she could make it through the service without breaking down. She was still raw with grief. And even though there were times when she didn't dwell on his death, it was always in the back of her mind.

She squeezed her eyes shut and tried to concentrate on the reading and the sermon on forgiveness.

Kate heard the pastor's words and was unmoved. She wasn't ready to forgive. She'd never forgive whoever had done this. And she wouldn't move on until the killer had been brought to justice. But she sat patiently listening, while her mind and heart rebelled.

At last, Reverend Norwith announced the final hymn, and minutes later they were all filing out into the sunny day. Almost immediately, clouds scudded over the sun and the sky become overcast.

A typical fall morning in New Hampshire, thought Kate, and it echoed her feelings. They stopped to say hello to the pastor, then Pru grabbed her arm and began propelling her down the front steps of the church.

"What's wrong?" Kate asked.

"Louis is standing on the sidewalk."

Kate gritted her teeth. "Aunt Pru, this isn't really the time—"

"Horse swaddle," said Pru, and pushed her inexorably toward the street.

Louis said hello and gave his condolences. Kate thanked him for the lovely arrangement she'd seen at the funeral home. Pru asked him to dinner that night.

Fortunately, he had a prior engagement. Unfortunately, the chief of police walked by at the exact moment Aunt Pru made her invitation.

Kate hadn't seen him in the church, probably because he was dressed in a gray suit, expertly tailored, maybe even designer. And he looked so . . . Kate felt a rush of embarrassment. Heaven help her. She was having inappropriate thoughts about the new chief of police.

"Yoo-hoo, Katie." Elmira jogged down the sidewalk. "Whew. I was afraid I'd missed you. We've got to get new choir robes, those darn zippers . . . What is it, dear?"

"The chief," Kate whispered. "He just passed by."

Elmira stood on her toes to see. "My, my, doesn't he look nice?" She snapped open her purse and pulled out a manila envelope. Kate took it and slipped it into her own bag.

What would the chief think if he'd seen them make the exchange? Drugs? Microchips? Classified information? Something like this could probably end her security clearance.

"I don't know how to thank you," said Kate.

"Don't think anything of it. Oh, there's my ride." She winked at Pru and was gone.

Kate looked up to see the chief watching her. The corners of his mouth tipped up, but his expression was more sardonic than friendly.

She felt the heat rise to her face. Sometimes she hated being a redhead.

Kate was anxious to get to the museum and start trying to solve the professor's Sudoku. But it seemed like everyone wanted to say hello or express their condolences. Some just wanted more details about the murder.

Kate shuddered at the thought that one of these "good" people might be a murderer. She was acutely aware of Chief Mitchell a few yards away, ostensibly talking to one of his young officers and his family, but she knew for a certainty that he was concentrating on her.

Trying to catch her in a lie? Or catch someone else.

When she finally managed to pull Aunt Pru away, the chief was not in sight.

Kate refused Aunt Pru's plan for brunch at the Olden Diner and had to make up an excuse about reorganizing the displays.

As soon as Pru dropped her off at home, she changed into jeans, her "Pobody's Nerfect" sweatshirt, and sneakers. She was tempted to look at the puzzle right away, but she knew the inefficiency of being overzealous. She'd wait until she got to the museum, set up a lab situation where she wouldn't be distracted, and then she'd solve the puzzle.

She made herself a peanut butter sandwich, grabbed a can of Coke from the fridge, picked up her bag and briefcase in the hall, and hurried out to her car.

The wind had kicked up, and the sky had grown dark with rain clouds. A storm was coming. She jumped into the Matrix and turned the ignition.

Nothing happened. She tried again. Still nothing. She checked the lights to see if the battery was dead. Everything seemed to be in order.

How could her car not start? It was new. It was a Toyota. She got out and looked up at the sky. Her only ride was on her way to the diner. She wasn't even sure Granville had a taxi service. She'd have to walk.

By the time she reached Hopper Street, it had started to drizzle. The drizzle quickly became a downpour. She ran up the front steps of the museum and made it inside just as lightning lit up the sky.

A panicked yowl met her as thunder rumbled overhead.

Al bumped his head against her ankles. She knelt down to pet him, and he tried to crawl into her lap. "Yeah, I know. Not your favorite sound. Come on. I'll get you something to eat."

She started down the hall, turning on lights as thunder rumbled overhead. Al trotted beside her, tail twitching, as they headed for the kitchen. She filled a bowl with fresh water and another with food. Shook the rain from her jacket and towel dried her hair. Then she headed to the office.

She immediately sat down at the desk, turned on the desk lamp, and opened the envelope. There was a piece of photo-grade paper and typed cover copy: *Color copy of original. A bit gruesome. But more accurate than b&w.* It was signed with the initials SS.

Cautiously, Kate slid off the top page. Her stomach lurched and she looked away. She took two long, controlled breaths and looked again.

In the photo, the grid was covered with dark red splotches, and she knew she was looking at the professor's blood. She closed her eyes. Took another deep breath. She had to do this.

She moved the lamp closer and made herself look past the blood to the numbers. Some were partially covered over, some were completely defaced.

It took a few moments before the professor's handwriting emerged into something readable. His crossed sevens, his open fours, the loopy way he made his sixes and nines. Just seeing them sent grief surging through her.

But allowing her emotions to overcome her would be self-defeating. She didn't have time for emotional response now. So she had to do something about that bloodied photograph.

She took the color copy over to the new all-in-one and made a black-and-white copy. Now the blood was black splotches across the page. A lot less gruesome but unreadable.

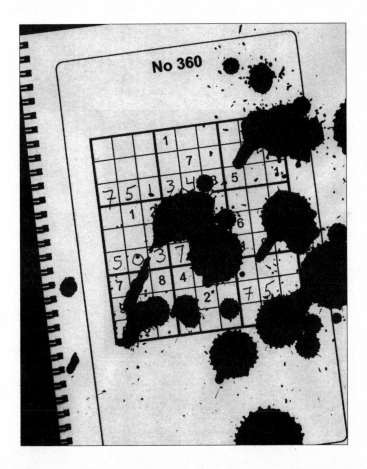

She placed her copy and Sam's copy side by side on the desk. She took the professor's magnifying glass from the drawer, flicked on its internal lamp, and began to peruse the color copy. She could see some of the numbers clearly beneath the film of blood.

She reached back into the drawer and found a bottle of Wite-Out. She dabbed away the black on her copy and began transferring the numbers from Sam's copy into the corresponding cells.

A printed six and seven in the upper right corner. A nine below the seven. And that was definitely a one at the end of row three. A seven, nine, and five at the bottom of column one. A three next to the five. All were preprinted clues, the "givens." The rest of that subgrid was blank.

A printed seven completed the four-two diagonal in subgrid eight. The rest of that square was also blank. She moved to the last subgrid. The professor's handwritten seven and five were the only numbers there.

The center of the puzzle was covered with the thickest blotches. Even so, she could make out the dim shape of printed numbers. Sam must have gotten the shot before the blood had finished drying. She sent her heartfelt thanks to the photographer. And to his aunt.

At length, she managed to decipher the remaining givens and fill in subgrids four through six. One, two, six, five in the fourth row. Four and six in the fifth. And five, zero, three, seven, nine, three, one, eight in the sixth.

She saw immediately that the structure was off. There were too many handwritten answers for the number of printed numbers, and they were all in the same rows. Almost as if the professor had been randomly filling in numbers.

Or trying to leave her a clue.

Be methodical, she cautioned herself, but she couldn't stop the thrill of anticipation that passed over her. Already she'd seen that the five and one in the first box appeared twice in the same row. And the seven twice in column one.

He'd written a zero in the sixth row. Zeros were never used in Sudoku, but it was too large to be the beginning of a six or an eight or a nine. She was sure he had done it on purpose.

Leaving the zero as an unknown variable, she studied the row. The number after the three had to be a seven.

But why had he stopped before crossing it like he always did?

Had the murderer surprised him? No. That didn't make sense. It wasn't like he'd been working a puzzle and was interrupted. He'd never been working this puzzle at all. *None* of his numbers were the product of deduction. He must have started writing them down after the murderer had confronted him. He must have known that his life was in danger. Why else put down these senseless numbers?

She drew back from the puzzle and that uncompleted seven, sickened by her next thought. Was the seven left unfinished because that's when the killer grabbed the letter opener and stabbed him?

She forced herself to keep looking, double checking to make sure she'd read the defaced numbers correctly. What she needed was an IR Reflectogram, and all she had was a magnifying glass. *And your wits*, she reminded herself.

When she was satisfied that she'd gleaned all she could from the color copy, she returned it to the manila envelope and slipped it into her briefcase. She began checking her copy for any patterns within the numbers. 751–3485 could be a phone number, but the exchange didn't look familiar. She took out her cell phone and punched in the numbers. The number didn't go through. She added the area code for New Hampshire and got no results.

If it was a number, it could be any state. The seven and five in the next to the last row might even be a country code. She remembered that Columbia was 57, but as far as she knew there was no country code 75. A city code? To search the entire world for area code and prefixes and the possible combinations would take one of the computers at the think tank. It was too complicated.

If you're about to be killed you don't have time to create something so arcane that nobody can figure it out. Not even the professor. He would use something common to both of them, like Sudoku. Something that could be solved with the intellectual tools she had. Providing, of course, that he'd actually tried to leave a message for her.

He'd called her to come to the museum. There was something he wanted to tell her. Was it here in the puzzle?

She pulled the combs out of her hair. Scratched her head, stimulating the nerve endings. Tried a new approach. She looked away from the puzzle, glanced quickly at it, and away again. Nothing stuck. No partially subliminal message. Nothing.

She stood up. Walked to the window and back. Sat down. Looked again.

The three-two-four pattern of social security numbers? If she left out the three and four, she would have 751-75-5037. But that was too arbitrary. The professor wouldn't have taken the chance on being misunderstood.

A date? A bank account? The combination to a safe? She even tried substituting letters for numbers and got *geacd, eoca* (or possibly *eocg*), and *ge*. Nonsensical. There were too many variables. No common thread.

But she knew for certain now that the professor had been trying to tell her something.

She looked over at Al, who was curled up on the back of the professor's chair. He yawned and blinked his eyes.

"Were you here that night?" Al just looked at her. "No, I guess not. The killer would be covered with scratch marks." She quickly sifted through the people she'd seen in the last week. The only scratches she'd noticed were on the police chief, and he'd received those when he was trying to get Al down from the bookcase.

She continued to study the puzzle while the rain fell steadily, and her eyes grew tired and the numbers began to waver. She'd maxed out. Felt dull and stupid. She needed something to take her mind off the puzzle for a while. Take a fresh look once her initial impressions wore off. She unpacked her sandwich and Coke and went out into the hall.

The room across the hall from the office had originally been the largest of the three main bedrooms. For years it had housed jug puzzles. It was now a storeroom, but Kate could just see the built-in oak shelves over the stacks of boxes.

It would make a great interactive room. Even if they did find a will, it could take months for the estate to be probated. People could continue to enjoy the museum until then. It was time these things came out of storage.

She put down her lunch and began dragging boxes out of the room.

The first box was filled with packing peanuts. She stuck her hand into them and felt bubble wrap. She pulled out the object and carefully unwrapped it. It was a pottery jug decorated with crudely rendered fanciful animals. Holes perforated the lip. Too old and messy for an interactive room. It had taken her half an afternoon to figure out how to drink from it without spilling the water it contained. Her clothes were drenched when she finally proudly showed the professor her achievement.

She rewrapped the jug and took out another object. This was flatter and circular, and she wasn't surprised when she uncovered a fuddling cup, an older form of jug puzzles. Its three drinking hollows were glazed in an opaque aqua.

The rest of the items in the box must be more jugs and teapots. She carefully returned them to the box and pushed the box along the wall until it was out of the way.

The next two boxes also held jug puzzles. She dragged these boxes down the hall to sit with the first. She went back to the office for a magic marker, carefully avoiding looking at the professor's puzzle. She marked each box with the contents it held while Al watched from his perch on the topmost box.

The day grew darker and the storm louder. Each time lightning cracked, Al grumbled and the windows rattled. They would have to be better sealed to protect the puzzles from moisture.

By the time she had the room half-cleared, her back was aching. She'd dislodged Al from his afternoon nap so many times that he finally stalked indignantly away. She'd broken two nails, and the hallway was lined with boxes, but she'd reached the center of the room.

Once it was completely cleared, there would be room for a big activity table and several smaller play stations. The high wall cases would be perfect for sorting the different puzzles. She'd buy some beanbag chairs to put beneath the windows. A few throw rugs for sitting on. Or better still, those foam interlocking squares. A comfortable place to play.

She continued to pull out boxes while rain kept a steady pounding rhythm on the windowpanes. The day grew even darker. Her body was aching, but her mind was clear.

It was time to go back to the professor's puzzle.

She made tea and took the Sudoku copy to her chair by the fireplace, wishing she had a fire to cast off the gloom. She wished she had the professor sitting beside her as they worked their puzzles.

She used one of the larger puzzle books as a desktop and looked at what she'd achieved so far. Nothing jumped out at her. She randomly opened the book to compare one of its puzzles to the professor's and again drew a blank.

Lightning cracked. She barely heard it, just continued to stare at the puzzle. She was certain now that he hadn't been attempting to solve the puzzle. So what was he trying to tell her?

The lights went out.

She sat still, waiting for them to go back on. They didn't. Thunder rumbled right over her head.

The lightning must have hit a transformer. A wire blown down? She looked out the window. The street lamp was on. Across the street she could see lights in the houses through the trees.

And now that she thought about it, the time between the lightning and the thunder had been too long for the museum to be struck.

It must be one of the old fuses. Which meant she'd have to go to the cellar to replace it. Her least favorite job. Why didn't lights ever go out in the daytime? She stuck the Sudoku between the pages of the book and left it on her chair. She felt her way across the room to the door. The hall was dark, too. There was no light coming from any of the open doors.

Surely the whole house hadn't been affected.

She tried the light switch. Flicked it up and down and up again. Nothing happened. She felt along the wall until she came to the staircase. Looked down into darkness. Every room was dark. The whole place needing rewiring.

She grasped the rail, and sliding the back of her ankle down each riser, she carefully made her way to the first floor.

She heard a thump behind her and knew that Al was following her down.

"If only you could change a fuse," she said to her unseen companion, "then I wouldn't have to go to the cellar."

Al didn't bother to reply.

She picked her way down the hall to the kitchen door and fumbled at the doorknob until the door opened. She nearly tripped over Al in the dark. He'd stopped just inside the door, and now she heard the low rumble that was his version of a growl.

"I know. I know. I don't like it, either."

She groped her way to the utility drawer, found a flashlight that worked. She reached back into the drawer, took out several fuses from the box, and stuffed them in her jeans pocket. She fervently hoped that updating the wiring was part of the proposed renovation.

She followed the flashlight beam to the cellar door, threw the bolt lock, pulled the door open. The door scraped along the floor as she pulled it wider, and stale, dank air invaded the room.

She aimed the flashlight into the cellar well. The light disappeared almost immediately. Something brushed past her leg, and she let out a squeak before she remembered that it was Al.

"Get a grip," she muttered. "A few spiders and you'll have light again."

"Yeow."

"Not you. I meant me, though I don't suppose you'd like to go down there with me?"

Al shot past her and dove under the table.

"Coward."

Repressing a shudder, she started down the stairs. They were wooden and creaked with each step. As soon as she reached the bottom, she shone the flashlight along the walls, spotted the fuse box across the room, and shuffled toward it.

Was it her imagination or was the flashlight growing dimmer? She mentally added batteries—lots of them—to her list. She opened the fuse box and heard a scrape. A slam. A click.

Impossible.

Something cold crept along her shoulders. Pure fear. She fumbled in her pocket for a fuse, but her fingers were clumsy, and it fell to the floor and rolled away. And suddenly she didn't care about the lights. They could change the fuses tomorrow after she'd bought some new batteries or a big floodlight. Heck, she would call an electrician, even if she had to pay for it herself.

She felt her way up the stairs. The door was closed. She turned the knob and pushed. The door didn't budge. She threw her shoulder against it. But still it didn't open.

You are not locked in, said her rational mind. *Try again.* She tried again. And then her gut feeling took over. She had to get out.

She rattled the knob, pushed against the door with all her might. The door wasn't stuck. It was locked. Someone had locked her in the cellar.

And no one knew she was here. Her car was in her driveway at home. Pru would think she was there.

"Let me out," she cried. "Help." Which she knew rationally was futile. If someone had bothered to lock her in, they wouldn't readily let her out. Who would do this? And why? How had they gotten into the museum?

Wild scenarios rose to her mind.

Janice out for revenge. She had a key. She might pull a trick like that. Let Kate sit in the dark all night and discover her innocently in the morning. But surely, Janice wasn't that mean.

Abigail might try to frighten her away. She probably had a key. She was the heir after all.

It might even be a burglar, taking advantage of the storm. And then a worse thought reared up in her mind. What if the murderer had come back?

She shrank against the wall.

Stop it. You're getting hysterical. There's a logical explanation for this. There's a way to get out. There has to be.

Was it true that murderers always returned to the scene of the crime?

Ridiculous. She had to stay calm.

And then she saw a light other than hers. It was moving along the storm wells on the opposite wall. Someone was outside. Making sure she didn't escape?

She flipped off her flashlight and held perfectly still until the light passed out of sight. She sank onto the stairs in relief.

Almost immediately she heard the first footsteps over her head. He was in the hallway. Coming toward the kitchen.

"Oh God," she whimpered. It wasn't an idle plea. She was afraid that only divine intervention would save her now.

Don't be stupid. Your survival depends on you.

She refused to wait for him like the sacrificial mathematician. She had a weapon. A flashlight could do serious damage if she managed to hit him hard enough. She stood up and nearly fell. Her knees felt like water, and the rest of her was stiff with cold and fear.

She crawled to the top of the stairs, listening for the smallest sound. Heard them again. The footsteps. They stopped, just outside the door. Kate gasped and threw herself against the cellar wall. The flashlight fell from her hand and clattered down the stairs. The sound echoed through the darkness.

So much for a weapon. She heard the bolt being drawn back. Surprise was her only weapon. She'd be dammed if she would go whimpering like a frightened animal.

The door scraped open. Kate launched herself at the killer.

CHAPTER

SIXTEEN

HE WAS HUGE and strong, and she was going to die. She twisted within arms that threatened to squeeze the life out of her. She headbutted him in the chest. It was the only part of him she could reach. It had no effect. She threw herself to the right. The arms just got tighter. She squirmed, bucked, jerked her head, looking for a place to bite. The beam of his flashlight bounced around the room as he fought to hold her.

She couldn't outfight him. If he'd only relax for a second. Kate went still, then let her weight fall.

"What—" His hold relaxed, and she bolted. He grabbed the neck of her sweatshirt, stopping her cold. She swung around, arms flailing, fists flying. One came in contact with his jaw. The blow reverberated up her arm.

Run, she commanded. *Run*. But she couldn't get her feet to move. His hands grabbed her upper arms, and she cried out in sheer surprise.

"Cut it out, you little termagant. I'm trying to help."

That voice. She shook her head. She recognized that voice. She stopped struggling. Made herself look up. Chief of Police Brandon Mitchell stood over her. The light from the flashlight turned his features into Boris Karloff.

She took a step back. "Oh."

"Oh," he mimicked. He stepped away from her, leaving chill air in the space between them. "Would you like to tell me what happened and why you felt compelled to clobber me?"

"I thought—" She swallowed, tried again. "I thought you were the murderer. Could you move that flashlight? It makes you look scary."

Chief Mitchell moved the flashlight.

It was suddenly easier to talk to him. "I thought he was coming back to kill me. And then I dropped my flashlight, and the only thing I could do was try to take him by surprise, but you weren't him, you were you."

"I'm still me," he said. "What were you doing in the cellar?"

She shook her head. "The lights went out. I went to change the fuses." She frowned up at him. "How did you know I was down there?"

"You were making an infernal racket."

"Oh. The flashlight. But why are you even here?"

"An anonymous tip."

"Someone called to warn you that he was going to kill me?"

"Someone called to say your lights went out suddenly. I was in the vicinity. Decided to check it out. Where do you keep the extra fuses?"

Kate reached into her pocket and pulled out the two she hadn't dropped. "There are more in the utility drawer." She pointed to it, realized he couldn't see her hand, and guided his flashlight to it.

He left her there, quaking. He rummaged in the drawer, brought out the box of fuses, and dumped the remaining fuses into his hand. "Christ, these are ancient. Stay here," he said, and went down the stairs.

Kate hugged the doorway. He'd taken the only light.

A few minutes later, the lights came on. Kate blinked against the glare, then hurriedly glanced around the room to make sure there was no one lurking there. Chief Mitchell appeared in the doorway. He was dressed in jeans and a zip-up sweatshirt. There was a bruise forming on his jaw.

She winced. She'd just tried to deck the chief of police. It gave a new meaning to the term *police brutality.*

"The fuses didn't blow. Someone unscrewed them. I don't suppose that was you?" He dumped the extra fuses on the table and turned to face her. His eyes snagged on her chest and stayed there.

Kate quickly crossed her arms. What was he looking at? Her cheeks flooded with heat. "Of course not."

The police chief finally pulled his gaze up to her face; one side of his mouth was lifted. "Nice sweatshirt."

Kate looked down at her Pobody's Nerfect shirt. "Oh." She tightened her arms and started to shake.

"Adrenalin overload," the chief said. "Take this." He unzipped his sweatshirt and pulled it off. He tossed it to her.

"I'm not cold," Kate protested as she caught the sweatshirt.

"Yes, you are. Zip it up."

She tried, but her fingers were shaking too much to grasp the little piece of metal. He pushed her hands aside and zipped it up to her throat.

"Thanks," she said, suddenly feeling warmer.

She pulled up the sleeves until her hands were free. "You're not going to arrest me, are you?" Kate asked between chattering teeth.

"Not tonight."

"How did you get in?"

He sighed. "You left the door open."

"I did not!"

"Hmmm."

"Hmmm? What does that mean?"

"Stay here." He started toward the door to the hallway.

"Wait. Where are you going?" Kate hurried after him.

He stopped so abruptly that she had to hop backward to keep from being stepped on.

"If someone was really here, they might still be here. I'm going to check. Stay put."

"No."

The chief's nostrils flared. She was pretty sure she could hear his teeth grinding.

"You are too damn stub—"

"I'm not stubborn. I'm scared." Kate scurried closer to him. "What if he comes back?"

"He's probably long gone. Come on, but stay behind me."

She followed him, keeping as close to him as she could. Matching him step for step. He stopped again; she let out a squeak and hopped back.

Chief Mitchell shook his head. "Not so close, Harpo." He turned and stepped into the hallway.

The heat rushed to Kate's cheeks, not because she was acting ridiculous but because he thought she looked like one of the Marx Brothers. It was probably her hair. *Inappropriate thought,* she warned. She was a mathematician. Mathematicians didn't worry about their hair. Especially not when there was a murderer at large. Still, she pushed it out of her eyes before hurrying after him.

The front door was wide open.

"Too late," said the chief.

"How do you know?" asked Kate, moving closer.

"I don't leave doors open." He stepped onto the porch, looked around.

"Neither do I," Kate said and followed him out.

"There were no signs of a forced entry."

"Then it was someone with a key. We display some very valuable puzzles. We always keep the door locked after hours."

"Who else has a key?"

She didn't like the tone of his question. It wasn't even a question, more like an accusation. Did he think she'd locked herself in the cellar? That would have been quite a feat, even for someone with her IQ.

"Well?"

"I don't know. Janice. Jacob Donnelly, maybe. He's president of the board." She remembered that Janice had stayed to open the doors for everyone the night of the board meeting. "Maybe not Mr. Donnelly. But Janice does. I suppose there could be others."

"And was Ms. Krupps here with you?"

"No. It's Sunday. The museum is closed."

"Hmmm."

She followed him up the stairs to the office.

The office was in shambles. Papers stuck out from partially closed desk drawers. Books and papers were spread in disarray across the desktop. Books had been pulled off the shelves and lay in a jumble on the carpet.

Kate could only stare in horror and anger while the chief called for additional officers. And a worse horror occurred to her. The original photo and the copy of the Sudoku puzzle had been in there.

She inched toward the desk.

"Don't touch anything. Just back out and stay in the hall," he told her as he listened to the voice on the other end of his cell phone. "Now."

She backed out. It was the only option she had.

He followed her out. "The night shift is on its way. We'll wait in the kitchen while they're dusting for prints. Not that I expect it will do much good."

He sat her down at the kitchen table and rummaged in the cabinets until he found the can of coffee. Kate watched numbly while
he poured water into the coffeepot. Watched the coffee drip into
the carafe and accepted a mug when he handed it to her.

His cell phone rang, and he went to the door to let the team in.

Kate heard the tromp of feet up the stairs. Then the chief was
back. He sat down across from her. Pulled a little notebook out of
his jeans pocket. "Tell me what happened."

She told him about the lights going out. About going to the
cellar. About the door closing. She faltered there.

"You're doing fine."

She turned on him. "I'm not fine. I'm pissed. Someone killed the
professor and now they're trying to kill me. And no one is doing
anything about it." She stopped, appalled at her outburst. "I
mean—"

"I meant that your testimony was fine. Very succinct. Logical.
Precise." He took a breath. "And contrary to your assumption,
there *is* an investigation in progress."

"Oh."

"Oh."

Patrolman Curtis stuck his head in the doorway. "We've finished dusting the office. Do you want us to do the display cases?"

"Any sign of a disturbance in any of the other rooms?"

"Just a bunch of boxes in the hallway."

"I was reorganizing the storage rooms," Kate said.

The chief nodded. "Anything else?"

"No. But we took some random prints just for the heck of it."

The chief winced and turned to Kate. "Many visitors in the
museum lately?"

Kate's mouth tightened. "More than usual."

"Figures."

"Why?"

"Morbid curiosity. Wrap it up here, Paul. I'll meet you at the station after Ms. McDonald goes through and sees if anything has been stolen."

The policeman's face fell. "Yes sir."

"And tell Wilson to wait for me here. He can take notes."

"Sir." He nodded briskly, and for a split second Kate thought he was going to salute.

Patrolman Wilson was standing by the stairs when Chief Mitchell and Kate came out of the kitchen. He followed them upstairs, and Kate couldn't help but think, *Now we really are the Marx Brothers,* and she had to suppress a gurgle of hysteria.

Kate walked inside ahead of the other two. She stopped by the desk, quickly glanced down at her briefcase, and nearly sank with relief. She saw the edges of the Sudoku photo and copy sticking out at an angle from the opening. She moved to the center of the room trying to take in the destruction, but she couldn't tell if anything was missing. "Why did he do this?"

"Obviously looking for something. And why do you keep saying *he*? Do you have information that you've failed to tell me?"

She shook her head. "No reason. It just doesn't seem like something a woman would do." She stopped. "Unless . . . "

"Unless?"

"What if it was Abigail looking for the will? Simon didn't find one. She's anxious to get the property. She even had surveyors here the other day."

"Hmmm."

She waited for him to elucidate, but he just looked around the room, keeping his thoughts to himself.

Kate waited, but the silence stretched on with only the sound of Patrolman Wilson's pen scratching across the page. When the chief started toward the door, she gave it up. "Hmmm what? You can't just say hmmm and then nothing."

He gave her a look and walked out the door. She hurried to catch up. Wilson fell in step again.

"It's a really irritating habit."

The chief stopped; Kate jumped back and stepped on Wilson's foot. "Sorry."

The chief shook his head. "You don't have trouble expressing your opinions, do you?"

He started walking again, past the boxes in the hallway to the stairs. The truth was, she normally did.

"Do you think it was Abigail? You don't think she killed the professor, do you? She's his daughter."

"I think we're going to turn out the lights, lock up, and you're going home." He started down the stairs.

"But I have to finish working. I can't leave boxes open in the hallway. There are valuable puzzles stored in them."

"You can finish in the morning."

"But the office—"

"In the morning."

"But—"

"You can't stay here alone after a break-in. Use your brain."

It was the same thing the professor used to say to her. But it was easier to take from him than this know-it-all policeman. It was obvious that he was only taking a minimal interest in the case. *Investigation in progress* her foot. By whom? His two junior detectives? They probably had their hands full citing jam makers and old ladies who rolled through stop signs.

She stopped. Put a hand to her mouth. She was beginning to sound just like the other inhabitants. And she knew better than to be beguiled into that kind of mindset. Preconceptions were lethal to clear thinking. And she'd never needed her wits more than she did now.

When all the lights were off, Patrolman Wilson left to make a

final circuit of the grounds. The chief walked Kate out to the porch
and waited while she locked the door.

"I'll have someone on the night shift make a few drive-bys, but
you should really have security lights."

"If it were mine, I would."

"Where are you parked? I'll walk you to your car."

"It's—" Then Kate remembered, she didn't have a car. "At home."
He looked incredulous.

"It wouldn't start this morning."

"And how were you planning to get home tonight?"

"Walk?" It had seemed like a good idea when the sun was out.
It was definitely out of the question in the dark. Not after the night
she'd had.

The chief sighed. "Get in the cruiser. I'll give you a ride."

Kate reluctantly accepted his less-than-gracious offer. They
didn't speak until they were driving up Porter Street.

"It's the white one with the lights on."

The chief nodded his approval. He pulled the cruiser into her
driveway and stopped behind the Matrix.

"Well, thanks," said Kate. She opened the car door. The chief
opened his.

"What are you doing?"

"Seeing you to the door."

"You don't have to."

"I know, but it's the polite thing to do. It's also the safe thing to do."

"Oh."

"Oh."

They both got out and walked up the porch steps. There was a
Market Basket floral box propped up next to the front door. *Oh,
great*, thought Kate. Now what would the police chief think about
her? Maybe he wouldn't notice. She hurriedly opened the door.

"You want me to come in and check the house for you?"

"You think he might be in there?"

"No. But if you'll feel safer . . . "

"No," said Kate. "Thank you. I'll be fine." She stepped inside and looked back at him. "Well, thanks for . . . the ride and . . . everything."

"You forgot these." He leaned over and picked up the floral box.

"Thanks." She snatched them from his hands.

He shook his head. The telephone rang.

"Answer your phone. And lock your door."

He stood on the porch until she went inside and turned the lock. Then she heard him walk away. She picked up the phone.

"Is that a policeman on your front porch?"

"He gave me a ride home from the museum."

"The museum?" Pru's voice turned suspicious. "What were you doing there? Your car was in your driveway all day. Did something happen? Are you all right? I'll come over right away."

"No," said Kate. "I mean, that isn't necessary."

"But a policeman—which policeman?"

"My car wouldn't start this morning. So I walked." Kate hurried on before her aunt could ask more questions. "Which reminds me. Do you know of a good mechanic in town? And can you give me a ride in the morning?"

"Mechanic . . ." said Pru. "Let me see."

Kate waited.

"I have just the man. Norris Endelman. Excellent mechanic. Owns his own repair and body shop."

Not now, thought Kate. Her nerves had taken about all they could take, and the direction of Pru's thoughts threatened to push her into meltdown. "Great. Can you give me his number?"

"Sure. But I can call him for you after I take you to the museum and wait for him to come tow the car."

"Thanks. Eight o'clock? I have some work to do before the museum opens."

"Eight o'clock," repeated Pru. "You'll like him. A real gentleman."

Kate groaned. "Thanks. I'm tired. I really have to go. See you in the morning. Goodnight." Kate hung up just as her aunt said, "Job security."

		4	7		3	2		
	3		5		2		6	
9				8				7
8		9				4		3
	5						9	
1		2				8		5
2				7				9
	1		9		4		2	
		7	6		8	1		

CHAPTER

SEVENTEEN

PRU'S OLD BUICK was at the curb in front of the bungalow at eight o'clock sharp. Kate grabbed a jacket, remembered the chief's sweatshirt, stuffed it into a brown grocery bag, and hurried outside.

"Sorry to keep you waiting," said Kate as she climbed up to the seat. She nearly fell out again. The heat was pumping. Pru was dressed in a flowing dress, patterned with huge pink roses. Her face was hidden by a wide-brim hat that might have come from the set of *Gone With the Wind*.

"Aunt Pru. It's October."

"The Garden Society meets this morning. The theme is Shades of Tara."

"You've taken up gardening?"

"Heavens, no. I just go to the meetings. No reason to start digging in the dirt at my age."

"You're not exactly old."

The big hat swiveled Kate's way. "Old enough to know better." This sounded like the old Pru, and Kate was sorry she had mentioned her age. The hat swiveled back to the front, and Pru pulled away from the curb.

Kate cringed; Pru hadn't even looked to see if a car was coming.

"Did you get your breakfast this morning? A girl can't survive on coffee. No matter. I have to pick up desserts for the meeting at Rayette's. You can have breakfast there."

Pru took the turn at the end of the street without slowing down. Kate grabbed the door handle to stay upright.

"I wrote down the number of Endelman's Garage. It's on that piece of paper on the seat. Norris said to call him after noon and he'll let you know what's wrong with your car." They'd come to Main Street. Pru rolled past the stop sign and into the intersection.

No wonder she'd gotten a ticket.

Kate took the paper. Her aunt may have had a change of life, but her stationery was still the same, watermarked lavender with tiny violets chained across the top. She put the number in her bag.

Pru parked the Buick in front of Rayette's, straddling two spaces. Ignoring the parking meter, Pru ushered Kate inside.

A few minutes later, Kate walked out with an extra large latté and a bag containing the largest sticky bun in the display case.

The day was pumpkin weather cold, and Kate hurried up the sidewalk, skirting puddles left over from yesterday's rain. And while she walked, she was planning.

She had to clean up the office, finish storing the boxes, and put the photocopies somewhere nobody could find them. Then she would continue to try to solve the professor's Sudoku. And hoped it led her to the murderer.

She couldn't place her trust in the chief of police. The professor hadn't placed faith in him. She knew he'd expect her to find his killer, keep the museum open, keep the dream alive. And a part of her whispered, *Stay.* But dreams, she knew, were for children. And she had her own work back in Alexandria. When the killer was caught, she'd go back there.

She let herself in and met Aloysius waiting at the door. In the excitement of the night before, she'd forgotten to feed him. Not that he couldn't stand to lose a few pounds.

He let out a reproachful "yeow" and padded down the hall toward the kitchen, stopping once to make sure she was following him. She paused only for a second before going into the kitchen to look around and make sure the cellar door was locked. She cracked the pantry door open and looked inside before stepping in to get the cat food.

She really had to stop imagining a culprit behind every door. She'd be a basket case before the day was out.

Al was sitting by his empty bowl looking like a disgruntled Fu Manchu.

"Sorry." She poured dry food into a bowl and opened a can of kitty sardines. "It won't happen again."

Al set to work on his food, and Kate took her coffee and sticky bun upstairs to start repairing the damage.

The office looked even worse than it had the night before, and anger and disgust rose inside her. She quelled it. It was time to work, not give in to emotion. She cleared off some desk space for her coffee and pulled the sticky bun out of the bag. She took a bite and gave in to the sweet, seductive taste. She took another bite, wiped her hands, and started picking the books off the floor. And while she cleaned, she kept an eye open for something that should be there but was missing. Had the burglar found what he was looking for?

The will? Simon had looked through the papers in the office and in the professor's apartment, but he hadn't looked in all the books. Though she knew if the professor had decided to hide his will, he would be more likely to hide it in one of his puzzles than in a book.

There were hundreds of vessel and box puzzles. If the professor had hidden it in one of them, it could take years to find it. And she didn't have years.

Aloysius poked his head out of the dumbwaiter door, meowed, and went to sit on the back of the professor's chair.

Kate returned the books to the first two shelves, then stopped to take a sip of coffee. She heard a gasp from behind her. She whirled around. Janice was standing in the doorway, hands fisted on her hips.

"What's going on here?"

Kate took a deep breath to settle her jangled nerves. Al jumped from the chair and came to stand behind her. "There was a break-in last night." She watched for a reaction, some sign that Janice was not surprised as she should be, but only saw of flash of deepening spite.

"They should never have given you a key. You can't even be trusted to lock up after yourself. I tried to tell them, but they wouldn't listen. Maybe now they will. You've wrecked everything he spent his whole life building. I hope you're satisfied."

Her words hurt more than a physical blow could have hurt her. Janice was a master at it. Kate should be used to it. But it still hurt, and all the nasty things Janice had ever said or done to her flooded back.

No, thought Kate. *No more.* Janice was a disappointed, vindictive woman, but she'd have to take it out on someone else from now on.

"No, Janice," she said as evenly as she could. "It isn't my fault. Someone with a key let themselves in while I was upstairs. They went into the cellar and unscrewed the fuses. And when I went down to see what had happened, they locked me in."

Janice's eyes flickered. Surprise? Or satisfaction.

"Does that surprise you, Janice? Does it please you? I'm sure it must." Kate took a step toward her. "Was it you, Janice? Did you sneak in last night? What exactly did you think you could accomplish? Was it to frighten me? Did you hope I'd fall down the stairs and you'd be rid of me at last? It didn't work."

Janice stepped back and crossed her arms. "You're crazy."

"Maybe I am a little," said Kate. She threw out her hand toward the bookcase without taking her eyes off Janice. "Did you do this? What were you looking for? Were you trying to hurt me? Or was it the professor you wanted to hurt?"

Janice raised her hand as if warding off a blow. "Don't come any closer. You're crazy." And with that she ran from the room.

Kate groped for the desktop and leaned against it. Her knees were shaking, her hands were trembling. She had to gulp for air. She *had* gone a little crazy. Bette Davis crazy. And for what? No confession from Janice. And if it had been Janice who locked her in, Kate knew she'd have to be watching her back from now on.

She dropped into the professor's desk chair and reached for her coffee cup. The paper plate was empty. The sticky bun was gone, and Al sat at the corner of the desk licking his mouth.

"Pig." And in spite of the fact that he'd just eaten her breakfast, she picked him up and held him close. "I've never done anything like that in my life," she told him.

"Yeow," he answered.

"Yeow is right. She scared me. I didn't even hear her come in. If I had, I might not have acted so irrationally. What I need is an intercom." She hoisted him back onto the desktop. An intercom. Then she could hear when Izzy Culpepper came with the mail.

She could also hear when patrons came and if Janice was badgering them. And she'd be warned if any other intruders attempted to break in. As soon as she finished here, she'd drive over to Radio

Shack—damn. She didn't have a car. She fished in her purse for the paper with the garage's number.

She punched in the numbers. Al jumped off the table and padded back to the dumbwaiter. He nudged the door with his nose, then slithered through.

She'd always wondered how Al managed to get up and down the shafts. She'd never figured it out.

The phone began to ring at the other end, and she began to pace as she waited for someone to answer. The dumbwaiter wasn't the only old-fashioned apparatus installed in the house. Behind the desk, two gaslight fixtures had been converted to electricity. And between the two lamps was a rectangular brass plate that covered the gaskets of the old calling tube system. There were four of them linking the office, which was originally the parlor; the foyer; the kitchen; and the butler's sitting room. She'd found the rubber ear tubes years ago, when she'd been cleaning out a closet. The professor had shown her how they fit into the covered gaskets in the wall. The plate was still there.

"Endelman's Garage. Norris Endelman speaking."

Kate identified herself.

"Sure, it's ready," Norris said. "Fixed it right there in your driveway."

"You did? What was wrong with it? It's only a few months old."

"Looks like you had a visit by some rambunctious teenagers. Someone had loosened the distributor cap."

Kate was silent for a moment. "Is that hard to do?"

"Nah, just annoying. Don't have a car alarm?"

"No." She always parked in a secure lot both at home and at work.

"Well, it probably won't happen again. It's usually a one-shot deal, and they move on to another neighborhood."

Kate wasn't so sure. Was it really kids or was it just another harassment to get her to leave town? Did Janice know anything about distributor caps? Kate certainly didn't. "Well, thanks so much. What do I owe you?"

"Your aunt already paid me."

"Oh, well, thanks again."

"Uh . . . "

"Yes?"

"She said . . . "

Kate groaned inwardly and waited for the inevitable.

"She said that you would, uh . . . "

The guy had never even seen her. "I can guess what she said. Don't worry about it."

"I'm not. I mean, I'd love to take you out to dinner some night. Maybe take in a movie. There's a tenplex out at the mall over in Manchester. Or maybe bowling. A bunch of us bowl on Thursday nights. Do you like to bowl?"

Actually she loved to bowl. But it was too soon after the professor's death. There was too much to do.

"Of course, I'll understand if you'd rather not."

She heard the embarrassment in his voice and said automatically, "I'd love to go." She could kick Aunt Pru for getting her into this. She could kick herself for getting sucked into her machinations. She didn't want to go on a date. She wanted to find a murderer and save a museum. But she also knew she couldn't spend nights here alone. Maybe a night out would be a good distraction. Plus, it would make Aunt Pru happy.

"Great. I'll pick you up around seven?"

"Sure." She was already having second thoughts. She didn't even know anything about him, except that he had job security.

"Great. See you then."

"See you." She hung up, thinking about how many times he'd said *great* during their brief conversation. She just hoped the evening would be as superlative as his vocabulary.

She pushed Norris Endelman and the date aside. She found a nail file in her bag and began to unscrew the brass plate. She lifted it off to reveal four holes stuffed with old newspapers. She pulled the newspaper out, checked to make sure nothing was important in their pages, and tossed them into the trash.

She went downstairs to find the other openings. Janice must have taken an early lunch because she wasn't on the first floor.

Fine by Kate. She'd be happy if Janice never set foot in the museum again.

The gasket in the foyer was hidden nicely by the pedestal chandelier. The one in the parlor had been completely covered with wallpaper. She left it alone. The laundry room next to the kitchen had once been the butler's pantry. She found that opening behind the dryer.

It wasn't ideal. Normally, the speaking and listening tubes would be plugged into the wall openings. Without a tube, she might not be able to hear distinctly, but she'd be able to hear something.

She went upstairs and waited for Janice to get back from lunch.

She could usually hear the bell if the office door was open. But today with the door closed, she heard the distant tinkle through the calling tube.

No one would be sneaking up on her again.

CHAPTER

EIGHTEEN

MARIAN TEASDALE MADE an unannounced visit to the museum that afternoon. Kate was crowding the last box of puzzles into the small back bedroom when she heard the entry bell. She tiptoed to the head of the stairs and listened to Janice's pinched greeting. And Marian's reply of "Good afternoon, Janice. No need to see me upstairs."

Kate quickly wiped her hands on her slacks and, pushing an escaped strand of hair behind her ear, went to meet her.

Marian looked up, saw Kate, and smiled. Holding the rail, she finished the last steps and looked into the newly cleared-out room.

"My goodness, what's all this?"

"It's going to be an interactive room. I moved all the storage boxes to the small bedroom." She stopped, suddenly wondering if she'd overstepped her bounds as interim curator. "I sort of promised some Girl Scouts that we would have a free Puzzle Day on Saturday next. I hope that's okay. I should have cleared it with the board."

"Nonsense. The daily operation of the museum is in your hands. You have every right to set up your interactive room. P. T. would want you to be in charge."

Kate smiled weakly. She was sure the professor had never given it any thought.

"He would. Believe me. So just go on doing what you think is appropriate. I—and Ginny Sue—will back you one hundred percent."

"Thanks," said Kate, honored and flattered and feeling very close to tears.

Marian lingered in the doorway. "I'd forgotten how large this room was." She sounded wistful. "It was the master bedroom when P. T. and I were children." She smiled and said, "The inner sanctum. It will make a wonderful interactive room. What are you planning for it?"

Kate explained about the various puzzle stations. She'd already chosen several puzzles from the boxes she'd inventoried, and they were lined up on the empty shelves.

"We'll have to start small at first." *At first.* She wondered if they would even be open next week. "And then we'll see."

"You'll need some funds for supplies, won't you?"

Kate was about to say she would use her own money, when Marian said, "Get Janice to advance what you need out of petty cash. Or better still, let me make a contribution. I'm sure Janice is being uncooperative."

"Rather," admitted Kate. "She never liked me, and she blames me for the professor's death."

Marian *tsk*ed. "She's a very bitter woman. She doesn't like me, either, so you're in good company."

Bitter, thought Kate. *Bitter enough to kill?* But the professor was the only person she seemed to care for. If Janice was going to murder someone, surely she would have killed Marian—or Kate, for that matter.

"Don't worry about it. We've managed to rub along for years. You will, too."

Years? She didn't have years. The museum was existing on borrowed time and so was she. Her next project would begin in just a few weeks. But as she looked around the room, empty except for dust and disuse, she wondered how she could ever leave. Of course, it wasn't up to her. Abigail was going to sell the house.

"Shall we go into the office?"

"Please," Kate said, and led the way.

Aloysius met them at the door.

"Good afternoon, Aloysius." Marian bent down and scratched him behind the ears. Al flopped on his back, and Marian rubbed his tummy. Kate quickly closed the speaking tubes. God forbid that Janice should hear their conversation. Did she even know about the tubes?

When she turned around, Marian was watching her, eyebrows raised.

The telltale flush rose to Kate's face. "We had a burglar last night. I remembered the calling tubes. I don't want to be taken by surprise again. But I don't intend to use them to eavesdrop," she added hurriedly.

"Or vice versa," added Marian. "Now what's this about a burglar? I assume he didn't take anything, or you would have informed the board."

"Of course." Kate knew she should have called them, but at the time she hadn't thought about it, and later she didn't want them to think that she was incompetent. "The chief of police came himself and we went through the rooms. They'd made a mess in here, but nothing appears to have been taken."

"I'm sorry you had to go through that. Chief Mitchell should have called one of us and not put you to the trouble."

"I was here when it happened. The lights went out, and when I went to the cellar to check the fuses, the intruder locked me in.

Fortunately someone called the police when the lights went out. Hence the listening tube."

"That's awful, Katie. I'm so sorry. I've been after the board to install an alarm system for years. They're slower than maple sap on a cold morning."

"It wouldn't have made a difference," said Kate. "They didn't break in." Kate felt a surge of renewed anger. "Whoever it was had a key." She stopped to gauge Marian's reaction. See if she was as surprised as she should be. But Marian only looked thoughtful. "I don't suppose Chief Mitchell caught him?"

"Unfortunately, no."

"Are you sure nothing is missing?"

"I don't think so. I haven't been able to find an inventory, so I'm doing another one as I go. The damage was mostly in here. Chief Mitchell thinks he was looking for something, and when he didn't find it, he trashed the place."

"What would someone be looking for?"

Kate deliberated. Surely Marian had come to the same conclusion that she had. Should she trust this woman with her suspicions? If she'd really been in love with the professor all these years, she would want to help. She'd have to take the chance.

"The will? I'm not accusing Abigail, but she might have the key. She's the professor's daughter, after all."

"I doubt if—I suppose it's possible."

Doubt what? wondered Kate. "Who else has a key?"

Marian's eyebrows went up, and Kate realized that her question had been abrupt. She'd never learn anything if she couldn't be more tactful.

"I do. But I never use it when Janice is here. And I didn't lock you in the cellar." She walked over to the window and looked out.

Kate watched her, afraid that she had offended her. Had her words sounded like an accusation? "I didn't mean you," she said hastily. *At least I hope it wasn't you.*

"Well, you should be suspicious of everyone." Silence fell over the office. Only the ticktock of the mantel clock measured the passing time.

Then abruptly, Marian left the window and retraced her steps back to Kate. She slowed as she passed the two wing chairs. She ran her hand along the back of the professor's chair.

"Oh God," she said, and turned away. She took a ragged breath, but when she turned back to Kate, she was perfectly composed.

Kate felt sad for her and yet relieved. That brief slip had been enough for Kate to understand the depth of her feelings for the professor. It was a cry of grief, not guilt, surely.

"Kate, you must be careful."

"I will be, but—" She was close to breaking down herself. "Why did this happen? Who would do such a thing?"

Marian smiled, sad, not reassuring. "What should I say, Katie? An interrupted burglar? A random crime by a stranger who just happened to know how to open P. T.'s letter opener? No. I'm afraid it's much closer to home."

It was what Kate had been fearing. That someone she knew was a cold-blooded killer.

"I'm sure Chief Mitchell is doing all he can."

"Are you?" asked Kate. "He seems to be at a loss. And no one is cooperating."

"I wouldn't let his bland exterior fool you. He knows what he's doing." She took out her checkbook. "Five hundred enough, do you think?"

"Yes, but—"

"If you need more, just ask." She tore off the check and placed it on the desktop. "Now, if you could write up a short press release, I'll take it over to George at the *Free Press* and have him put an announcement for your Puzzle Day in Thursday's edition.

"Which reminds me. I'm planning to introduce you at the meeting tonight. Just say a few words about yourself, then announce your Puzzle Day. Stir up some enthusiasm, because it's going to be a free-for-all after that."

"At the town meeting?"

Marian nodded. "There's an open forum on the mall issue. Everyone and their opinions will be there. This will be our biggest chance to influence the fence sitters."

A speech, thought Kate. She would have to speak in front of the whole town. All her old insecurities surged up again. She ruthlessly pushed them away. She could do it. She would do it. It would be the perfect opportunity to see who was on which side and who might have a motive for murder.

At five o'clock, Aunt Pru picked Kate up and drove her home. "You'll have to get a wiggle on if you're coming with me. The courthouse will be packed, and I want to get a good seat." She was already dressed in a red, white, and blue knit pantsuit, with her DAR pin and an American flag prominently displayed on the lapel.

Prudence McDonald was dressed for battle.

"Marian Teasdale wants me to say a few words about the museum tonight."

Prudence nodded. "So you should. Something inspirational. Something that knocks them on their you know whats. That's just what we need." She lifted both hands off the steering wheel. "Save our town's integrity."

"Uh, Aunt Pru?"

Pru's hands returned to the steering wheel, and she turned to look at Kate. "Yes, dear?"

"Nothing." Kate stopped gripping the door handle and sat back in her seat. She didn't say anything else during the ride home. She was afraid they might not get home if she distracted her aunt again.

"Why don't I pick you up? My car's fine now," Kate suggested when Pru stopped the Buick in front of the bungalow.

"Norris didn't even have to take it to the shop. Fixed it right here. Wasn't that clever of him?"

"Yes," said Kate, sorry she'd brought up the subject.

"He's a lovely young man. Has job security. People have to get their cars fixed."

"Yes, Aunt Pru. I know. We're going bowling Thursday night."

"Lovely. Pick me up in twenty minutes."

Kate got out of the car, and Pru peeled rubber, cut a diagonal across the street, made a forty-five degree turn into her driveway, and sped up the driveway until the Buick disappeared behind the house.

Kate watched in amazement, not a little horrified. Pru wasn't old enough to be so erratic. Was this speed demon part of the new Pru? Or just old habit. No wonder the chief had ticketed her.

Kate showered and changed and was outside Pru's house in eighteen minutes. Pru came down the front steps before she had time to honk.

Watching from the window, thought Kate, feeling a pang of sympathy for her aunt. It was the main source of entertainment for Pru and Alice Hinckley and many of the older Granvilleites.

The museum needs a senior citizens' night. She quickly amended the thought. God forbid they would all be driving at night. The police chief would never forgive her. Senior Citizen Saturday. No, that should be reserved for the kids. Weekday mornings would probably work best, or early afternoon. She'd get Rayette to cater.

Aunt Pru opened the car door and dropped like an elevator onto the low-slung seat. "This is some car," said Pru as soon as she'd gotten herself settled. "How's the gas mileage?"

"Good," said Kate, conjuring visions of Pru in a low-to-the-ground red convertible, scarf flying behind her like Isadora Duncan. "But . . . "

"Too small for me, I think."

"Yes," Kate agreed. "Absolutely."

She drove down Porter Street and turned left toward downtown, carefully keeping to the speed limit and obeying traffic signs while she tried to come up with a catchy name for Seniors' Day so she could add it to her speech.

At Main Street, Pru said, "Watch the stop sign. That new police chief probably has someone hiding out just to harass decent citizens." She twisted in her seat and searched for lurking police cars. "Big night tonight. Everyone will be out. One way to fill the town coffers." She faced front again. "All clear."

Kate stopped at the sign but had to pull forward to see around the rose bushes.

Senior Sudoku, thought Kate, as she made the turn and began looking for a place to park. That was catchy and not insulting to the older members of Granville society. She'd mention it right after Puzzle Saturday.

"There," said Pru, pointing to a small rectangle of space between two cars right in front of the town hall.

"It's a fire hydrant," said Kate.

"It's fine. Everybody including the volunteer firemen will be at the meeting."

"It's against the law."

"Look around you. What's going to catch on fire?"

Had there always been this callous disregard for obeying the rules in Granville, wondered Kate. Or was she just noticing it because she'd been gone. No wonder the police chief was so uptight.

"I'll let you off and find another spot. Save me a seat."

"Use the bank parking lot. It's after hours," said Pru, staying put.

Kate waited for a blue Volkswagen bug to pass, then turned left into the side street and right into the parking lot behind the bank. Several cars were already parked in spite of the sign that read BANK

CUSTOMERS ONLY. ALL OTHERS WILL BE TOWED. A middle-aged couple was getting out of a light pink Cadillac.

"That's the mayor, Charlie Saxon, and his wife, Sarah."

Kate nodded. If the mayor was using the lot it must be okay. Kate found a place, and they got out of the car. Kate punched the lock button on her key chain.

"This is Granville," said Pru. "Nobody locks their cars. And if we vote down the mall, there won't be any need to do different."

But they hadn't had their cars tampered with, thought Kate, and kept walking.

When they reached the corner, a man was unfolding himself from the blue Bug. He'd parked in front of the fire hydrant.

The assembly room was on the first floor. Even though they were a half hour early, two-thirds of the seats were already taken. A long oak table ran across a raised dais at the front of the room. Eight microphones were positioned at equal intervals, and water glasses had been placed by each seat. Only two of the chairs behind it were occupied.

"You're up front," said Pru, and pointed to where the first two rows of chairs were cordoned off. "There's Marian Teasdale waving at you. See you afterward." Pru waved at someone across the room and began crawling over knees to get to her place.

Kate walked past a standing microphone that was placed in the aisle, presumably for speakers. *That would be me,* thought Kate as her stomach began to flutter.

"All ready?" asked Marian.

Kate nodded and sat down. Her mouth was suddenly dry. What if she made a fool of herself? She reached in her bag for her notes. She didn't really need them. She could see every single word in her head.

Members of the town council began to file onto the dais and

take their places at the table. The row where Kate and Marian were sitting was almost full. Behind her the buzz of conversation and the scraping of chairs indicated a full house. Kate swallowed the lump in her throat and hoped that she wouldn't make any blunders in front of the entire town of Granville. *Katie is a ge-ek.*

The taunt was quieter now. Which was good. She'd probably only let it sneak back into her brain because Darrell Donnelly had just passed them and taken a seat at the end of the row. Kate was pretty sure she knew which side of the mall issue he would be speaking for.

As the room filled up, it grew stifling hot. People began to strip off jackets and sweaters. Kate was beginning to feel lightheaded, and she looked at the pitchers of water on the council table with envy.

"Is there a water fountain?"

"Too late," said Marian. "The meeting is beginning. You'll do fine."

Mayor Saxon took his place at the center of the table and tapped on the microphone. Several fuzzy thumps echoed through the room. "Is this thing on? Can you hear me?"

He was answered by a reverberating "Ayuh" and then laughter. Obviously, a Granville ritual.

"The meeting of the town council will now come to order. Carrie, will you read the minutes from the last meeting?"

The evening proceeded while the room grew warmer and Kate grew more and more nervous.

The old business was dealt with, then the new. And finally the call for announcements.

"The Meet and Greet at the community center is being postponed to October 23 due to a broken pipe."

"The parish Friday night bean supper is looking for volunteers to serve between the hours of six and eight."

"Meals on Wheels needs drivers, please call . . . "

The announcements seemed to take forever, but when Marian stood up and walked over to the microphone, Kate wished they had gone on even longer.

She hardly heard what Marian said as her nerves jumped into warp speed. And suddenly Marian was saying, ". . . I give you Katie McDonald."

Kate. My name is Kate now. Kate stood up and realized immediately that if she stood at the microphone she'd be facing the council, and she wanted to talk to the people. But if she spoke to the audience, her back would be to the council. No good choice here.

When she reached the microphone, she saw that the mike could be taken from the stand. She lifted it off and walked to the corner where she could speak to the whole room.

She swallowed, picked out four spots on the far walls to focus on so that it would look like she was speaking to everyone. She cleared her throat, and the sound rumbled into the quiet room.

"Hi," she said. *Dumb. Dumb. Dumb.* She took a deep breath. "There are several things I'd like to announce tonight. But first, I'd like to thank Marian Teasdale and the Avondale Museum Board of Directors for their support in keeping the museum open after the professor's—P. T. Avondale's—untimely death. The professor was my dear friend as well as a valued member of our town. The Puzzle Museum is a part of Granville's history, and I hope it will be part of Granville's future."

She saw Marian's nod of approval. Darrell's condescending smile. Jacob Donnelly, who was sitting next to the mayor on the dais, had no expression at all.

"You can rent space in the new mall," shouted someone in the back of the room. He was quickly hushed.

She cleared her throat again. "So with that in view, I'd like to announce several events that the museum is planning. In two weeks, we will hold our first free Puzzle Saturday. There is a new interactive room where kids of all ages can test their ability to unlock unlockable boxes, find pictures within pictures, work jigsaw puzzles and word puzzles, or create puzzles of their own.

"Watch for posters around town or read Thursday's *Free Press* for details. The Senior Sudoku Club will meet Tuesdays at ten.

"It has been proven that Sudoku enhances logical thinking, prevents the onset of—" *Don't get complicated.* "It will be a fun time to test your skills with other Sudoku fans. Or just come and learn what all the fun is about. Refreshments to be catered by Rayette's Bakery." She hoped Rayette wouldn't mind.

Everyone else seemed to think it was a good idea. A murmur of approval floated through the room.

"What about crosswords?" The voice was high and thin. Kate looked out over the audience. It was Izzy Culpepper.

"Crosswords on Wednesdays," Kate said rashly. And decided to end her speech before she was tempted to make any more promises she might not be able to keep.

"Do we get Rayette's on Wednesday, too?"

Everyone laughed.

"Absolutely. So watch for announcements of events coming soon." She carried the microphone back to the stand, turned to go back to her seat, then changed her mind.

"Just one more thing." She knew she was out of order and might undo all the good she thought she had just done. But she wouldn't get another opportunity to talk to this many people at once. "The professor was not only a friend, but my mentor. He helped shape what I am today. He was cut down by a vicious killer when he had so many more years to give. If anyone saw anything, heard anything, please contact the police. Thank you."

She practically fell into her seat. But she didn't miss the scornful look that Darrell flashed at her before looking away. *Katie is a ge-ek.*

So what if she was. If it took a geek to catch the professor's murderer, then she'd gladly accept the onus.

"Well done," whispered Marian as Kate sat down.

"If there are no further announcements," said Mayor Saxon, "I'll open the floor to discussion about the outlet mall proposal."

"Here we go," Marian whispered. "Hold on to your seat."

		1				8		
5	3						6	9
		8	6		9	7		
3				5				8
		4	3		1	5		
2				4				1
		9	7		6	2		
7	6						1	4
		2				3		

TALKING ERUPTED EVERYWHERE. The mayor banged his gavel on the table. He was ignored. He banged it again. "If you don't quiet down, there won't be any discussion."

The noise gradually died away.

"That's better. Now, I'm going to recognize the speakers who signed up in advance first. And if you behave yourselves, I'll give the floor to as many others as we have time for. The first speaker is Ernie Tate." The man sitting next to Kate got up and went to the microphone.

"State your name and address for the record."

"Ernie Tate. 324 Grove Street. And I'd like to say that we need some new business around here. Our young people are leaving in droves. Why just this past June, my niece and her husband packed up their entire family and moved down to Connecticut."

Boos, hisses, groans.

The mayor banged his gavel.

"That might not mean a lot to some of you folks, but they're practically all the family I got left. Dick couldn't find any work to support a growing family around here. But if they build the mall, there will be lots of jobs for us, and it might even bring new people to town."

"Don't need no new people."

"We need more jobs."

The mayor banged on the table.

"Don't need anymore GDTs mucking up our land."

"What tourists?"

More laughter.

The mayor's gavel went unheeded.

Ernie Tate grasped the microphone stand. "That's just what I'm saying. The only time we get people from the south is to look at the leaves. That's two weeks a year. A man can't live on two measly weeks of tourist trade."

"You forgot P. T.'s Folly."

"Save the museum!"

"To heck with the museum. Save my house."

"Ah, sit down."

"I'm just saying," said Ernie, and returned to his seat.

The mayor finally restored a semblance of order, and the next speaker took his place at the microphone. Darrell Donnelly. He walked past Kate without a glance.

"Thank you, Mayor Saxon. Mr. Tate is correct about the state of Granville's economy. I'm loan manager at the Farm and Mercantile Bank, and I've seen firsthand what the sluggish economy has done to our town. It's affecting every one of us, our friends, neighbors, loved ones. Our very quality of life. That's why I'm speaking in favor of the proposed mall. It's estimated that it will generate 500 new jobs for our citizens. The influx of year-round tourism will jump-start businesses that already exist." He paused. "Rayette will have to start mass-producing her sticky buns."

Laughter.

Kate seethed. He sounded so sincere, but she didn't believe him for a second. She knew what he really was. She looked around the room, saw some nods, some thoughtful expressions, and hope dwindled.

"So I urge you to support the mall referendum. And give Granville a better quality of life."

He sat down, and Mayor Saxon called Jacob Donnelly Senior.

Kate clenched her fists. It was a rout. Wasn't anyone going to talk against the mall?

Donnelly stayed seated but gave his name and address. "Darrell here has brought up some good points. Everyone knows we could use a little bump up in our economy."

"Sure could."

"'Bout time, too."

"But he forgot an important issue that the new mall would affect." He looked over the crowd. "Taxes."

Shouts of "no" and "not again" erupted around the room. The mayor banged his gavel.

"The surge in traffic would require the widening of Main Street."

"More jobs," someone shouted.

"That we'll have to pay for."

Donnelly Sr. held up his hand. "If you'll let me finish." The room quieted.

"It would also mean a larger police force, a professional fire brigade. Which means considerably higher taxes. The mall food court is projected to hold thirty eating establishments. Those along with the outlets stores themselves will virtually kill business downtown."

Kate could hardly believe what she was hearing. She glanced at Marian, but she didn't seem surprised. Darrell, on the other hand, had straightened to the edge of his seat and was glaring at his grandfather.

"So I urge you to consider carefully before voting in favor of the mall. Thank you."

"Alice Hinckley," said the mayor, and looked out over the audience. "Alice Hinckley," he repeated louder. "Well, if Alice isn't here, Dave Renquist can take the floor."

The back doors swung open and Alice Hinckley burst in waving a poster with the word MALL circled and crossed over in red. More people poured through the doors. All carrying signs. SAVE OUR MUSEUM. VOTE QUALITY OF LIFE, YES—CHEAP JUNK, NO. NO MORE MALLS. BUILD IT IN MAINE. There were at least fifteen of them, all women, and none of them younger than seventy. They were all wearing red sashes with the initials GAB printed in gold.

Alice marched down the aisle, followed by her supporters on walkers and canes, even several in wheelchairs, whose bobbling posters endangered their ambulatory comrades. The audience burst into a new fit of heckling.

Alice reached the microphone, and the rest of her group crowded in behind her. "Sorry we're late," she yelled over the noise. "Some blue Volkswagen parked in my usual place.

"But now that we're here, the Granny Activist Brigade has one thing to say. No new mall!" She pumped her sign in the air. "No new mall," echoed the other GABs.

Others took up the chant. "No new mall! No new mall!" Reedy voices, deep voices, warbley voices, all chanting and pumping signs.

Chants of "Progress! Progress!" rose up around the room.

"No new mall!" shouted the GABs in unison.

"Go home where you belong," yelled a man sitting on the aisle.

Alice turned on him and jabbed her poster at him. "No new mall!"

"Order. Order," yelled the mayor, growing red faced as he hammered his gavel on the table.

The man jumped from his seat and tried to grab Alice's sign. Alice smacked him in the head with it. He fell back into the seats, and the man next to him hit the floor. The GABs crowded around her, walkers, wheelchairs, canes, and orthopedic shoes making one united front. "No new mall! No new mall!"

The man struggled to his feet and grabbed the sign. Alice staggered back. A little man in the next row jumped up and yelled, "You can't hit a granny!" and socked the man in the nose.

Others jumped from their seats and formed a protective circle around the GABs. An equally large group barred their way back to the microphone. The GAB group pushed forward. The pro-mall group pushed back. One of them broke rank and dove into the group of GABs. A malacca cane came down on his head.

"No new mall! No new mall!"

The gavel banged away, unheeded. Kate stood up to get a better look. The chief of police was pushing his way through the crowd. Though what a single man could do against that crowd was anybody's guess. His patrolmen stood at the perimeter of the room, mouths hanging open, not making a move to restore order.

"Police," the chief yelled over the din. "Cease and desist."

Kate rolled her eyes. That would really stop them.

A pocketbook swung near his head. The chief ducked, and Kate saw her aunt wind up for another swing.

"Aunt Pru. No!" Her cry was drowned out as more shouting rose from the crowd.

"Stop now, or I'll arrest you."

That did the trick. The shouting stopped. Slowly the crowd turned on him, Pro-Malls, Anti-Malls, and GABs alike glaring at the sole source of reason in the room.

"Stay out of this, Chief. Isn't your business."

"Keeping the peace in this town is my business. Now return to your seats immediately or leave the premises."

"Better than the movies," said Marian as a fist whizzed by the chief's ear.

The chief caught the arm and yanked the owner out of the crowd. "You're under arrest for attempting to assault a police officer." He looked around for backup and found his department standing at the wall.

"Curtis. Wilson. Owens. Now." The young officers jumped as if they'd been goosed, then waded through the crowd to their chief. He thrust his detainee at them and turned back to the crowd.

"Who's next?"

Kate grinned. It *was* better than the movies.

"Order," yelled the mayor, and he banged his gavel.

"Aw, Chief Mitchell, you can't arrest Sneedins. Everybody knows he couldn't land a punch even with his glasses on."

"Ayuh," yelled the pro-malls.

"Ayuh," yelled the anti-malls.

"Let him go," yelled the GABs.

"This meeting is adjourned," shouted the mayor, and he banged his gavel once more before climbing down from the dais and leaving by a side door. The other council members followed him. Only the police chief and his three inexperienced patrolmen were left to restore order.

"Now look what you've done," someone said.

"Ayuh," agreed the crowd, their differences forgotten as they glowered at the chief of police.

The chief opened his mouth, then closed it. He shook his head and said, "Let him go." Officers Curtis and Wilson stepped back, looking relieved.

Someone handed Sneedins his hat, which he slapped against his thigh before stuffing it onto his head. People began to congratulate the GABs, and others congratulated the pro-mallers. Then everybody congratulated each other.

No one even glanced at the chief of police.

"You've just witnessed a typical New Hampshire town meeting," said Marian, gathering up her belongings.

They joined the crowd converging toward the back door and met up with Ginny Sue and Rayette halfway there.

"There seems to be a traffic jam ahead," said Marian. "Can you see what's holding us up?"

Ginny Sue stood on tiptoe to look over the heads in front of them. "Oh Lord. It's Chief Mitchell and Alice Hinckley."

"He's probably giving her a summons for marching without a permit," said Rayette. "I better go do something."

They all squeezed their way through the throng and reached the GABs just in time to hear Alice say, "Arrest me. Go ahead, I dare you."

The chief offered her his arm. "I'll escort you to your car, Mrs. Hinckley."

"I'd rather you arrested me," said Alice, staring at the proffered arm as if it were the serpent in the garden. She huffed and turned on her heel; walkers, canes, and orthopedic shoes fell in behind her.

The chief jerked his head toward his patrolmen. "See that they all get in their vehicles safely."

"Yes sir." Looking considerably happier, they hurried after the grannies.

The chief ran a hand through his hair. He turned around and came face to face with Kate. He nodded at her, at the other three, then cut through the rows of chairs toward the side entrance.

Outside the assembly room, the hallway was packed with arguing people. Kate perused the crowd looking for Pru and saw Abigail Avondale at the center of a knot of people. When she turned back to Marian and Ginny Sue, she found herself alone.

Ginny Sue waved over a mass of moving bodies. "See you next week." She disappeared into the crowd.

Kate began navigating toward where Abigail was standing. But when she got there, Abigail was gone.

Darrell was there. Almost as if he'd been waiting for her.

He stuck his face close to hers. "Well, you and Alice Hinckley certainly created a diversion tonight. It won't work. Abigail is going to sell the house. The mall will be built. And you'll just be a geek without a job. Go back to your think tank and leave us normal people alone."

He walked past her, knocking against her shoulder, and she flashed on the night of the murder . . . being hit, falling back. Could it have been Darrell?

In her heart, she wished it were Darrell, but her mind said two words that won out. *No evidence.*

But he was wrong about her. She was as normal as anybody. Just smarter. Stinging with hurt and indignation, she muscled her way through the double door to the outside. She found Pru talking to Simon beneath the lit statue of Abelard Granville.

"What a riot," said Pru. Her cheeks were flushed. "Can't remember when I had so much fun."

"Aunt Pru. You attacked the chief of police."

"And I almost got him, too," Pru said proudly.

"You could go to jail for that."

"Pooh. I'd like to see him try."

"Well, I wouldn't."

"Nor would I," said Simon. "Really Pru."

"Oh really, yourself. Don't rain on my parade."

"Wouldn't think of it."

"I think it's time we went home," said Kate as Simon and Pru continued to bicker under the streetlight. Kate finally had to pull her away.

There were two people walking ahead of them toward the parking lot. At first Kate thought it must be the mayor and his wife. But as they rounded the corner of the building into the parking lot, the security light caught their profiles.

"That's Jacob and his no-good grandson," said Pru. "I thought Darrell would have a fit when Jacob stood against the mall." Pru snorted. "Served him right, too. I remember how mean he was to you in high school. McDonalds don't forget."

"Shh, he'll hear you," said Kate as they followed the two Donnellys into the parking lot.

The two men stopped abruptly in the middle of the asphalt. Darrell turned on his grandfather.

"Just what the hell do you think you were doing?"

Kate grabbed Pru. "Wait."

"You'll wreck everything. People listen to you. Are you crazy?"

"You forget yourself." Donnelly Sr. looked back over his shoulder.

Kate pushed Pru between two parked cars and pulled her down to the pavement

"What are we doing?" asked Pru.

"Looking for a killer." Kate peered around the fender of the car.

Donnelly Sr. poked his finger into the younger man's chest. "I told you not to count on this. There are other agendas in this town that don't include your greed."

Kate could feel her aunt pressing close behind her. "What's he talking about?" she whispered.

"Shh."

"And what would that be, old man? Your agenda? You'd think you'd be satisfied now that the old coot is dead."

"You insolent—" Donnelly Sr. raised his hand.

Darrell stepped out of the way. "You wouldn't dare hit me." He turned his back and strode across the lot to his car. Donnelly Sr.

stood looking after him, then slowly shook his head and went to his own car.

Pru started to stand up, but Kate held her back. A silver Porsche sped past them and screeched into the street. It was followed by a black Cadillac.

"Okay. It's safe now." Kate took her aunt's elbow and helped her up. She turned around and came face to face with a scowling chief of police.

"And you would be doing what?" he asked dryly.

"We were just, uh—"

"She dropped her keys," said Aunt Pru, lying like a hardened criminal instead of a good Presbyterian.

Kate was impressed.

"They're in her hand," said the chief.

"Just found them," said Pru. "It isn't a crime to drop your keys in a parking lot, is it?"

"Aunt Pru," warned Kate between her teeth.

"No," he said. "But it could be dangerous eavesdropping on people who bear you ill will."

"The Donnellys?" said Pru, surprise making her drop her defensive stance. "Don't be ridiculous. I've known them all my life. Our families go back for generations. There's no ill will between us." She wagged her finger at his nose. "And you'd know that if you were from around here."

Kate cringed.

He turned to her. "So did you learn anything?"

"She certainly did not," interrupted Pru. "We weren't eavesdropping. We were looking for keys."

"I was looking for keys." It wasn't a total lie. Not if the Donnellys held the key to the professor's murder.

"Then I'll see you to your car." He waited for them to lead the way. Kate blipped the doors open. Pru went around to the passenger side. The chief opened Kate's door, but when she started to get inside, he stopped her. "I'll stop by the museum tomorrow, and we'll have a little chat."

Kate swallowed as the blood rushed to her face. At least it was dark. If the chief saw her reaction, she'd be back on his suspect list.

	6	1		3	7			
	7	9						
3					4			2
			2					9
	3			7			6	
5					8			
8			9					6
						9	5	
			4	6		7	1	

CHAPTER

T W E N T Y

THE NEXT MORNING, Kate went back to town hall. She didn't know why she hadn't thought of coming here before. Too much distraction, she guessed. It had taken the council meeting for her to realize she'd failed to research the most basic factor of the situation.

She walked across the wooden floor and perused the directory of offices. The land title office was on the second floor.

She climbed the stairs and stopped before a frosted glass door that said TITLES, PERMITS AND LICENSES, and below it, MARRIAGE, ANIMAL, DIVORCE, DEATH, and a line below that, AUTO, BUILDING, AND PROPERTY.

She read it again. Not quite believing that all this could take place in one room. One stop shopping for a lifetime of licenses.

Inside, a counter ran across the front of the small room. A bell sat next to a sign that said RING FOR SERVICE.

Three wooden desks were crowded into the small, windowless room. One of the desks was occupied by a woman who had passed a healthy weight a hundred or so pounds ago. She was wearing a shirtwaist of geometric patterns, topped by a white cardigan. Straight gray hair was pulled back with a barrette and hung to her shoulders.

She was reading a copy of the *Granville Free Press*.

Kate cleared her throat.

The woman looked up. "Good 'n you?"

"Good, thank you," Kate answered automatically.

The clerk began to rock herself up from her chair. The chair creaked as she made a final push to her feet and leaned on the desk to balance herself. She took several long breaths before hobbling over to the counter.

"Swollen ankles," she said. "How can I help you?"

It took Kate a second to answer. She was used to hearing "Next" as a typical bureaucratic greeting.

"I'd like to see a list of recent house sales, if that's possible." She noticed the woman's name tag, half-hidden by the folds of her sweater. "Mrs. Partridge."

Mrs. Partridge smiled for the first time. "You're Pru McDonald's niece, aren't you? Saw her at the Market Basket the other night. She said you'd come home. That's what we like to see around here. Our young people moving back instead of away. Good for you." She stopped to wheeze in air.

"The property list?"

"Oh, ayuh. And you're in luck. 'Cause I can actually find them. Had that new police chief crawling around in the stacks for an hour last week." She chuckled, then narrowed her eyes at Kate. "He didn't send you, did he? No, of course not," she continued without pausing for Kate to answer. "Heard he tried to lock you up for P. T. Avondale's murder. Dang fool."

"Not ex—" Kate began, then thought better of it. If everyone thought the police chief and she were at odds, they might be more inclined to cooperate. So she shut her mouth, shrugged, and tried to look sinned against.

"Well, you just come right on back, and I'll get them for you." She pointed to a swinging half door at the far end of the counter. It was hanging from one hinge.

Mrs. Partridge sidestepped her way toward it, squeezing between the desk and counter. She lifted up the end and pulled it toward her. Kate slipped through.

"Don't say it. Ordinarily, they woulda fixed it the same day I called it in, but they got Mr. Higgins working over at the police station for two weeks now. Leaves us without a screw to drive, if you know what I mean."

Kate knew.

"Just through that door. You'll have to go first. Not room to turn around in there." She reached past Kate and pushed the door open. The two of them crowded inside.

It was hardly bigger than a pantry. The far wall was covered with floor-to-ceiling metal file cabinets. Open shelves created a row down the middle and were filled with stacks of cardboard file boxes. Unfiled folders were piled high on a small table.

Mrs. Partridge took several folders off the top. "Never had a chance to refile them yet. But you'll probably want to take them into the outer office. Too dusty in here.

"No one uses the other two desks. Sally Marsh quit two months ago. Haven't bothered to hire anyone else." She shook her head. "Heck, I've been trying to retire for the last two years. Can't find anybody to work. And everybody complaining about there being no jobs. They can have mine." She shoved the stack toward Kate.

Kate took them and backed out the door.

She sat down at one of the empty desks and glanced through the folders. The chief had made her search a lot simpler. She was looking at nine parcels all within the historic district. She opened the first folder.

Property number 7. Sold by Benjamin Corsi to GN Enterprises. Kate pulled a small notebook from her purse and wrote down the name of the company. She opened the next. Sold to GN Enterprises. She put that file aside and opened the next expecting to see the same thing. She was surprised to find Darrell Donnelly's name on the buyer's line. A big chunk of the picture fell into place.

No wonder he was so anxious for the loan to fail and for the museum to go to auction. He was buying up property himself. But how could he afford to outbid the mall people, who Kate assumed were represented by GN Enterprises?

She went back to the first folder and looked at the date of transfer. Darrell had bought this property last spring. Nearly a year before GN had purchased their first property. He'd gotten a jump on the mall consortium. Inside information?

She knew that by the time rumors started in a community, there were always a few people who already knew. And if it were something that could be taken advantage of, someone would. Darrell seemed to be that person.

She continued on to the next folder. GN Enterprises again. Then Darrell. He'd bought up three properties. He'd gotten them for a song.

Cheated the buyers. What else had he been willing to do to buy up the district?

There were four properties not sold. Alice Hinckley's and the professor's on the Hopper Street block. Jason Elks one street over. And the Grosses at the far end of the district. But they were all pivotal. Alice's and the professor's were on the prime end of the block, and Jason's abutted the museum. The Grosses had the nearest access to the county road that led to I-90.

Kate sighed and leaned back in her chair.

"That chief of police had the same reaction as you," said Mrs. Partridge from her desk. "Sat right there and sighed. Didn't you find anything? Are you investigating?" Her voice had suddenly taken on a thrill of interest.

Kate turned around to see her leaning over her newspaper, her head craned forward with curiosity.

"Goodness, no." All she needed was for it to get back to the chief that she was looking into the situation on her own.

She quickly turned back to the stack of deeds. She turned to a fresh page in her notebook. Who was GN Enterprises? Why had they let Darrell buy or outbid them on property that they obviously needed. Were they working together? Or was GN a front for Darrell Donnelly? Was he responsible for the anonymous letters and the graffiti and burning Alice's shed?

"Mrs. Partridge? Do you happen to know anything about GN Enterprises?"

The clerk put her paper down. "That Mitchell fellah asked the same thing. Never heard of them."

Kate straightened the folders into a neat stack and stood up. She'd have to go back to the museum and Google it.

"Finished already? The chief took much longer. Course, he's not as smart as you." Mrs. Partridge nodded, agreeing with herself. She took the folders from Kate.

"Thanks so much." Kate lifted the half door inward and squeezed through, then dragged it until it shut.

She was beginning to wonder if Chief Mitchell was as clueless as they all believed. She hoped she would never have to put it to the test. Too bad he was so uncooperative. She bet between them, they could find the professor's murderer, and then she could— Could what? Go back to Alexandria? She should. She would. But a part of her was beginning to like being home.

You can't stay here, she told herself as she jogged down the stairs.

You have important work to do. With numbers. Numbers don't leave you. Numbers don't change. They don't turn on you no matter who or what you are. They're dependable.

Yeah, but . . . She shook herself. Pushed that irrational voice back to where it belonged—in the dark recesses of her mind. She would get the job done and get going.

Take care of the puzzles. The professor's voice suddenly replaced her own. She grasped the newel post as she reached the bottom step. Held it tightly as the words echoed inside her. *Take care of the puzzles.*

Had he known that his life was in danger? Had he been expecting the confrontation that had led to his murder? Or was it just an old man's wish to see his legacy carried on?

Should she confide that conversation to Chief Mitchell? She hadn't thought it significant at the time, but now she wasn't so sure. Of course, he'd probably think she was trying to divert attention from herself.

She had to take the chance. She headed toward the police station.

She heard the buzz of voices before she'd even gotten inside. The lobby was packed with people. Elmira was looking harassed. When she saw Kate, she jumped from behind her desk and hurried over, calling over her shoulder, "Just fill out the form, Carol." She grabbed Kate's arm and pulled her down the adjacent hall and into the ladies room.

"What's going on?" asked Kate.

"Everyone and his uncle is in here giving tips about the murder."

Kate flushed. She knew before Elmira told her that it was because of her plea at the town meeting. "Is he upset?"

Elmira gave her a look. "That's the understatement of the decade."

"I need to talk to him."

"He's holed up in his office. But I wouldn't go in there if I were you."

"It's because of what I said at the council meeting last night." Kate hung her head like a guilty child. "I only wanted to help."

Elmira patted her shoulder. "I know, dear. And don't you worry about it. You did your civic duty. It's just that some vindictive fool—I'm not mentioning any names, mind you, but someone whose truck was confiscated last spring—got to talking at the Bar and Grill last night after the meeting. He came up with the 'idea' to help out the chief. Then everybody got on the bandwagon. If there's a valid tip in that mess, we'll be hard put to find it. But don't you start blaming yourself. They would've come up with it on their own eventually."

"You like him, don't you?"

Elmira hesitated. "He'll pass once I get him trained. Come on. I'll take you back."

There was a surge in volume as they pushed through the crowd of people surrounding Elmira's desk. Elmira knocked on the door and opened it. She pushed Kate inside.

"Someone to see you, Chief."

Voices echoed down the hall.

"Hey, Chief Mitchell, you really need to hear what I know."

"Me, too."

"No, listen to this."

"Gotta go." Elmira backed out of the room and shut the door. The noise ceased. The chief looked up.

"You."

"I know this is my fault. I'm sorry."

"Sure you are."

All the contrition Kate had felt evaporated instantly. "You know, if you were friendlier to the people in this town, they might not have it in for you."

The chief's jaw tightened. Kate could almost see him counting to however high he had to count to gain control of his temper. She bet it was a pretty high number. She might be standing there for a long time.

"Look, I'm really sorry. I was just trying to help."

"Well, don't." He narrowed his eyes, looking intently at her as if he could find answers there. But the answers to what? "Why are you here?"

"If you think it's to gloat over the consequences of my appeal last night, you're wrong." She hesitated. She knew she was going to sound just like all the other crackpots in the waiting room. But she had no choice. "I thought of something."

The chief sighed. Closed his eyes.

And Kate thought, *He's going to blow*. She felt an insane urge to laugh. It was awful. But the whole situation was absurd.

"So tell me."

"What? Oh." Kate took a breath, fought for composure. "Well, maybe it's nothing, but—"

"Trust me, it won't be my first false lead of the day."

She gave him her iciest look.

It had absolutely no affect. "The day before the professor was killed, he made me promise to take care of the puzzles."

"Well, you are taking care of them. You're the curator now that he's dead."

She didn't like his tone and what it inferred. "Just acting curator, and just because I know the exhibits better than anyone else."

His interest suddenly picked up; she could see it in his eyes. But whatever had caused that sudden spark faded almost immediately.

"You think I killed him to become curator of a museum that's about to be torn down?"

Chief Mitchell shrugged. "People kill for all sorts of reasons, sometimes for no reason at all."

She wanted to shake him. How could he be so complacent? Didn't he have any feelings at all? "Well, you're wrong."

He leaned forward, looked at her like she was a remedial student. "Figure it this way. You show up in Granville after a nine-year absence, you go straight to the museum, the proprietor is murdered less than a week later, and you're named curator. You're the mathematician. You add it up."

Kate opened and shut her mouth, incapable of speech. "You're nuts."

"Probably. What else did he say?"

He was maddening. "That's all. To take care of the puzzles. I thought he meant if he couldn't save the museum. Or when he was too old to do it himself. But now I think he might have known his life was in jeopardy. I mean, why tell me something like that when I had come back to help him save them?"

Finally the chief's look changed from complacency to speculation. "Is that why he asked you to come?"

"No. He just said he needed help."

"And you dropped everything and drove to New Hampshire."

"Yes." When all she got was a bland, disbelieving look, she said, "The professor was my friend and mentor. My only friend when I was growing up. We may have not kept in touch like we should have, but I would do anything for him. So when he asked, I came."

"The part about the lonely kid. Nice embellishment."

"Oh, for Christ's sake." Kate clapped her hand over her mouth. She'd been so careful not to swear. She knew she was expected to act like the good young lady who'd left Granville. But she wasn't the same girl now. She'd poured out her soul, and he'd stomped on it. She was sick of this arrogant civil servant.

"I didn't embellish. I make my living by being precise. There are no embellishments in science. That would be immoral."

He quirked an eyebrow.

"Damn it. Don't you trust anyone?"

He just shrugged, his lack of interest reading loud and clear.

"How's this? Don't think you can throw me off the scent by all these diversionary tactics."

"What?"

"The EMTs, the cellar, the call for tips from the townspeople."

"Grr-r-r." It was the only response she was capable of. He still thought she was guilty of murder. She whirled around and yanked the door open.

"Stay out of trouble," he called after her.

"Out of your way, you mean." She slammed the door and marched past Elmira's desk and out the front door. She stood on the sidewalk, fuming.

He'd made her lose her temper, and she hated losing her temper. And he'd made it clear, he didn't want her help and he wouldn't cooperate. But damn it, he needed her help.

He might be stupid. Or just cagey. But if he thought he could just ignore her, push her to the back of the pile of other witnesses, he could think again. She didn't give up that easily. At least not in her business. Numbers might not talk back to you, insult you, or send you packing, but they could be just as stubborn and unforgiving as a certain chief of police. And she knew how to handle numbers.

She turned on her heel and marched back into the police station. Elmira looked up. "Forget something?"

"Yes," said Kate. "To give the chief a piece of my mind. Don't get up. I'll announce myself."

Elmira grinned, her face crinkling into a hundred fine lines. "You go, girl."

"Thank you." Kate lifted her chin and strode down the hall to the chief's office.

She had to stop outside the door to gather her wits and take a deep breath. Her heart was pounding. She knew the coming confrontation might be a serious setback to building her people skills, but some things were just more important.

She rapped twice on the door and, hearing a resigned "Come in," stepped inside.

"Just listen to me."

The chief groaned. Not a quiet groan, but loud enough to make her take a step backward.

She regrouped. "You could use some help. I'm willing to help. But you're so damn stubborn, you can't see the picture for the pixels." Ugh. Not only had he made her lose her temper, but he'd made her sound like the geek she was. "A pixel is a—"

"Amazingly enough, I know what a pixel is," said the chief.

"Well, then. . . ." she stalled. Adrenalin had peaked and drained, and she was tired. "I want to help."

The chief's jaw tightened. He picked up a pencil and began to roll it between his fingers.

She hurried on. "I don't mean actively, just that maybe I know something that could lead to the murderer."

"Something you didn't tell me before?"

Kate sat down, since he seemed to have forgotten his manners. "I don't know. That first night I barely remember anything that happened except for—" Her voice caught. "And then Saturday with all the interruptions . . . and now with all the tips you've been getting."

The pencil snapped. They both looked at it.

"I guess everybody's been giving you a hard time."

He tossed the pencil pieces in the trash can.

"They're good people. Usually. They don't mean it personally. It's just any newcomer has to earn their place. Jason Elks moved here before I graduated from high school and they still give him a hard time. You know how it is."

"I know that your townspeople are thwarting my investigation with all these tips. If you or they are protecting someone, you can tell them for me that it won't work. I always get my man—or woman." He leaned forward and leveled dark, intense eyes at her.

A cold chill crept up her spine. "I would never. They wouldn't." Or would they? She'd wondered that herself. The professor was well loved. It was like Rayette said, they'd take their own vengeance.

Vengeance. Revenge. Did he know about the rift between the professor and Jacob Donnelly, or the professor and his daughter?

"Just listen and don't interrupt me, please. Maybe you already know all this, but just let me say it."

The chief nodded. He pushed a portable tape recorder across the desk and looked at Kate. She nodded, and he flipped it on.

Kate took a breath, letting her thoughts settle into order. "Jacob Donnelly and the professor, Professor Avondale, were best friends until college. Then something happened, and they've been enemies ever since."

The chief nodded slightly. He knew this.

She tried not to feel intimidated. "Just bear with me. Jacob is the president of the museum's board of directors. He devised the plan to renovate the museum, and he arranged for the loan. The payments haven't been made, and the bank is threatening to foreclose. Jacob Donnelly is also the bank president."

There, she thought. How was that for a succinct bit of logic.

"Was," said the chief. "He retired ten years ago."

"Oh," said Kate, suddenly deflated. "But his grandson is the loan manager. When I went to the bank to try and trace the payments, he said they hadn't been paid. He seemed glad that the professor was about to lose his home and his museum. I thought maybe he's joined the feud, whatever it is."

"Conjecture," said the chief.

"I know it's conjecture. It's also conjecture that he might have caused the loan to default so he can buy the property. He already owns three others."

"Checked the land office, did you?"

"I finally thought of it last night after the meeting."

The corner of his mouth twitched. "Slow, but methodical."

She ignored him.

"And the morning after I returned to Granville, when I got to the museum, Abigail Avondale was there. She was threatening to have the professor committed."

The chief's eyes flashed. She'd finally gotten his interest. "Why didn't you tell me this before?"

Kate looked at her hands. "I don't know. I'm not sure what I said. Everything was so awful, and I was confused. That's why I came back today." At least part of the reason. "And I know this is conjecture, but I thought maybe she wanted the property to sell to the mall consortium." Kate sighed. "And now she has it."

"Not yet."

"But it's just a matter of time, isn't it?"

"Pretty much. Unless they find a will that leaves the museum to someone else. She's the only living relation that has been found to date."

His voice had softened a nano-degree. He seemed to catch himself and lifted his chin at her. "Anything else?"

Kate shook her head. "Just conjectures." She caught his smile before he looked away. "I do have a question."

"Ask it."

"Where's Harry?"

8			2	4				
	1		6		8			
6	4	7						
9			7	8				
		6				3		
				9	4			5
						2	7	8
			5		3		4	
				1	2			3

CHAPTER

TWENTY-ONE

HARRY PERKINS WAS now listed as a missing person, wanted for questioning in the murder of Peter Thomas Avondale. *Scary enough to keep the kid in hiding, if he was even alive,* thought Kate.

She hadn't asked Chief Mitchell about the identity of GN Enterprises. They had somehow achieved a shaky truce, and she didn't want to push her luck. She stopped by Rayette's for takeout.

"Glad you stopped in. Are you meeting someone?" asked Rayette, wiping her hands on the towel at her waist. Her aim was getting better. There were fewer flour marks on her skirt today.

"Just takeout, thanks."

Three women were standing at the register. One of them was Janice Krupps.

"There she is," said Janice in a whisper that carried throughout the room. "She's caused more trouble in the last week than we've had in the last ten years." A whimper, then a muffled, "It's her fault that he's dead."

Her two friends closed around her, murmuring condolences. Kate's cheeks suffused with heat.

Rayette moved closer to Kate as the three women passed by on their way to the exit.

"People have been sued for less, Janice Krupps. If you're smart, you'll keep your mouth shut. And don't bother to come in here again. An attitude like yours sours my half and half."

"Well," said one of the women, and they all bustled out the door.

"Don't pay them any mind," said Rayette. "Bored, lonely, bitter. All three of them. Managed to find each other in a town of six hundred. Go figure."

"I'm sorry," said Kate. "I shouldn't have come. I don't want to alienate your customers."

"Customers? If they come in here once a month, I'd be surprised. They're lousy tippers. And I don't like them. What's the use of owning your own restaurant if you can't decide who gets to eat in it?"

Kate sat down at her desk and unwrapped her sandwich. *Her desk.* It wasn't hers. It wasn't even the professor's anymore. It belonged to Abigail Avondale, and Kate was here on borrowed time.

She booted up her laptop and searched for GN Enterprises while she picked pieces of crabmeat from the homemade bun. She found three newspaper articles from the *Portsmouth Herald* that mentioned the sale of property in Granville to GN Enterprises in a series of articles on the changing landscape of New Hampshire. Nothing to tell her who GN represented.

She Googled the *Granville Free Press* only to discover that it didn't have a Web site. No surprise there. Granville wasn't exactly rushing to modern ways of doing things, except for the proposed mall.

There was no listing for GN Enterprises in the Granville phone book.

Surely there had to be information somewhere.

She took a bite of sandwich and looked down at Al who sat at her feet, looking expectant. She dropped a piece of crab to him.

"A terrible habit, so don't get used to it."

She'd reached a dead end and hoped that Chief Mitchell was having better luck than she was. And there were other things she needed to be taking care of.

She needed to find those endorsed (or not endorsed) checks. She needed to find Harry. Puzzle Saturday, not to mention Crossword Night and Senior Sudoku, was closing in on her. She must have been crazy to think she could pull it off.

And she was no closer to finding the professor's killer. She'd been so sure he'd left her a clue. But she'd tried just about every possibility and drew a blank.

She dropped her sandwich onto the paper and, on a whim, typed in Abigail Avondale's name. There were several listings. On the fourth she hit pay dirt.

A mention of Abigail's association with a real estate firm in Exeter. *Well, that made sense.* Abigail had won salesperson of the year and had been feted by the mayor for service to the community.

In the last paragraph, Kate found her answer. *Abigail Avondale is the daughter of Gloria Neale Avondale formerly of Boston, now deceased.*

Gloria Neale. GN Enterprises. Was it possible? It was too coincidental not to have validity.

GN Enterprises had to be a cover for Abigail Avondale. Abigail must be buying up the property in the historic district. For the mall consortium? Or was Abigail the mall consortium? The implications were staggering.

And then Kate remembered her at the funeral, sitting next to the Donnellys. Together again at the reception afterward. Darrell demanding that Simon find the will. And talking together in the courthouse hallway after the town meeting.

It was possible that Darrell wasn't a rival but a partner. Had they gone into partnership in an attempt to buy up the town? Had they resorted to murder in order to get what they wanted?

Whoa. She was jumping way ahead of the proof. It was merely a postulation. But postulation was a step ahead of conjecture. *Take that, Chief Mitchell.*

Had he arrived at the same conclusion? She wouldn't be surprised. She wished she could ask him, but like Ginny Sue said, he didn't play well with others.

Well, that was fine by her. She usually worked alone, too.

She went back to the possible relationship between Darrell and Abigail Avondale.

If Abigail really had the power to have the professor committed, she would have done it, and she'd be in possession of the museum right now. But if she didn't, she might try to frighten him into leaving the house.

The thought sickened her. His own daughter. But Kate balked at making the next step. Abigail committing patricide. Granville wasn't Thebes and a mall complex wasn't the Trojan War.

But this still didn't answer the question of who had killed the professor. And would they kill again?

And how did she fit into the equation? Just a tangential figure or someone whose return forced the killer to act?

Kate was hit by a wave of disgust, followed by a stab of guilt. The professor was surrounded by enemies, and not just his known enemy, Jacob Donnelly. If she'd come back sooner, if she'd not gone on that date, if only . . .

Woulda, shoulda, coulda. Not exactly the scientific method. Not a useful way to think.

There was a knock on the door. Ginny Sue came in, carrying a huge cardboard box. "Hi. Thought we might need some supplies." She put the box down on the floor.

Kate glanced at her watch. Three-thirty. She'd lost track of time. "Finish your lunch first. What's left of it."

Kate looked at the forgotten sandwich. Only the bun was left. Al was nowhere in sight. "I'm done," she said and tossed the remains in the trash can.

"Marian put an announcement in the *Free Press*. We arbitrarily decided 10 a.m. to 4 p.m. would be a good length of time. Hope you don't mind."

"Fine."

"That way, the museum can be cleared out by the time the Arcane Masters meet. *If* they meet."

"What is it exactly?" asked Kate. "I've been meaning to ask, but with everything else . . . "

"The cream of the puzzle-solving cream. P. T." She stopped. "Sorry. Jacob Donnelly, Jason Elks, Erik Ingersoll, Obadiah Creek from over near Laconia. And a couple of professors from Dartmouth. They work diabolically hard loci puzzles, Sudoku, sequencing, stuff like that."

"You're not a member?"

"I'm not in their league. But I'll come to crossword night. Besides, there are no women in the group." Ginny smiled wickedly. "Maybe you'll change all that. Now where shall we start?"

Kate threw up her hands. "Pick a place, any place. I have a lot of puzzles unpacked, but we'll need some more simple ones. Jigsaws, paper mazes. Assembly puzzles for the little kids."

"I can get those at the teachers' supply store. They have some big floor puzzles that would be good for the younger children. Though let's stay away from the books of puzzles. We want to create something that they can't get anywhere else."

"Good idea. Marian donated a check, but I haven't had time to cash it."

"No problem. I'll charge it, get my teacher's discount, and you can pay me back later. Want to see what I brought?"

"Sure."

She began unloading reams of paper, pencils, crayons, rulers, stickers in bright colors that said, "GOOD JOB! AWESOME! WOW!" Ginny smiled sheepishly. "The kids at school love them. I thought we could stick one on each of the puzzles the kids make. If you think it's a good idea."

"I think it's wonderful. You're incredible. " Kate hesitated, then asked. "You will be here on Saturday?"

"Wouldn't miss it for the world. What's next? Have you done anything about the posters?"

Kate shook her head. "I thought I'd call Alice Hinckley and see if she and the GABs would be interested in helping out. Their posters at the town meeting last night were very impressive. Though they might be too busy."

"Those girls? They're never too busy. And I'm sure they'd love to be part of anything that would help save this town from the mall. I'll call her right now." Ginny Sue rummaged in a giant book bag and came up with a hot pink cell phone.

The call only took a minute.

"She'll be right over. Knew she would. Where shall we put them?"

"Them?" asked Kate, feeling a little overwhelmed.

"She's calling a few of the others."

"We could use the boardroom. The table is big enough for several people to work at once."

They went downstairs to wait. Janice barely looked up from *Love's Slave* as they passed her on their way back to the boardroom.

"Should she be reading that at the front desk?" asked Ginny Sue.

"No," said Kate. "But I think she does it just to annoy me. Surely she has the good sense to hide it when visitors come in."

Alice arrived ten minutes later, armed with poster board and a plastic Dollars Galore bag filled with magic markers.

"The others are on their way."

Kate took the poster board from her. "Thanks so much, Alice. I—we really appreciate your help."

"Think nothing of it," said Alice, perusing the boardroom. "Good. Lots of table space. Command Central. What do you want us to say on the posters?"

Together the three of them came up with all the information needed to put in print.

The "few" others turned out to be eleven and they came en masse. "We'd have been here sooner, but Beatrice couldn't find her hearing aid," explained the cane wielder from the council meeting.

"Elmira has to work late," said a short, muscular woman who didn't look old enough to be a grandmother and who introduced herself as Tanya.

"That makes twelve of us," said Alice. "I'm shooting for a baker's dozen. Where's a phone?"

"You can use my cell." Kate handed it to her.

Alice turned it over in her hand and frowned at it.

"Just punch the numbers in and press the green arrow. It'll connect you. When you're finished, just push the red arrow."

Alice nodded, squinting as she pressed in the phone number.

"Prudence McDonald. Alice Hinckley. Get your un-granny backside over to the museum and help your niece with her Puzzle Day."

Without waiting for a reply, she pushed the End button and handed the phone back to Kate.

"The way to get things done is not to give 'em time to say no." She turned to the GABs. "Man your battle stations." The ladies scurried to find seats, crossing canes and walkers in an alarming way that had Kate closing her eyes.

Finally they were all settled, and Alice handed around the page of information.

"Okay, you know the drill. Hup . . . " The GABs nodded in unison.

"We'll be upstairs setting up supplies," said Ginny Sue. They let themselves out of the room and closed the door on twelve gray, white, and blue heads bent over their work.

When they returned two hours later, the room was filled with brightly colored posters and the twelve GABS had become thirteen.

"I don't know why you didn't say you needed help," said Pru, looking up from a poster she was busily coloring. She'd misspelled *museum*.

She caught Kate looking. "I ran out of space. Put an apostrophe instead of the *eu*. Takes up less room." She held up the poster.

"It looks great," said Kate, looking at the crooked red letters and the big MUS'M that ran across the bottom.

"Hasn't quite got the hang of it," said Alice. "See, Pru? If you'd been with us on the mall campaign, you'd be an expert by now."

"Pooh," said Pru, and went back to filling in her letters.

"They all look great," said Kate, then took a sharp breath when she saw FREE REFRESHMENTS written at the bottom of each one.

"Feed 'em and they'll come," said Alice. "Don't worry. What Rayette can't handle, we'll take care of. Carrie Blaine." She paused while Carrie waved from the other side of the table. "Makes the best orange bundt cake in town."

"In the whole county," said Carrie in a raspy voice.

"Like I said, the whole county. Tanya is the brownie queen." Alice paused to yell at Tanya, who was collecting markers and putting them back in the bag.

"And no nuts. Don't need any allergic reactions on our first Puzzle Saturday." Alice shook her head. "Don't know why so many people are suddenly allergic to nuts. Never happened in my day."

"I'll make my maple cream cake," said Pru, tossing her red marker into the bag. "That'll draw the crowds."

Alice turned on her. "Well it's about time you got in on the act."

"You could have called me sooner," spit Pru.

"Your trouble is you don't know how to activate."

"I do too."

"I mean more than wearing clothes that oughta be reserved for someone a third your age."

"Alice Hinckley, if you knew anything at all about fashion, you wouldn't wear those old granny shoes," said Pru, jutting out her chin.

"I am an old granny. And proud of it. Save your energy for what counts."

"I have more energy now than you had when you were on the girls' kayaking team," retorted Pru. "A lot more."

"Well then it's about time you put it to good use." Alice nodded, her pink face growing pinker.

Just when Kate thought she might have to intercede, Alice said, "Get off your high horse and get moving." She pumped her fist in the air. "And no nuts."

Pru scowled across the table at her. "I never put nuts in my maple cream cake."

"Then let's leave these young ladies alone to get their own work done. Tea, cookies, and strategy planning at my house. You too, Pru."

The GABs marched, hobbled, and rolled themselves out the door.

Grumbling, Pru followed them out. "I'll be next door. Don't stay here alone."

Kate promised she wouldn't, and Pru was swept away by the others.

"If you need me, call me. Call me when you leave. Don't let Ginny Sue leave without you. You can protect each other." She would have continued except that Kate adopted Alice's technique.

"I will," she said, and closed the door.

"Will you be ready to leave soon?" asked Ginny Sue. "I want to get to the teachers' supply store before they close."

"You go ahead," said Kate. "I just need to get my laptop and straighten up a bit."

"I'll wait."

"Go ahead. I won't be long. Aunt Pru is right next door. And if anyone tries to lock me in the cellar, I have my cell phone in my pocket and twelve and a half GABs next door to save me."

"Well, if you're sure."

"I'm sure. I have no desire to stay here alone—especially not after my little episode in the cellar."

"Then I'll say goodnight. I'll drop by tomorrow after school. Lock the door behind me."

"I will." Kate locked the front door, double-checked it, then went upstairs to the office. She opened all the calling tubes, even though she only planned to be there a few minutes. She closed her laptop.

Al appeared and jumped up to the desktop.

"Well, Al. It looks like we've got ourselves a Puzzle Saturday."

"Chi-uh-rp," said Al. He walked over the laptop, then sat down on it and stretched his neck to have his ears scratched.

It happened almost immediately. The faint crash, the sound of breaking glass.

Kate froze. Al's ears pricked up, and he turned his head, listening. Neither of them moved after that, just listened to the sound of more breakage, a rustling, a thud.

"In the kitchen," Kate whispered. Someone was in the kitchen.

Kate gripped the back of the desk chair. Strained to hear more. Silence.

Someone had broken the kitchen window. And now they were inside the house.

She crept over to the door and locked it. She turned back to the desk.

Al was sitting upright, alert, and he was sitting right in front of the open calling tube.

Kate put her fingers to her lips. Not that she had to warn Al. He was tense; his growl was a vibration, not a sound. She carefully took her cell phone from her pocket and dialed 911.

Holding her hand over the phone to muffle her voice, she whispered, "Someone has broken into the Puzzle Museum."

A young male voice asked, "Are you at the museum?"

"Yes. Please send someone."

"Yes ma'am. We're on our way."

Kate hung up and tiptoed to the calling tube. She put her ear to the opening and heard rummaging sounds. She breathed out slowly. Now if the police would just hurry.

She didn't hear sirens or even car doors slamming. The first she knew the police had arrived was when a deep voice called, "Police. Freeze."

The sound of scuffling and a tenor voice crying, "Let me go."

Kate rushed to the door, fumbled with the lock, then ran downstairs, Al bounding ahead of her.

She reached the first floor just as a blur of bodies tumbled past her. They both fell to the floor, and Kate recognized one of them as Chief Mitchell.

The other man was tall but slight. The chief grabbed him by his sweatshirt and hauled him to his feet. Kate took an involuntary step backward. He was filthy, and the stench that pervaded the hallway was nearly overpowering.

The chief thrust him toward Kate. "Kate McDonald. Meet Harry Perkins."

3	8							
			7		9	3		
	6	2					4	
1				5				
		4	3		8	7		
				1				5
	7					2	8	
		3	6		5			
							6	1

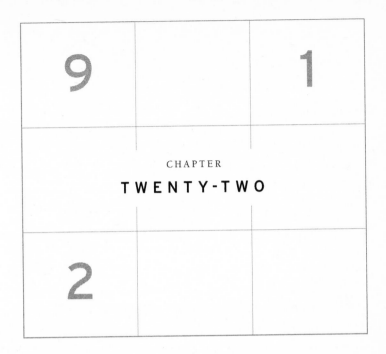

CHAPTER

TWENTY-TWO

KATE STARED.

"Let me go. I have to see the professor," said the boy, and he tried to wrench away.

The chief took a firmer grip but kept him at arm's length. "You can't, so stop struggling. I don't want to hurt you."

"I have to see him—I have to, before it's too late."

"Before what's too late?"

"Let me go. Professor! Professor! It's Harry!"

This was Harry Perkins, the professor's protégé? His sweatshirt and jeans were caked with mud and dirt and God knew what else. His face was streaked with dirt, and his hair was matted down with filth.

Where had this boy been and for how long? And he was just a boy, only fourteen, though he was close to six feet, too thin for his frame, even accounting for a huge growth spurt. He must be starving.

"Who are you?" he asked, suddenly becoming aware of Kate.

"I'm Kate McDonald, Harry. I was the professor's apprentice once and his friend."

Harry's eyebrows wrinkled. "You?"

Kate nodded.

"Where is he? I have to warn him." He began struggling again, but the chief held on.

"You can't see him," said Chief Mitchell. "The professor is dead."

Kate cringed. Didn't the man have any sensibility at all? "Chief Mitchell—"

"You're lying!" Harry wrenched himself away and bolted toward the door. But he wasn't trying to escape. He grabbed the newel post and clambered upstairs.

Chief Mitchell watched him go; his eyes narrowed, but the rest of his face remained impassive.

"How could you be so cruel? You're horrible," said Kate, and started after Harry.

"And you're gullible." The chief slipped past her, unclipping his holster as he took the stairs in measured steps.

"Don't use that," Kate yelled, and tried to catch up.

They reached the second floor in time to see Harry rush wildly from the office.

"Stay back," said the chief.

Kate stayed on his heels.

Harry ran up the next set of stairs two at a time, stumbled and fell near the top, and scrambled up the remaining stairs on his hands and knees.

When Kate and Chief Mitchell reached the landing, Harry was pounding on the door to the professor's apartment, crying desperately, "Professor! Professor! Open the door. Open the door," over and over until his words were cut off in a sob.

He slid to the floor and huddled there, clutching the doorknob. "I'm too late," he said. "Too late."

The chief moved toward him.

Al leaped past him and stood between him and the boy.

"It's okay, Al," said Kate, and knelt beside the sobbing boy. She lightly touched his shoulder. He flinched away and buried his head in his arms.

"I'm sorry, Harry. Someone killed the professor, a week ago. I'm so sorry."

Harry raised his head just enough to look at her. "A week ago?" Tears streaked his filthy face. The words were soft, high, and boyish.

She nodded, too choked up to speak. She was vaguely aware of the chief standing over them, and she could imagine his skeptical expression. Well, to hell with him. He was a cold so-and-so, and she wouldn't let him harass a grieving child.

"Friday before last," she said. "Come downstairs and I'll fix some cocoa and tell you what happened."

She helped Harry to his feet. The smell of sweat and dirt was overpowering. The chief had turned away from them, so she led Harry back down the stairs. A mathematician and a filthy boy, both grieving for the professor, for themselves, for the rituals they would never experience with their mentor again.

Harry hesitated at the office door, emotions warring on his face. He didn't want to go in, but he didn't want to leave. And she understood.

"Let's go to the kitchen," she said. He didn't move, just stared through the open doorway. Finally, she pulled him away. "Come on."

They took the stairs to the kitchen, Al loping along beside them. She could hear the chief following at a distance.

He watched from the doorway while Kate scalded milk and Harry washed his face and hands at the sink. When Harry was finished, he neatly folded the towel, put it on the counter, and turned around. With the tear-streaked grime rinsed away, he looked even younger.

The chief stepped into the room. She cut him a look that warned him not to start picking on the boy. "Would you like some cocoa?"

He hesitated, narrowed his eyes at her. Did he think she might poison him? "Sure." He sat down at the table across from Harry and leaned forward on his elbows. It reminded Kate of the interrogation room. She hastily got three mugs from the cabinet and placed them on the table, leaning between the chief and Harry in order to give the chief a look that she hoped warned him to go gently.

The chief closed his eyes as resignation filled his face.

She was doing it, too, she realized. Bullying the chief just like everyone else. She had to stop falling back into her Granville ways. Even if he did deserve it. The man was sorely lacking in people skills. *Like you,* she reminded herself. *Be nice.*

She stirred cocoa into the milk and poured it into the mugs while the chief and Harry sat silently at the table. Occasionally Harry sniffed and ran a sleeve over his nose. Kate handed him a paper towel; the chief almost cracked a smile.

When she sat down in front of her mug, Harry asked, "What happened?"

She glanced at the chief, who to her surprise nodded.

She told Harry everything. How she found the professor stabbed at his desk. His bottom lip trembled when she mentioned the letter opener. They both dropped tears when she told him how she'd tried to revive him.

The chief just stared into his cup until she was finished.

"He said you would fix things," Harry said, his lip quivering. "But you'd didn't come in time."

Kate shook her head as new tears welled in her eyes.

"Stop it. Both of you." The chief's voice was so harsh that they both jerked their heads toward him. He was glaring at them, somehow managing to take them both in with a steely frown.

"You can indulge in regrets later. Right now I need to know where you've been and why." He turned toward Harry, effectively blocking Kate out.

Harry looked at Kate.

"He wants to help," said Kate, trying to reassure Harry but not totally believing it herself. Brandon Mitchell was one cold, unfeeling chief of police. And his manner was doing nothing to make Harry trust him.

And then she realized he didn't want Harry to trust him. *He wants to provoke him,* thought Kate. What was he after? Surely he couldn't think that Harry had anything to do with the professor's death.

She nodded at Harry, hoping she was doing the right thing. "Tell us."

Harry shifted his eyes to the table. "In the shed."

"What?" the chief and Kate asked simultaneously. The chief shot her a dampening look.

"He locked me in."

"Who?" asked the chief.

"My uncle."

Kate saw the chief's jaw tighten, but other than that, he displayed no surprise or any other emotion. "When was this?"

Harry shrugged. "I don't know. A week, maybe more. I kinda lost track of time."

Locked in a shed. Kate shuddered as she remembered her few minutes in the cellar. But to be locked in for days . . . it was unimaginable. She suddenly remembered the shiny new padlock on the shed in Buck Perkins's front yard. Her scalp prickled as cold revulsion passed through her. Had Harry been locked in there when they'd gone to confront his uncle? Had they'd driven away and left him imprisoned? Thank God the professor would never know.

"Let me get this straight," said the chief. "Buck Perkins locked you in the shed on his property."

"And didn't let you out for a week."

"Maybe more."

"Seems to be a popular pastime around here."

Kate glared at him.

"Huh?" said Harry.

"Someone locked me in the cellar," explained Kate. "But only for a few minutes. Not like you. You were very brave."

She heard the chief suppress a groan.

"He never let you out?"

Harry shook his head, and his lip quivered. The chief played with his cup. He hadn't taken one sip. Finally, he asked, "Why?" And this time Kate caught an undertone of anger.

"Somebody paid him."

Kate gasped. The chief leaned forward on his elbows. "Do you know who? Or why?"

Harry shook his head. "I just heard them talking in the yard. He asked whomever it was if they had brought his money. And then—" Harry's voice cracked. Kate pushed his cup of cocoa closer to him, and he took a sip. "He asked him how long he had to keep me and what he was—" He stopped again, gripped the cup. "What was he supposed to do with me afterward."

"Christ," said the chief.

Kate took his cup and quietly went to reheat it.

"You have no idea who hired him?"

Kate's back was to them as she stood at the stove, but Harry must have shaken his head, because the chief said, "No idea at all?"

Kate poured the reheated cocoa into the chief's cup and placed

it in front of him. Then she topped off Harry's cup and returned
the pan to the stove before sitting down again.

Harry watched her every move. His eyes were swollen, red, and
bleak. "You were supposed to fix it."

"I'm sorry." She hadn't protected the professor. She might even
have forced the murderer's hand.

"She tried," said the chief. "She tried her best."

Kate blinked. Was Chief Mitchell actually defending her? His
number one suspect? She didn't dare look up for fear that it was
not real, just an auditory hallucination based on her need to be
reassured. Or a trap.

The chief stood up. "It's late. I'll take you down to the station.
You can get a shower there while I call social services. They'll give
you a—"

"No!" Harry shot up from his chair. The chair crashed to the
floor; hot cocoa spilled across the tabletop.

The chief had him in a firm grip before he'd taken two steps.

"Do you want me to take you back to your uncle's?"

This time it was Kate who yelled. "No! You wouldn't."

"He's a minor. And if he won't return to his legal guardian . . . "
He held up his free hand. "And I'm not suggesting that he should.
But he'll have to become a ward of the state until arrangements can
be made. Do you have any other relatives?"

"No," mumbled Harry. "But I can stay here. The professor
always let me."

"The professor . . . Ah hell. You can't stay here."

Harry looked desperately at Kate.

"He can stay with me," she blurted out without thinking.

"No, he can't."

"Why not?"

"Because we only have his word for what happened."

"It's the truth," said Harry, turning sullen. "And I won't go to social services. I'd rather go to jail."

"That's an option," the chief answered. "And until I check out your story, that may just be the place for you."

Harry lurched away from him. The chief yanked him back.

"You can't believe that he murdered the professor."

"I didn't," cried Harry.

"Chill," said the chief, giving him a shake. "I'm not accusing you of anything." The "yet" resounded silently in the air.

"I'll keep an eye on him," said Kate.

"And who's going to keep an eye on you?"

"Me?" she said indignantly.

"Did it ever occur to you that if our friend here escaped, he might have people looking for him?"

"Oh."

"Oh," he repeated.

She narrowed her eyes at him. This was not the time to make fun of her. She was on overload. Ready to crack, explode, at least have a fit.

And then she had an idea. "He can stay with *you*."

Harry and the chief both turned on her, shaking their heads like a pair of bobbleheaded car ornaments.

"It's a great idea. You can watch Harry, and he can have a safe place to stay until you catch whoever might be after him."

"No," said Harry.

"Absolutely not," said Chief Mitchell.

"Absolutely yes," said Kate.

"I have a job. I can't be responsible for a kid."

"And Harry has school. And after school he can come here. You can pick him up after work. It's perfect."

"I want to stay here," said Harry. "Someone has to look after the puzzles. Someone has to—"

"Chief Mitchell will bring you back tomorrow, won't you?" She went on without looking at him or waiting for a reply. "And you can help me get ready for Puzzle Saturday. There's lots to do."

"They're not going to tear down the museum?"

Kate sighed. "Not before next Saturday. But after that, I don't know. There isn't a will, so his daughter Abigail can't close us down immediately. Then, I just don't know." Kate looked gloomily into her cup, trying not to think about the day when the professor's puzzles would pass out of her hands.

She almost missed Harry saying, "There is a will."

Slowly she looked at him, the words beginning to register. "There is?"

Harry nodded.

"Do you happen to know where it is?" asked the chief, his demeanor firmly back to impersonal.

"In the coffin."

"What coffin?" asked the chief.

"The Cofanetto," said Kate. She'd disassembled the silverware, but the professor had stopped her before she'd opened the inner casque. Because the will had been inside? Was it still inside?

"Yeah. He said if anything happened to him, you'd know where to find it." Harry hung his head. "But I didn't know if you would be smart enough, so I peeked. He put it in the coffin."

The chief visibly shuddered before he said, "If anything happened to him. Was he expecting something to happen? Was someone threatening him?"

"I don't know," blurted Harry. "He should have told me. I would have protected him." He hung his head.

Kate glared at the chief. "It's not your fault, Harry." *And please, God, don't let it be mine.* "Let's go upstairs and find the professor's will."

4	5		9					3
				7		6	5	
	9	6	8					
1	6					5		
		2					7	1
					1	2	3	
	7	3		2				
5					6		4	7

CHAPTER

TWENTY-THREE

HARRY CARRIED THE Cofanetto to the desk. "It's in here."

It was hard for Kate to believe. The future of the museum had been sitting in front of her for a week. She'd even opened it. *But the professor stopped you,* she reminded herself. And then she thought of something even more unbelievable.

The chief was already looking at her suspiciously.

She took a breath and delivered her confession to the chief's forehead. "My fingerprints are on it. We used the utensils for lunch one day. But I didn't open the inside." But she had years before, many times. How long did fingerprints last, anyway? Ten years? She nodded to the Cofanetto. "May I?"

The chief was looking at her strangely. Then he bowed slightly. "By all means."

Ignoring what she knew was a sarcastic piece of chivalry, she sat down at the desk and began removing silverware pieces. She lined them up in order on the desktop. When the outer level was clear, she opened the casket. Inside were the sections for two silver-plated goblets. She gently lifted them out to reveal a small ornate tray.

Harry and the chief moved closer and peered over her shoulder. She lifted out the tray, and there on the bottom of the casque was a white envelope with the words LAST WILL AND TESTAMENT OF PETER THOMAS AVONDALE.

Her throat closed. She heard Harry's intake of breath. She reached for the envelope.

"No," said the chief.

She drew her hand back.

"Don't touch it. I'll call Simon Mack." He pulled his cell phone off his belt and pushed speed dial.

Interesting, thought Kate. *He has Simon's number on speed dial. Why?*

Simon agreed to come over. Then the chief moved them away from the desk to the wing chairs.

"Sit," he said.

They sat. Kate didn't even hesitate before she dropped into the professor's chair. The chief paced between them and the desk. *Like a guard dog,* thought Kate. Every couple of passes he stopped to frown down at them. The man was tall. And forbidding. Kate hugged herself and tried not to look guilty for whatever his look was accusing her of now.

Simon arrived a few minutes later, accompanied by Officer Curtis, who must have been waiting downstairs to let him in.

He was wearing another three-piece suit, this one with gray and black stripes. His hair was groomed. He even looked like he'd shaved. Kate glanced at her watch. Only twenty minutes had elapsed. It seemed like hours.

"I called Pru to say you had been delayed and were all right," Simon said reprovingly.

Aunt Pru. Kate had forgotten that she'd told her she was going right home. "Thanks, Simon, I—"

"Yes, I know. Something came up." He looked over to Harry, and his nose wrinkled. "I suppose that smell, young man, is you?" He didn't wait for an answer, but crossed to the chair where Harry was sitting. "And what do you have to say for yourself? You've caused us all a good deal of concern. Where have you been? And what on God's green earth have you been doing?"

"It isn't his fault," said Kate.

"I'll fill you in later," said the chief. "The will is over there. We left it *in situ*. I would like to have the envelope dusted for prints before you take it."

Simon nodded, and Chief Mitchell nodded to Officer Curtis, who produced a metal box and proceeded to do whatever he needed to do in order to get prints. Kate twisted in her chair trying to see, but the chief's wide shoulders effectively hid the procedure.

It only took a few minutes, then Simon lifted the envelope and put it in his inside jacket pocket.

"I'll have a look, check its bona fides, and if all is in order, I'll gather the legatees together for the reading. I suppose the sooner the better?"

Chief Mitchell nodded. "I'd like to be present at the reading."

"Of course. Will there be anything else?"

"Not at this time."

"Then I'll see Katie home."

"I'll do it," said the chief. "There are still a few things we need to discuss." He held up a preemptory hand. "Nothing that requires the presence of her lawyer. Though you're welcome to stay."

Simon looked from him to Kate.

"It's all right, Simon. It's just some logistics." She angled a glance toward Harry. "Isn't that right, Chief Mitchell?"

"Right." He didn't look happy. He knew what logistics she had in mind.

"Well, then, if you'll excuse me, I'll take my leave. I confess, I'm anxious to see the will and have it validated."

The will, thought Kate. She crossed her fingers. *Please let the professor have left the museum to the town.* It was against the odds, of course. If the talk was true, the museum was the only thing he had left to leave his daughter.

She glanced at Harry. He was looking back, and she guessed he was thinking the same thing. His face was grim.

"May we get up now?"

"No." Chief Mitchell came to stand before them, looking down from his forbidding height as if they were two delinquents. Well, maybe one of them was, but she didn't have to take this treatment. She opened her mouth.

The chief beat her to it. "You didn't know that the will was there."

Kate leaned back in her chair. *Here we go again,* she thought. She should have had Simon stay.

"I told you I didn't."

He shifted his eyes to Harry.

"I didn't touch it," said Harry, bristling.

"Fine." The chief's jaw tightened. "It's late. You'd better come with me."

"No." Harry jumped up. Chief Mitchell pushed him back into the chair and gave him a long look.

"Son. We can play this two ways. You give me sh—a hard time, you go to social services tonight. You ease up and you can stay with me. For tonight."

Kate jumped up. "Thank you. Isn't that great, Harry?"

Harry didn't look like it was great at all.

"I guess."

"Make sure he gets a shower and some clean clothes."

The chief gave her a look. "Those are two things I'm not likely to forget. Now, let's lock up and I'll—" He stopped and narrowed his eyes at Kate. "You do have your car tonight?"

"Yes."

"Lucky you. We'll follow you home."

Kate didn't argue. So much had happened that she'd welcome the company. "Just let me put the Cofanetto back together and we can go."

Chief Mitchell and Harry followed her home. The chief let Harry sit up front in the squad car, but not until he'd opened all the windows.

Kate couldn't help smiling, though she did feel a pang of sympathy for the chief's nose. Well, that would be remedied as soon as Harry got a bath.

When she turned into her driveway, the chief pulled in behind her and got out of the car.

"You don't need to see me in. I'm fine. Thanks."

"Well, I'm not. I could use the fresh air." He walked her to the door.

She unlocked the front door but didn't go right in. "Really, thank you for taking Harry. He's been through a lot, and he could use some TLC."

"My specialty," said the chief. "Go inside."

Kate went inside. When she started to close the door, she saw that the chief was still standing on the porch, watching her. He was smiling.

Kate's pulse did a little flutter. "You should do that more often."

The smile vanished. "What?"

"Nothing. Thanks for taking Harry. Goodnight," she said.

"Goodnight."

He was still standing there when she shut and locked the door.

"Again?" exclaimed Pru as soon as Kate answered the phone, which began to ring as soon as Kate was inside. "I don't like this. That's twice I've seen him on your porch."

"Aunt Pru, he was just making sure I got home safely."

"Where was Ginny Sue? I thought you were leaving together. I've been worried sick."

"Something came up. Actually, Harry Perkins. His uncle has had him locked in his shed for over a week. He managed to escape and came to find the professor."

There was silence at the other end, then, "Poor boy. I didn't think he'd run off like people were saying. But I still don't like that police chief hanging around."

"He isn't hanging around. He's just doing his job. And you have to respect that, even if he did give you a ticket."

"His job, my foot. If you ask me, he has designs on you. And not just legal ones."

"Aunt Pru," said Kate. "Really, you have nothing to worry about."

"He's too interested in you. And if he doesn't still consider you a suspect, it can mean only one thing."

"I don't think—" began Kate.

"Well, I do. Nothing good will come of this."

"Why? Because he gave you a ticket?" Why on earth was she defending Chief Mitchell? She certainly didn't have any designs on him any more than he had designs on her. But he did have a nice smile. And he had taken Harry home with him. "He's not so bad."

Pru groaned. "I knew it. Kate, don't. Police have no job security. They're always getting shot."

"Is that what you're worried about?"

"Isn't that enough?"

Kate sighed. "Why are we even having this conversation? He was just doing his job."

"Well, you just make sure he sticks to that."

"I will," said Kate. "I'll talk to you tomorrow. Goodnight." She hung up the phone and went down the hall to bed . . . smiling.

* * *

When Kate got to the museum the next morning, she found Harry sitting on the front steps.

He was scrubbed and wearing jeans and a sweatshirt much too large for him.

"Why are you sitting out here? Isn't Janice here yet?"

"Yeah, she was opening up when the chief let me off. But she wouldn't let me in."

"Oh." Kate tried not to let her anger show. Harry didn't need any more violence in his life. "Don't you have a key?"

"I did. My uncle took it."

So there was a key floating around. "Did you tell Chief Mitchell?"

"Yeah," said Harry, sounding unenthusiastic. He stood and hoisted his jeans up. They were too long and too big. They must be the chief's.

Kate grinned. "I think we need to do a little shopping."

"The chief said he'd take me after work today."

"Oh," said Kate. That sounded good. "Did you discuss, um, the future?"

Harry shrugged. "He said since I managed not to murder him in his sleep, he might let me stay for a while. But he says I have to go back to school on Monday."

"Oh, Harry, that's great."

"Yeah, but what's gonna happen when he gets tired of me?"

He sounded so vulnerable that it was everything Kate could do not to promise to take him in, but that would be foolish. She didn't even know what was going to happen with her.

"We'll worry about that later," she said instead.

"He doesn't like me."

"Sure he does. He's just not very good at getting people to like him."

"He isn't?"

"No."

"Kinda like me." Harry shuffled up the last step to the porch.

Kate caught up to him at the door. "All the other kids, uh, guys treat you like you're a geek?"

Harry looked up. "How did you know?"

"You're looking at a fellow geek."

He looked so grateful that Kate had to look off into the trees and blink furiously to keep from bursting into tears.

She felt an awkward pat on her shoulder, but when she turned around, Harry's hands were stuffed into his jeans pockets.

"Come on," she said. "Let's go inside."

They stopped at Janice's desk.

"Harry is my assistant. As soon as I get a chance, I'll have a key made for him. Until that time, please treat him accordingly."

Janice snorted but didn't bother to look at either of them. "He'll rob you blind."

"Enough," said Kate, her temper finally getting the better of her. "Harry isn't responsible for the stealing that's going on around here. Come along, Harry."

She marched up the steps, fuming, with Harry right behind her.

As soon as she'd closed the door to the office, Harry said, "I didn't steal anything. She's lying."

"Don't pay any attention to her."

"What was stolen?" he asked, looking worried. "I swear, I didn't take anything. She's always had it out for me because she didn't want me around. She wanted the professor all to herself."

From the mouths of babes, thought Kate.

"She treated him like he was senile or something. Always fussing over him. He hated it. So did I."

"I don't blame either of you. I'd hate it, too." She had hated it when Janice castigated her for taking the professor to see Harry's uncle. "She's mean and jealous."

"So fire her."

"I'd love to fire her, but I don't think I have the authority. Besides, I think she's been helping herself to the petty cash and maybe some of the loan money, and I want to keep an eye on her until I can figure out how—and why."

"Shi—uh—wow," said Harry.

Kate bit back a smile. The chief must have put it to him about his language. "So we'll just have to make the best of it until then."

"Old Krupsy, a thief. Did you tell Chief Mitchell?"

"Not yet," said Kate.

Harry grinned. "The chief said you were a nightmare." He lowered his eyes. "But I think you're . . . well . . . okay."

"Thanks, Harry, and Chief Mitchell is just frustrated with this case. No one is cooperating with him, and he was hoping that I was the murderer so he could solve the case quickly."

"No way!"

"I'm afraid so."

"He doesn't still think you—you murdered the professor?"

"I don't know. I hope not."

"So are we going to find out who's stealing the money?"

Kate hesitated, then jumped in with both feet. "We're going to try, but we have to be very discreet."

"You mean, don't tell Chief Mitchell what we're doing. Cool."

Kate nodded, but reluctantly. She was pretty sure she shouldn't be getting a teenage boy involved in what could turn out to be a dangerous situation. She was pretty sure she shouldn't be getting involved herself.

"He needs our help, he just doesn't like it. And if we find out anything, anything at all, we'll tell him immediately. We will not put ourselves in danger." She narrowed her eyes at him until he mumbled, "Sure."

"I mean it, Harry. Nothing dangerous."

"Okay. Nothing dangerous."

"In the meantime, we have a museum to run, at least for now, and a puzzle event to organize."

"That's easy. We used to have stuff like that before they decided to renovate. Everything got shot to shi—I mean, all messed up after that. So what have you done so far?"

"About Puzzle Saturday?"

"About who killed the professor."

Kate deliberated and decided Puzzle Saturday could wait. Two heads were better than one, and when they were hers and Harry's . . . a no-brainer. She took her notes from her briefcase. He could help her figure things out, and she wouldn't let him get into any trouble. "I've made some notes. See if any of it sounds important to you.

"First there are the anonymous letters. We need to find out who wrote them and if they're connected to the professor's murder."

"How do we do that? The professor threw them all away. They were cut out of *Sports Illustrated*, *Newsweek*, *Popular Mechanics*, and the *Free Press*." Harry shrugged. "But those can be bought anywhere."

"How do you know which magazines the letters were cut from?"

"Geez. By looking at size, texture, and font. Baby stuff. I'd show you if we had any of the letters."

"We do," said Kate. "At least one. I received two since I came back. The chief took one, but I saved this." She reached into her briefcase.

"You did? Let me see."

She handed over the letter, and Harry hurriedly opened it. He frowned at it for several seconds, then shook his head. "This is different."

"How so?"

"Different magazines." He pointed to several letters. "These were cut from the *Free Press*, but I don't know where these others came from. They don't look familiar. But they all came from the same magazine."

"Oh," said Kate, disappointed. She knew it had sounded too easy.

"I can go down to the drugstore. If they have the magazine, I'll recognize it."

"Impressive."

"Piece of cake." Harry took another look at the anonymous letter and handed it back to Kate.

"You don't need this?" asked Kate, relieved. She didn't like the idea of Harry walking around with a letter that could incriminate someone.

"Nope." He pointed to his temple. "Got it right here."

Kate broke into a broad smile. Another photographic memory.

"*Glamour*," said Harry, bursting into the office an hour later. He pulled a magazine from inside his sweatshirt and tossed it onto the desk.

Kate picked it up and looked at the cover. "You paid for this, right?"

"No—but I would've. The professor didn't like me stealing. I checked it out of the library." He made a face. "Seriously compromised my reputation. You owe me big time."

Kate picked up the anonymous letter and opened the magazine. Same type, same quality paper.

"Harry, you're a genius."

"Nope," said Harry. "But close."

He grinned at her, and she felt a wave of affection for this resilient boy who'd managed to keep his wits while living with his abusive uncle and who was holding up under an uncertain future and a staggering grief. Thank God the professor had found him, or he had found the professor.

Well, they wouldn't have to ever think about Buck Perkins

again. Harry would not be going back to him, ever. She would make sure of that. She'd just have to convince Chief Mitchell to keep him until she could figure out what was best for him.

"So what do we to do next?"

"I'm not sure. Why would a person suddenly change magazines?"

"They were afraid of becoming too predictable?"

"Possibly. Or because they were sent by different people."

"I didn't think about that."

"The ones sent to me were written by a woman."

"The *Glamour*. Hot damn." His eyes widened. "Sorry. Don't tell the chief. He said I had to clean up my language or else."

Kate nodded. She wondered what the "or else" had been.

"So now what do we do?"

Kate considered, then said, "I won't tell the chief about your language if you won't tell him that I searched Janice's desk one night."

"No sh—kidding. You broke in?"

"Not exactly," said Kate. "I have a key."

"Geez," said Harry, clearly disappointed. "So did you find any incriminating evidence?"

"Just an inordinate price for stationery and a bulletin board." Something niggled at her. "She reads romance novels," she said more slowly, conjuring up the contents of the drawer. "There was a bottle of perfume."

"Stinky," said Harry, passing judgment on Janice's taste in scents.

"The petty cash ledger and . . . magazines. Magazines." She turned to Harry with a grin. "And guess what one of them was?"

"*Glamour*."

"*Glamour*."

"It isn't proof," said Kate. "Lots of people read *Glamour*."

"It is if there are letters cut out of it."

"I know. But I'm not sure we should—"

"And you have a key."

Janice went to lunch, and Kate and Harry searched her desk while Al stood guard at the door. At least that's what Harry said he was doing. Kate thought he'd just gotten tired and plopped down for a nap in front of the doorjamb.

They found the *Glamour* magazine in the bottom drawer, just where Kate had first seen it. Several pages had letters cut out of them.

"We've got the proof and the ledger," said Harry. "Are you going to fire her?"

"Not yet."

"But why not?"

Kate pursed her lips. She was just as eager as Harry to have Janice out of the museum, but it would have to wait. "Because," she said, "if she's been writing anonymous letters and helping herself to money that doesn't belong to her, she might be involved in this more than we know."

Harry's eyes widened. "You think she murdered the professor?"

"I don't know. But I'm not letting her get away until I find out."

4	2				7		3	
				5		8		4
7		8			6			
8	9					4		
		1					9	5
			9			1		3
5		3		1				
	4		8				5	2

CHAPTER

TWENTY-FOUR

THE READING OF the will took place on the following morning. Kate dutifully appeared at nine o'clock, though she could hardly imagine why both she and Harry had been called.

Simon lived in a two-story stone house a block from the court-house on an alley called Primrose Way. His office was in a white wooden addition that had been built at the side of the house. It had its own entrance that was reached by a brick walkway. Dark gold asters grew in profusion on both sides of the door.

Harry was already there when Kate entered the office. He was sitting in a chair at the end of a line of chairs that had been arranged in a semicircle in front of Simon's desk.

He was wearing a Lacoste shirt and chinos. A brown leather jacket was draped over the back of the chair. Chief Mitchell's doing, Kate was sure. The chief stood behind Harry's chair.

Protectively, thought Kate as she crossed the room. Kate gave him a quick smile to show her thanks.

He acknowledged her with a slight nod, then walked away.

Kate sat down next to Harry. He smiled shyly at her, looking even more freshly scrubbed and younger than the day before.

Almost immediately, the door opened, and Abigail Avondale came in, followed closely by Janice Krupps. The women didn't acknowledge each other or Kate, but sat down in the middle of the row, leaving an empty chair between them.

Kate's stomach growled from sheer anxiety. She pressed her arm over it and stared straight ahead, trying to prepare herself for what lay ahead.

In a few minutes, Simon would read the will. Abigail would inherit, and the museum would pass into oblivion. And what would happen to Harry? She felt an overwhelming urge to put her arm around the boy, which would totally embarrass him, so she pressed her arm harder against her stomach.

She felt a hand on her knee. Harry gave her an awkward pat, then pulled his hand back.

She smiled at him, trying to be reassuring. If the professor had left Abigail the puzzles as well as the property, Kate would find a way to buy them. She and Harry would open the museum somewhere else. The GABs would help. Ginny Sue and Marian would help.

Until this moment, she hadn't consciously made a decision to stay. She'd been steeling herself to let go, to return to Alexandria and get on with her life. But now she knew that no matter what happened, her life was with the puzzles, and she would do what she had to do to keep them.

Marian Teasdale was the last to arrive, looking solemn in a lilac wool suit. She took the seat next to Kate. She smiled at Kate and leaned over to smile at Harry. She didn't seem surprised to see him.

Had news of his return already hit the Granville grapevine?

Simon entered the room at precisely ten o'clock. He sat down at his desk and took them all in with a comprehensive glance.

"Thank you for coming to this reading of the last will and testament of Peter Thomas Avondale." His voice was even, and he carefully avoided looking at any of them as he began to read.

"To Janice Krupps, secretary of the Avondale Puzzle Museum, for her many years of service, I bequeath ten thousand dollars."

Kate heard Janice's sob. She couldn't tell if the sound was surprise, grief, gratitude, or disappointment.

So Pru was wrong. The professor did have some money. And if the professor had ten thousand to leave Janice, maybe he had provided in some way for Harry. She sneaked a look at him, but his head was lowered, and his lips were clenched, only a slight quiver at one corner. He was fighting hard to control himself.

Kate empathized. Once the will was read, not only would the museum be gone, but so would the professor.

"To Marian Teasdale, the contents of safety deposit box 213 at the National Bank of Exeter. Marian," Simon took a breath. "Marian, my dear friend, you will know what use to make of its contents."

Everyone, including Kate, turned to look at Marian, but she kept her eyes focused on her lap.

"To Abigail Avondale . . . "

Kate clenched her arms tighter around herself. She felt Harry tense beside her. It was closure. But not the kind she'd hoped for.

" . . . her mother's jewelry, which is to be found in safety deposit box 178 at the Farm and Mercantile Bank in Granville."

Abigail shifted in her seat and sat straighter.

"To Harry Perkins, a trust account, established in his name to be administered by the executor of my will, Simon Mack, Esq., for his continued education."

Harry's breath caught. He pressed himself back into his chair as if he wanted to disappear.

"The house and property at 63 Hopper Street, the contents of the house and the holdings of the Avondale Puzzle Museum, as well as all my worldly possessions, I leave to Katherine Margaret McDonald, who shared my puzzles and taught an old man to love."

Kate's breath stopped. The room went out of focus. She was vaguely aware of Abigail's cry of outrage. But it seemed distant.

The professor had left the museum to her. It was impossible. She couldn't have heard correctly.

"This is nonsense," cried Abigail. "He was coerced. How do we know that he even wrote this? It's an obvious fraud perpetrated by this woman."

"Ms. Avondale—" began Simon.

Abigail was on her feet. "You'll be hearing from my lawyers." She whirled to face Kate. "Don't think you'll see a dime from that house."

Harry jumped up. "You leave her alone. She was the professor's friend."

"Ms. Avondale, please," repeated Simon.

A shadow passed in front of Kate.

"Ms. Avondale, if you can't restrain yourself, I'll have to ask you to leave." The voice was Chief Mitchell's. Maybe that was why he was here. To keep things sane.

"Oh, don't worry. I'm leaving. But I'm not finished. And if she attempts to remove one thing from that house, I'll have her arrested."

"Ms. Avondale, constrain yourself," said Simon in an incisive voice that Kate had never heard before. "This will was witnessed by the president and vice president of the National Bank of Exeter, February 5, 2004. I have spoken to both of them, and they have attested to its validity."

"Undue influence." Abigail grabbed her bag and coat. "My father was mentally incompetent."

She turned on Kate. "Don't touch a thing in that house."

"Abigail," said Marian Teasdale, her voice quiet but hard. "It was always P. T.'s intention to leave the museum to Kate. I was"— she paused and took a breath—"privy to his intentions. I'm sorry, but the will is valid."

"This is a conspiracy. You'll be hearing from my lawyers." Abigail swung around. Her purse slammed into Janice, who was just standing up. Abigail didn't stop, but strode to the door and out of the room.

A minute later, Janice followed her, but not before throwing a caustic look at Kate.

Harry stood up awkwardly. He didn't speak but crossed the room in measured steps. When he reached the door, he broke into a run.

"Harry," Kate called and stood up, but Chief Mitchell was already at the door.

"Well, Kate," said Simon, coming around his desk to stand beside her. "What do you say to all of this?"

She shook her head, still not believing it. "I had no idea. Is it true? How can that be?"

"It's what P. T. always wanted," said Marian. "The museum, the house, everything belongs to you now."

"But what about Abigail? Doesn't she have a legal claim?"

"She has the right to contest the will," said Simon. "But P. T.'s wishes are what count, and he wanted you to have the museum. I just wish he'd made them known earlier. Unfortunately, we'll now have to wait out any petitions of contention."

"No, we won't," said Marian. "Abigail is not his daughter."

Her words fell into silence as Simon and Kate both stared at her.

Marian looked incredibly sad. "For years, I told P. T. to tell her the truth, but—" She smiled tightly. "At first he was too angry at Gloria for having trapped him into marriage with another man's child. But he didn't want to hurt the child. He kept putting it off.

Now look at the mess he's left." She took a steadying breath. "The proof is in the safety deposit box. I was hoping not to have to use it, but if Abigail persists in contesting the will, I'll have no choice."

"Good God," said Simon. "That poor woman."

Kate walked out of Simon's office in a fog. The professor had left everything to her. Even though she repeated it over and over, it still hadn't sunk in. It seemed impossible. He'd never given any indication that he was planning this. They'd hardly even communicated in the last few years.

The only emotion Kate felt at the moment was pity for Abigail Avondale. Abigail wasn't the professor's daughter. Marian and Simon were on their way to Exeter to open the safety deposit box that contained the proof. What proof could there be? A confession. A DNA sample? It was all too sordid. And tragic in its own way. Gloria Avondale wrecked four lives when she'd lied to the professor. Her own, his, Marian's. And not satisfied, she'd wrecked her child's by lying to her about her father.

Harry and Chief Mitchell were standing on the sidewalk next to a utility pole with a bright poster announcing Puzzle Saturday stapled to it. The chief was looking her way, but Harry was looking down at the ground.

His education was provided for, which was great. But college was still several years away. Who would take care of him until then? He couldn't be sent back to his uncle, and she would fight to keep him out of foster care. But he couldn't live with her. She didn't know anything about kids.

She didn't even know what to do about herself. Was she really ready to give up her career, to move back to her hometown to run an ailing museum? Until a few minutes ago, she'd been ready to give up everything to fight for the museum's continued existence. Now that it was hers, she was riddled with ambivalence.

Where was the sense of accomplishment she'd felt when the GABs helped her prepare for Puzzle Saturday? Her excitement over her nascent plans for the future? The delight she took in Harry's interest in the interactive room? Now the responsibility seemed to engulf her, and her first impulse was to run.

Then another, more ominous thought hit her. She was now responsible for repaying the loan. Her shoulders slumped at the sheer immensity of the situation.

"Congratulations." Chief Mitchell's face didn't look congratulatory, but suspicious. And who could blame him?

She straightened up, met his look.

"I know what you're going to say. You can add the inheritance to the rest of the stuff against me." Her voice broke. "I'd suspect me, too."

"I wasn't going to say that."

"You were thinking it."

He didn't answer.

"I swear I didn't know about this," she said, more hurt by his silence than she wanted to admit. "I'm not even sure I want the museum."

Harry finally looked up. "Sure you do. Don't you?"

Kate shrugged. She seemed incapable of reassuring him—or even herself.

"It's been a shock, and it's too early to make serious decisions." Chief Mitchell looked at both of them. "The fate of the museum is still not out of the woods. Abigail Avondale—"

Kate shook her head, cutting him off. "She isn't the professor's daughter." Kate pushed her hair away from her face, drying an escaping tear as she did. "Marian just told us. She has proof."

The chief let out a low whistle.

"It's wonderful about your trust fund, Harry."

"I guess."

"Are you okay?"

"Yeah."

Kate tentatively put a hand on his arm.

He pulled away. "You don't have to worry about me. I can take care of myself."

"Harry," snapped the chief.

"Of course you can," said Kate. "But you don't have to. I need you to help me run the museum." It was out before she realized what she was saying, but it sounded right.

"You don't even know if you're staying."

Kate hesitated. "I'm staying. It's just scary. What about you?"

"You bet. I mean, well, I don't know." He cast an anxious glance at the chief.

"One thing at a time," said the chief. Then he relented. "We'll see."

He didn't elaborate, but Harry looked relieved, and it was pretty clear to Kate that the chief might be getting a permanent boarder. She was so pleased that she could have hugged him.

Though of course, she didn't.

Chief Mitchell went back to work. Harry and Kate walked back to the museum.

Janice was already there, packing up her desk. "I'll be out of here within the hour," she said without looking up.

Kate felt Harry's head snap toward hers.

She hesitated. It was tempting. But if she let Janice leave now, she might never be able to recover the missing funds. And then they'd really be up the creek. They'd just have to put up with her until they figured out their next move.

"I'd like you to stay until I can find a replacement, or until you find another job." There, it was said, even though it galled her to have to say it.

Janice looked up, not grateful as she should be, but triumphant. Without a word of thanks, she began returning her things to the desk.

Kate motioned to Harry to go upstairs.

As soon as the office door closed behind them, Kate put her finger to her lips and tiptoed over to the calling tube. She closed the opening and turned back to Harry.

"I can't believe you're letting her stay. We know she wrote those letters. She's trouble."

"I know, but we have a more urgent problem than Janice. The bank is about to foreclose on the house for nonpayment of debt."

"That's stupid. The professor isn't—wasn't in debt."

"Well, the bank doesn't have evidence of payments for the bank loan the museum board took out. And I can't find any bank statements or endorsed checks."

"Did you ask old Krupsy?"

"Harry."

"Sorry."

"Yes, I did ask her, and she said the professor had them. But he didn't. And I haven't been able to find them. I've searched."

"The professor doesn't have the checks. He wasn't interested in that stuff. He signed a bunch and gave them to her. She wrote in the rest."

"Wait a minute," said Kate. "You're saying he signed blank checks and let Janice . . . I don't believe it." Genius had its drawbacks. How could the professor have been so sloppy when he was so meticulous in everything else?

"He just kinda lost interest in the everyday bullshit."

"We've got to find out what happened to the missing money. And get it back if we can."

Harry sank down on the edge of the desk. "If we don't, you can have my education fund. I don't need it."

"Thanks," said Kate. "But you do need it. You don't want to end up an uneducated almost-genius, do you?"

"I guess not, but where should we look next?"

"I've already looked everywhere," said Kate.

"At her house?"

Kate made a face. "No. But I don't think we have enough evidence against her to ask Chief Mitchell to get a search warrant."

"I know how we can get them."

Kate didn't miss the excitement in his voice or the glint in his eye, though he quickly looked away.

"Absolutely not," said Kate. "It's illegal."

Harry gave her an innocent look.

"It's dangerous."

"Nah."

"You live with the chief of police."

Harry shrugged. "Save the taxpayer's money. Easy to find me if I get caught. But I won't get caught."

"No! I forbid you to do anything dangerous or illegal." *Or jeopardize the chief's trust.* "Besides, I have something else I need you to do."

"What?" he asked suspiciously.

"Finish the interactive room. Ginny Sue and I started it, but it needs a lot of work. And now that it seems we might really have a Puzzle Saturday, it has to be the best."

Harry looked unconvinced.

"Someone has to go through the professor's things. Maybe the checks are in his apartment."

"I'll do the interactive room," Harry said too quickly. "If that's okay."

"It would be a big help."

* * *

Kate stood outside the apartment door, key in her hand. She was afraid to go in. Afraid that that it would be too hard to face. Too sad. Too familiar. Or too different. Or a dozen other excuses she could think of. The truth was she didn't want to have to say this final good-bye.

She inserted the key, gave it a twist, and pushed the door open. She found herself looking into one large, airy room. The walls were a pale blue and made her think of the sky. It didn't jibe with the dark wood and decor of the rest of the house.

Kate stepped inside. There was an alcove kitchen to her right, a small sitting area under the eaves. The rest of the room was unfurnished except for a large brass bed that was covered with a patchwork quilt. Two bedside tables each held a stack of puzzle books, and an old-fashioned wardrobe stood between two dormered windows.

Kate closed the door and came face to face with a Victorian mirror, cloudy with age and black where the underfinish had flaked away. Next to it was a rolltop desk with the top closed.

Kate sat down gingerly in the chair and slowly raised the wooden slats.

The desktop was neat, cleared of papers. Only an ink bottle and nibbed pen were placed in the back corner. A large, blue canvas checkbook sat dead center. It was the kind that held three checks per page that could be torn along a perforated line to separate it from the stub.

She hadn't expected to find it this quickly, and her fingers trembled as she opened it. There was a half inch of pay stubs running along the inside seam. There were still three checks on the top page, all signed with the professor's familiar scrawl. The rest of the lines were blank.

Kate shook her head. Anyone could have been taking checks and writing them for anything they wished. Anyone who had access to the checkbook, that is. And as far as she knew, that was only Janice and the professor. Did she come here to get the checks? Or did the professor take them down to her?

The latter, thought Kate. She couldn't imagine the professor letting her in. Not even to write checks. Kate knew of no one who'd visited him here. Certainly not when she was his apprentice, at least not while she was around.

She began looking through the check stubs. They were filled in with the professor's shorthand. Cramped to fit into the small space, but it was the professor's writing. *Utl, mag, groc*—utilities, magazine subscriptions, and groceries. She also found entries for the three missing loan payments.

That was some vindication. Now if she could find the endorsed checks. She leaned back, caught off guard by the sense of relief those last stubs gave her. At least the professor had meant to pay them. Which in Kate's mind left only one possibility. Janice.

But it wasn't usable proof. She had to somehow connect Janice to the missing checks.

She stood up to look around the room. Aloysius was curled up on one of the pillows on the bed. He slowly blinked his eyes at her. She walked over to pat him and saw a framed picture on the bedside table, nearly hidden by the stack of books. She picked it up.

It was a young man, the professor, his arm linked in the arm of a young woman. They were smiling at each other, seemingly unaware of the photographer. Kate peered at it, wondering what kind of woman he had married, but the eyes that smiled at the professor were not Gloria Neale's. They belonged to Marian Teasdale. Kate put the picture back, embarrassed to have intruded on such intimacy.

Next to it was a picture of Kate, taken when she was ten or eleven, at the Halloween festival. She was dressed as Pippi Longstocking with wire run through her braids so that they stuck out from her head. And a photo of Harry, younger and small, looking like an urchin right out of *Oliver Twist.*

She crossed to the wardrobe and pulled both doors open. On one side, a stack of wooden drawers held socks and underwear and other miscellaneous items. On the other, slacks, shirts, and jackets hung neatly side by side.

Kate ran her hand over the tweed of his favorite jacket. And then she did something she would never have done before. She reached into the pockets. She found a Sudoku paperback in one, a crumpled grocery list in another. She methodically went through all the clothes, carefully removing the pieces of scratch paper the professor used for writing notes to himself and placing them on the desktop. A reminder to buy cat food, to get his hair cut. None of them offered a clue to his murder.

Al jumped down from the bed, padded over to her, and began figure-eighting around her ankles. She sat on the floor and pulled him into her lap. He was heavy, warm, safe.

"He's not coming back, Al." Al answered with a plaintive "chirrup." Her mouth twisted. "I'm sorry."

She buried her face in his fur. They sat there for a long time, until Al's fur was wet with her tears. Then she heaved a sigh and rolled Al onto the floor.

He immediately returned to his place on the professor's pillow and curled up to sleep.

She opened the door to a small closet, which held a winter coat and a stack of cardboard boxes. She pulled out the top box and guided it to the floor. Then she sat down and opened the flaps. Rubik's Cubes—big ones, little ones, plastic ones, and older wooden prototypes. She took each out, held it in her hand, then placed it on the carpet next to her.

Beneath them was an old leather scrapbook. Kate set it on the floor and flipped through the pages. Sepia photographs of the professor's parents. The professor in knickers and a sailor-collared shirt. He and Jacob Donnelly as teenagers, winner and runner-up of a regional chess tournament. Marian, Willetta, Jacob, and the professor on Cape Cod dressed in summer whites. Another of their faces smiling out of holes in a board painted with bathing beauties and lifeguards.

A newspaper article and picture of six young men, among them Jacob and the professor, members of a Boston University club called the Brain Trust. The professor had been president, and Jacob vice president. Is that when this thing between them started? Jacob always second to the professor's first? Was it based on jealousy? The next page displayed his diploma from BU, summa cum laude.

Several pages were devoted to newspaper articles. Another insight to her mentor's life. He must have already been interested in collecting puzzles while he was in college. There was an article about a puzzle museum opening in Great Britain, another article about a stolen chalice, and two about the discovery of a cache of stone sequence puzzles in an ancient Chinese tomb. Kate scanned each one of them, soaking in all the things that made up her mentor's life.

She came to a blank page, though Kate could see where the little black corners had been glued, and she guessed what pictures had been torn away.

On the next, she found an article about the opening of the puzzle museum with an accompanying picture of the professor watching the Avondale Puzzle Museum sign being installed. He was tall and handsome, but seemed a little sad. There was no date, but she guessed it was after his marriage to a woman who didn't love him, and his loss of the woman who did.

Kate took a shuddering breath. Maybe numbers *were* better than people. They, at least, were safer. And though sometimes she was tempted to cry out of frustration, it was never over a broken heart.

The next page held an invitation to the wedding of Marian

Teasdale and Arthur Compton. There had been no wedding pictures or any pictures at all of his own married life.

She turned the page. And found herself. Several pages of herself. Standing in the maze in uneven pigtails, clutching her Rubik's Cube. She didn't remember him taking that. She and the professor standing on each side of a gigantic pumpkin. They'd come closest to guessing the pumpkin's weight. One hundred sixty-three pounds, she remembered. Kate winning a puzzle contest, being named National Merit finalist.

He'd saved everything she'd ever done.

On the next page there was a Polaroid of Harry, proudly displaying a cipher to the camera.

After that, the pages were blank. There should have been more. Many more as Harry grew up under the tutelage of his mentor. And Kate raged at the injustice of it all.

She closed the book, put it back in the box, and covered it with the Rubik's Cubes. She closed the flaps, closing off the past. Then she rested her forehead on the top.

A noise made her look up. Harry was standing in the open door, looking alarmed, and next to him stood Brandon Mitchell, looking expressionless as always.

Kate pushed to her feet, stumbled as her foot gave way, then was covered with tiny pinpricks of pain.

Harry rushed forward. "Are you okay?"

"My foot just went to sleep," said Kate. Her voice sounded shaky. She was embarrassed. She wished they would go away and leave her with her memories.

"The chief is taking me for pizza. We, uh, thought you might like to come. Thursday nights you get free root beer."

She doubted if that had been Chief Mitchell's idea, but what the hell. She could use dinner and just to be away from here for a while. "Thursday? Oh no!"

"What?" asked Harry, sounding scared.

Kate grimaced. She had a date to go bowling with Norris Endelman that night. She'd forgotten all about it.

"I'm sorry. I'd love to, but I have other plans."

Harry looked disappointed.

Chief Mitchell looked like he couldn't care less. He knew what "other plans" meant. And she knew exactly what he thought about a woman dating when she should be in mourning.

Well, to hell with him. If he listened to gossip instead of being the stuck-up prig he was, he'd know that it was Aunt Pru's doing.

9   1

CHAPTER

TWENTY-FIVE

2

THE DATE WAS great, according to Norris. He and his friends had a great time, laughing and roaring and doing all the things the other bowlers up and down the lanes were doing. Kate bowled an impressive game, only she wasn't comfortable jumping up and down with success. She was too busy calculating where she stood within the other scores, or how long the game would take, or what the outcome would be. Old habits were hard to break.

Norris was nice looking and muscular. He had good manners. Everyone was friendly, and they all went for a beer afterward, where they laughed about the game and quickly segued into other subjects—George's new four-by-four, Helen's newest customer at the beauty salon, Norris's tickets to the upcoming Patriots' game.

Kate smiled and nodded and wished she were back with her math geeks talking probabilities and abstract numbers. She even wondered if Harry and Chief Mitchell were enjoying their pizza. Though she guessed she'd feel no more at home with them.

She replayed the entire evening as she drove to the museum the next morning and came to one conclusion. She didn't fit in. Disgusted with herself, she resolved to do better the next time, if there was a next time.

Harry was waiting on the steps again.

"Morning, Harry. Janice lock you out again?"

Harry shook his head. "I don't think she's here yet."

"Good," Kate said and opened the door. "I'll get a key made for you today."

The phone was ringing, and she hurried over to Janice's desk to answer it. It was Darrell Donnelly.

"Hello, Katie. I'm sure you must realize that the loan is due on Monday. If you could stop by the bank this morning."

"Certainly," said Kate. News traveled fast in Granville. He must know that her hands would be tied until the lawyers fought out the legality of the professor's will. She glanced at her watch. "Eleven o'clock?"

"Fine. See you then."

She hung up.

Harry was frowning at her.

"The bank. Don't worry. I'll think of something." She headed for the kitchen, Al and Harry following behind. She didn't have a plan. She didn't have the least idea how to stall until something, anything—the loan money appearing out of nowhere, winning the lottery, finding a hidden treasure—happened to save the museum. She snorted at her own unscientific thoughts. She'd better come up with something better than leprechauns before her trip to the bank.

"What?" asked Harry.

Kate shrugged. "Just trying to come up with a plan." She poured out cat food and placed the bowl on the floor. Al fell on it like he hadn't been fed in ages.

"Do you think Kru—Ms. Krupps spent all of it?"

"We don't even know that she took it."

"We would if we could find those checks."

"No," said Kate, looking stern.

Harry grinned. "You look funny when you screw up your face that way."

Kate sighed. It was obvious that Harry needed a stronger hand than hers. She wondered if there was any way to convince the chief to keep him.

At ten to eleven, Kate stopped by the interactive room to tell Harry she was leaving. He was arranging three bright red beanbag chairs by the window. There was a worktable in the center of the room, and plastic bins were lined up on one shelf filled with puzzle-making supplies. The other shelves were filled with puzzles of all shapes, sizes, and colors.

"This is incredible, Harry."

Harry shrugged, but his face beamed with pride.

"I'm going to the bank now."

His face fell, then he brightened. "I'll go with you and stop at Rayette's for takeout."

Kate kept forgetting that Harry was a growing boy and needed to eat all the time. "Good idea."

They walked to Rayette's, and Kate handed Harry a twenty. He went inside and Kate continued to the bank. Her stomach was tense; adrenalin coursed through her. She still didn't have a plan. She'd have to ad lib, a technique that ran counter to every part of her training. But she was desperate.

Darrell didn't come to meet her, but had the receptionist lead her down the hall to his office. Kate couldn't help but make the analogy of the cowardly lion on his way to see the wizard. But *that* lion wasn't really a coward, and *that* wizard was a fake.

When the receptionist announced her, Kate had a smile on her face.

"Come in." Darrell only half rose from his chair and motioned Kate to the one opposite him.

She sat down. *That wizard was a fake.*

"Well now," said Darrell. His tone was condescending and smug. He had the upper hand, and he knew it.

Kate kept silent and smiled at his forehead while she calculated what balance would remain if she dumped all of her savings into the account. Not enough to save the museum, plus it would leave her without a means of survival.

Darrell shifted impatiently. "I must say, news of old P. T.'s will has taken the whole town by surprise."

Kate held her tongue.

"But of course, you'll never own the house or its contents. Abigail will contest. You don't have a leg to stand on."

And neither does Abigail, thought Kate. But that news must not have hit the Granville airwaves yet. It would though—eventually.

"You seem to be stuck between a rock and a hard place."

Kate bit her tongue to keep from enlightening him. It would give her more time to weigh her options if he was in the dark.

Darrell placed his elbows on his desk and leaned toward Kate. "You can't possibly keep the house, even if you did miraculously win the case. The house will have to go to auction." He paused, apparently considering something. "Not that it will bring very much. Probably not even enough to cover the outstanding loan."

She had an idea where he was going, so she said, "I imagine whoever wants to flip it to the mall consortium will pay handsomely." She watched for a reaction but saw none. She'd have to press more. "Though I think it strange that no one from their office has attempted to contact either me or the professor when he was still alive."

Darrell leaned back in his chair. He was regrouping. And suddenly in a burst of intuition, Kate knew the mall consortium wasn't Darrell and Abigail. There was a real consortium. They just hadn't decided on a location.

The mall was contingent on Darrell and Abigail being able to offer a complete package. And receive a healthy middle-man commission?

She might be wrong, but that was the only explanation that answered all the variables of the situation. She stood up. "I'm not selling. Good day."

She'd taken him by surprise. And for a second, he just looked blankly at her. She headed for the door.

"Then you'll lose it," he said as she shut the door.

She walked down the hall, willing herself not to hurry, just in case Darrell was watching.

She had three days. It might as well be three hours, or three minutes.

She stepped out into an overcast day. They were in the thick of fall. The days were sunny and calm one minute, and stormy and windy the next.

She stopped at the hardware store and had an extra key made for Harry.

Janice was coming down the steps of the museum when Kate opened the gate.

It was barely noon, an hour earlier than her usual time. She knew her days at the museum were numbered. Whether the house was sold or Kate became its true owner, Janice would soon be looking for a new job, and she didn't bother to acknowledge Kate, just squeezed past her and walked off down the street.

There was a wrapped sandwich and bottle of spring water waiting for her on her desk, but no sign of Harry. She sat down and picked up the sandwich, revealing a stack of checks, held together by a blue rubber band.

And beneath them she could see the blue corner of a savings passbook.

She looked at it first. It belonged to Janice Krupps, and the balance came to three hundred thousand and change. The payments had begun years before with small deposits of twenty-five to a hundred dollars every few weeks—until the last six months, when they suddenly jumped to outrageous amounts, which added up to far more than the three loan payments. Janet had been engaging in some serious embezzlement.

Kate dropped the passbook and pulled the rubber band off the checks. She rifled through them, separating the ones with the professor's signatures, and totaling them mentally as the pile grew. Over two hundred thousand dollars.

How on earth had she managed to get away with it without anyone noticing? Except that the professor was completely uninterested in financial matters, Willetta Donnelly was too ill to fulfill her duties as treasurer, and Jacob was too preoccupied with his wife's health to realize what was happening.

At least Janice hadn't spent it, but why she hadn't was beyond Kate. Saving it for a rainy day? Her retirement? Well, whatever it was, it was all about to come tumbling down. But first she wanted to talk to Harry.

She locked the checks and bankbook in her briefcase and went to the interactive room. It was empty, as were the other exhibit rooms. He wasn't in the kitchen, but as she turned to leave, she heard the sound of pruning sheers coming from outside.

She looked out the window. The opening of the maze had been enlarged, and there was a pile of cut branches lying nearby.

She went outside and followed the sounds of the shears into the maze. She found him several yards and two turns away, gathering up a bundle of freshly pruned limbs.

"Harry."

He looked up. "Hi." He started carrying the branches past her.

"Harry."

He kept going, talking over his shoulder. "I thought I would clean up the maze so we could open it for Puzzle Saturday."

Kate followed him out into the yard where the sun was once again peeking through the clouds.

"You broke into Janice's house."

"It's a pretty big job, but I might be able to finish it by then. The kids will love it."

"Breaking and entering is illegal, as you well know. What if you'd been caught?"

"I was thinking maybe I could get some help with the pruning." He dropped his load of twigs on the pile and turned to face her. "She stole the loan money. She sabotaged the museum. She probably killed the professor. I hate her."

It was finally beginning to hit him. The professor was dead. He'd been coping so well, but now he looked young and lost.

He wiped his sleeve across his face, leaving a streak of dirt. "Now at least they can arrest her."

Kate shook her head. "I'm not sure they can use illegally confiscated goods as evidence."

"That's not fair."

"No, but I think it's the law."

"I can put them back and then tell the chief where to find them."

"No," said Kate. "Chief Mitchell would skin us both alive. I have a better idea."

Harry frowned at her. "What?"

"We'll make her pay it back."

"How?"

Kate wasn't sure, but she tried out a hypothesis. "We'll confront her when she comes back from lunch. Threaten to take them to the police. Even if they can't use them, news will spread all over town and she'll be shunned by her friends." Kate smiled bitterly. "They might even ride her out of town on a rail."

"Okay," said Harry, not totally convinced. "But what if she murdered the professor? How are we gonna find that out? That stupid money won't bring him back."

"No," Kate agreed. "But it will give us more time to figure out who did kill him. And it might just save the museum."

Harry kicked at the grass with his sneaker. "All right. I guess. Let's do it."

Kate and Harry were waiting for Janice when she came in from lunch. She looked at both of them, then started up the stairs.

"Janice," said Kate.

Janice glanced over her shoulder. "I need to powder my nose."

"Janice," Kate repeated, trying to sound authoritative. She was feeling sick just anticipating the confrontation. "Harry and I have something to say to you."

Something in her tone must have come through, because Janice came back down the stairs. She stopped at the bottom and gave Kate a considering look. Her mouth straightened into an unpleasant line. "Yes?"

Kate held up the checks.

Janice's eyes widened, then she rushed across the room. "Give me those." She lunged at Kate.

Harry stepped in front of her and she stumbled. He grabbed her elbow, breaking her fall, but when he'd set her on her feet, he grabbed her shoulders and shook her. "You stole the professor's money, and you're going to pay it back."

Not exactly the tactics Kate had planned. "Harry!"

Janice twisted away. "I'll do no such thing."

"Yeah you will, or we'll tell, and everyone will hate you," said Harry, his lower lip trembling.

"And you'll be arrested for embezzlement," said Kate.

"You can't prove anything."

"No?" Kate held up the passbook.

"You stole my bankbook." She turned on Harry. "It was you, you little ingrate. You'll be the one going to jail."

"I think not, Janice." Kate's cool words bellied the undercurrent of nervousness that made her weak in the knees.

Janice sneered at Kate. "You'd drag your beloved professor's name through the mud? It's his signature on those checks, not mine. I didn't even know they were in my account."

"Bullshit." Harry clenched his fists, and Kate began praying he wouldn't use them on Janice. "The professor would never take anything that didn't belong to him. You did. Did he find out what you were doing? Did he threaten to turn you in so you murdered him?" Harry's face was suffused with blood, his features contorted with anger.

For the first time, Janice's demeanor slipped. Her mouth twisted. "I'd never kill P. T."

"Then why did you take his money?"

"I didn't."

Kate interceded. "Give it up, Janice. Put it back or go to jail. It's up to you."

Janice hung her head. "We needed that money. P. T. needed me to take care of him. But it was no use. He would never leave his precious museum." Her head snapped up. Her eyes lit with venom. "Take it and be damned. It's no use to me."

Harry, looking disgusted, opened his mouth to say something.

Kate quelled him with a look. What could you possibly say to a woman that deluded? And Kate didn't want to lose the advantage.

"We're going to the bank now," said Kate, trying not to feel any sympathy for the woman. "And you're going to transfer all two hundred fifty-seven thousand dollars and thirty-six cents into the loan account. I don't know how you got the rest, saving it or dipping into petty cash, but that you can keep."

Janice cast a final bitter look at Kate, but the fight was gone out of her.

The three of them walked to the Farm and Mercantile Bank. Kate and Harry stood beside Janice as she transferred the money back into the loan account. Kate was pretty sure that the whole town would know about it before nightfall, but it wouldn't be from her or Harry.

As soon as they were back on the sidewalk, Janice pushed them away and started down the street in the direction of the museum.

"Come on," said Harry. He took off down the street.

"What are you doing?" called Kate, jogging to catch up to him.

"Making sure she doesn't steal anything." He loped off without waiting for her.

By the time Kate reached the museum, Janice was coming down the steps carrying her tote bag. Harry stood in the doorway, arms crossed over his chest.

Kate waited for her just inside the gate and stepped in front of her as she passed. "Janice, I'll send you two weeks' severance pay. But I'll have to ask you for your key."

Janice fumbled at her key chain and took a key off the loop. "Take it. I hate the place. I never want to see it again." She flung the key at Kate.

Kate snatched it out of the air and tossed it to Harry.

They watched her struggle with the gate.

"Should we let her go?" asked Harry.

"I don't see how we could stop her, even if we wanted to."

"But what if she killed the professor?"

"If she did, the chief will arrest her."

Janice opened the gate and reached the sidewalk just as a silver Lexus pulled up to the curb. The passenger door opened, and Kate saw Abigail Avondale leaning over the seat.

Convenient that she was so close, thought Kate. And since when had she and Janice become such good friends?

"Go inside, Harry."

"But—"

"Please. I'll just be a second."

Reluctantly, he turned back to the house.

"Don't think this is over," Abigail said past Janice, who'd stopped on the curb to give Kate a triumphant look.

Empty threat, thought Kate, then thought again. Two bitter women allied together could make big trouble, even if neither of them was the murderer. She had to do something to diffuse the danger.

"I know you're both upset and hurt. So am I, but —" She meant to say they could solve their differences amicably, then changed her mind. "But if anything happens to anyone I care about, I won't stop until someone pays."

Both of the women looked at her as if she had sprouted horns, then Janice got into the car. The door slammed, and the Lexus peeled away.

Kate watched until it reached the corner and turned out of sight. Had she really just threatened them? She'd never threatened anyone in her life. She backed up and grasped the wrought iron gate as her knees gave way.

She was appalled at herself. At first. Then she started to feel better. *There,* she thought. *A little backbone. Just what the situation warranted.* As a people skill it was lousy, but as a deterrent it worked just great.

			1	8				5
2								
			7					
	7	1					8	
	3			9			2	
	5					6	4	
					6			
								1
4				3	2			

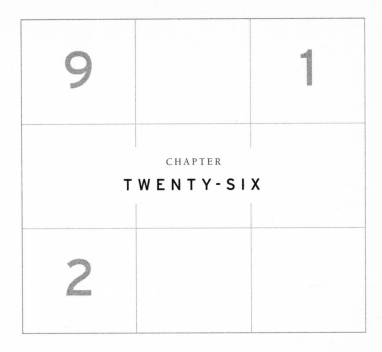

CHAPTER

TWENTY-SIX

KATE FOUND HARRY sitting at the professor's desk, propped on his elbows, his head resting in his hands. She watched him for a minute, then asked, "Are you okay?"

"Huh?" He didn't look up.

"I said, are you okay?"

"Yeah." He scratched his head, and Kate realized he wasn't upset, he was reading.

"What are you doing?"

"Looking at this puzzle. I found it stuck between the pages of your book. What is it?"

"It's a photocopy of the puzzle the professor was working the night he died."

At first Harry didn't move, then he sat up, distancing himself from the paper. "Ugh."

"I know. I wasn't going to show you."

He took a deep breath. "It's okay. What are you looking for?"

"I thought—hoped—the professor might have left a clue as to who killed him."

"Like in an old movie," said Harry, peering at the puzzle again.

"Pretty far-fetched, huh? Nobody about to be killed would have the wits to leave a clue in a puzzle."

"Except the professor," said Harry. "He could have done it."

"That's what I was hoping. I knew something was off. I was too upset that night to really notice, but something about the puzzle kept needling my subconscious. I know now that the professor wasn't trying to solve the puzzle. His numbers aren't positioned in the right place. Some of them he didn't even have enough information to place anywhere, much less where he did. Now I don't know what to think."

"What does the chief think?"

"The chief?"

"Chief Mitchell. You got it from him, right?"

"Sort of."

"Sort of?"

"Kind of."

"You stole it?"

"No," Kate protested. "Not exactly. I, uh, appropriated a copy of the original photograph. I printed this out in black and white."

Harry turned pale, but he said, "Cool. Where's the photo?"

"In an evidence bag somewhere."

"Seriously cool. But I meant the original copy."

"In my briefcase. But Harry, it's pretty detailed."

"I can take it."

Kate unlocked her briefcase and reached for the envelope. When she pulled it out of the briefcase, she realized that the picture Sam Swyndon had sent her wasn't inside. It was still in the briefcase. She lifted it out and straightened a corner that had been bent. She handed it to Harry.

"Ugh."

"I know," said Kate. "That's why I've been working from the black and white."

"Good idea." Harry handed the photo back to her. He looked a little pale.

"I wouldn't have shown it to you, but I'm stumped. If there is a clue, it has to be in the puzzle, or else it was stolen the night of the break-in." She stopped. The photo had been in the envelope that night. She hadn't looked at it since then; she'd kept her briefcase always locked after that night.

"The night I broke in?"

"What?"

"The night I broke in?"

"No. Several nights before that. Someone else broke in and ransacked the office. I thought it might have been Abigail looking for the will. But . . . to give the devil his due, Chief Mitchell thought they might have been looking for something that would incriminate them."

"So how do we know if they found what they were looking for?"

She hesitated while she re-created what she could remember of that night. She distinctly remembered putting the photo in the envelope. It was no longer in the envelope. Ergo, someone had found it and looked at it.

The intruder or the police?

Kate thought she knew. Had the murderer figured out the meaning of the puzzle? Or was he afraid Kate had? Had she put their lives in danger?

"Kate?"

"What?"

"You're looking kind of weird."

"Sorry. We don't know. But if there's an outside chance there is a clue in this puzzle, we need to solve it." Before the murderer did.

She scooped up the photocopy and returned it to her briefcase. This time she made sure it was locked.

"How's your Sudoku?"

Harry shrugged. "The professor taught me. It's okay, but you just end up with a bunch of numbers that don't mean anything."

"A closed system."

"Yeah. I like ciphers better. At least they tell you something."

Kate sighed. "I was hoping the puzzle would tell me something. See? The numbers aren't aligned right. When I solved the puzzle using just the printed numbers, the steps diverged after the first few numbers."

"Hmmm," said Harry, sounding awfully like Chief Mitchell. "I do know you can't use zeros in Sudoku."

"At first I thought it was the beginning of a six or nine, maybe an eight. But now I don't know what to think."

Harry looked at the paper with renewed interest. "Maybe it stands for a date."

"Or zip codes, phone numbers, addresses. I tried them all. Do you know how many potential combinations there are for nine numbers?"

"A lot."

"More than that. And I don't think the professor would have left something too complicated. He'd want us to find his murderer."

"But he'd have to make it hard enough so the murderer couldn't figure it out." Harry frowned. "You think the murderer knows Sudoku?"

"Doesn't everybody?"

They spent two hours trying to find a plausible solution to the professor's numbers. They only got more frustrated.

"It's impossible." Harry got up and started opening cabinets.

Kate watched him for a few minutes until curiosity got the better of her. "What are you doing?"

"Looking for clues."

Kate leaned back in the chair. Stared at the ceiling.

They'd done everything they could. She'd didn't know what else to do.

Harry continued to open and close cabinets.

"Take a break, Harry. I've already searched."

"Then I'll search again. There has to be something. If it's not in the puzzle, it has to be somewhere. And I'm going to find it if I have to turn this place upside down."

He slammed the cabinet door, opened another.

Upside down. Kate sat up straighter. *Upside down.* She looked at the numbers she'd been studying for days. "Upside down."

"What?"

Slowly she turned the puzzle around until she was looking at it upside down. She stared at the new orientation of the numbers. "Harry, I think you might really be a genius."

"No, I—what?"

He came over to the desk and looked over her shoulder. Kate looked down at the newly oriented page and shifted her eyes in the same way the professor had taught her to look at the hidden pictures, but this time she was seeing hidden letters.

"Not sevens, but Ts."

"Wow," said Harry, and leaned closer. "And the threes are Es."

"The fives are Ss."

"St.—" Harry began.

"The zero was intentional." Kate shook her head. "And I thought he'd made a mistake. It's *St. Leo's.* That unfinished number wasn't a one or a seven, but an *L*."

Harry smacked his forehead. "Heist. The four is an *h*. The last word spells *heist.* It's been here all this time. Next to backward writing, this is the simplest code there is, and I didn't see it."

"Nether did I," said Kate. But now that she did, it was all coming together. "The professor was depending on his two apprentices to figure it out. And we did it." Relief flooded through her. "St. Leo's Heist."

"But what does it mean?" asked Harry.

Something flickered across her brain. St. Leo's. It was gone. "I don't know, but we're going to find out."

She pushed the paper aside and opened her laptop. Typed in the words *St. Leo's* and got over six hundred thousand hits. Added *heist* and shaved off a few thousand. Tried substituting *robbery* and found the answer.

A newspaper clipping from the 1960s about a valuable jeweled chalice stolen from the safe at St. Leo's Cathedral in downtown Boston.

"I don't get it," said Harry. "What does this have to do with anything?"

"Shh." Kate scrolled down and found an article dated three weeks later. Neither the thieves nor the chalice had been found. Another article, this one right after the theft, and a picture of the stolen chalice. And Kate knew.

She'd seen the same article in the professor's scrapbook.

She did some quick calculations. The professor had been a sophomore at Boston University that year. Did he know something about the theft? Did he know the thief? Was that why he was killed? But why now? And who?

What did she know about the professor's current associates? Jacob Donnelly, Sr. had been at Boston University with the professor. Marian had been a student at a nearby college. Surely not one of them. Someone else had been at BU and had met the professor there. Kate picked up a pencil and began to doodle.

"What?" asked Harry.

She shook her head to quiet him. It was at the board meeting. One of the men.

Jason Elks. That was it. He'd met the professor at BU. They'd met again at a puzzle conference after that and struck up their friendship. Jason had retired here fifteen years ago.

Was his moving to Granville significant?

Could one of these people possibly be the thief? Could the professor have been involved? A chill ran across her shoulders. No. He would never steal anything. He must have somehow stumbled over the truth. It would be just like him to see the article about the theft and worry it until he came up with a solution. But why didn't he contact the authorities in that case?

She thought of Chief Mitchell. Maybe the professor had told the authorities and they'd brushed him off, just like the chief had brushed her off.

And where was the chalice now?

The telephone rang. Both she and Harry jumped.

It rang again, and Kate realized there was no one downstairs to answer it. She picked it up. "Uh, Avondale Puzzle Museum."

"Katie, is that you?"

"Aunt Pru."

"I heard that you fired Janice Krupps. Good for you. Time you started using your authority as owner and curator."

"Aunt Pru . . . "

"I'm not going to bother you. I just wanted to let you know that Elmira has invited us to go to the bean dinner at the community center tonight."

"I don't—"

"And her nephew Sam is coming with us. He's got a very nice photography business, when he's not called out on some awful job by that policeman. It was very kind of him to get that copy of the puzzle for you. Not just any man would. . . . And he's got great job security, weddings and graduations and anniversaries . . . "

Kate closed her eyes as the inevitable gripped her. "What time?"

"Seven-thirty. They're picking us up. Bye."

Kate hung up the phone. Her concentration was destroyed, but Harry was leaning over the computer, clicking on sites and taking notes.

"You left the door open again."

Kate and Harry both jumped. They were beginning to look like a comedy routine.

Chief Mitchell stepped into the room. "It's past closing time and the two of you are sitting here with the museum unguarded and oblivious to your surroundings. What's so interesting?"

He moved toward the desk. Kate slapped the lid of her computer down. She glanced at Harry. He looked guilty as sin. She imagined she did, too.

"What are you two up to?"

"Nothing," they said together.

The chief grunted and lifted the computer lid. He tapped the mousepad, and the screen lit up. He looked at it for a long moment, then looked at Harry.

"Damn it. Have you been hacking my files? So help me—"

"No," said Harry. "Why should I?" He didn't sound convincing.

Kate didn't want to confess what they'd learned to the chief quite yet. It wasn't conclusive, and there were still too many suspects. Then the chief's words hit her. "You have files on the cathedral robbery?"

The chief didn't answer, but his expression, even blanker than usual, said it all.

"Oh," said Kate.

"Oh," he repeated.

"Well, what do you think?"

The chief clicked out of Netscape and closed the computer. "I think I should confiscate your computer and put you both behind bars before you get yourselves into serious trouble. There is a murderer at large. Leave the investigating to the professionals."

Harry and Kate unconsciously cowered together.

The chief sighed. "I'm not the enemy, contrary to popular belief. And contrary to popular belief, I will solve this case." His voice tightened. "But you could screw this up big time, not to mention get caught in the crossfire, so stay out of it." He looked from Harry to Kate.

There was a momentary standoff, then they both nodded.

"And don't talk about this to anyone."

They both shook their heads.

"So how did you figure this out?"

Harry shrugged and looked at the floor. Kate followed his lead. She couldn't lie. Especially not to a police chief. And especially not to this particular police chief. But she couldn't get Elmira and Sam in trouble.

"I'm waiting."

She swallowed. "We—I, uh, got it from the puzzle."

Chief Mitchell frowned. "What puzzle?"

"The one the professor was working when he was killed?"

"Is that supposed to be a question?"

It was supposed to have gotten him off the track. Another dismal failure on her part. "I have a photographic memory." That wasn't a lie. It also didn't redirect the chief's thoughts.

"And you remembered the numbers. And the numbers led you to the theft?"

"Yes."

He looked at the desk, saw the puzzle copy, and picked it up. "St. Leo's Heist. How?" His expression changed, and he turned the paper upside down. "Very clever."

Kate breathed again.

"Is that how you figured it out, chief?" asked Harry.

Damn. They'd almost been home free.

"No," said the chief. "I did it by investigating the evidence and following the leads as they developed." He turned to Kate. "Pretty good, your photographic memory. Not only the numbers, but the blood stains, too." He dropped the copy onto the desk before her. "How did you get this?"

Kate shrugged.

"You bribed Sam Swyndon, or Elmira, or both."

"I didn't bribe anyone," Kate said indignantly.

"No, of course not. You merely had to ask." There was a touch of bitterness in his voice.

Something that he would never have done, thought Kate, and she felt a stab of sympathy for him. It wasn't even his fault. It was just that he was an outsider.

"Don't be mad at them."

"I should fire both of them."

"No," said Kate. "Please. It's just the way we've always done things. It will just take time for things to change."

"Right."

"It will. And Elmira likes you. She really does. So don't fire her."

"I'm not going to fire her. I doubt if I could find anyone to replace her."

"And don't be mad at Harry. He didn't know anything about it."

"Yes, I did. Not until later, but that makes me an accessory after the fact. So if you're going to arrest Kate, you'll have to arrest me."

Chief Mitchell pushed his fingers through his hair. "I'm not going to arrest either of you, though I'm tempted to lock you both up for your own good."

"And you won't send Harry away?" Kate looked pleadingly at the chief.

He didn't answer at first.

"Let me stay. I'll make it up to you. Promise." Harry's lapse from bravado to supplication cut right through Kate's heart.

It seemed to have worked on the chief, too. "I'm not going to do anything with you, yet. Except take you to the bean supper."

Kate groaned.

The chief shot her an ironic look. "I suppose you'll be there, too. Who is it tonight? The grocer, the mechanic, or the candlestick maker?"

The chief confiscated the copies and the photo and erased her search sites before he and Harry walked her to her car. She drove away with them watching. She was thinking, not about the discovery they'd just made but about how the chief had known about her date with Norris Endelman.

Inappropriate, she reminded herself, and began to think of ways of avoiding being seen by the chief with Sam and Elmira, and how to discover who had stolen the St. Leo's chalice.

As luck would have it, Harry and Chief Mitchell were the first people Kate saw when she entered the community hall with Aunt Pru, Elmira, and Sam. They were standing halfway across the room, talking to Jason Elks. She couldn't help but stare. Were they questioning him about the murder?

The chief turned his head and looked straight at her. His eyes flicked past hers to Sam and Elmira. His reaction was sardonic at best.

Hers was total embarrassment. Color rushed to her face, and she was only glad he was too far away to get a good look.

Unfortunately, she had the same reaction when she saw him the next morning at the museum. She was in the kitchen feeding Al when she heard Harry working on the maze. She went outside to see how he was progressing and came face to face with Chief Mitchell.

"Oh," she said.

One side of his mouth quirked up. "Oh."

"I wish you wouldn't do that."

"What?"

"Say 'Oh' every time I say it."

The other side of his mouth quirked up. "Irritates you, does it?"

"Of course not. It's just a stupid thing to do."

Instead of getting angry, he broke into a full smile. It was dazzling.

"I have to go inside," mumbled Kate, and she went.

Aunt Pru was in the kitchen scrubbing the counters down to the finish. "Glad to see that man can do an honest day's work." She lifted her chin toward the window.

Kate deduced she was talking about the chief. Of course, she just had to peek to make sure. He was carrying a huge pile of branches to the side of the house. He'd taken off his flannel shirt and was wearing a navy blue T-shirt.

Kate turned away right into Aunt Pru's lifted eyebrow. "Things to do," she said, and hurried out of the room.

"Katherine Margaret McDonald."

Kate froze, then slowly turned around. For someone who was about to turn thirty, she sure felt like a child. "Yes, Aunt Pru," she said primly.

"I saw you looking at that policeman last night."

"I looked at a lot of people last night."

"Yes. But not the way you looked at him."

"I accepted a date with Sam, didn't I?"

"Well, I suppose you did."

The front doorbell jingled.

"Then don't worry. Gotta go. Someone's at the door." Kate fled.

The GABs were crowded onto the circular front porch armed with brooms, mops, vacuums, and furniture polish.

"Gotta get a jump on things," said Alice Hinckley, rolling an ancient Hoover. She began barking out orders, and the GABs dispersed.

Kate climbed the stairs to where Ginny Sue was putting the finishing touches to the interactive room, arranging bins with scissors, paper, cardboard, markers, crayons, and glue sticks. A sign printed in primary colors was tacked to the wall beside the door.

P. T.'s PLACE

"It was Harry's idea," said Ginny Sue.

"It's perfect," said Kate. "I can hardly believe it's actually happening. I just wish the professor were here to be a part of it."

Ginny Sue smiled sympathetically. "How do you know he isn't?"

Kate lifted an eyebrow, just like Pru would do.

"I know you're a mathematician and everything, but . . . don't you feel his spirit?"

Kate smiled. She *was* a mathematician. She didn't dwell on spirits and holy ghosts and stuff like that. But she had to admit, she felt the professor in every room. Not his spirit, of course, but his essence, or something.

"You will," said Ginny Sue, and went back to her puzzle bins.

Kate wandered into the office, feeling a little at loose ends. Everybody was busy, and she seemed to be doing nothing but thinking—and missing the professor.

She hadn't heard from Darrell. She wondered if he'd discovered that the loan was up to date and a large amount of the principal had been repaid. Surely he wouldn't attempt to foreclose now that they were up to date. And if he tried, she was sure Donnelly Sr. would have something to say about it.

Everything seemed to be proceeding like clockwork. And now that she realized that Brandon Mitchell also had discovered the chalice theft, she had every confidence that he would catch the professor's murderer.

Puzzle Saturday was only a week away. All around her, Aunt

Pru, Ginny Sue, the GABs, Harry, even the chief were busy, and it seemed like she should be doing something, too. And she knew where she had to start.

She hadn't rearranged anything in the office, but left it just as it was before the professor's death. The room had grown dusty over the weeks, but she didn't want to clean the last of his presence away, and she wouldn't trust the job to anyone else.

It was time to stop trying to recapture something lost. It was time to move on.

She started with the desk, relegating the unneeded papers and books to one of the cupboards. She polished the furniture, then returned the Cofanetto to the cabinet.

It wasn't an easy task. Just touching it brought back memories of the professor. But almost immediately her sadness gave way to a feeling of companionship. They'd spent many happy meals using the puzzle's utensils, and those times would always be a part of the Cofanetto and of her.

She windexed the windows. Dusted the furniture. She borrowed the old Hoover and ran it over the carpet until it was wrenched out of her hands.

Aunt Pru turned it off, and Kate's ears rang in the sudden silence.

"A curator has no business vacuuming; now go make yourself curatorish."

But Kate watched from the door while Pru ran the vacuum over the old oriental carpets. When she finally turned off the vacuum, the rug looked almost new.

"Are you still here? You run along, dear. I'll just dust a bit."

"I already dusted," said Kate.

Pru started to run her hand over the crystal ball.

"Don't."

"It's filthy. I'll be careful."

"It isn't that," said Kate. "It's just that I was never allowed to touch it."

"That's because you were a child. Now go on and don't worry. I promise I won't move a thing."

Kate sighed. It was useless to argue with Pru about cleaning. And besides, she was right.

Kate realized that she and Harry would no longer have that refuge. The office belonged to the future. And anyway, the professor wasn't contained there. He was present everywhere in the museum.

She closed the office door on Pru and her vacuuming.

"It's going to be great," she said to herself, aware that she was also speaking to her mentor.

She glanced into the new P. T.'s Place, bright and clean and kid friendly, and went downstairs breathing in the scent of Pine-Sol, Pledge, and ammonia. She passed the hidden picture room. It had new lights and had been vacuumed and polished, but she wasn't tempted to look inside. She wasn't ready to confront the faces there.

The professor's murderer was still free.

	9			5		4	1	
						7		
2			8					
			2		3			8
		3		7		5		
6			5		9			
					1			9
		4						
	7	5		3			2	

CHAPTER

TWENTY-SEVEN

PRU INSISTED THAT she would drive to church the next morning. Kate was afraid that she had ulterior motives, only one of which was to keep her away from Brandon Mitchell.

This morning she was wearing a rust-colored suit and a hat covered with feathers of the same hue.

Kate jumped in, and Pru gunned the engine. She coasted through the stop sign at the end of the street. A green, dented pickup truck screeched to a stop to their right.

Pru waved. "Looks like Roy got his truck back."

Kate shuddered. Pru and Roy Larkin on the road at the same time. It was a frightening thought. A police chief's nightmare.

"What are you smiling about?"

"Me?" asked Kate.

"You see anybody else in this car?"

"Just that the museum looks pretty good, don't you think?"

"I do. And Rayette is all lined up to contribute to the food table.

Though I'd forgotten how bossy Alice Hinckley is." Pru cut across two lanes and turned into the church parking lot. Fortunately there were no oncoming cars.

Kate got out and straightened her dress. It was a gray wool that she'd bought last year at Filene's Basement. She'd packed it just in case the weather turned cool while she was in Granville. It had. It was fall—and she was still here.

They greeted their way into the church and down the aisle to their usual place. She gave Harry a lift of the eyebrows as she passed by the pew where he was sitting. He was dressed in a suit, white shirt, and tastefully striped tie, just like the man sitting next to him. She tried not to look at him, but she couldn't help herself.

"There's Jacob Donnelly," whispered Pru as she retrieved a hymnal from the pew in front of them. "Poor soul. They say Willetta's taken a turn for the worse."

"That's too bad," said Kate. That must be the reason Jacob hadn't been working on the museum's behalf lately. He looked exhausted, and she felt a wave of compassion even though he'd been the professor's enemy.

He sat down next to Darrell. They didn't speak. Not good blood there, either. *Why can't people just get along,* wondered Kate.

The choir filed in, followed by Reverend Norwith. The congregation stood, and Kate's eyes wandered to the chancel and the communion plate and chalice set there. Who would steal a chalice? Granted, the St. Leo's chalice had been worth a fortune, but it seemed like such an odd thing to choose. And the cathedral had just installed a state-of-the-art security system. Why not just rob a jewelry store? It would have been easier.

She hadn't gone back on the Internet. The chief had scared her enough to make her keep her promise. But she had reread the article in the professor's scrapbook. It had been important enough to keep all these years. Important enough to kill for?

Aunt Pru nudged her in the ribs. "You're not singing."

Kate sang. But she was also thinking. *Why now? Where was the chalice?* As far as she knew it had never been found.

She barely heard the sermon. There was too much rumbling around in her head. She fervently wished Chief Mitchell would arrest someone and get it over with. She surreptitiously looked around the congregation. The Donnellys, Marian Teasdale, Ginny Sue were all there. Jason Elks went to the Methodist church down the street.

Rayette winked at her. Kate smiled then turned a little farther in her seat, just enough to catch a glance of Harry and the police chief. He was looking over the congregation, too.

Their eyes met. Kate turned around and concentrated on the rest of the sermon.

After church, Pru held her usual court on the sidewalk. Jacob Donnelly stopped on his way to his car.

"I didn't have a chance to tell you how happy I am that the museum is in your hands now."

"Thank you," said Kate, acutely aware of Chief Mitchell a few feet away.

"How's Willetta?" asked Pru.

"As well as can be expected."

"Well, you just tell her I asked about her."

"Thank you." He walked slowly away toward the parking lot.

"A shame," said Pru. "And after all those treatments. Thy will be done."

Harry and the chief stopped long enough for Harry to tell her he'd meet her at the museum after lunch.

"You can take a day off if you want," said Kate. She turned to the chief. "He's been working like crazy . . . Oh." She flinched, but he only stood there. "I meant to thank you for helping with the maze."

The chief merely nodded. He was looking warily at Pru, who was frowning malevolently at him.

But Harry wasn't at the museum when Kate got there at two o'clock. He still wasn't there at three. She didn't want to be over-protective, but . . .

She looked up the number to the police station. As she suspected, the chief was working. The dispatcher put her through.

"I just wondered if Harry was coming today," she said before he could think she was calling for any other reason.

There was silence on his end of the line. Then, "I dropped him off two hours ago."

"Oh. Well, he must have gone out for something."

Another silence.

"What is it?"

"He said he was going to mow the grass. We bought gas for the mower on our way."

"I'll go look out back," she said. She might be overreacting, but she was worried.

"Kate."

She froze. He'd just called her Kate. Had she finally been declassified from number one suspect?

"His uncle called here twice last week. He's obviously heard about Harry's inheritance. He's insisted on having him returned to him."

"No."

"I told him he'd have to go through legal channels. But I'm driving out there now. I'll call you as soon as I know if he's taken him. Until then, go home."

"I'll be at the museum. In case it's a false alarm and Harry comes back."

"Then lock your doors. All of them."

He hung up. Kate went to the backyard. The gas can was there, but the lawn mower was still in the shed. She went back inside. Called out to him. Checked in all the rooms. Even opened the professor's apartment and looked in. Harry was nowhere in the museum.

She tried not to imagine Buck Perkins forcing him back to that awful trailer. Harry would never stay, unless he was locked up again. She didn't want to think about how traumatic that would be. She knew the chief would make short work of Buck Perkins, and she vowed that Harry would never go back there even if she had to adopt him herself.

She went back to the office. She was met by a yowl from Al. He rubbed against the bookshelf and padded over to the desk. "Yeow," he repeated, and went back to the bookcase, bumped it with his nose, and looked back at her.

"What is it, Al?"

"Yeow."

"Yeah, great, but where's Harry?"

Al bumped against the bookcase. The telephone rang. She grabbed for it.

"It's Brandon Mitchell. I just left Buck Perkins. He doesn't have Harry. Not here at least. Have you heard anything?"

"No."

"I'll cruise through town, then come to the museum. I should be there in a half hour." He hung up.

"Yeow," said Al.

"What," said Kate, anxiety making her voice shrill. "Find a mouse? If you could just find Harry."

Al gave her a look and bumped against the bookcase.

"Stop it. You're making me crazy."

Al pattered back to the desk and jumped in her lap; his claws dug into her jeans. She pushed him off. "That hurt."

"Yeow." He went back to the bookshelf, and this time Kate followed.

She heard a muffled thump-thump from the other side. Held her breath and listened. Another sound, this one a human voice, but sounding very far away.

"Harry?" She pulled books from the shelf and knocked on the back panel. The knock was returned. "Harry, where are you?"

There was nothing on the other side of that wall but the two bathrooms. Was he stuck in the bathroom? She rushed into the hallway and knocked on the men's room door. Getting no answer, she peered inside.

It was smaller than the women's room, not as deep, and there was no window, just a solid wall.

She went back to the office and pulled more books off the shelf. "Harry, can you here me?"

"Yes," was the muffled reply. "Get me out of here."

"I'm trying. But how?"

"The ball."

"What?"

"The crystal ball."

"Okay." Kate spun around. The crystal ball was where it had always been. It had been dusted—and polished. Aunt Pru had been thorough. It positively gleamed. Kate stepped closer and peered at the glass.

Could it be possible that some mechanism on the ball or plinth opened a secret compartment? Gingerly, she placed both palms on the glass. It felt cool and hard. She lifted it, or tried to. It didn't budge. She tried again, but it didn't even wobble. It was cemented to the pedestal.

She leaned over and discovered a tiny groove on the top surface of the wooden pedestal. It was sheathed in tarnished brass. She felt around the base of the ball until she felt a small appurtenance, but it was a quarter rotation around.

She tried turning the ball clockwise. It didn't budge. But when she switched directions it slid silently around until the catch was in line with the groove. She pressed it down and it clicked into place.

Kate looked back at the bookcase. It hadn't moved. She looked back at the crystal ball, rapidly searching her brain for similar puzzles. She tried to lift the ball again. Nothing except a slight lift in the pedestal itself.

She pushed up on one side of the crystal ball. It rose, taking the base of the pedestal with it. She pushed it all the way open until the ball and plinth were hinged against the back of the pedestal. Inside was a secret compartment. Just like many of the puzzles on display.

There was the switch plate screwed into the wood. "Stand back," she called to Harry, and flicked the switch.

There was a groan, a creak, and the bookcase swung open. Harry fell into the room.

"Thank God," said Kate, weak with relief.

"Wait till you see this," said Harry, and motioned her to follow him back inside.

"Wait. How did you find this? Did it lock by itself?"

"I was looking up at the bookshelves. I thought maybe I could find a secret compartment or something."

"Well, you did."

Harry looked embarrassed. "Yeah, but it was a mistake. I mean, I was backing up to get a better look and I guess I sort of backed into the crystal ball. It started to wobble and I grabbed for it, and it just opened up."

Pru's dusting must have realigned the catch, thought Kate. "And you saw the switch and had to try it."

"Of course. And then the bookcase opened and—you've gotta see this." He began pulling her inside.

"Wait. How did it close again?"

"I don't know. It just did."

"Then wait a minute." Kate looked around. "Help me move one of these chairs in the opening, just in case it's on some sort of timing mechanism."

They dragged the professor's chair into the opening, then stepped inside.

It was like being on the inside of a puzzle box. The walls were intaglio, carved with intricate leaves and vines, fruit and fanciful figures, rococo curlicues. There was a light switch inset into the wood near the opening.

"Amazing," said Kate.

"More than amazing. Look at these." He pointed to a small incongruous shape camouflaged within the carvings. And then to another. At first they appeared to be purely decorative. But soon Kate made out a pattern.

"They're symbols," she said. "Hundreds of them hidden in the designs."

"Yeah, but look at these over the entrance. I almost missed them."

They were carved of the same colored wood and formed into a curling vine, but when Kate shifted her eyes, they stood out in strong relief. Four of them formed a vague line through a grapevine.

"Numbers," she said. "Three, five, one, four."

"You think it's a code?"

"I think it's a combination to a lock."

"But there are no locks, I've checked." Harry peered around the room. "Unless. The first number was three, right?" He walked slowly around the room, frowning at the designs. "Here." The Celtic triquetra." He touched a small symbol of three interlocking circles. "It turned!"

"Oh my God. It did. Look for five."

They both started scanning the walls. Kate was the one to find the pentagram, in the center of a medallion of astrological figures. She touched it and it shifted to the right a bare centimeter.

They found several circles and one ankh.

"Two kingdoms," said Harry.

"But only one ruler. You'll have to try to reach it though. It's too high for me." It turned between Harry's fingers. "Four," he said in an awed whisper.

They started in opposite directions looking for a symbol for four.

"There." Kate pointed to a Chinese geometric pattern. In the center was an equal-sided cross. "The four directions, the four temperaments."

"You try it," said Harry.

It didn't turn. It didn't move to either side. "It doesn't work," she said, disappointed beyond reason. "Unless." She pushed it in and turned. It slid easily in her fingers.

"Just like an aspirin bottle," said Harry. "But now what?"

"Nothing," said Kate, and removed her hand from the cross.

A square of paneling popped open at her feet. She dropped to her knees and stared at the steel safe that it had hidden. "Oh, Professor. No more games."

"Wait," said Harry. "There's no lock. Just pull the handle."

She did, and the door opened to reveal a deep-set, lidded box.

Together they pulled it out and set it on the floor between them. They looked at each other, then Kate lifted the lid.

It was dazzling. Gold embedded with rubies, emeralds, sapphires.

"The chalice," said Harry. "But what is it doing here?"

"I don't know," said Kate, but her mind was already collating the facts she knew. The professor had kept the article all these years. The chalice had been stolen while he was a student in Boston. Her mind recoiled at the deduction she made. Not the professor. Never.

"What's it doing here?" Harry asked again, his voice frantic. He had come to the same conclusion and was having as much trouble as Kate admitting it.

"Waiting for me," said a voice behind them.

Harry and Kate spun around. A dark silhouette was framed in the opening.

"You," said Harry, and jumped to his feet. "I heard you with my uncle. You're the one that had me locked in the shed."

"No harm done." A silver pistol appeared out of the darkness. "I'll take the chalice now."

Kate shook her head. "You don't really want it."

"No, but I need it."

"To pay for your wife's medical expenses."

"Yes," said Jacob Donnelly. "I'm sorry, Katie, but I have no choice."

"Of course you do," said Kate. "A person always has a choice."

"You killed the professor," Harry cried, and lunged at him.

The barrel of the pistol caught him on the temple. He fell to the floor and lay there, unmoving.

"Harry!"

"Stay there, Katie. I don't want to hurt you. Just give me the chalice." He was holding a briefcase, and he thrust it toward Kate. "Put the chalice inside and hand it back to me."

"How did you know where it was?" asked Kate, not reaching for the briefcase.

"I didn't. But when I saw your photograph of the Sudoku puzzle, I was sure P. T. had left you a message. You really shouldn't leave something like that in an unlocked briefcase."

"I knew someone had looked at it, but I just didn't know who. And it was you who locked me in the cellar?"

"I'm sorry, Katie. I confess, I got the idea from Buck Perkins. But I had to look for the chalice. I couldn't leave Willetta alone at night, and you were always here during the day. I would have let you out, except Brandon Mitchell beat me to it."

"And I suppose you locked Harry in here, too," said Kate, trying to think.

He shrugged slightly. "It seems to be my modus operandi. Simplistic, but very handy, I must say."

"And those vile letters, were they handy, too?"

"I didn't write those letters."

"But—" Of course. Not the grandfather. The grandson. The bully. "Darrell."

"The boy never outgrew his mean streak. Or his greed."

"And what about yours? That's why you insisted on the renovation. You didn't care about the museum. You thought you could find the chalice while restoration was taking place."

"Everything has worked against me. If only P. T. had relented." The gun wavered, but he recovered himself. "Take the briefcase and do as you're told. I've already killed once. It's academic if I have to do it again."

And he would have to kill them. He couldn't let Harry and her live, knowing what they did. Kate made a quick calculation. It had been at least twenty minutes since she'd talked to Brandon Mitchell. He'd said he'd be there in a half hour. But could she trust him to be prompt? Would he walk into a trap? Donnelly would have to kill him, too.

She reached out her hand for the briefcase, lowered it to the floor, and opened it. If she could just stall, maybe the chief would get there in time to save them—or be killed with them.

"Why did you steal it?"

Jacob blew out air. "It was part of an initiation into the Brain Trust, an exclusive university club we wanted to join."

Kate remembered the photo in the professor's scrapbook and felt sick. "We?"

"I and P. T. Oh yes, your mentor. But don't blame him. We were supposed to disable their state-of–the-art security system and steal the chalice, show it to the club members, then return it without getting caught. We did, too. And without any computers or other high-tech toys. Just our brains." He sighed. "Unfortunately, before we could put the chalice back, the church discovered the theft.

"They let us in the club, but we were stuck with the chalice. I wanted to sell it, but P. T. balked at that. He hid it and refused to tell me where." He took a painful breath. "Katie, please."

Kate glanced toward Harry. He hadn't moved, but surely that blow hadn't killed him. If she could get Donnelly out of the room, he might be spared. She had to think, and looking at a pistol aimed at you wasn't conducive to clearheadedness.

"You won't be able to sell it," she said. "Someone will recognize it."

"Katie. For such a bright girl, you are incredibly naïve. There is always someone willing to buy stolen art. In fact, it's a booming business. Now hurry, please."

He was nervous. He was sweating copiously. He might panic and shoot.

Kate lifted out the chalice and placed it in the briefcase. She closed the lid and slowly stood up, letting the briefcase drop by her side.

Brandon, where are you? Kate strained to hear the sound of a car, anything, but the chamber was well insulated. She had to get out. Somehow lead Donnelly away from Harry.

Or die trying. There weren't too many alternatives—die cowering in fear, or die trying to escape. It was a no-brainer.

"Katie." Donnelly held out his hand. It was trembling.

"Here." She swung the briefcase as hard and fast as she could. It hit Donnelly's shoulder, and he staggered back. In that second Kate darted past him and ran for the hallway.

Please follow me. Don't kill Harry first. "Jacob! I have the chalice!" She ran for the stairs, took them two at a time, and had just reached the first floor when a report exploded in the air and a piece of the front door splintered.

She swung around the newel post and raced down the hall to the kitchen. She didn't stop, but snatched the back door open and barreled into the yard.

The maze stood directly in front of her. Closer than either side of the house where she would be an open target.

She ducked through the opening, sending thanks to Harry and the chief for their hard work in opening the maze and praying the chief would get there in time to save them. Then stopped as she stepped on freshly strewn gravel. It crunched beneath her feet. It might as well have been a megaphone announcing her whereabouts. But it couldn't be helped.

Moving as quietly as she could, Kate took the first right turn and threw herself against the hedge. She held her breath, listening, hoping that he would think she'd made a dash for the front yard.

If he didn't . . . She tried to remember the layout of the maze. Just in case. And then she heard it. The crunch of gravel, and she knew that she hadn't been able to fool him. She was inside, but so was he.

	7	8						1
			4					8
		5		6				
1								2
	3			5			6	
8								4
				7		9		
4					2			
7						4	3	

CHAPTER
TWENTY-EIGHT

KATE BARELY BREATHED as she listened to the footsteps come nearer. If she remembered correctly, there should be another turn just several yards away. If Harry had managed to cut it open.

Regardless, she couldn't just stand there like a trapped rat. She began to ease along the hedge, trying not to disturb the fresh gravel beneath her feet. She heard the other footsteps slow, then stop. He was listening, too.

He was at the first turn. If he looked, he would see her.

Donnelly turned the corner. Kate flung herself at the hedge and fell into a newly opened passageway just as another shot exploded in the air.

He must be crazy. Someone would hear the shots. The police would come. He couldn't get away.

But it might be too late for her. He was desperate.

Kate tried to calculate where she was and where the next leg of the maze might start. If she wasn't careful, she'd run into a dead end or end up where she started—with Jacob Donnelly there to meet her.

She saw the hedge shiver and knew he was in the next passageway, just on the other side of the hedge. He was waiting, listening, moving carefully down the path.

Kate began to run to where she thought—hoped—the next opening would be. Only she ran into branches. The opening was merely a slit. They hadn't pruned this far into the maze.

It would have to do. She pushed herself sideways into the hedge and was swallowed up by darkness and stiff, tangled branches. She forced her way through, the twigs catching at her clothes, scratching her face. Her hair caught on a branch, and she wasted several seconds trying to free it before she yanked her head away. Her eyes stung as hair was pulled from her head, and she stumbled blindly forward.

She fell into open space, landed on hands and knees, and gulped for breath.

She pushed to her feet, looked left and right, and ran to what she thought was an open path. It was open, but she caught a flash of gray jacket just ahead of her. She spun around and raced back the way she came, past the slit in the hedge she'd used before. She remembered another way, not to the center of the maze but a shortcut to the exit.

She ran. And came straight to a dead end. She looked around. There had to be an opening. Or at least there had been once. But there was nothing but green, overgrown hedge reaching high above her. She dropped to her knees, saw a dead spot in the lower branches, and crawled inside.

She saw light through the branches. She crawled toward it and miraculously found herself in another cleared path. She started to stand when her ankle was gripped by a large hand, and she was being pulled back into the bushes.

"No," she cried and struck out with all her might.

"Kate? Kate. Where are you?"

Harry's voice. *Please don't come in here,* she prayed. She kicked out, and for a moment the grip loosened. She propelled herself forward.

She knew where she was now, and she knew where she needed to go to get out. She just hoped Jacob Donnelly didn't.

She moved along the hedge, trying not to give her direction away. But she heard the footsteps echoing hers on the other side of the hedge.

"I helped plant this maze," said Jacob from the other side. "You won't escape me."

Kate kept moving. They were going to meet at the end of the passage, but she couldn't stop. There was no other way.

Jacob beat her to the end. He stepped out into the space before her and raised his pistol. He stepped toward her, his gaze focused not on her face but on her hand, and she realized that she'd somehow managed to keep hold of the briefcase. She gripped it to her chest. Not that it would stop a bullet, but he'd have to kill her for it.

"Kate! Kate, where are you?" Harry's voice was hysterical.

She could call out, tell him to run for help, but she couldn't seem to make a sound, only stare as Jacob Donnelly moved inexorably closer.

Above her head, the wind rippled the branches, and Kate thought, *That's the last sound I'll hear before I die.*

But Donnelly didn't shoot, just kept moving closer. "Katie," he said coaxingly. "I don't want to hurt you. Just give me the briefcase and you can go."

She shook her head. No way could he let her go.

"What's going on in there, young man? Is somebody shooting?"

Another voice, but not the one she longed to hear. Alice Hinckley had come to see what was going on.

"Where's that darn police chief when you need him? Even called the station. Elmira said he wasn't there. Figures. Is Katie in there?"

Kate couldn't hear Harry's answer, she just knew that Brandon wouldn't get there in time. Resigned, she started to close her eyes. A blur of black and gray flew past her head and landed on Jacob Donnelly's shoulder.

Jacob screamed. The gun fell from his hand.

Al had come to the rescue. He clung to Donnelly's coat while Donnelly flailed madly to shake him off.

Kate forced herself to move. Keeping her eye on Jacob and Al, she crept close enough to snag the pistol and step back.

Donnelly gave a final fling, and Al flew through the air. He landed on his feet several feet away and poised for another attack.

"Kate!"

Finally. He'd made it after all. Kate nearly dropped the gun from sheer relief.

"Here." It hardly came out. She tried again. "I'm in here."

"Are you all right?"

"Yes. But hurry." Her hand was shaking. Donnelly's gaze flicked back and forth from her to the sound of Brandon's voice.

"Please, Mr. Donnelly. Don't make me shoot you." And then a blue uniform came around the corner, looking large and strong and angry. His gun was much bigger than hers.

"Face down on the ground. Now."

For a moment Kate wasn't sure who he was talking to, then Jacob lowered himself stiffly to his knees.

"All the way."

Donnelly lay face down on the pathway. Brandon pulled a pair of handcuffs from his back and deftly snapped Donnelly's wrists together.

He glanced up at Kate. "Are you sure you're okay?"

She nodded. She began to shake all over.

"Then please put down that pistol. Slowly. By your feet. And for heaven's sake, stay away from Mr. Donnelly here."

A few seconds later, patrolmen Owens and Wilson came around the corner.

After a moment of shocked recognition, they hauled Donnelly Sr. to his feet and took him away.

Brandon Mitchell looked at Kate and stretched out his hand, and she ran into the security of his arms.

"Thank God," she said. "I was afraid you wouldn't get here in time."

He pulled her closer, but it was only to get a look at his watch. "Exactly thirty minutes since I called." He blew out air. "And not a minute to spare."

"Katie." Alice Hinckley rounded the corner and stopped so quickly that gravel spurted out from her feet. Harry barely was able to stop before plowing into her.

Kate jumped away from the chief.

Alice scowled up at him. "And just what do you think you're doing?"

"He was—"

"Your men just arrested Jacob Donnelly. He's one of our finest citizens. We won't put up with this kind of behavior. Don't think we will. And put that magnum away."

Chief Mitchell holstered the gun.

"Now, you have some explaining to do."

"Mr. Donnelly murdered the professor," said Harry.

"Harry," warned the chief.

"No," said Alice. "He wouldn't kill anybody. He was president of the bank for thirty years"

"Well, he did. And he's going to jail."

"Harry."

"Because he wanted the chalice. It's in that briefcase. He and the professor stole it."

"Harry!"

"No. Let me see." Alice started for the briefcase that was lying on the ground where Kate had finally dropped it.

The chief stepped in front of her. "Evidence, ma'am, unless you want your fingerprints on file with the Granville PD."

"You wouldn't." Alice's head was tilted so sharply to look at him that Kate was afraid she might topple over backward.

The chief didn't answer, but the glint in his eye said he meant business.

"Hmmph," said Alice. "I don't believe any of this. I'm going home." She tottered away, her shoes wobbling in the gravel.

"Go with her."

Harry saluted and took off after Alice.

"She might not believe it, but all of Granville will know about it by nightfall."

Kate smiled sympathetically. "It's the Granville way. You'll get used to it."

He closed his eyes, took a breath, and held it.

"How far do you have to count?"

"To what?"

"To keep your temper."

"Higher than we have time for. What the hell were you thinking?"

"About what?"

"About attempting to apprehend a suspected murderer?"

"You suspected Jacob Donnelly?"

"I'm the police chief!"

Kate stepped back. "You don't have to yell. He was chasing me. He was going to kill me."

"You should have left it to the police."

"Well, I would have, but you weren't here."

"I mean you should have left the investigation to the police."

"I know, but I wasn't sure . . . "

"That I could do it."

"It's not that. But I knew people wouldn't cooperate and—"

"I was close to an arrest."

"You were? How did you figure it out?"

He gave her a long-suffering look. "Police training."

"He's a computer geek," said Harry, rounding the corner. "You should see his house. It's incredible. He has a—"

"Harry."

"Well, you do."

Kate smiled; the smile broadened into a grin. "You're a geek? No wonder your people skills are so awful."

"I'm not a geek. And what's wrong with my people skills?"

Kate and Harry exchanged looks.

"You needed us," said Harry. "If we hadn't found the secret room, you might never have found the chalice."

"What secret room?"

"I'll show you. And if Kate hadn't hit him with the briefcase and made him chase her, he might have gotten away. We expedited things for you."

"Expedited," repeated the chief.

"Helped?"

"You nearly got yourselves killed." He switched his focus to Kate. "Do you even know how to shoot?"

"Everyone in New Hampshire knows how to shoot," said Harry.

"She lives in Virginia. Do you?"

Kate shrugged. "I know about propulsion rates, trajectories, and speed to force ratios."

"Oh my G—"

"Chief," warned Harry.

"Promise me you will never do something like this again."

"What are the odds," began Kate.

"I don't want to hear about odds, just promise."

"We promise."

"Good. Now as soon as County gets here to take the damn chalice—"

"Chief," warned Harry.

Sirens sounded in the distance. And soon a team of county police came through the entrance.

"Wow. How did you do that?" asked Harry, watching them spread out through the maze. The briefcase was bagged and carried away.

The chief smiled.

Kate's toes tingled. "You're not clairvoyant or anything?"

"Nope," said Brandon, leading them out of the maze. "I'm just an ordinary cop. I radioed ahead."

CHAPTER

TWENTY-NINE

PUZZLE SATURDAY TOOK place as scheduled. And though the town was still reeling from the news of Jacob Donnelly's arrest, it didn't keep them away.

It was a crisp fall day, cold enough for hot apple cider but not too cold to enjoy the maze. There had been a steady line outside the entrance since they'd opened that morning.

Kate had made her first major expenditure when it became obvious that Harry wouldn't have time to finish the pruning. Fortunately, Mike Landers of Mike Landers Landscaping was a happily married fifty-six-year-old with six children and two grandchildren on the way.

The exhibit rooms were packed. There were some curious gawkers, but for the most part, children and adults, babies and grandparents, went from room to room admiring, questioning, and having a good time.

By early noon, Ginny Sue had hung fifty homemade puzzles along the wall waiting for the judges to declare a winner later that day.

Harry manned the door like a pro, directing people to the visitor book, which was placed on a table next to forms for membership and a pickle jar for donations. He'd already emptied it twice.

Even Izzy had gotten in on the act by offering to guide visitors through the Paper Puzzle rooms.

It was a wonderful, successful day, and yet Kate felt at loose ends. Everyone was busy, and it seemed like she had nothing to do except smile and accept congratulations.

She wandered outside to where two long banquet tables, covered with orange tablecloths, held an array of goodies, including Pru's maple cream cake, Tanya's brownies, and Rayette's apple fritters. And donuts, pumpkin bread, muffins, and cookies. Pru, Alice, and several other GABs were kept busy overseeing the food while Rayette dispensed coffee, hot chocolate, and cider.

Everyone was having a great time.

She caught sight of Brandon Mitchell in the crowd. He was actually talking to a small group of people. *Please don't let him be arresting someone.* He looked up and saw her, and the next thing she knew he was striding toward her. *Had the GABs all gotten food handlers licenses?*

"Pretty impressive," he said, coming up to her. "How does it feel to be curator of your own museum?"

She gave a half-smile. "Good, but a little scary." She sighed. "We're not out of the woods yet."

"Well, if you're worried about the mall, don't be. The deal was contingent on GN Enterprises offering a whole package."

"Wow," said Kate, trying to take it in. "What's going to happen?"

"My guess is Maine will be seeing a new outlet mall, and Darrell and Abigail will be unloading some very beautiful Federal and Victorian houses."

"All that emotion for something that didn't even happen. You know, I just don't get people sometimes."

The chief fought a smile.

"It isn't funny."

"Thinking about the professor?"

Kate nodded. "It's just so hard to believe that a man who was kind to me, so important in my life, could have been a thief."

The chief shrugged. "As a shirt I once read put it, 'Pobody's Nerfect.'"

Kate gave him a look. "I'd expect better from you."

"It's the truth. And it doesn't take away from what he did for you or Harry."

"You think he took us in to make amends?"

"I think he took you in because he saw what he could have been in the two of you."

Kate watched a group of children come running out the front door and crowd around the refreshment table. "I'm grateful to him. It's just . . . I don't know."

"Your hero is a little tarnished. Doesn't mean he can't be a hero."

"But to have kept the chalice all those years. Why?"

"That's something that even Jacob Donnelly doesn't know."

"If he'd only given it back he might be alive to see all this. What will happen to Jacob?"

Brandon looked out over the crowd. "He'll go to jail for the rest of his life."

She sighed. "He did it for Willetta. And now what is she going to do?"

"Murder always affects more than the immediate victims."

"Like a pebble dropped into the water."

"Don't get all poetic on me. I'm just figuring out your logical side."

"I wasn't. It's the ripple effect." Kate looked up and saw Pru making a beeline for them. "Oh no."

Brandon took a step back. "I'd better make myself scarce."

"Too late." When Pru was several feet away, Kate said, "Aunt Pru, we were just discussing the logistics of Puzzle Weekend."

Brandon shot her a wary look. "We were?"

"Chief Mitchell has agreed to provide the police force for it."

"No, I—"

"Isn't that wonderful?"

"Yes, dear. I'll make my maple cream cake. But—"

"We'll advertise it all over the county."

"Kate."

"That's nice, dear." Pru took Kate by the elbow and began dragging her across the lawn. "But first there's someone I want you to meet. A real gentleman."

Kate looked back over her shoulder at Brandon Mitchell.

He grinned and shook his head.

"A great future, job security . . ."

Katie McDonald returns in

SUDDEN DEATH SUDOKU

A regional Sudoku championship is the setting
for a different kind of puzzle!

AVAILABLE NOW IN HARDCOVER
From Running Press Book Publishers

SOLUTIONS

PAGE 28

1	3	6	8	7	5	2	4	9
9	8	7	3	4	2	5	1	6
2	5	4	6	9	1	7	8	3
4	6	1	5	2	7	9	3	8
8	2	3	9	6	4	1	7	5
7	9	5	1	8	3	6	2	4
5	7	8	2	3	6	4	9	1
3	1	2	4	5	9	8	6	7
6	4	9	7	1	8	3	5	2

PAGE 54

2	1	5	8	4	9	6	3	7
4	9	7	6	1	3	2	5	8
6	3	8	7	2	5	4	9	1
3	6	9	5	7	8	1	4	2
8	5	4	1	6	2	3	7	9
7	2	1	3	9	4	8	6	5
1	4	6	2	5	7	9	8	3
9	7	3	4	8	1	5	2	6
5	8	2	9	3	6	7	1	4

PAGE 62

9	6	3	4	5	7	8	2	1
2	1	7	6	8	9	4	3	5
4	8	5	1	3	2	6	7	9
8	7	1	3	4	6	9	5	2
5	4	9	2	7	1	3	6	8
3	2	6	8	9	5	1	4	7
6	9	2	5	1	4	7	8	3
7	5	8	9	6	3	2	1	4
1	3	4	7	2	8	5	9	6

PAGE 76

5	8	7	9	6	1	3	4	2
2	9	6	3	4	8	7	5	1
1	4	3	2	7	5	9	8	6
6	7	4	8	3	2	1	9	5
3	5	2	1	9	4	6	7	8
8	1	9	6	5	7	2	3	4
9	3	1	4	8	6	5	2	7
7	2	8	5	1	3	4	6	9
4	6	5	7	2	9	8	1	3

PAGE 85

1	8	9	7	2	3	5	4	6
2	3	6	9	4	5	1	7	8
7	4	5	8	6	1	9	2	3
4	1	8	2	3	7	6	5	9
3	5	2	6	9	4	8	1	7
9	6	7	5	1	8	2	3	4
8	9	1	4	7	2	3	6	5
6	2	4	3	5	9	7	8	1
5	7	3	1	8	6	4	9	2

PAGE 100

1	4	8	9	5	3	7	2	6
9	6	3	2	8	7	5	1	4
7	5	2	1	4	6	3	8	9
8	2	6	3	9	4	1	7	5
5	1	7	6	2	8	9	4	3
4	3	9	7	1	5	8	6	2
6	8	5	4	7	9	2	3	1
3	7	1	5	6	2	4	9	8
2	9	4	8	3	1	6	5	7

PAGE 140

1	6	8	9	4	3	5	7	2
2	7	3	5	6	1	9	8	4
9	5	4	2	7	8	1	3	6
3	4	1	7	8	9	6	2	5
5	9	7	6	3	2	4	1	8
8	2	6	4	1	5	7	9	3
7	8	9	3	5	4	2	6	1
4	3	2	1	9	6	8	5	7
6	1	5	8	2	7	3	4	9

PAGE 160

9	2	5	1	4	3	7	6	8
1	8	7	9	5	6	4	3	2
4	3	6	8	2	7	9	1	5
3	6	1	4	9	2	5	8	7
8	7	9	3	6	5	1	2	4
2	5	4	7	1	8	3	9	6
6	1	2	5	7	9	8	4	3
7	4	8	6	3	1	2	5	9
5	9	3	2	8	4	6	7	1

PAGE 188

6	8	4	7	9	3	2	5	1
7	3	1	5	4	2	9	6	8
9	2	5	1	8	6	3	4	7
8	7	9	2	6	5	4	1	3
4	5	3	8	1	7	6	9	2
1	6	2	4	3	9	8	7	5
2	4	6	3	7	1	5	8	9
3	1	8	9	5	4	7	2	6
5	9	7	6	2	8	1	3	4

PAGE 210

6	9	1	5	7	3	8	4	2
5	3	7	4	8	2	1	6	9
4	2	8	6	1	9	7	5	3
3	1	6	2	5	7	4	9	8
9	8	4	3	6	1	5	2	7
2	7	5	9	4	8	6	3	1
1	4	9	7	3	6	2	8	5
7	6	3	8	2	5	9	1	4
8	5	2	1	9	4	3	7	6

PAGE 222

2	6	1	8	3	7	4	9	5
4	7	9	6	2	5	3	8	1
3	8	5	1	9	4	6	7	2
7	4	8	2	1	6	5	3	9
1	3	2	5	7	9	8	6	4
5	9	6	3	4	8	1	2	7
8	1	7	9	5	3	2	4	6
6	2	4	7	8	1	9	5	3
9	5	3	4	6	2	7	1	8

PAGE 236

8	9	3	2	4	7	5	1	6
5	1	2	6	3	8	4	9	7
6	4	7	9	5	1	8	3	2
9	3	5	7	8	6	1	2	4
4	7	6	1	2	5	3	8	9
1	2	8	3	9	4	7	6	5
3	5	1	4	6	9	2	7	8
2	8	9	5	7	3	6	4	1
7	6	4	8	1	2	9	5	3

PAGE 248

3	8	7	2	4	6	1	5	9
4	5	1	7	8	9	3	2	6
9	6	2	5	3	1	8	4	7
1	2	6	9	5	7	4	3	8
5	9	4	3	6	8	7	1	2
7	3	8	4	1	2	6	9	5
6	7	5	1	9	4	2	8	3
8	1	3	6	2	5	9	7	4
2	4	9	8	7	3	5	6	1

PAGE 258

4	5	7	9	6	2	1	8	3
2	1	8	4	7	3	6	5	9
3	9	6	8	1	5	7	2	4
1	6	4	2	3	7	5	9	8
7	8	5	1	4	9	3	6	2
9	3	2	6	5	8	4	7	1
6	4	9	7	8	1	2	3	5
8	7	3	5	2	4	9	1	6
5	2	1	3	9	6	8	4	7

PAGE 272

4	2	5	1	8	7	9	3	6
9	1	6	3	5	2	8	7	4
7	3	8	4	9	6	5	2	1
8	9	2	5	3	1	4	6	7
6	5	4	7	2	9	3	1	8
3	7	1	6	4	8	2	9	5
2	8	7	9	6	5	1	4	3
5	6	3	2	1	4	7	8	9
1	4	9	8	7	3	6	5	2

PAGE 300

7	4	3	1	8	9	2	6	5
2	9	5	6	4	3	7	1	8
1	6	8	7	2	5	9	3	4
9	7	1	2	6	4	5	8	3
6	3	4	5	9	8	1	2	7
8	5	2	3	7	1	6	4	9
5	8	9	4	1	6	3	7	2
3	2	6	8	5	7	4	9	1
4	1	7	9	3	2	8	5	6

PAGE 316

7	9	8	3	5	2	4	1	6
5	3	6	1	9	4	7	8	2
2	4	1	8	6	7	9	3	5
4	5	9	2	1	3	6	7	8
8	2	3	4	7	6	5	9	1
6	1	7	5	8	9	2	4	3
3	6	2	7	4	1	8	5	9
1	8	4	9	2	5	3	6	7
9	7	5	6	3	8	1	2	4

PAGE 330

3	7	8	9	2	5	6	4	1
6	1	2	4	3	7	5	9	8
9	4	5	8	6	1	2	7	3
1	5	7	6	4	9	3	8	2
2	3	4	7	5	8	1	6	9
8	9	6	2	1	3	7	5	4
5	8	1	3	7	4	9	2	6
4	6	3	5	9	2	8	1	7
7	2	9	1	8	6	4	3	5